"What ... what are you doing?" Susanna sputtered in panicked disbelief.

"I'm undressing you, my love."

"Don't you ever call me 'my love' again! You don't love me—"

"You're right, I don't," Adam lied, certain that he saw a flicker of pain cross her lovely features as he slowly advanced upon her. "But I've desired you since the first moment I saw you, and I believe you want me, too. Come to bed, wife."

"No. I'll scream if you so much as touch me—"

"Only in pleasure," he countered. "Only in pleasure . . ."

# DEFIANT IMPOSTOR

## MIRIAM MINGER

AVON BOOKS ◆ NEW YORK

DEFIANT IMPOSTOR is an original publication of Avon Books. This work has never before appeared in book form. This work is a novel. Any similarity to actual persons or events is purely coincidental.

AVON BOOKS
A division of
The Hearst Corporation
1350 Avenue of the Americas
New York, New York 10019

Copyright © 1992 by Miriam Minger
Inside cover author photograph by Priscilla E. M. Purnick
Published by arrangement with the author
Library of Congress Catalog Card Number: 91-92998
ISBN: 0-380-76312-5

First Avon Books Printing: February 1992

AVON TRADEMARK REG. U.S. PAT. OFF. AND IN OTHER COUNTRIES, MARCA REGISTRADA, HECHO EN U.S.A.

Printed in the U.S.A.

RA   10  9  8  7  6  5  4  3  2  1

For my friends,
who despite time and distance,
are always with me

and

For my loyal readers,
who endlessly inspire me

# Prologue

*London, England*
*Autumn 1736*

"**Y**er late, ye little bitch!"

Nimbly dodging her father's swinging fist, her heart thundering, Susanna Guthrie skittered barefoot across the dirt floor and took refuge behind a lopsided table.

Daniel Guthrie was drunk again.

In the hazy light cast by the smoking oil lamp, his watery eyes were red-rimmed and his once-handsome face was flushed and bloated. The stuffy air reeked of cheap gin, sweat, and urine. Shattered liquor bottles littered the tiny cellar, a sure sign of her father's explosive anger. An anger which the long-unemployed foundryman would easily vent upon Susanna if she was foolish enough to come within arm's reach. Her bruised young body still ached from the cuffing he'd given her yesterday; her thin shoulders still stung from last week's lashing.

"Where the 'ell 'ave ye been, girl?" Daniel slurred thickly, staggering toward her. "Ye know me rules. Yer t' be back 'ere by sunset with yer day's earnings. 'Twas dark two 'ours past!" Lurching into the table, he glared at her furiously. "Answer me, ye chit, and stop starin' at me with those big green saucers o' yers! Where were ye?"

Susanna swallowed hard against the fear that was

1

paralyzing her throat. She drew some courage from the hope that her explanation for her tardiness would soothe his temper.

"Covent Garden Theatre, Papa," she blurted in a nervous rush. "An op'ra was playin' there tonight, so I went t' the front entrance t' do me beggin'. Look!" She fished into both pockets of her filthy, tattered skirt and withdrew two handfuls of gleaming coins. "I tied one leg up under me dress joost like y' taught me and limped 'round with a wooden crutch under me shoulder. I must 'ave been a truly pitiful sight, for two fine ladies with tears rollin' down their rouged cheeks gave me a shillin' apiece. A kind gentl'man, too!"

"Dump the money on the table," Daniel commanded, his eyes alight with greed and his fury clearly forgotten as he plopped heavily onto a bench. "That's me clever girl. All of it now, and show me yer pockets."

Susanna quickly obliged him. In her fumbling haste to turn her pockets inside out and prove that they were empty, she tore a hole in one of them.

"Friggin' flimsy fabric," she muttered under her breath, poking her forefinger through the offending tear. Now she would have to mend her only skirt before she set off to beg in the early morning, and she hated sewing!

Intent upon the pocket, Susanna did not look up in time to see her father's sudden movement. His sharp, unexpected box to her ear sent her reeling to the floor.

"I'll 'ear no more cursin' from ye, Susanna Jane!" Daniel shouted, retaking his seat with a grunt. "Yer mother's foul tongue, the devil rest 'er soul, was the bane o' me life, and I'll not 'ave the same from ye! 'Tis bad enough ye remind me of 'er, the witch, wi' yer honey hair and wanton's face."

Her head ringing from the painful blow, Susanna gripped a table leg and rose shakily. Hot tears burned her eyes, but she stubbornly forced them back. She wouldn't give her father the satisfaction of seeing her cry, no matter how much he hurt her. She had learned early that tears didn't help anyway. They seemed to make him madder, and he would hit her again, just for good measure.

Instead, as she silently watched him count the coins and test their metal between his rotted teeth, Susanna thought for the thousandth time of leaving Daniel Guthrie and his brutality far behind her. But where could she go? He had warned that if she ever ran away, he would not rest until he found her, and she believed him. Oh, how she believed him. She could well imagine the beating he would give her then.

Sighing, Susanna darted a glance around the shadowed cellar.

At least here she had a roof over her head, a bed of straw, and one meal a day, which was far better than sleeping cold, miserable, and starving in doorways and dark alleys. As for her father's abuse, his very presence did offer her some measure of protection from others who might seek to do her harm.

At twelve going on thirteen, she was experiencing most perplexing changes in her body, including a bloody flux that came every month, starting five months ago, and budding breasts and gentle curves she could not hide. She had seen the leers lately on the faces of male passersby, the hungry, speculative looks that made her shudder. She would be a fool if she left this place to spend the nights alone on London's streets, prey to any ruffian or footpad who might take a lustful fancy to her.

No, she was safer here, at least until she found a position as a scullery maid in some gentry household. Her father could hardly object to the steady work and wage, which couldn't be found in the begging trade, and she wouldn't be running away from him. He would know exactly where she lived and would share in her earnings. Mayhap he would even be pleased with her new status.

She, for one, had no intention of remaining a beggar forever. Not Susanna Jane Guthrie.

She had big dreams. Dreams of putting this miserable existence behind her and making a better life for herself, and, if she was lucky, in a few years finding a skilled tradesman to marry. It wasn't so important that they love each other, just that he be a good, honest man. A man she could trust and put her faith in. A man wholly unlike her father. Together, if they worked hard enough, maybe they could afford a place of their own someday, a small business or a shop. Aye, a shop with a fine bow window would be grand—

"Ye did well this day, chit," Daniel said, his gruff voice jarring Susanna's daydreaming. He scooped the stacked coins into a small leather pouch and stuffed it inside his stained shirt. "But I've a way ye can do even better, and God knows"—his bleary eyes raked her appraisingly, lingering on her swelling bodice—"yer old enough now."

"How's that, Papa?" Susanna asked, growing uncomfortable under his queer scrutiny.

"Never ye mind. Take these two pennies upstairs t' Nellie Brice in the gin shop and buy yerself a pitcher of 'ot water, then bring it down 'ere and clean yerself up. Oh, aye, and fetch me another bottle o' gin. We've a fine gentleman caller comin' t' see y' tonight."

Confused, Susanna stared at him. "A gentl'man . . . t' see me?"

"Aye. Mr. Keefer Dunn. Enough questions now. Go on wi' ye."

She tensed, growing wary.

Keefer Dunn was no gentleman, but a well-known scoundrel and king of thieves who had grown wealthy from the sale of stolen goods. She had seen him leaving the cellar just the other day as she was returning home from a day's begging. With his ruddy face marred by the pox and his crooked gap-toothed smile, he was not a pretty sight, and the disturbingly possessive way his strange amber eyes had roamed over her had filled her with disgust. Even more repulsive had been the pungent smell of sweat and stale ale that had emanated from him as he passed her on the street, the odor heightened by his sickeningly sweet cologne.

"I don't understand, Papa. Wot does Mr. Dunn want wi' me?"

Too late, Susanna realized she'd asked her father one too many questions. His face had grown so red it had taken on the hue of an overripe berry, and looked fit to burst at any moment.

"Are ye daft, girl?" Daniel exploded, jumping up from the bench so suddenly that it crashed to the floor. "Surely y' didn't think I'd waste yer beauty upon the beggar's trade! Ha' ye not looked into a mirror o' late? Yer bloomin' into a fine-lookin' wench, and ye've caught Keefer's eye, ye 'ave! He's bought ye for the night and paid me a pretty price, too! I was at me wit's end when ye didn't come home, and 'im probably on 'is way t' see ye even as we speak. Now get yer bloody arse upstairs so ye'll be ready when 'e comes t' call! 'E wants a virgin, and a clean one!"

Susanna was thunderstruck, his words searing into her brain like red-hot pokers. She felt ill, her meager lunch of dry, days-old bread and sour milk roiling in her stomach.

Her father had sold her to Keefer Dunn! He wanted her to whore for him! What a fool she was to have believed she was safe here. After years of his abuse, she should have guessed he would do something like this—

"Keep in mind, chit, that if ye please Keefer b'neath the sheets tonight, 'e might take ye on for a while as 'is mistress," Daniel added coarsely, oblivious to her horrified distress. "Joost think of it! Fancy clothes, plenty o' food t' put some flesh on those skinny ribs o' yers, and money t' buy whate'er yer 'eart desires. You and me can make a right pretty penny t'gether."

"No!"

Daniel gaped at her in stunned surprise, his face turning an even deeper shade of red. Finally he managed to choke out, "Tell me I 'eard ye incorrectly, Susanna Jane. Y' know bloody well the price for disobeyin' yer father. Now I'll 'ear an 'Aye, Papa' if ye please."

Susanna shook her head, her knees quaking so badly she could almost hear them knocking together. She had never crossed Daniel Guthrie before. It was both heady and terribly frightening, yet this time he had gone too far. She would not be his whore!

"Ye heard me right, Papa," she said, her heart beating violently in her chest. Commanding her limbs to move, she began to edge around the table. "I won't do it. I've begged fer ye since I was only four years old and picked pockets time and again, but I will na' whore fer ye." She glanced in panic at the door, which seemed miles away instead of a few short feet, then back to her father, "I 'ave dreams, Papa. I—I was plannin' t' find work as a scullery maid—"

Susanna shrieked in terror as her father dashed the table out of the way with an enraged roar and lunged crazily at her.

"Bitch! I'll teach ye t' cross me! Do y' think I care a whit about yer friggin' dreams? Ye'll do as I say, and like it! 'Twill be over me corpse that ye become a bloody maid!"

If Daniel hadn't been drunk Susanna wouldn't have had a chance, but the copious quantity of gin he had already consumed gave her the slightest advantage. As he lost his balance and went down on one knee, she eluded his flailing grasp and fled to the door.

"Oh, God. Oh, God, please 'elp me!" she prayed, clawing frantically at the rusty latch.

It gave way just as she felt her father's large hand clamp upon her shoulder. With raw fear flooding her body, she turned her head and bit his nearest finger as hard as she could. He bellowed in pain and practically ripped her dress from her back before he suddenly released her. Panting like a wild animal and gripping her torn bodice to her breasts, Susanna threw open the door. She scrambled up the damp stairs to the street and flung herself into the foggy lamplit night.

"Whoa there, me pretty pet! Where do ye think yer off to? I've come t' pay ye a little visit. Didn't yer father tell ye?"

Susanna stopped short just before crashing headlong into a grinning Keefer Dunn, who materialized out of the swirling mists like one of Satan's own evil minions. She gaped at him in horror, despair filling her heart as her father cried out close behind her, "Catch 'er, Dunn! Catch 'er. She's runnin' away!"

"Wot the 'ell?" Keefer's leering smile faded instantly and he made a grab for her arm. "Come 'ere, girl!"

Without thinking and desperate to escape, Susanna sidestepped him and ran straight into the middle of the street. She did not hear the sharp clattering of hooves upon the paving stones, or the coachman bellowing to make way. All she knew was that her father and Keefer Dunn were hard upon her heels like rabid, slathering dogs, determined to bring her down.

It took a woman's high-pitched scream to jolt her from her frenzied daze. She heard someone cry, "Look out, wench—oh, Lord, look out! The carriage!" Glancing over her bare shoulder, she saw the black hackney coach bearing down upon her at the same moment that she was pushed violently from behind.

Gasping, Susanna pitched forward onto the cobbled street and rolled over and over, striking her forehead against one of the posts that railed off the pedestrians' walkway. As something warm trickled down her face, she heard her father's voice eerily cut off as he cursed and shouted her name, horses neighing in fright and carriage wheels grinding to an abrupt halt. Then a stocky, blurred figure was standing over her and rasping breathlessly, "Ye didn't think . . . ye'd get away from Keefer Dunn, did ye, chit? I paid good money . . . fer yer favors."

Susanna's mouth opened in a soundless scream, then all reality ceased and she was swallowed by blessed darkness.

"I believe she's waking up, your ladyship. Shall I fetch her some hot tea and broth?"

"Not yet, Mary. Give the poor child a few moments

first. She might fall right back to sleep. I wouldn't be surprised if she did, what with that nasty bump on her head and all those awful bruises. For shame! I always knew London was a wicked town, but I'm more convinced of it than ever. We'll be leaving in the morning for Fairford, of that you can be sure. Our sleepy little Cotswold village may be quiet and provincial, but at least one can walk safely in the streets.''

"Aye, indeed. Ah, there we go, she's opening her eyes, and what a lovely green color they are, too. Almost like Camille's, wouldn't you say, your ladyship?''

"So they are. How are you feeling, child?''

Wincing at the painful throbbing in her head, Susanna licked her dry lips and stared with confusion at the petite, gray-haired woman sitting so straight beside the bed.

Dressed in shimmering blue silk with a triple strand of gleaming pearls around her neck, she had a stern countenance but her hazel eyes were kind and full of concern. Behind her stood another woman, stout and dressed quite simply, with a starched cap pinned atop her brown hair and a blindingly white apron tied around her ample waist. She smiled at Susanna and said gently, "Answer her ladyship, child. You've nothing to fear from us.''

"Me—me 'ead 'urts," Susanna stammered, her tongue feeling strangely thick and heavy. "Like someone's poundin' on it with a 'ammer.''

The silk-clad woman nodded sympathetically. "Yes, I'm sure it's quite dreadful, but the physician has assured me the pain will fade before long.'' She leaned forward in her chair and lightly patted Susanna's head with a cool palm. "Now, my child, if you're feeling up to it, perhaps we could talk about what happened earlier this evening. I must say that you do look a bit better to me, not half so pale. Perhaps you've had enough sleep for a little while.''

As if she hadn't heard, Susanna's eyes wandered from the older woman's direct gaze and patrician features to the quilted ivory-colored canopy overhead, then to the embroidered satin spread covering the huge bed. She fingered the smooth fabric, having never felt anything so fine before. Soft down pillows cushioned her head; clean, sweet-smelling sheets were tucked around her chest; and she was wearing some sort of fleecy white garment that felt incredibly warm and soft against her skin.

Still caressing the bedspread, Susanna let her gaze drift around the well-appointed room: rose-papered walls, a cheery fire in the hearth, candles glowing in shiny silver holders, thick carpets upon the floor. She had never seen such richness. Surely she must be dreaming, unless . . .

She gasped, her eyes darting back to the two women. She looked incredulously from one concerned face to the other. "Yer angels, ain't ye? I've died and gone straight t' 'eaven!"

"Good gracious, no, child," the older woman said with a small laugh, glancing up at her quietly chuckling companion. "I've garnered some praise for my charitable works in Gloucestershire, but I've never yet been called an angel."

"Well, if yer not angels, then ye must be . . ." Susanna's eyes widened fearfully as she drew the bedding up under her chin, her sense of wonder supplanted by dread.

Oh, no. Who could have thought the devil's lair would be so lovely? She should never have picked those bloody pockets!

The sumptuously dressed woman's voice held a faint touch of amusement. "My dear girl, whatever you may be thinking, you're quite earthbound, I can assure you. You're very much alive and, as the physician informed me, in amazingly good health, despite those bruises and strap marks upon your back . . ." She cleared her throat delicately, her expression sobering. "Mary, fetch the tea and broth, and some sweet biscuits. I think Susanna Guthrie is ready for some nourishment now."

"Aye, my lady."

"How do y' know me name?" blurted Susanna, her apprehension all but forgotten in her amazement.

"Mind your manners, child," Mary interjected kindly yet with a firm, no-nonsense tone, "and address Lady Melicent Redmayne, the Dowager Baroness of Fairford, as either 'my lady' or 'your ladyship' from now on." Then she gave a wink. "I'm Mary Sayers, Lady Redmayne's waiting-maid. You may call me by my Christian name." With that, Mary bustled from the room, leaving the door slightly ajar.

"One of the witnesses at the unfortunate accident this evening, a young woman who said she was married to the proprietor of a gin shop, told me your name," Lady Redmayne explained, "and that you lived with your father in their cellar."

"Aye, that would 'ave been Nellie Brice," Susanna said, adding as an afterthought, "yer ladyship."

"Yes. Well . . ." Lady Redmayne paused, drawing her lips together, as if she was uncertain how best to proceed. "Susanna," she began after a long moment, "you narrowly escaped being run down by my private coach this evening. My grandniece and I were on our way home from the opera when . . ." Again she stopped, reaching for Susanna's hand. "My dear child, I don't know how else to tell you this other than straight out. Your father was killed tonight. He fell beneath the wheels and was trampled before the coachman could bring the carriage to a halt."

Thoroughly stunned, Susanna felt her face grow warm, but she said nothing.

"The local constable was summoned, and between his small knowledge of your family and the information Mrs. Brice willingly offered, I soon gathered that you had led a most wretched life. Of course I would not hear of it when the constable suggested that, as an orphan, you should be sent to a workhouse. I feel responsible for what happened—it was my coach, after all—but in your case, I do believe that divine providence intervened and saved you from a cruel and brutal man."

Aye, Daniel Guthrie had been a cruel man indeed, Susanna thought, feeling no grief at this startling news of his death. Instead, euphoria mixed with relief was rising from some deep place inside her. It was probably a terrible sin for her to feel this way about her father, but she had the most unseemly urge to fling back the covers and jump up and down upon the bed.

He couldn't hurt her anymore! Never again would he kick her awake and shove her out the door to beg before the sun had risen. Never again would he try to sell her for some man's pleasure!

Misreading Susanna's silence for shock, Lady Redmayne gently squeezed her hand and gave a reserved smile, which appeared to be something she was not accustomed to doing very often. "My child, I can think of only one way to make amends for your loss of home and hearth. I offer you a place within my household. I fully expect that, with proper training, you will make an excellent waiting-maid to my eleven-year-old grand-niece, Camille. She's a good, gentle girl who also wants very much to help you. As we're leaving London to-morrow, I can't give you much time to think it over—"

"I'd be 'appy t' live in yer 'ousehold, milady," Susanna exclaimed in a breathless rush, astonished by her good fortune. A waiting-maid! In this fine lady's home! And she had believed she'd be lucky if she found work as a scullery maid, scrubbing dirty pots and pans. "I learn fast, I do, y'll see. Y' won't regret yer kindness t' me, I promise." Then a sudden shadow, black and menacing, fell over her heart, and fear thickened like a lump in her throat. "Yer ladyship, there was another man at the accident. 'E—'e must 'ave been the one who shoved me out o' the way o' the coach."

Lady Redmayne shook her meticulously coiffured head. "When I was helped from the carriage, I saw a man standing over you, but he disappeared into the fog when shouts went up for the constable. Why, child? Was he a friend of yours? Perhaps you would rather we find him—"

"No!" Susanna bit her lip at Lady Redmayne's astonished expression, and she quickly sought to explain her rude outburst. "Forgive me fer raisin' me voice, yer ladyship. What I meant t' say was, well, 'e was no friend o' mine, no matter that 'e saved me life. 'E was cut from a worse cloth than me father, if y' know wot I mean. That's why I was runnin' away. Me father 'ad sold me t' 'im. That man wanted me to—to—"

"I can well imagine," Lady Redmayne interrupted gently, her eyes full of pity which nonetheless quickly faded. She squared her delicately boned shoulders, her spine ramrod-straight as her tone grew brusque but not unkind. "So we're decided, then. You will remain with us. As for this night's unfortunate incident and its unsavory cast of players, we'll put it all behind us, shall we?"

Susanna nodded vigorously, grateful tears in her eyes. God willing, she prayed, she had seen the last of Keefer Dunn and his filthy, lusting kind.

"Is she going to be all right, Aunt Melicent?"

As Lady Redmayne turned in her chair, her silk skirt rustling stiffly, Susanna's blurred gaze flew across the room to where a young girl with honey-gold curls peeked shyly at her from behind the door.

"Yes, Camille. Susanna is going to be just fine." The baroness beckoned to the girl with a wave of her jeweled hand. "Come closer, my dear. There's no reason to be so bashful."

To Susanna, the girl walking gracefully toward the bed looked like a delicate china doll in her pastel-pink silk dress, slippers, and matching lace-trimmed cap. And to her amazement as Camille drew closer, Susanna found herself staring into a pair of deep green eyes that were remarkably like her own.

"Camille, meet Susanna Guthrie. When she's ready, Susanna shall be your new personal maid."

Camille rested her small white hands on the plush wine-colored velvet back of her great-aunt's chair. "Hello."

" 'Tis pleased I am t' meet ye, miss."

"Camille has been living with me since she was three years old. Her father, James Cary, sent her here to England for her education, and rightly so." Lady Redmayne sniffed in disgust. "He lives in the uncivilized wilds of Tidewater Virginia. Vile, barbarous, unhealthy place."

"The American colony?" Susanna asked, her curiosity piqued. She had often overheard sailors and merchants telling fascinating stories about America. Stories about red-skinned people who wore feathers and beads in their hair and adorned their bodies with paint. Fearless fur trappers who disappeared into the wilderness only to return months later with hundreds of glistening pelts. And tale after tale about the amazing richness of the land, and all it had to offer England.

Camille nodded solemnly, then, still half-hiding behind the chair, she pointed to Susanna's puffy, bruised forehead. "Does it hurt very much?"

Susanna shrugged. "Only a little." In truth, it scarcely seemed to hurt at all anymore.

Camille looked relieved, and offered a timid smile.

Susanna smiled back, convinced she was, indeed, in the company of angels.

# Chapter 1

*Aboard the brig Charming Nancy*
*Summer 1743*

**"I** don't want t' 'ear another word from ye about dyin', Camille, not another bloody word! I know yer feelin' poorly, but y've already come through the worst o' the fever. I'd swear on me father's black 'eart that y'll be enjoyin' some fresh air and sunshine on the deck by week's end. Now give yer Susanna Guthrie a smile, or I'll joost take m'self straight back t' Bristol!"

"And how will you do that?" Camille Cary asked, forcing a smile as she swallowed painfully. She inclined her head upon the sweat-damp pillow and watched Susanna soak a linen cloth in a basin of cool water. "Swim?"

"Aye, either that or I'll catch a ride on a dolphin, I will! Or a spoutin' whale. Joost watch me!"

Susanna was rewarded with a soft laugh, the first she'd heard from Camille in several days, but it quickly became a hacking cough. She set the basin upon the gently swaying planked floor and moved to the head of the narrow bed, where she lifted and supported her young mistress's quaking shoulders and back until the spasm passed. Then she helped Camille to lie down, tucking the blanket around her too-thin frame.

"Better?" Susanna asked, feeling guilty that she had inadvertently brought on another coughing spell. She had only wanted to lighten the mood in this stuffy, dank-smelling cabin. Anything to get Camille's mind off her illness!

Camille nodded weakly, a ghost of a smile upon her pale, cracked lips. "Dearest Susanna. You've always known how to make me laugh. I can never keep a straight face when you talk like you did when we first found you in London. I would have thought after all these years, and Aunt Melicent's constant insistence that you speak proper English, that you'd have forgotten how."

Susanna shrugged lightly as she wrung out the cloth and pulled her chair nearer the bed. "I guess some things you just never forget."

Camille's feverish eyes met Susanna's as the damp cloth covered her forehead. "Speaking of forgetting, you never said how Captain Keyes is feeling today. Is he better?"

Susanna concentrated upon wringing out another cloth. "Oh, yes, doing quite well," she lied, sparing Camille again from the true horror that gripped the *Charming Nancy.*

Five weeks out of Bristol a terrible pestilence had struck the huge vessel, and within a fortnight it had become a floating death ship. There weren't enough provisions to turn back to England, and even if that had been possible, they were already closer to the colonies. Flushed with the fever and barely able to stand, Captain Samuel Keyes had ordered his men to sail with all haste to Yorktown, Virginia.

Now the grizzled captain was dead, buried at sea just that morning along with three more crew members and a half dozen passengers, two children among them. Susanna had watched silently on the top deck as the shrouded mummylike figures had plummeted into the choppy gray sea with scarcely a prayer to guide them into the hereafter, the ship's parson having died late last week.

She couldn't blame what remained of the frightened crew for not performing some semblance of a burial service. They simply wished to rid the ship as quickly as possible of any diseased corpses.

So she had mumbled a prayer, for the dead who were finally free of their earthly suffering; for her dear Camille, that she would grow well again and healthy; and for herself, that she might be spared the killing fever. Then she had returned to their cabin with the day's ration of thin barley soup and stale bread, wishing Camille hadn't been so generous in sharing with the ship's cook the extra food supplies Lady Redmayne had insisted they bring with them for the long voyage.

That was just like Camille. Generous and caring to a fault, yet so shy she had hardly left the cabin until she heard that a little boy down the passageway had taken sick.

Offering what medicines she possessed and all of her gentle comfort, Camille had sat up with the distraught parents through the night, only returning to the cabin at dawn with the sad news that the child had died. The next day, she had been struck with the fever, and she hadn't risen from her bed since. That had been almost ten days ago. Susanna didn't have the heart to tell her that the boy's parents had also sickened and died during that time, an ominous misfortune upon which she didn't wish to dwell. Oh, why, why wasn't Camille getting any better?

"Susanna."

She lifted her head at the sound of the beloved voice that had grown so feeble, only a whisper of its former melodic strength, and she immediately felt her cheeks begin to burn. Camille was staring at her so intently she could swear her closest friend could see right into her soul.

"Captain Keyes is dead, isn't he?"

Susanna knew any further attempt to lie would be futile. She nodded, wondering what she had done to give herself away.

Sighing, Camille glanced at the wall. "It's just as well."

Susanna was shocked. "It's not like you to say such

things, Camille Cary. The captain was a longtime friend of your family. He knew both your parents and your grandfather. Why, he braved late-winter seas to bring you the news about your father.''

"I know, I know, and I can only hope that heaven will forgive me for saying it,'' Camille murmured. She clutched Susanna's arm with a hand so pale that the thin blue veins stood out in sharp relief against her white skin. "We must talk, Susanna. I've been thinking about something since last night. Something important. I couldn't sleep because of it. But you mustn't tease me as you did a few moments ago when I tried to tell you. This is serious.''

"All right, no more teasing,'' Susanna agreed, sensing she had failed to divert Camille's attention from her suffering. "Now, what's so important that it's robbing you of precious sleep?''

Camille's gaze grew almost pleading. "I know you won't want to hear this, Susanna, but you must listen to me. If something happens to me, if—if I die, I want you to go to Virginia in my place as Camille Cary and accept my inheritance. I want you to accept Briarwood, my father's tobacco plantation, as your own.''

Susanna stared at her incredulously, so stunned she didn't know what to say. Finally, gathering together her frayed emotions, she said with quiet vehemence, "Nothing's going to happen to you. I won't let it! In a few days you'll be feeling better, then everything will go on just as before. When we reach Virginia, you'll find a husband, just as your father wanted you to, and you'll settle down happily at Briarwood and raise lots of children, just as you always wanted to—''

"Perhaps,'' Camille interrupted softly, squeezing Susanna's arm. Tears welled in her eyes and tumbled down hollow, wasted cheeks. "But if I don't get better, promise me that you will do as I ask. You've been like a true sister to me, Susanna Guthrie, and a truer friend. My only friend. I want to know that you're well provided for. You've already been dealt more than your share of unhappiness. I don't want to worry that you might find yourself in as terrible a situation as you knew in London. You deserve so much more.''

Deeply touched, Susanna opened her mouth to protest, but she was silenced by a weak flutter of her mistress's hand.

"No, listen to me, Susanna. There's another reason and, I admit, it's a selfish one. If you refuse, Aunt Melicent will inherit Briarwood, and she has sworn never to set foot in the colonies. She'll sell the plantation without ever having seen it, and then everything my father and grandfather worked so hard to build out of the wilderness will be lost. I can't allow that to happen! Briarwood meant so much to them. It means so much to me. Cary sweat and blood are in that soil, my family's hopes and dreams."

Camille drew a ragged breath. "Aunt Melicent never had a good thing to say about Virginia. No, not even once. You heard her protests when I received Papa's letter just after Christmas, saying it was time I wed and summoning me home by autumn. Then Captain Keyes brought word in April about Papa's death, and I decided to accept his kind offer of escort and leave England even sooner than she had expected . . .''

Camille grew silent, grieving for a father she had rarely seen but whom she had loved dearly.

Aye, Susanna thought, Lady Redmayne had never minced words about Virginia, calling it a cursed and barbarous place peopled by savage Indians, traitors to the Crown, and the dregs of England's society. Yet Susanna had never understood the baroness's intense dislike for a place she had never visited until Camille had told her the full story.

Lady Redmayne had never forgiven her adventurous brother, Camille's grandfather, for selling their family estate in England so he might start a new life in America. Then when Camille's mother, Constance, and two older brothers had died of a strange malady known only to the colonies, the baroness's low opinion of Virginia had been forever sealed.

Susanna shook her head, becoming angry with herself. None of this mattered. Camille was going to get better, and that was that!

"Even if something did happen to you, which it won't," Susanna objected with characteristic stubbornness, clasping Camille's chilled hands tightly, as if she could will some of her own strength and warmth into them, "such a farfetched plan would never work."

"It will," Camille insisted. "I wouldn't have suggested it to you if I had any doubts. We're almost the same age and we look so much alike, Susanna—you know that, though you're by far the prettier one."

"Camille . . ."

"Shhh, you know it's true. And the last time anyone saw me in Virginia, I was only three years old. Papa's last visit"—her voice caught and she composed herself before continuing—"his last visit to England was two years ago. If he has described me to anyone since then, he could have been describing you as well."

"My temperament falls quite short of your sweet and gentle nature," Susanna said with wry self-deprecation. "In that respect, we're no more alike than night and day. Someone would surely guess that I was an impostor."

Camille gave a very small laugh, which sounded more like a congested rattle. "You'd manage, Susanna, I'm sure of it. I always wanted to be more like you, so clever and headstrong, and now, in a sense, I'll have my chance. How I always admired the way you filled that great, somber house with your laughter and drove Aunt Melicent to distraction with your antics. Remember the time you invited all the village children to Sunday supper, and the time you collected that jar of spiders and emptied them out on Mistress Plumb's desk after she scolded me during a lesson—"

"Or when I convinced you to climb out onto the roof with me so we could see the stars better, giving Lady Redmayne the scare of her life," Susanna broke in, recalling the stern dressing-down they had both received, once safely back inside Camille's bedchamber.

"Aye, I'm sure there were many times she wished she had left me in London's slums."

"That's not true, Susanna, and you know it. She was very fond of you. She always hoped that some of your joie de vivre would chase away my shyness, and perhaps it did, a little. You faced such adversity as a child, yet your spirit remained undaunted. I couldn't help but be encouraged and inspired." Camille's expression grew pensive. "Even so, I don't think Aunt Melicent ever accepted the fact that I'd never be the belle of the Cotswolds. After she spent so much time teaching me to be a lady, I truly disappointed her when I proved to be such a timid homebody. I got to be quite good at avoiding all those dreadful balls and card parties, didn't I?"

"Yes," Susanna agreed, still hoping to convince Camille of the absurdity of her plan, "but Lady Redmayne didn't always take no for an answer. You had a few social acquaintances in Fairford. In Gloucestershire, for that matter. What makes you think none of them will ever travel to the colonies?"

"And trade their comfortable country lives for a dangerous sea voyage and the unknown wilds of America? If any of my acquaintances possessed a daring streak, I'm sure Aunt Melicent would quickly persuade them from their folly with her talk of red savages, mysterious dread diseases, and the terrors of ocean travel. No, the only person who could have hindered my plan was dear Captain Keyes . . . and he's dead—"

Strangling on the last word, Camille looked truly frightened. She clutched Susanna's hands as if she would never let them go and added in a tremulous voice, "I almost wish Aunt Melicent had convinced me to stay in England. I—I'm not very brave, Susanna."

Swallowing the sudden hard lump in her throat, Susanna had to fight back helpless tears.

Don't let your fear show, Susanna Jane, she chided herself. Camille needed her comfort and courage, not doubt and weakness. She would have to be brave enough for the both of them!

"Everything is going to be fine," Susanna said with conviction, truly believing it. "You'll see. I promise."

Easing her hands from Camille's weakening grasp, Susanna busied herself with changing the cloth on her mistress's forehead, which felt much warmer than it had that morning. Camille looked so weary, the dark smudges beneath her eyes more sharply drawn. It was clear their lengthy discussion had taxed her strength.

"Camille, you must rest. We've talked enough for now."

"I will, but only after you swear, Susanna. Swear that you'll go to Virginia in my place if anything happens to me. Please. It would mean so much to me to know . . ."

Susanna met Camille's desperate eyes and relented, if only to humor her so that she might get some sleep.

"Very well. I swear it. Now I don't want to hear any more talk of dying. Are we agreed?"

Camille's thin shoulders slumped back upon the pillows in relief, and a gentle smile curved her lips.

"Agreed."

Susanna sat numbly in her chair, staring at the narrow bed, Camille's bed, which looked so huge in its emptiness.

For the past week she had been unable to bring herself to sleep in it, as if by doing so she would commit some sacrilege or gross act of disrespect. Instead, heartbroken, she had slept upon her cot against the opposite wall, telling herself each night before she snuffed the lamp that Camille would be in that bed when she awoke in the morning, and everything would be as it had been before.

Of course in the morning the bed would still be empty, and she must reconcile herself to the fact that Camille would never come back.

The killing fever had claimed her after all.

Death had come like a silent thief one beautiful, sunny afternoon when Susanna had been convinced Camille was getting better. Her cough had lessened, her skin had been cool to the touch; even her pale cheeks had held two rosy spots of color. Yet Camille must have sensed that the thief was in their cabin, for her last words were a poignant, whispered good-bye.

"Remember, Susanna . . . you swore. When you get to Virginia, marry wisely, as I would have done, and live happily. Please . . . don't forget me."

The remainder of that day was an awful blur in Susanna's memory. Her only vivid recollections were the unsettling exchange of her dress and apron for one of Camille's simpler gowns, the excellent fit being no surprise since they were virtually the same size; then later, Camille's hasty burial at sea. Rather, Susanna Guthrie's burial at sea, for so it had been recorded in the ship's records.

In her grief, some small part of herself had been rational enough to identify herself as Camille Cary when she had gone to report the death, the deceased being her unfortunate waiting-maid, Susanna. No one had asked questions. Camille had been such a recluse that few people aboard ship except Captain Keyes had ever seen her. Thus Susanna had fulfilled her sworn promise and her dearest friend's dying wish. There would be no going back.

Susanna sighed heavily, her gaze dropping to her folded hands in her lap.

They were idle, purposeless hands now that she no longer had Camille to wait upon, fine gowns to be laid out and arranged, hair to be dressed, pillows to be fluffed, or tea to be poured and served. She didn't know quite what to do with herself. As she wondered for the hundredth time what her life would be like when she reached Virginia, doubts crowded in upon her.

How could she, a waiting-maid, former beggar and pickpocket, possibly act the part of a real lady?

It was true that through her seven years of service to Camille her speech and manners had become proper. She had been taught to read, write, and do some arithmetic by Camille's staid governess, Mistress Plumb, yet she lacked any musical talent whatsoever and was

all thumbs at needlework—besides hating it anyway!—
two prerequisites for refined ladies of quality.

She hadn't been trained to be a "decoration for society" like Camille, although they had used to play that
they were both grand ladies until Lady Redmayne had
caught them and lectured Susanna severely on her correct place in life. What was even worse, she knew absolutely nothing about tobacco! How could she, a
bloody waiting-maid, run a huge plantation? She was a
fool to have sworn to enact this insane masquerade!
Surely she could have been more forceful in persuading
Camille that it was sheer folly to even think such a plan
could work—

Susanna started at the sharp rap on the door and fairly
flew out of the chair.

"Who—who is it?"

"Captain's mate, Miss Cary. I've been goin' 'round
to the passengers to tell ye that we've sighted land. We
should make Yorktown by tomorrow mornin' if the
winds hold up. God be praised, I'd say! A good ev'ning
to ye.'

Land, Susanna thought, pacing the cabin before retaking her seat rather shakily. Soon her lifelong masquerade would begin. Could she manage it?

All she had to do was remember the fervent plea in
Camille's eyes to have her answer.

"What the devil's the matter with you, Susanna
Jane?" she suddenly chided herself aloud, slamming
the flat of her palm down so hard upon a side table that
her skin stung. "You've never been one to shrink from
anything life handed you! Why don't you just accept
your good fortune and do the name of Cary proud?''

Aye, and so she would, Susanna vowed, feeling more
like her normal optimistic self than she had since Camille's death.

Preserving Briarwood was the least she could do for
a dear friend who had played a part in rescuing her
years ago from an abusive, drunken father and a miserable life of prostitution. Why, she owed it to Camille!
What better way to thank her for the happiness she had

known in Fairford, the sense of belonging, the security and comfort, and most of all, their friendship? Perhaps this new life would even help her distance herself from her bitter childhood memories and the terrible nightmares that still plagued her; nightmares that caused her to wake in a sweat, sometimes screaming, her flesh on fire from a phantom lashing that seemed terrifyingly real.

Susanna shuddered and quickly shoved away her thoughts of bad dreams, purposely reflecting instead on what lay ahead for her. She was a quick learner and a good mimic. Surely if she watched other young ladies, she would manage to discern the fine points of Virginia's social behavior.

Suddenly Susanna felt a nervous flutter in her stomach as she recalled the reason Camille's father had summoned her home to Briarwood.

James Cary's last letter had said it was time his daughter found a husband, and he had even mentioned that he had someone in mind, although he hadn't given a name, writing instead that they would discuss it when Camille arrived in Virginia in the fall. Oh, dear, that meant *she* was now to be wed! Susanna thought. And he wouldn't be the skilled tradesman of her long-held dreams, either. Not anymore. Not for an heiress, and a very rich one at that.

Lady Redmayne had thoroughly coached Camille on the criteria for finding a suitable husband once she was in Virginia, stringent rules which Susanna knew she must now adopt. She could still hear the baroness's dignified recital as if it had been directed straight at her.

"An heiress like yourself, Camille, must marry into both money and position. Marrying for love is a luxury only the poor can afford. That is not to say, of course, you will forego your share of happiness. You and your husband will undoubtedly discover a congenial contentment that quite often leads to genuine affection. My marriage to Baron Redmayne, God rest his soul, was most agreeable even though we were barely acquainted when we wed. Am I understood thus far, Camille?"

"Yes, Aunt Melicent."

"Good. You must wed a gentleman who is your equal, one who can bring as much, if not more, material wealth to your marriage than you yourself bring. First and foremost, your husband, without any assistance from your own inheritance, must be able to support you in a manner befitting your birth. Always remember, my dear, that you've the Cary reputation to maintain, albeit in the barbarous wilds of Virginia."

Camille had never questioned these dictums, fully believing that they would help her to enrich Briarwood's fortunes, and neither would she, Susanna thought as she moved to a large trunk full of her mistress's belongings. If she chose a husband wisely, she would surely find not only security and social acceptance among the Tidewater gentry, but happiness as well. It all made perfect sense.

She had never planned to marry for love anyway. In that, Lady Redmayne had been wrong. Even for a poor woman, it made more sense to wed a good, hardworking man whom she didn't love than to fall in love and marry a handsome rakehell with few or no prospects, as her mother had done with her father. Their love had quickly soured and turned to hatred in the face of his drinking and constant unemployment. Susanna had sworn to herself long ago that that would never happen to her.

She and Camille had talked about her also finding a husband in Virginia. She had never entertained any thought of settling down in Fairford, although she had caught many a young man's eye, wanting as she did to travel with Camille to the fabled American colonies one day. They had decided that "her man" would have to be associated with Briarwood so the two women would never be far apart. James Cary had mentioned in his letters, and during his last visit to the Cotswolds, an industrious, trustworthy young man named Adam Thornton who had been working at Briarwood, first as an overseer and then as the plantation manager, and Susanna had been eager to meet him. But all that had changed now. A hired man would hardly make a proper husband for an heiress.

Susanna wished Mr. Cary had mentioned in his last letter the name of the particular gentleman he had had in mind for Camille. It would have made her task so much easier. Now she would probably have to choose from a wealth of eager suitors, and with only Lady Redmayne's strictures to guide her.

"I'll simply marry the richest, most prominent, most eligible gentleman I can find," Susanna vowed, lifting the trunk's heavy brass-bound lid. Such a union could not help but preserve the Carys' fine reputation and, most importantly, fulfill her promise to Camille.

Susanna drew out a folded whalebone hoopskirt. She was determined to practice walking in the unwieldy garment until she could do so gracefully. But it tumbled with a crisp swoosh to the floor when she spied the top of a gilt frame tucked toward the back of the trunk.

Tears dimmed her eyes as she was assailed by fresh grief. She had forgotten all about the portrait. Slowly, and with trembling hands, she withdrew a small, exquisitely framed painting of Camille.

Meant as a gift for her father, it had been commissioned by Camille shortly after she had received his last letter and before she had learned he had been killed in a hunting accident. She had debated giving it to her aunt instead, but at the last moment had decided to bring it with her to Virginia, thinking the portrait would make an appropriate wedding gift to her future husband.

Susanna gazed into a pair of serene jade-green eyes, and wondered if she could find it within herself to destroy her only image of her beloved friend. The painting would surely label her as an impostor if it fell into the wrong hands. Despite their many physical similarities, she and Camille had not looked so much alike that she could pass the portrait off as one done of her . . .

No, she could not part with it, Susanna decided firmly, her throat tight with suppressed emotion.

Instead, she found a razor-edged letter opener and deftly slit the painting from the heavy gilded frame. After rolling the canvas carefully, she buried it deep inside the trunk beneath mounds of lingerie and accessories. When she reached Briarwood, she would simply find a good hiding place for the painting. No one would ever discover it. She would see to that.

It was well past midnight when Susanna finally crawled into the narrow bed, abandoning at last the cot in which she had slept since the ill-fated ship had left Bristol. She was exhausted from hours of trying on Camille's beautiful gowns and from her tense, late-night walk upon the upper deck, where she had dumped a large cloth bag containing her few personal belongings, maid's clothes, and the costly frame into the blackened sea. Then she had returned to the cabin and done her best to bathe and wash her hair with the small bucket of precious water each passenger had been allotted.

Now, dressed in a lacy nightrail that still carried the delicate lavender scent of Camille's perfume, Susanna felt a moment's unease as she drew the embroidered coverlet up over her shoulders, both for the place she was usurping and the unknowns she would face in the morning. But her determination to honor her dearest friend's last wish proved much stronger than her niggling misgivings.

"Go t' sleep, Camille Cary," Susanna whispered drowsily as she reached over and snuffed out the lamp.

# Chapter 2

*Yorktown, Virginia*

Squinting in the brilliant July sunshine, Adam Thornton dismounted from his lathered chestnut stallion and intently scanned the line of passengers peering over the railing of the *Charming Nancy*.

Thanks to Elias, a Cary slave who had been quartered in the town to watch for the ship's arrival, word had traveled swiftly to Adam that it had finally arrived earlier that morning at the Yorktown docks. Elias had also informed him that the vessel had been struck with typhus fever during the ocean crossing, and that no one would be allowed to disembark until the town's physician had discovered if there was still a threat of disease on board. Adam had ridden the fifteen miles from Briarwood to Yorktown at a hellish pace, not knowing if Camille Cary, the young heiress he intended to marry, was alive or dead.

"Damn," he muttered darkly, a hard knot forming in his stomach as his gaze shifted from one passenger to the next.

Several young women were scattered along the railing, but none with honey-gold hair that he could see. James Cary had boasted many times about his daughter's fair tresses and sea-green eyes, so Adam had some clue as to her appearance. He ignored the blatantly appraising glance of one pretty, saucy-eyed wench, a lady's maid judging from the plainness of her clothing, and, growing more agitated, tethered his heaving stallion to a post.

Adam's athletic, solidly built frame felt like a tightly coiled spring as he strode with the slightest limp toward a somber-faced group of men standing just beyond the lowered gangplank. He recognized several neighboring tobacco planters, while the others were local merchants and townsmen who no doubt had goods aboard the large sailing vessel.

"Adam, my boy, hold up!"

Out of the corner of his eye, Adam saw Robert Grymes, another neighbor, descend from an open carriage and rush along the dock to catch up with him. Reluctantly he paused and waited for the portly planter to reach his side.

"Grymes," he acknowledged, resenting the delay. He was in no mood for conversation. He wanted to see if the other men had any information about the survivors.

"What brings you here this fine morning?" Robert asked jovially, clearly unaware of the *Charming Nancy*'s plight. "I would have thought you'd be in the tobo fields tending to Cary's Finest." The planter wiped his sweaty face with a silk handkerchief and added in a low aside, "Word has flown that you've shipped another handsome crop of sweet-scented to England, eh, Adam? Quite a tribute to James, I'd say, poor bastard. By the by, if you ever tire of managing Briarwood, I'd be happy to hire you on at my place. Just name your price. I'd pay a pretty sum to have a crop master like you supervising my leaf."

Adam had to fight the instinct to tell Grymes he'd do far better cultivating turnips in his impoverished soil, but he held his tongue. The last thing he wanted to do right now was discuss tobacco.

"I'll keep your offer in mind," he lied, eager to end their discourse. "Excuse me."

Resuming his powerful strides, he didn't care if the somewhat affronted planter kept up with him or not. As Adam approached the group gathered near the gangplank, Benjamin Carter, a wealthy town merchant as stout as Robert Grymes, nodded a greeting and stepped aside to admit Adam to their circle.

"I heard about the fever," Adam said tightly, shooting another glance at the crowded railing, only to be disappointed again. "Has the physician finished his inspection of the ship?"

"Not yet," answered the heavily jowled older man, his expression grim as he shook his bewigged head. "Nasty bit of business, this. At least half the passengers lost and two-thirds of the crew, including Captain Keyes. Damn pity. He was an honorable man. Traded with him for years, just like the Carys."

So the feisty old salt had finally met his end, Adam thought, distressed by this news. He had liked Samuel Keyes, almost as much as he had liked James Cary. He had listened to the two men swap many a tale in front of a roaring fire at Briarwood. Now they were both gone. And Camille?

His every muscle taut, he found it difficult to voice his next question. "Is there a list of surviving passengers? James Cary's daughter was to be on this ship. Captain Keyes had gone to England to fetch her home."

"Cary's daughter, you say?" blustered Robert Grymes, who had joined their group and been listening to their exchange in openmouthed disbelief. "Good God!"

Benjamin Carter's face was even more grave as he held out a rolled document. "The physician's aide just brought us their official list. Perhaps you might want to take a look first . . ."

Adam took the document from the merchant, his breath dammed in his chest as he ignored the apprehensive glances from the silent men surrounding him. He unrolled the stiff paper and read quickly, his eyes drawing like a magnet to one name.

Camille Cary.

A tic flashed across his tightened jaw, and he tried not to show his immense relief.

She was alive. His ambitious plan for revenge was still intact.

"Well?" came Robert Grymes's demanding query.

"She's on the list." Adam's pronouncement was greeted with a collective exhalation of breath.

"Splendid!" Robert enthused, a smile splitting his round, sunburned face. "I shall extend an invitation this very day for her to share supper with us at her earliest convenience. I'm most eager for Miss Cary to meet Matthew, my eldest son."

I'll wager you are, Adam thought dryly, noting the shrewd, speculative gleams in the eyes of several of his companions, whom he knew to have unmarried sons.

As one of the richest heiresses in the Tidewater, Camille was already creating a stir and she hadn't even set foot on Virginia's soil. Yet she had been causing a tumult in his own life since he had learned that the wealthy tobacco planter James Cary had an only daughter being educated in England who would return to the colony one day to be wed. When his period of indenture had finally ended and he had become a free man, Adam had looked no further than Briarwood for a job.

He had hired on as an overseer five years ago at the age of twenty-four. Even then he had known that he would somehow marry her, and no one would keep him from it. Not Matthew Grymes. Not any other planter's privileged, indolent son with his eye on marrying an heiress. Not Satan himself. Camille formed the very heart of his plan. He couldn't enact it without her.

Everything Adam had done since that first day at Briarwood, everything he had become, had been for one reason: revenge. Not a swift revenge settled by sword or pistol, but a long, tortuous revenge like the slow oozing of blood from a tiny puncture wound. Until he destroyed Dominick Spencer, the planter who had made his life a horrible nightmare during his eleven years of indenture, the man responsible for the senseless deaths of his parents, he would never be at peace.

Perhaps he would find no peace even then. His body,

mind, and heart bore permanent scars from Dominick's cruel abuse. He would never forgive, or forget.

Just to be standing here among these prosperous merchants and planters, and treated as an equal, had taken years of backbreaking work. He had come a hell of a long way since his days as an indentured servant laboring in the tobacco fields with a hoe in his callused hands.

Within two years as an overseer at Briarwood, he had been elevated to plantation manager and James Cary's trusted right-hand man, yet that hadn't been enough for him. He had worked even harder and become renowned as a crop master, a man possessing superior judgment in the production of tobacco, a man called upon for advice by other planters even though he owned no land himself.

This title had won him respect and entrance into the Tidewater's highest social circles, but it still wasn't enough. Only when he possessed his own plantation would he have the wealth he needed to set into motion his plan for revenge, and he wanted Briarwood, one of the richest and most fertile plantations along the York River.

There was only one way to get it: Camille.

Upon hearing that she had finally been summoned home to Virginia, Adam hadn't been surprised when James Cary had given him permission to court her; the planter had been pleased that Adam had asked, saying he would wholeheartedly recommend the match to Camille when she arrived. James had taken a liking to him and had always treated him like a son, having lost his own two young sons many years ago. Adam had used this affection to his advantage. He had done everything in his power to prove to the planter that he could be trusted, that he was worthy to be considered as a suitor for his daughter, and as damn good as any other man who might offer for her.

At first, considering his motives, Adam had experienced some guilt for the strong bond that had developed between them, but it had faded in the knowledge that when he owned Briarwood, he would respect and care for the house and land as well as James Cary had and make it prosper as never before. Adam had allowed himself to grow close to his employer, as close as he had been to anyone since the death of his parents.

Only a few months after Adam had received permission to court Camille, James Cary had been killed in a hunting accident, or so it had been concluded by the county constable. Although Adam had no proof, he believed it was murder. Now he had another score to settle with Dominick Spencer.

He had seen the two men arguing heatedly the day before the ''accident,'' and had already learned from James that Dominick also wished to court his daughter, a desire James vehemently opposed. James Cary had made no secret of his intense dislike for the man, especially after seeing the jagged, crisscrossing scars from numerous whippings that were permanently etched across Adam's back.

Adam's suspicions about Dominick Spencer made him all the more impatient to woo Camille quickly and marry her. He would let nothing, and no one, least of all that conniving bastard, stand in the way of his revenge.

''Careful, man, you're crushing the passenger list!''

Robert Grymes's exclamation pierced Adam's dark reverie. He opened his tightly closed fist and handed the crumpled document to the planter, and was saved from making a reply by the dull thud of footsteps descending the gangplank. As everyone turned expectantly, Adam could tell at once from the relieved expression upon the physician's lean, craggy face that the news was good.

''Well, can the ship be unloaded or not?'' one of the merchants demanded. ''I've a full year's income of goods in that hold!''

''Yes,'' the physician replied, then added pointedly, as if to reprimand the man for his mercenary concerns, ''and the passengers and crew may also disembark. I see no signs of the fever among them, thank God.''

Adam had to restrain himself from brushing past the physician and bounding up the gangplank to meet the young woman who would become his wife. Yet he didn't want to startle her; James had told him she was painfully shy. He planned to court her gently, albeit swiftly.

He had always had a way with women; it was not conceit to think so, just a fact. He had a gift for sensing what a woman wanted, and he had warmed his bed with lonely, neglected wives seeking discreet diversion, and with willing waiting-maids desiring a night's pleasure. He already knew that Camille shunned social events, preferring a quiet, sheltered life. He planned to offer her the same, along with his protection. By promising her the serenity she wanted, and backed by her late father's approval, he was certain that in no time he would easily win her hand in marriage.

If she was the romantic sort, his wooing of her would be even easier. A few kisses and well-chosen words would only hasten her into his arms. He would do anything, even tell her that he loved her, to ensure his success. Admittedly, such a measure would be despicable—he had never before intentionally misled a woman's affections—but he had worked too damn long and hard to leave anything to chance.

"Mr. Thornton."

Hearing the familiar deep baritone voice, Adam turned to find a strapping black man standing just off to one side.

"Good, Elias, you've returned with the carriage."

"Yes, sir, it's right over there," Elias said, nodding to the glistening black coach near Adam's tethered horse. As the slave glanced with anxious dark eyes at the ship, he twisted his tricorn hat in his huge hands. "Any word about Miss Cary?"

"She's aboard and well, as far as I know, but I haven't seen her yet," Adam replied. He stepped back as some passengers began walking down the gangplank, their trunks and other goods being hoisted to the dock by the remaining crew.

"That's good news, Mr. Thornton! Good news!" Elias exclaimed, a grin cutting across his face. "I'll go wait by the carriage. Just give a nod when you want me to load the trunks."

"Thank you, Elias." As the big man strode away, his broad back proud and straight, Adam ignored the disapproving looks of his neighboring planters. He had heard it all before. Familiarity with your inferiors will only breed contempt and disrespect. But that had not been James Cary's creed, nor was it his.

It was well-known throughout the Tidewater that Cary slaves were treated humanely; many of them had earned their freedom and remained by choice as paid workers at Briarwood. As for himself, Adam had served long enough under the whip to know that cruelty and mistreatment were the surest ways to inspire hatred. None of the overseers at Briarwood owned whips. He could not stomach the sight of them.

Adam watched intently as more passengers filed off the ship, their sickly pallor and uncertain gait suggesting they had narrowly escaped the fever's dread clutches. Yet everyone seemed happy to be setting foot upon dry land once more, especially that pretty, dark-haired lady's maid who had eyed him so lustily a short while ago. As the giggling wench followed a stout matron down the gangplank and onto the dock, her slim arms laden with floral-papered hatboxes, she passed by Adam and tripped. The next thing he knew she was in his arms, hatboxes tumbling to his feet.

"Oh, thank ye, sir, what a fine, handsome gentl'man ye are!" she gushed, smiling up at him through charcoal-black lashes as she pressed her hands against his hard, well-muscled chest. "I would have taken a nasty tumble for sure if y' hadn't caught me." Wetting her lips seductively, she made no effort to extricate herself from his embrace, adding in a rush, "Me name's Polly. Polly Blake. Me mistress and I are on our way to Williamsburg. I don't s'pose y' might have a residence there, too?"

Wryly amused by the wench's boldness and the open

invitation in her flirtatious dark eyes, Adam was equally relishing the stirring sensation of her pert breasts pressed against him. But he pushed her away when he realized that they were creating a scene, from his companions' laughter and the matron's shocked stare.

"Allow me to help you with your packages, Miss Blake," he offered, bending to retrieve the hatboxes.

As he straightened and handed them to the flattered maid, he spied the glint of honey-gold tresses trailing down the slender back of an elegantly dressed young woman who had just passed him. She continued a short way, swaying ever so slightly, as if she was having difficulty adjusting to walking upon a stationary surface, then she stopped and seemed to study the long line of carriages and wagons just beyond the dock.

Adam began to follow her, leaving behind a forgotten and insulted Polly, who stared sulkily after him. His intuition told him it was Camille, but he couldn't be sure until he saw her more closely. James had told him that his daughter was of medium height and passing fair, but with limpid green eyes that mirrored the color of a calm sea. Adam's plan for revenge didn't rest upon her appearance, but if she was somewhat attractive, he wouldn't complain. They would be sharing a bed, after all. He wanted heirs.

Adam was almost upon the young woman when she turned and gifted him with a silhouette that set his pulse racing. A gust of wind swirled her voluminous skirt around her, affording him a view of trim, shapely ankles, and as she reached up to hold the brim of her small silk hat, he caught an even more tantalizing glimpse of her creamy breasts swelling against her square-cut bodice demurely trimmed with lace.

"Miss Cary?"

Strangely, she seemed not to hear him. Adam drew even closer, so near that he could have easily reached out and touched her. So near that he could smell the skin-warmed scent of her lavender perfume. His gaze wandered over her, the soft swell of her slightly parted lips, the long curve of her throat, her temptingly slender waist. He had to admit that so far he liked what he saw. A lot.

"Miss Camille Cary?"

She whirled to face him then, and Adam's breath snagged almost painfully in his chest as their eyes met.

He had never seen a lovelier woman. Not beautiful in the classic sense, but with arresting features: sultry, wide-set eyes of an unusual opalescent green framed by thick, dark lashes; slightly arched brows; a fine, straight, almost aristocratic nose; and lips perhaps a shade too full but incredibly inviting. With her fair hair blowing around her face and stunning figure swathed in rich blue silk, she looked lush and radiant and capable of turning any man's head. Clearly James Cary's assessment of his daughter's beauty had been a modest understatement, or perhaps she had blossomed since his last visit to England. Blossomed like a luxuriant red rose in the warm morning sun. The mistress of Briarwood . . . his future wife.

"You are Miss Camille Cary," he stated with quiet certainty, knowing it was so as he stared into her questioning eyes.

Yet, oddly enough, for a fleeting instant he had the vague impression that she thought he was asking for someone else. She seemed unsure and unsettled, almost surprised. Then, as she lowered her head and clasped her white-gloved hands nervously, realization flooded Adam.

She *was* terribly shy, he thought, noting how she chewed her bottom lip. He could swear she was nearly trembling. Yet with her striking looks and gracefully erect carriage, her timidity seemed incongruous.

He shrugged off the odd thought, satisfaction filling him, mixed with a strong protectiveness. This timid mouse would give him no trouble at all. He was smiling as she glanced up at him and said, "Y-yes. I'm Camille Cary."

# Chapter 3

❧ ∽ᎧᎧ∽ ❧

Susanna had never felt so nervous. The words were barely off her tongue when she was besieged again by doubts, but she forced them down as she stared at the confidently smiling stranger who was standing so close to her.

He was very handsome in a rough, rugged sort of way, and one of the few wigless men on the dock other than the crew members and workers unloading the ship. His thick brown hair, a dark mahogany which shone with reddish highlights in the sunshine, was rather long and tied in a queue at his nape, and he had the most piercing brown eyes she had ever seen.

In fact, he was studying her most intently, Susanna realized in agitation, which made her feel even more uncomfortable. She took a step backward—certainly it wasn't proper manners for two complete strangers to stand so close together, even though this man seemed to know who she was—and one of her heels dropped into a large knothole between two planks.

"Oh! Oh, dear!"

Tottering, she gasped in surprise when he caught her arm and easily prevented her from falling; she blushed at the iron strength in his grip. When he merely smiled again, she could only wonder at the impression she was making. He seemed undisturbed by her obvious discomfiture, almost as if he expected it.

"Easy, Miss Cary. You'll get your land legs back, but it might take a while. You've been at sea a long time. Now, if you would lean on my shoulder for a moment . . .''

Susanna swallowed as she obliged him, trying hard not to dwell on the play of his sinewy muscles beneath her fingertips. Surely their position must appear undignified! She watched wide-eyed as the man sat on his haunches and, cradling her small foot in his hand, gently released her heel.

''There now, step down.''

Carefully regaining her full balance, she met his eyes when he rose beside her once more. He was much taller than she was, but he stood no more than an inch or two above six feet. Fleetingly she marveled that he seemed so much bigger, but perhaps that was because his shoulders and chest were so broad, his physique so powerful beneath his black riding coat and white lawn shirt.

Blushing anew, she looked away, thinking how unsure of herself she must seem. Then again, Camille would have acted nervous and flustered, and she was supposed to be her dear Camille, after all.

James Cary had probably told everyone that his daughter was extremely shy, which might explain this man's reaction to her. Susanna certainly didn't want anyone to think her behavior was out of keeping with James's description. Although being timid and docile were two traits wholly foreign to her nature, she would simply have to feign them until she was more comfortable with her new life. Then, as she learned how to act properly in Virginia society, she could gradually lose her veneer of shyness like a butterfly shedding its cocoon and become more like her true self.

Get hold of yourself, Susanna Jane, and consider it a game, she chided herself. Or pretend you're an actress in a play. Just remember, everything you do is for Camille's sake.

''I hope you didn't turn your ankle. Does it hurt?''

Susanna shook her head and offered her attractive rescuer a faint smile. Feeling calmer and in more control of her wits, she suddenly saw him in a new light and felt a twinge of tense excitement.

Might this man be a wealthy tobacco planter? From the fine cut of his coat and breeches, lacking adornment though they did, and his black leather jackboots, an expensive pair from the looks of them, it was possible. And he knew her. Had he been a good friend of James Cary's, perhaps a prominent, unmarried friend?

Susanna demurely lowered her lashes as she had seen Camille do countless times, and, ready to begin the game, murmured, ''You were very kind to help me, Mr.—''

''Thornton. Adam Thornton. Forgive me for not introducing myself sooner, Miss Cary.''

Of course. Adam Thornton, she thought, intensely disappointed, her earlier hopes fading. Not a rich planter, prominent personage, or even a true gentleman—but a hired man. Mr. Cary's plantation manager. It made sense that he had been the one to greet the *Charming Nancy*. And to think she had been so eager to meet him, might even have welcomed his attentions at one time. But that was before—

''Perhaps your father mentioned me in his letters. I've been the plantation manager at Briarwood for several years now, and I've certainly heard a great deal about you. I'm glad that we've finally had the chance to meet.''

Disconcerted by his deep, husky voice, Susanna noticed that he was still holding her arm, his fingers exerting a gentle pressure that felt almost like a caress. Dizzying warmth rippled through her, but she quickly attributed it to the hot late-morning sun.

Surely it was most unseemly for him to be touching her in such a possessive manner! She was no longer in any danger of falling. And why was he still looking at her so intently?

''Yes, yes, I know of you,'' she said softly, doing her best to stifle her irritation at his boldness and to remind herself that she must act like Camille. ''Papa . . .'' How strange it sounded to call the late Mr. Cary

"Papa." "My father did mention you in his letters, Mr. Thornton. Many times, actually. He spoke highly of everything you've done for Briarwood."

And how often Camille—intent upon playing the matchmaker—had speculated about this Adam Thornton as a potential husband for her, Susanna thought, recalling Camille's prediction for her future in the Virginia colony.

"Mr. Thornton must be a good man, Susanna, or Papa wouldn't have employed him for so long. And you've always said you want an honest, hardworking man with promising prospects for a husband. I know what we'll do! After my wedding, we'll plan one for you. How about in the springtime? Oh, you'll make the prettiest bride! 'Mrs. Susanna Thornton' has a lovely sound to it, don't you agree?"

But then, just before she had died, Camille had told her to marry wisely as she herself would have done, Susanna remembered with heartrending clarity. Camille must have realized that Adam Thornton was no longer a proper match now that Susanna was to take her place in Virginia. A hired man wasn't good enough to marry an heiress. It was as simple as that.

"So this must be Miss Cary!" a loud voice boomed from across the dock, bringing Susanna's attention back to the present. As she watched a rotund gentleman approach them, she felt Adam's grip tighten on her arm and draw her closer to his side. She thought to protest this new and puzzling affront, but again she held her tongue. Camille would have borne it meekly.

"My dear girl, allow me to introduce myself," the richly dressed gentleman enthused, bowing and taking her hand. "My name is Robert Grymes. I was a good friend of your father's." His friendly face clouded and he squeezed her fingers in sympathy. "Such a tragic loss, James's death. So unexpected. My sincerest condolences to you, Miss Cary."

Susanna mustered a small smile. "Thank you."

Robert Grymes cleared his throat and, releasing her hand, he clapped his soft palms together, his wide grin reappearing. Clearly his expression of grief was short-lived.

"I'm pleased to say that I'm a neighbor of yours, Miss Cary, though my plantation is downriver a good ways from Briarwood. My wife Charity and I would be delighted if you'd come by for supper within the week and meet the rest of the family. I've a daughter about your age, Celeste, and three sons, Tyler, Francis, and Matthew, the eld—"

"Miss Cary will probably need at least a week or more to recuperate from her voyage," Adam interrupted coldly. "If you recall, Grymes, she's had a harrowing trip. We're fortunate that she was spared the fever"—his arresting eyes, flecked with shards of gold, flickered over her appraisingly—"and has arrived in such remarkably vibrant health."

Susanna glanced at him in shock, hardly believing he would speak for her as if he had the right to. Who did he think he was, anyway?

"Oh, yes, of course," Robert said, nodding his head so vigorously that the curls of his powdered wig bobbed. "Forgive me, Miss Cary. It was not my intent to inconvenience you. Please come and visit us, but only when you're rested enough to do so . . . Oh, and don't feel you must wait for a formal invitation. We Virginians rarely use them. We pride ourselves upon our hospitality, a code of courtesy you might say, and welcome visitors whenever they chance by."

"Thank you, Mr. Grymes," she murmured through clenched teeth, pointedly ignoring Adam's hard look of disapproval. But she said nothing more and did not commit herself to any visit, knowing Camille would have wished to stay at home. She sensed the planter must have heard of her shyness, though, when instead of excusing himself, he persisted by trying another tack.

"Come to think of it, I have an even better idea, Miss Cary. Perhaps my family and I might take it upon ourselves to visit Briarwood. Such an arrangement would spare you from any unnecessary traveling. The summer is a rather tedious time for us planters since the tobo is ripening in the fields, which gives us some respite for amusement. Why, we could make a grand welcome ball of it, say, on Saturday which is almost a full week away, and invite some of your other neighbors, who I'm sure are eager to meet you. I would think you'd be well-rested by then—"

"I have it upon excellent knowledge that Miss Cary is not one for social gatherings," Adam interjected again, his tone even more rude. "She prefers more peaceful pastimes."

"Nonsense," Robert objected with a good-natured chortle, clearly undaunted or perhaps just accustomed to dealing with Adam's surly manners. "What young lady doesn't like such amusements? Why, my pretty Celeste was a shy one until her fourteenth birthday, then when she saw what fun all the other girls were having, she came around. I believe the best cure for such a malady is to expose oneself to frivolity on a regular basis. I'm sure Miss Cary will find there is no harm in meeting her neighbors."

"Sorry, Grymes, but it won't be possible. Now if you'll excuse us, Elias is waiting with the carriage to take us back to Briarwood. I'm sure Miss Cary is eager to see her home."

Susanna felt Adam's insistent tug on her arm as he attempted to steer her away, but she chose to ignore it and remained right where she stood. How dare both of these men talk over her head as if she wasn't there, as if she didn't have a tongue with which to speak! What in bloody hell was going on here? She was so angry that this time it was difficult to keep her voice mild and steady.

"I think a house party at Briarwood on Saturday would be delightful," she said, glancing from Adam to Robert Grymes and then demurely at the ground. "Papa would have wanted me to meet my neighbors."

When she received no ready reply, Susanna peeked through her lashes to find the planter beaming from ear to ear and Adam glowering, his jaw taut. She knew he couldn't argue with such a statement. Of course she would want to meet her neighbors, whether she was shy or not.

She was eager to fulfill her promise to Camille by launching herself into the Tidewater's social whirl so she might find the right husband, but she would have to move slowly if she was to maintain her deception. A reputedly timid young woman would not become a popular belle overnight, yet a welcome ball would be a good way to start and it could lead to other outings. She had always dreamed of attending such an event, but as a lady's maid, it had been out of the question. Now she would have her chance.

Before long she ought to feel right at home among the gentry and be able to drop this unpleasant part of her masquerade. She had barely arrived, yet already acting so unlike herself was beginning to chafe, no thanks to the overbearing Adam Thornton, who seemed determined to go beyond the bounds of social propriety with his unseemly possessiveness. She looked forward to giving him a good dressing-down, but for now, she must exercise patience, not one of her stronger traits. Heaven give her the strength to curb her tongue and her temper!

"Splendid, Miss Cary!" Robert exclaimed, finding his voice at last. "Absolutely splendid!" He waved his hand with a wide flourish toward the gentlemen still gathered near the gangplank. "If I may, I shall tell the others. What a wonderful day it will be!"

Susanna gave a slight nod, and the planter hurried away.

"House party, my foot," Adam grumbled under his breath. "You're going to have a blasted mob on your hands. Every single male in the county will be there."

"Did you say something, Mr. Thornton?" she asked innocently, though she had heard him well enough.

She didn't understand his obvious resentment. Why should it matter to him if she met some eligible young gentlemen? Surely he knew James Cary had summoned Camille home to find an appropriate husband.

"I said, if you would point out your trunks, Miss

Cary, I'll have them loaded onto the carriage and we'll be on our way," Adam replied, unsettled by how quickly his plans had gone awry.

He had wanted to have Camille all to himself for the next few weeks, which would have given him plenty of time to court her without any outside interruptions. Now that was not to be. Leave it to that fool Robert Grymes to pressure the girl into something she didn't really want to do. He would just have to inform her of his intention to marry her a little sooner than he had planned, and before any other bastards had a chance to meet her.

Maybe he would tell her tonight and be done with it, Adam thought. If he worked fast enough, he might even announce the betrothal at this welcome ball. By God, he could imagine the look on Grymes's face at the news. He could just as easily imagine the look on Dominick Spencer's face if the planter had the audacity to show up at Briarwood. Adam would sell his soul for such a moment.

"My trunks are over there, Mr. Thornton."

Adam signaled to Elias, who was still waiting patiently by the carriage. The huge black man rushed forward and lifted one after the other of her three trunks, carrying them back to the coach as if they contained nothing but feathers. After the luggage was secured, he re-tethered Adam's mount to the vehicle and called, "All's ready, Mr. Thornton!"

"Have you no maid?" Adam queried, it suddenly dawning on him that of course Camille wouldn't have traveled such a distance alone. "I recall Mr. Cary saying you had a devoted waiting-maid about your age named Susanna Guthrie. Where is she?"

Susanna felt the color draining from her face. She had never thought to hear her own name mentioned in Virginia. It was an eerie sensation, especially since she knew no one would ever call her that again.

"She died a little over a week ago. The fever . . ." It was simply too painful to say more. Susanna fell silent, her gaze fixed on the river.

"I'm very sorry, Camille. Come, I'll take you home."

A few moments ago, Susanna might have taken offense that he called her by her first name. Now, it didn't seem to matter.

Turning away from the *Charming Nancy,* she allowed him to lead her to the carriage, which was drawn by two magnificent dappled grays. He lifted her inside, his strong, tanned hands easily encircling her waist, and took a place beside her on the plush wine-colored velvet seat. She didn't look back as the coach jolted into motion and rumbled away from the bustling dock. She never wanted to see that cursed ship again.

# Chapter 4

$\diamond\!\!\!\diamond\!\!\!\bigcirc\!\!\!\bigcirc\!\!\!\diamond\!\!\!\diamond$

Susanna said little during their journey to Briarwood, which seemed to make no difference to
Adam.

When he had ascertained by her soft-spoken "No"
that she remembered nothing about her place of birth—
which was entirely believable since Camille had been
only three years old when she was sent away to England—he kept up a steady and interesting commentary
about Yorktown and the rest of the colony, until, after
a while, she felt her melancholy begin to lift. The coun-
tryside was beautiful, although lacking the lush rolling
hills of the Cotswolds, and it felt so good to be on dry
land again. Only at one point did she venture to ask a
question, her avid curiosity getting the better of her.

"I heard there are still Indians in Virginia. Do you
think we might see any?"

A low chuckle rumbled from his throat. "Not unless
you travel far to the west and into the wilderness. The
Indians retreated from this region years ago when the
white men became too plentiful." His gaze traveled
slowly over her features, lingering overlong upon her
lips, then he looked directly into her eyes, his expression sobering. "Don't worry, Miss Cary. If any wild
savages chance to cross our path, have no fear that I
will protect you."

Feeling her cheeks grow warm at the strange intensity of his gaze, Susanna was tempted to retort that she
wasn't worried or frightened. She would have liked to

see some Indians, but since that would hardly be something Camille would have said, she directed her attention out the window, becoming increasingly exasperated with herself.

Dear Lord, what was it about this man that so easily pricked her temper? It didn't make sense. She had known him for perhaps two hours! Maybe it was because he seemed so sure of himself, and so completely sure of her. Or perhaps it was his condescending attitude that most irked her; that, and the tone that crept into his voice sometimes, as if he was speaking to a child instead of a young woman.

Susanna hazarded a glance at him to find that he was still looking at her. He smiled, his teeth a startling white against his tanned face. As she quickly turned back to the window, flustered anew, she decided that he must spend a great deal of time out-of-doors to have skin so darkened by the sun. She imagined his chest and back must be bronzed as well, in keeping with his job as a plantation manager. She had no doubt that he stripped off his shirt to work as any hired man might in the summer heat. She could almost picture him . . . his golden-brown skin glistening with sweat, the muscles across his shoulders and upper back bulging powerfully as he lifted the ax or hoisted a heavy barrel—

Susanna gasped as Adam suddenly leaned against her, his arm grazing her breasts as he pointed out the window, his hard muscled thigh pushing against her leg.

"See those trees?"

"Y-yes."

"They form the southern boundary of Briarwood. Welcome home, Miss Cary."

Flushed with embarrassment and not daring to breathe or move, she kept her gaze trained upon the towering oak trees, but she scarcely saw them. Her senses were blinded to everything except the heat of Adam's body pressed against her and the compelling scent of him, clean yet slightly musky.

She had been so close to a man only once before, a

few weeks before leaving Fairford, when a handsome village swain who had taken a fancy to her had cornered her in the Redmayne coach house. He had kissed her full on the mouth, his passionate ardor nearly dragging the breath from her body until she had stamped upon his foot and he had abruptly released her. Then she had slapped his face and run away. But some wild part of herself had wanted to feel his hands roaming over her body and his hard desire pressing through her skirt.

Susanna rolled her eyes, dismayed by her wanton thoughts.

This wasn't the same thing! Adam was this close to her merely because he was pointing out something of interest to her. The boundary of Briarwood, for God's sake! She could hardly grind her heel into his foot or slap him for that. His nearness was entirely innocent . . . or was it? Oh, when would this carriage ride be over?

Susanna couldn't relax even when Adam abruptly drew back and settled against the seat once more. Nor did she look at him; she was worried about how she might react if that same insufferably confident smile was upon his face. She kept her gaze fixed out the window, and was more than a bit relieved when the coach turned onto a wide, poplar-lined drive. As a magnificent brick mansion came into view, flanked by outbuildings half-hidden by flowering shrubs and trees, she was swept by nervous excitement, the previous moment's incident temporarily forgotten. She could not believe she was finally here.

Briarwood.

It was grander than she would ever have imagined, the formal approach a beautifully landscaped prelude to the ivy-clad, two-story house that lay beyond. This place was even finer than the Redmayne country estate, which now held a solid second place in her estimation. Briarwood was truly the loveliest spot on earth.

As the carriage pulled around a large circle edged in boxwood that terminated the drive, Susanna saw the front door open, and a host of black servants hurried down the broad stone steps to a wide walkway, where they formed a well-ordered line. Several footmen dressed in splendid blue-and-gold livery rushed forward to meet the coach. It seemed everything was happening so fast, the door opening and Adam climbing down so that he might assist her. Then she was walking with him toward the servants who, from their warm, expectant smiles, seemed genuinely pleased to see her.

It was an unsettling moment. She, who had done the waiting upon, was now the mistress of a large household, with servants to see to her every need. What was she to say to them? How should she act? Would they somehow sense that she was actually one of them?

"Your house servants," Adam explained in a low voice, his hand firmly—and impertinently, she decided—upon her elbow as he steered her toward them. "You probably know from your father that some of them are slaves while others have earned their freedom, and have chosen to remain here as paid help. The same can be said for the rest of the workers at Briarwood."

Actually, Susanna had heard of this unusual arrangement from Camille, who had been proud of her father's lenient and fair-minded attitude toward his slaves. She, however, didn't like the idea of anyone owning another human being; it wasn't right. Yet when she had expressed her opinion, Camille had said it was simply the way things were done in Virginia. Briarwood would never have achieved its greatness without the several hundred slaves who toiled in the tobacco fields. At least they were luckier than most to have James Cary as their owner.

But now you are their owner, Susanna thought, the reality of the situation not sitting well with her. Yet there didn't seem to be anything she could do about it, except to continue on as James Cary had done, allowing slaves to earn their freedom and then giving them the choice to stay on at the plantation or to set out on their own.

As Adam continued speaking, Susanna noticed that

his voice had grown strangely harsh. Why, she couldn't imagine.

"There are also some indentured servants here from Britain who are primarily craftsmen, but their numbers are few. Your father ceased to buy indentures several years ago, at my urging." He said no more upon the subject, but began to introduce her to the servants, the first a very stout woman with an enormous bosom. "This is Prue. She's the head cook here at Briarwood, and an excellent one, I might add."

"Hello," Susanna said softly, offering a small smile.

"We're so glad you're here, Miss Camille,' the woman said with obvious sincerity. "The house has been so empty since your papa . . ." She couldn't finish, her large dark eyes misting. "Well, will you look at me? A happy occasion and all."

Susanna's heart went out to her. It was clear James Cary had been very well liked, and was still sorely missed.

"I'm happy to be here," she said rather shyly, attempting her best imitation of Camille. "Thank you for your kind welcome, Prue."

The woman's friendly smile returned and she drew herself up, her emotions once again under control. "I'm preparing a nice welcome dinner for you, Miss Camille. Master Cary always liked to dine straight up at three o'clock, but if you'd like to eat a bit earlier or later—"

"Three o'clock will be fine. It is not my intention to change the way my father did things at Briarwood."

Her answer seemed to please the woman, who beamed broadly. "Good enough, Miss Camille. Good enough."

Susanna moved quickly along the line as Adam made more introductions, so many that the names of kitchen maids, chambermaids, laundry and dairy maids, the valet, a steward who kept the plantation's books, and numerous others were soon swimming in her mind. The last person she came to was an older black woman with short, graying hair beneath her starched cap. Her deeply lined face was still striking, although she appeared to be perhaps sixty years old or more. She regarded Susanna with a kind, hopeful expression.

"Do you remember me, Miss Camille? You've surely changed since I saw you last. You were just a little one then, no taller than my knees. I wouldn't have known you except for your pretty hair and eyes. My, you've grown into a fine beauty, just like your mama."

Taken aback, Susanna had no idea who this woman was. Adam did not readily come to her aid but seemed somewhat surprised himself that she did not know the woman's name.

"Ertha," he finally murmured, after an awkward silence.

Susanna flushed warmly, embarrassed that she'd forgotten all about Camille's childhood nurse.

Camille had always spoken of Ertha fondly—the woman had been like a mother to her, Constance Cary having died when Camille was barely one year old—but she had never really given Susanna any clear description of her. Camille had been so young when Captain Keyes had escorted her to England that her recollections of the woman were uncertain at best. Camille had simply remembered Ertha for her warm, constant presence; her soft, crooning voice singing her to sleep with lullabies.

Hoping to compensate for her blunder, Susanna turned back to the woman, who looked crestfallen, and took her hands, squeezing them gently.

"Of course. Forgive me, Ertha. I don't know what came over me. It's been so long . . ."

"Don't trouble yourself, child," Ertha said graciously, although some of the light had left her eyes. "It was a long time ago. I shouldn't have expected that you might remember me."

Again silence fell between them, broken when Adam interjected, "Ertha has been Briarwood's head housekeeper for fifteen years now. She has a gift for making everything run smoothly and a firm but gentle knack

for keeping the others in line. I'm sure you'll be pleased
with her work.''

''I know I will,'' Susanna replied, wishing there was
some way she could make up for her unintended slight.
Releasing the woman's hands, she looked up at Adam,
hoping she appeared convincingly fatigued.

In truth, she did feel drained. Her new position in
life was so overwhelming and her responsibilities so
great that her well-meaning masquerade suddenly
weighed very heavily upon her. She needed some time
alone to gather herself together. ''If you don't mind, .
Mr. Thornton, I would like to see my room now. I
could use a short rest before dinner.''

His deep brown eyes were concerned, but she also
sensed his agitation. ''You're not ill . . .''

''No, simply tired.'' Then, feeling the need to reassure everyone present when she saw some nervous
sidelong glances, she added, ''The physician gave me
a clean bill of health before I left the ship. You mustn't
worry about me.''

Yet when Adam still appeared unconvinced, irritation tweaked at her. What was he so concerned about?

''You seem troubled, Mr. Thornton,'' she said a bit
too curtly, forgetting herself. ''Perhaps you think I
should not set foot in my house until you're certain that
I'm free of disease?''

''I wasn't thinking that at all,'' he replied, his expression one of curious surprise. Then he smiled
slightly, as if amused. ''By all means, go in. Ertha's
had the household staff working for days to have everything ready for you.''

Silently cursing her heedless tongue and telling herself she must be more careful so as not to arouse
suspicion, Susanna softened her tone, although she
remained annoyed. ''If you'll kindly excuse me, then.''
Without waiting for him, she walked up the stairs to
the door. She certainly didn't need him to escort her
everywhere, especially not into her new home.

''I'll see you at dinner, Miss Cary. Enjoy your rest.''

Susanna glanced over her shoulder to find Adam

striding back toward the carriage, and for the first time, she noticed that he walked with a slight limp. Yet his bearing was straight and strong, his pace powerful; it was obvious that his disability did not hamper him as he untethered the spirited chestnut stallion and led the animal away.

Had he suffered some injury? she wondered, stepping into the spacious hall. And what did he mean by saying that he'd join her at dinner? Since when did the hired help sit at the table with their employers? She had never eaten one meal in Lady Redmayne's elegant dining room, but had always dined with the other domestic servants in the kitchen.

"If you'll follow me, Miss Camille, I'll show you upstairs to your room," Ertha said, gesturing to Elias to unload the trunks as she followed Susanna into the hall. With another wave of her hand, the other servants scattered, returning to their assigned tasks. "Miss Camille?" she repeated.

Susanna heard the housekeeper, but she felt as if her feet were rooted to the floor as she gazed in rapt awe about her. From what she could see while standing in the hall, the interior of the house was not in the least stuffy or somber, as Lady Redmayne's country manor had been. Golden sunlight pouring from open doorways reflected upon the fine furnishings and polished parquet floor, the hospitable scene easing Susanna's fatigue.

She heard a soft chuckle and turned to find Ertha smiling at her, the housekeeper's good nature clearly restored after the earlier awkwardness between them.

"How about a quick tour of the house, Miss Camille? I'd be pleased to show it to you. Since you were so little when you were here last, it will be like seeing it for the first time."

Susanna nodded, and eagerly followed Ertha from one sumptuously decorated room into the next: the dining room, dominated by a huge mahogany table that could seat twenty; the library, filled from floor to ceiling with richly embossed, leather-bound books; a game room with a large billiard table and tables for playing cards; a splendid forty-foot long ballroom with mirrored walls and crystal chandeliers; a small music room in which she planned to spend little time at all, especially since she could not play the harpsichord; and a drawing room graced by elegant yet comfortable furnishings, its papered walls hung with family portraits.

She paused before the largest painting, a charming family scene, and with a sharp pang realized that the pretty blonde toddler seated atop her mother's lap was Camille while the two boys, perhaps six and eight, were her brothers who had died so young. Behind them, proud and straight, stood a bewigged and handsome James Cary, his hand placed lovingly upon his wife's shoulder.

"Those were happy, happy times," Ertha murmured, then she turned and gazed directly at Susanna. "Now that you're home, Miss Camille, we'll know those times again. I'm just sure of it."

Susanna's throat constricted with emotion. Her lips curved into the most confident smile she could muster, though she knew it also held sadness. With a last glance at the painting, she moved toward the door, feeling as if all Cary eyes were upon her, especially Camille's.

"I hope you don't mind me saying so," Ertha continued as they walked together into the hall, "but what this house needs is little children again, their laughter filling the rooms and the sound of their feet running up and down the stairs. It's been too quiet here for too long. I hope you find a husband soon, Miss Camille."

Susanna met the housekeeper's eyes. "That is my plan, Ertha," she said honestly. "It's what my father wanted and what I want. A husband and lots of children." Glancing at the sweeping black walnut stairway that led to the second floor, she added softly, "We're going to have a welcome ball here on Saturday, for the Grymes family and some of the other neighbors. Would you see to the preparations?"

How strange, Susanna thought, as Ertha's wrinkled face split into a surprised yet radiant smile. That was her first request as the mistress of the house, and it hadn't been difficult to give at all. In fact, it had seemed quite natural. Maybe from watching Lady Redmayne give orders to servants so many times, she had actually learned something.

"Why, of course I will!" the housekeeper enthused. "It's been too long since we had a house party at Briarwood, and if Mr. Robert Grymes is coming, I imagine he'll tell everyone within shouting distance about it. That man has a real fondness for revelry, and so does his oldest son, Matthew. You can be sure that there will be plenty of young men here on Saturday eager to make your acquaintance. You'll have that fine husband of yours in no time at all!"

Ertha's pleased laughter ended abruptly, her eyes growing wide. "Oh, my, I've so much to do. Believe me, I've a feeling this ball will be the Tidewater's social event of the summer. I have to talk to Prue at once. We've got to plan the menu, and—"

"Why don't you go and speak to her right now, then," Susanna interrupted kindly, sensing the woman's eagerness to be about her work. "I can see my way upstairs. Just tell me which room is mine."

"Are you sure, Miss Camille? It doesn't seem right, me not showing you to your room, what with you just arriving and all."

"I'll be fine. Really."

"Very well, if you say so. You'll find your room at the very end of the hall, facing the rear of the house. It's the same one that used to belong to your parents. I'm sure Elias has already taken your trunks upstairs. I'll send Corliss to wake you in an hour or so, and she'll help you dress for dinner."

With that, the housekeeper hurried away, talking excitedly under her breath. Susanna, smiling, climbed the stairs, looking forward to being alone for a while. Yet at the top of the stairway, her curiosity was aroused again by the sight of four closed bedroom doors in addition to hers down the carpeted hallway.

As long as she was taking a tour of the house, she

might as well see these rooms, too, she reasoned. If they were even half as lovely as those downstairs . . .

She was not disappointed. The first guest bedroom was spacious and well-appointed, with white walls, blue brocade draperies at the tall windows, and a matching spread upon the double bed. She crossed the hall to the opposite room and, turning the silver-plated knob, stepped inside.

"What in bloody blazes . . . ?" she breathed to herself.

She stared in stunned confusion at a room that appeared not only occupied, but also in a state of wild disarray. The huge four-poster bed was unmade, the pillows scattered, and the rumpled sheets strewn with clothes, while a pair of dusty jackboots lay nearby on the floor—

Jackboots! And that was a shirt and a pair of breeches tossed upon the bed, not a gown and lace undergarments. Why, this must be a man's room . . . unless she had stumbled upon the site of a carnal tryst and the lover had fled without his clothing.

No, that was ridiculous, Susanna thought as she moved still further into the room. Her gaze skipped from an upended tricorn hat and a leather belt lying atop a richly upholstered chair to a massive wardrobe, its doors half-open. Even from where she stood, she could see full-sleeved white lawn shirts, dark riding clothes, and even a fine forest-green coat and gold brocade waistcoat hanging inside.

This *was* a man's room. But whose? Was there an overnight guest visiting Briarwood, someone Ertha had failed to tell her about in the commotion of her arrival?

"I hope you can forgive the mess. I left in quite a hurry this morning to meet the *Charming Nancy,* and it appears the servants neglected to straighten my room in all the excitement."

Susanna spun, her heart hammering in her throat. She gaped at Adam, who stood leaning against the doorjamb. He was smiling that same self-assured smile, his arms crossed casually over his chest.

"Y-your room?" she stammered in disbelief, her thoughts racing. Who had ever heard of such a thing? A hired man living under the master's roof? The mistress's roof? *Her* roof?

"Yes. My room," he stated with emphasis, his smile fading into a look of irritation and his eyes growing hard. "It's been mine since I became the plantation manager three years ago. A quaint custom in the Tidewater, and obviously one you're unfamiliar with. If there's a spare bedroom in a planter's house, it is often given to either the tutor or the manager, both highly esteemed positions on a plantation. Since there are no children here, and thus no tutor, I was given the honor."

"Oh . . ." Susanna barely managed to say, shocked by such an arrangement. She could just hear Lady Redmayne's snort of disapproval!

Her place had always been in the servants' wing—except for that one night in London when she had slept in that lovely feather bed—although Camille had often begged her aunt to allow Susanna to move into the smaller bedroom next to her own. Lady Redmayne would hear none of it. Although she knew they were best friends, the baroness had insisted that there remain a firm distinction between mistress and waiting-maid.

"I also eat my meals at the planter's table and drink his wine," Adam continued tightly. "Another fine custom. And if you're a crop master, the rewards are even greater."

"Crop master?" she asked. She shifted nervously as he walked toward her. So he would be dining with her, just as he had said. A hired man!

"Yes, crop master," he repeated, his tone growing angrier, his eyes demanding that she look at him. "A title bestowed upon only a few men, usually planters. I acquired it by learning as much as I could about tobacco. It's the kind of knowledge that impresses the Tidewater gentry. Earns a self-made man their respect." He came even closer, his gaze not wavering from her face. "That title has given me something else,

Miss Cary, something which you've always possessed. The gentry see me as one of their own now. I can go to their house parties, ride in their horse races, and even court their women—''

"Ex-excuse me, Mr. Thornton," Susanna cut him off, giving him a wide berth as she hurried to the door. Her words emerged in a distracted torrent. "I didn't mean to pry. I didn't know this was your room. I thought I would just look at all the bedrooms since I haven't seen them before . . . I mean for so long . . .'' She tore her gaze from him and didn't look back, acutely aware that he was watching her, and growing all the more flushed because of it. She hastened down the hall to her room, and leaned breathlessly against the door when she was inside.

She had a madman sleeping down the hall from her! she thought wildly. Either that or Virginia was a very strange place indeed. She had never heard of such customs! And why had he become so angry? How direct and rude he had been, considering she was now his employer. She couldn't make sense of all he had said, and right now, she didn't even want to try. All she wanted was to lie down and give her whirling thoughts a rest!

Adam shut the door, cursing under his breath.

Now you've done it, he berated himself, tearing off his coat and tossing it on the chair. If this was his idea of wooing Camille gently, then he was failing miserably, and it was his own damn fault. He had clearly upset her, but then he had meant to. If only she hadn't stared at him so incredulously when he had said this was his room. He could just imagine what she had been thinking.

A hired man sleeping only a few doors away from her? Well, he wasn't just any hired man! And the sooner she knew about his intention to marry her and that her father had approved of the match, the better. Yet somehow he would have to compensate for the less than fine impression he had just given of himself.

Growing more disgusted with his behavior, Adam leaned against the window, blind to the bustle of activity outside.

Dammit, he shouldn't have been so hard on her. Of course she wouldn't know of the Tidewater's customs, being a gently bred young woman raised in England. The social distinctions so rigid there were more blurred in Virginia, and more easily scaled. How could he have expected her to know that? Maybe she had simply been surprised, not insulted or disturbed, to discover that this was his room. He had to admit, the arrangement was unusual if he looked at it from her perspective.

Patience, man, you'll make amends, Adam told himself as he changed into rougher clothes and his workworn jackboots for the long, dusty ride ahead of him. Too bad it couldn't be over dinner.

He had been looking forward to spending more time her with, especially after what he had seen of her so far. He suspected that passion lurked beneath her shy exterior, although she kept it well-hidden. Yet in the carriage when he had leaned against her soft, lush body, there had been no mistaking the heightened color of her cheeks and the rapid pulse at the base of her lovely throat. Her reaction to his nearness had pleased and excited him; he could tell she was easily aroused by a man's touch, knowledge which he would use to his advantage.

He had been sorely tempted to kiss her then and there, to see if he could unleash more of that hidden passion, but he had restrained himself, thinking it would be too much too soon for his timid heiress. He would observe the proper niceties first and tell her of his plans for them, then kiss her. But now that moment would have to wait a while longer, Adam thought with regret.

There was trouble in the outlying tobacco fields because of a newly hired overseer who had exceeded his bounds with the slaves. Josiah Skinner, one of his head overseers, had just informed him in the stable that the man had been using the lash even though he knew no whips were allowed on Cary land. If the accusation was true, the bastard would be thrown off the plantation. Adam would not tolerate any deviation from his orders.

As he stepped into the hallway, he glanced at Camille's door, wondering if he should say anything to her now. Then, remembering how weary she had looked, he decided against it. He would let her rest. He wanted her to be fresh and receptive when she heard what he had to say.

# Chapter 5

Susanna felt a gentle nudge on her shoulder and opened her eyes with a start, at first not knowing where she was. "What . . . ?"

"I'm sorry, Miss Camille. I didn't mean to wake you so sudden-like. Ertha sent me to help you dress for dinner. My name's Corliss, if you recall. I'll be your waiting-maid—that is, if you like me well enough."

Time and place came flooding back to her, and Susanna realized from the crick in her neck that she had fallen asleep in the rather stiff chair near the fireplace. She remembered exploring briefly the luxurious suite with its huge canopied bed, separate sitting area, and curved balcony overlooking beautiful gardens that led down to the river. Then she had plopped down here, her enjoyment of her surroundings tempered by her unsettling encounter with Adam. She must have leaned her head back and nodded off.

"I'm sure we'll get along just fine, Corliss," she finally replied, hoping to reassure the pretty young woman who looked to be about the same age as herself. She knew she had succeeded when the maid grinned happily.

"I already laid out a few gowns for you to choose from," Corliss said in a rush, clearly eager to please, "and there's hot water in the basin if you want to wash. Now if you'll stand up, Miss Camille, I'll help you out of your traveling clothes."

Susanna did as Corliss asked, thinking how strange

it was to have someone waiting upon her like this. But she supposed she would have to get used to it. The household servants would wonder if she insisted upon seeing after her own personal needs.

As she washed and changed into a beautiful emerald-green gown—the stays laced to within an inch of her life, and the satin skirt buoyed by the same stiff whalebone hoop-petticoat she had practiced walking in last night—Corliss fluttered around her like a butterfly, arranging and fussing and making flattering comments.

"You're a true beauty, Miss Camille, I knew it the first moment I saw you. I swear you're going to make the other misses jealous when they see you at the ball on Saturday. If they're engaged to be married, they better hold on real tight to their menfolk, that's all I have to say. One look at you could easily change any gentleman's mind and bring him running like a hound panting after a fox."

Embarrassed at such talk, Susanna quickly sought to shift the focus of discussion to another topic as she sat down at the elegant dressing table. Now that she had gotten some rest, her mind was much clearer, and her thoughts returned to her troubling encounter with Adam. Her curiosity about him mounting, she wondered if perhaps the talkative Corliss could enlighten her about this puzzling and most infuriating man.

"Corliss, is it really a common practice in Virginia for a hired man . . . a plantation manager to have a room in the master's house?"

"You mean like Mr. Thornton?" the maid asked, whisking a brush through Susanna's thick hair.

"Yes."

"Well, Miss Camille, I'd have to answer yes, at least as far as I know. 'Course if you don't like it, being the new mistress and all, you could make him move out, but I don't think you'd want to do that. A good plantation manager is hard to come by, and Mr. Thornton is said to be the best around. He might take it into his head to leave Briarwood if he isn't treated nice. I 'spect he could find himself another job real easy, since he's a crop master, too.''

There was that strange title again, Susanna thought as Corliss concentrated upon sweeping her hair back from her forehead and fastening it with an ivory comb. Then the maid reached for a small heated iron with which to curl her long tresses into ringlets, a fashionable style borrowed from the Dutch. Susanna had arranged Camille's hair in ringlets countless times.

"What is a crop master?" she queried.

"Someone who knows everything there is to know about tobo, like Mr. Thornton.''

"Tobo?"

"Tobacco. Mr. Thornton's got planters coming from miles around looking for his advice about growing good leaf. He knows all about transplanting and cutting, curing and prizing. That's all these Virginians care about, growing their tobo, and they respect any man who can bring in a high-quality crop, year after year. Why, it's because of Mr. Thornton that your papa's tobacco has come to be known as Cary's Finest. Did you know that, Miss Camille?''

"No. No, I didn't." James Cary had never been one for bragging, at least not in his letters to his daughter. Susanna could not recall ever having heard anything about the special quality of Briarwood's tobacco, just that the plantation was doing very well.

"It's true, sure as I'm standing here," Corliss went on. "Your papa always treated Mr. Thornton well, probably to thank him, probably because he liked him, too. Treated him just like a son, if you ask me. I remember Master Cary saying once that if there were more planters that worked as hard and as honest as Mr. Thornton, there would be a lot better men in Virginia.''

Mr. Cary treated Adam like a son? Susanna wondered in disbelief. Surely not. Corliss must be exaggerating.

"I know Mr. Thornton thought well of Master Cary," the maid continued, her cheerful tone growing somber as she put the finishing touches on Susanna's hair. "You should have seen him after the accident. When he found out what had happened to your papa, he punched his fist right through the stable door. He raged and carried on until poor Ertha thought she might have to send for the doctor. After that, he didn't talk to anyone for days, just kept to himself . . ." Corliss sighed as she set down the curling iron. "I'm sorry, Miss Camille. Here I am carrying on myself, talking your ear off."

"It's all right, Corliss. I don't mind," Susanna said, absorbing everything the maid had told her.

It wasn't difficult to imagine Adam in such a rage. He seemed to have a lot of emotion boiling inside him, and he was prideful to boot. Yet she supposed she owed him an apology for giving him the impression that he didn't belong in the house. From what Corliss had said, it sounded as if Adam deserved a lot of the credit for Briarwood's recent prosperity. If James Cary had granted him a room under his own roof, it wasn't her place to take it from him.

Of course, once she was married that might have to change, Susanna quickly amended. Her husband might have his own plantation manager, and then crop master or not, Adam would have to go. Maybe her husband might even be a crop master himself—Adam had said the title usually went to other planters—which would certainly mean that Adam's services would no longer be needed. She would just have to deal with the situation when she reached it. For now, Adam Thornton could stay.

"Which pinner would you like to wear, Miss Camille?" Corliss asked, holding up two circular caps, one made of delicate cream lace and the other bordered with an emerald ribbon.

"I think the one with the ribbon."

"That's the pinner I would have picked, too," the maid replied, her voice lighthearted again. "It'll match your gown just perfect."

Susanna watched in the large oval mirror as Corliss carefully pinned the cap on the crown of her head. She was satisfied with everything she had learned about Adam so far, but one thing was still bothering her. "Corliss," she said, looking down at her hands, "you said that Mr. Thornton was well-respected by the planters, didn't you?"

"Yes, I did, Miss Camille. Why, you'd think he was a rich planter himself, they treat him so well, accepting him practically as one of their own kind."

"How so?"

"Well, he's invited to their doings, for one thing. Balls and picnics and such, though he ain't got much time for it. Like I said before, any planter would hire Mr. Thornton easy if he could only be coaxed away from Briarwood. I've heard tell of rumors going around the county that a few planters might even be willing to part with their daughters and some land to have a crop master like Mr. Thornton in the family."

So, that would explain what Adam had said about courting the gentry's women, Susanna thought, feeling a sudden shiver. It was simply amazing to her that a planter would allow his daughter to marry so beneath herself, and all for the sake of growing better tobacco. Then again, from what she knew of the English gentry, their daughters were often married off for such mercenary reasons. Yet would one marry a common hired man like Adam Thornton, with no land of his own and probably little money?

"A planter's daughter would surely be a prize for a man who used to wield a hoe in the tobo fields," Corliss added, stepping back from the dressing table to survey her handiwork. "An indentured servant one day, marrying into the gentry the next."

"Mr. Thornton was an indentured servant?" Susanna asked, startled.

She had once considered selling herself into indenture, years ago when she was only eleven, another wild scheme she had briefly entertained as a way to escape her father's brutality. But when she had found out that she would not be free again until she was at least twenty-one years old, she had changed her mind. So

many years in servitude seemed too dear a price to pay
to one so young, no matter how desperate.

Nodding, Corliss gave a final twist to one of Susanna's curls. "Mr. Thornton has never said a word about
his servant days, Miss Camille, 'cept that he worked in
the fields. I did overhear him telling Master Cary not
long after he hired on here that he came from England
with his parents when he was thirteen and that their
indentures were bought by another planter, Mr. Dominick Spencer. I didn't hear anything else because Ertha
caught me listening outside the library door and boxed
my ears good." She chuckled softly. "I was only thirteen then myself."

Intrigued by this new information, Susanna couldn't
seem to stop her questions. "Does this Mr. Spencer
live around here?"

A knowing smile crept over Corliss's lips. "Not too
close, but not too far, either. His place is about fifteen
miles upriver, near the town of West Point. He's a widower, you know, and as rich as the day is long. He's
got the finest house on the York, 'cept for this one, the
finest racehorses, the finest everything. He's real handsome, too, and a well-respected gentleman. Member of
the governor's council."

Susanna hadn't expected such a complete list of the
man's attributes. "Corliss, how do you know all of
this?"

The young woman shrugged, her dark eyes full of
humor. "We talk in the kitchen, Ertha, Prue, and the
rest of us housemaids. We know you'll be looking for
a husband soon, and he's said to be looking for a wife.
We just put two and two together, though don't take me
wrong, Miss Camille, I'm not saying he's the right one
for you. You might very well want a younger man, seeing as Mr. Spencer is in his forties—"

Corliss fell abruptly silent when someone knocked
softly on the door.

"Miss Camille, it's Ertha. I just wanted to let you
know that dinner will be served in a few minutes."

"Oh, no, I've kept you too long with all my chatter.'' Corliss glanced at the china clock on the mantel, which read exactly three o'clock. "Ertha will scold me for sure.''

"No, she won't,'' Susanna said with a reassuring smile as she rose from the dressing table. "I'll just explain that we were becoming acquainted.''

She took a last look at herself in the mirror and was amazed at her transformation. Now that she had some-one to help her dress and arrange her hair, she looked like a real lady. She could hardly wait until Saturday to see the reactions of the gentlemen, young and old, who might come to call.

"Did you enjoy the meal, Miss Camille?'' Prue asked, clasping her plump hands together as she stood at one end of the lengthy dining table. Her expression was doubtful as she surveyed Susanna's plate, which remained nearly full.

"The food was wonderful, Prue. Really,'' Susanna said, feeling bad that she hadn't eaten more.

In truth, the little of the braised lamb, herbed vege-tables, and buttered new potatoes she had tasted had been excellent, but after subsisting on thin, watery soup and dry bread for the past several weeks, she had only half her normal appetite. Between that and the tightness of her stays, she had managed only a few bites before she was full. No wonder Camille had always eaten like a sparrow. And Susanna had thought it was simply due to proper table manners!

"I'm sure I'll be able to eat more in a few days, once I'm used to good cooking again,'' she explained, glad when Prue's face brightened. "The food aboard ship . . .'' She grimaced, which seemed to convince the cook that her expertise was not at fault.

"I can well imagine it was terrible. I don't know why I didn't think of it,'' Prue said sympathetically, cluck-ing her tongue as she removed Susanna's plate. "I'll just save the wild strawberry tart for a light supper, then, and the rest of the food for Mr. Thornton. I'm sure he'll be hungry when he returns later in the day.''

"That will be fine, Prue. Thank you."

Susanna glanced at the empty chair to her right where a place setting had been laid for Adam. Ertha had already explained why he would be absent for dinner. It seemed the life of a plantation manager was a demanding one.

Actually, when she had heard that he had ridden out to deal with a problem in some distant tobacco fields, she had been disappointed. She had wanted to apologize to him for her behavior earlier, and, more selfishly, to see his reaction to her appearance. He wasn't a gentleman, but he was a man, after all. If he liked the way she looked, she could imagine what her prospective suitors would think on Saturday.

Determined to become better acquainted with her new surroundings, Susanna went into the library, where she spent several pleasant hours browsing through the vast collection of books. She was so glad that she had learned to read, for she enjoyed it immensely.

A favorite pastime of hers and Camille's had been to curl up in the window seats and read to each other—poetry, Shakespeare, and occasionally a romantic novel if Susanna could buy one from a traveling bookseller. Lady Redmayne had caught her with such a book once and before tossing it into the fire had proclaimed it complete drivel and a poor excuse for literature. But Susanna and Camille had known better.

They had laughed and sighed and even shed tears over the trials and tribulations of the heroes and their beautiful ladies, and rejoiced when the lovers were happily united in the end. Yet, when the book was closed, both of them knew in their hearts that such romantic love had little to do with their own lives, where pragmatism and a sense of duty ruled. It was still pleasant, however, to escape once in a while into a world where love and its fulfillment need be the only considerations.

After a while, Susanna began to feel restless and decided a walk outside in the fresh air would do her good. It was almost six o'clock, but there was still plenty of sunlight left to this long summer day.

As she exited the French doors at the rear of the house, she thought how wonderful it was not to feel a ship swaying and pitching beneath her feet. She strolled quietly along the bricked paths and resplendent flower beds all the way down to the riverbank, where she sat upon a marble bench beneath a gigantic spreading oak tree and gazed out across the water.

It was so peaceful here in the shade. Instead of thundering waves, creaking wood, and the coarse cries of sailors going about their work, she heard sweet, trilling birdsong, the gentle lap of water against the grassy shoreline, and the distant muted sounds of plantation life. The air was warm, but not too much so, and fragrant with the scents of roses and gardenias carried upon a gentle breeze.

Susanna could have sat there for hours, not thinking about anything in particular, just enjoying the tranquillity of her surroundings as the daylight softened and shadows lengthened, the sun slowly setting behind the trees. She was so engrossed in her private reflection that she did not hear the fall of footsteps behind her, nor did she sense that she was no longer alone.

"Has anyone ever told you how beautiful you are?"

She froze, Adam's deep, husky voice eliciting a strange excitement within her that surprised her almost as much as his unexpected presence.

"Do you always creep up behind people like a thief, Mr. Thornton?" she replied with feigned lightness, ignoring his presumptuous question.

"Ah, I startled you. Forgive me. I was so struck by the enchanting picture you made that I was loath to disturb you."

He came around the bench to stand in front of her, and in spite of herself she could not help thinking how attractive he was. His features were rugged like the man himself, dark brows over deep-set eyes, a slightly hawklike yet pleasing nose, a mouth that appeared uncompromising yet undeniably sensuous over a strong cleft chin, and the hard planes of his face faintly shad-

owed with dark stubble. How much—deceivingly so!—
he looked like a true Virginia gentleman.

He had clearly dressed with care in a finely cut blue
coat, silver brocade waistcoat, and matching breeches
that fit his taut, muscular body to perfection. Yet his
tanned face held a fine sheen of perspiration and his
dark hair, although tied in a queue, appeared unruly
and windblown, as if he had arrived only moments ago
from his ride and changed in a hurry. His intense gaze,
which held the slightest hint of wry amusement—at her
obvious appraisal of him? she wondered—caught and
held hers.

"You have still to answer my question," he observed
huskily, "although I would imagine many young gentlemen have praised your beauty."

"Actually, no, none have been so . . . bold," she
stressed, hoping he would see that he was far overstep-
ping his bounds.

"Then they were fools. Allow me to be the first to
tell you, Miss Cary, you are very lovely. Bewitchingly
so."

Susanna blushed hotly, her cheeks burning, not as
Camille would certainly have done but because she herself was truly, and unbelievably, flattered by his brash
compliment. She should have known that he wouldn't
be deterred by her pointed remark. She had hoped for
some reaction from him about her appearance, a smile,
a look of approval, but she hadn't expected this!

When his eyes fell to her breasts, she followed them,
and was shocked to discover her skin was flushed pink
clear down to her low-cut, rounded bodice. Silently
seething, furious with herself for having given her emotions away so easily, and still feeling his impertinent
gaze like a hot wind upon her flesh, she refused to lift
her head to look at him.

"May I sit down?" came his low-spoken query, confident, assured.

Susanna wanted to tell him he could bloody well sit
in the river for all she cared, but she bit back the response. How dare he compliment her so audaciously

and then let his eyes roam over her body as if she was not the new mistress of Briarwood, but . . . but some kind of tart! She nodded, not trusting herself to speak.

"Thank you."

As he sat, not at the other end of the bench as would have been proper but right next to her, she stiffened, her thoughts running away with themselves.

Who did this hired man think he was? Was it possible that he believed he had some special privileges where she was concerned because he had known Camille's father? Some special right to such unseemly and bold familiarity? Here she had been ready to offer him an apology for her earlier behavior, yet surely his own behavior was most inappropriate and, come to think of it, had been since the moment they met!

"I'm sorry that I missed dinner. I can imagine that Prue outdid herself for your first meal at Briarwood."

"Yes, she did," Susanna said, flustered at his nearness. She raised her eyes just a bit to stare unseeing at the grassy riverbank. He was not sitting so close to her that their legs were touching, as had happened in the carriage, but she could feel his presence almost as if they were.

"I also want to apologize for the way I acted earlier this afternoon. I'm sure you were surprised to find that your father had given me a room in his home, but you'll soon discover that things are done somewhat differently here than they are in England. I had no right to become angry, though. I can only explain it by saying that you had seemed so shocked that I took it to mean you might be troubled by such an arrangement. I truly hope that that was not the case. But then, it won't really matter before long."

Now what did he mean by that? Susanna wondered.

When she made no reply but stubbornly continued to look at the ground, a charged silence fell between them which was broken only by the sounds that a short while ago had so charmed her. Everything seemed to be irritating her now, and she was about to excuse herself and return to the house when he took her hand, caressing her fingers with his thumb. Susanna almost choked.

"I was going to wait a few days to tell you what I have to say, but I find that my impatience will not allow it. First, I want you to look at me, Camille."

Susanna started when she felt his other hand gently cup her chin, his fingers callused yet surprisingly warm, and lift her face to him. She was so shocked that he would call her again by her first name, so astounded that he would dare to touch her in this way, almost tenderly, that she could only stare incredulously into his eyes.

"A few months before your father died, I requested his permission to court you, and he granted it with his full blessing. Camille, it is my intention for us to marry." His expression serious, he paused to stroke her cheek, then his finger lightly traced her lips. "I know this is very sudden. You don't have to say anything right away, just hear me out."

Doing her best to ignore the strange, dizzying sensations elicited by his feather-light touch, Susanna was so flabbergasted she couldn't have said anything. Court her? Marry her? Camille's father had given Adam his blessing? Surely the man was mad!

"Your father told me a lot about you. You're very shy, just as he said—"

When Susanna drew in her breath and looked away, relieved to hear how well her masquerade had convinced him, Adam misread her action entirely.

"I didn't mean that as a criticism, my love. I find your timid nature . . . most beguiling."

*My love?* Susanna thought, glancing back at him in total astonishment. How quickly she had gone from Miss Cary to Camille to *my love!*

"Your father also told me that you prefer a quiet life, much to the despair of Baroness Redmayne, your Aunt Melicent. He said she was forever encouraging you to attend balls and go on outings while all you ever wanted to do was stay at home. Is this true?"

"Yes," she replied, her voice sounding oddly hoarse.

Adam took both of her hands in his large ones, his vivid brown eyes burning into hers. His touch held restrained tension, which only added to her disquiet.

"I promise you this, Camille. I'll never force you to do anything you don't want to do. Allow me to give you the kind of life you desire, peaceful and protected, just as your father wanted for you. I'm not a rich man, and I don't own any land, but I do have one thing. Your father's approval. He knew that I would do well by you and that under my care Briarwood would continue to prosper. You know how much this plantation meant to him. We'll make it prosper together, my love, you and I, just as your father would have wanted."

Susanna was dumbfounded, Adam's low, impassioned words echoing in her mind.

Was it really true, then, what Corliss had told her about some planters being willing to allow Adam to court their daughters because he was a crop master? she thought dazedly as he studied her face. Had James Cary intended for Camille to be courted by and then married to this man? Surely he would have mentioned Adam's name in his last letter if that had been the case. He had said that he had someone in mind for Camille, that they would talk about it when she arrived in Virginia . . . but Adam Thornton, his plantation manager?

No, she couldn't believe it! The idea was simply too incredible. James Cary couldn't have agreed to such a thing for purely mercenary reasons. He loved his daughter too well. He would have wanted her to marry a gentleman, to follow the rules Lady Redmayne had so painstakingly taught her. Surely a planter with wealth and position could help Briarwood prosper ten times more than any hired crop master.

Susanna's gaze fell from Adam's face. She could tell from his increasingly impatient expression that he was waiting for her response. Yet what could she say to him?

Suddenly all the puzzling pieces were fitting together. The possessive way Adam had been treating her, his overconfident manner, his absurd protectiveness, his telling Mr. Grymes that she didn't like social gatherings, then his resentment . . . all of it leading to his unsettling proposal. Even his behavior upstairs in his room made sense. He had become angry because she was looking at him—and rightly!—as a hired man when he believed himself to be so much more. Her friggin' future husband!

Susanna's anger whirled inside her like a brewing tempest that was becoming ever more difficult to contain.

The nervy, conniving, opportunistic bastard! He truly expected her to agree to his proposal just as Camille might have accepted it if she had been faced with such an argument. Her dear, meek, obedient Camille would have done anything her father wanted, she loved him so much. If she had believed Adam's story, she probably would have become Mrs. Thornton. And to think Camille had thought of Adam as the perfect husband for *her!*

But Camille wasn't here, God keep her, and neither was James Cary. Only Susanna. And she didn't believe Adam for a bloody minute. Mr. Cary might have treated him well, even liked him as Corliss had claimed, but surely not enough to grant Adam his daughter's hand in marriage. It was all a lie, a grand scheme concocted by a very ambitious man with nothing to lose and everything to gain: Briarwood.

There had to be some way she could stall him, Susanna thought, her mind working fast. Some way to make him think she was seriously considering his suit until she could find a proper husband. She couldn't say no outright. Adam would leave Briarwood, and she would have no one to manage the plantation. Perhaps if she could make him understand that she wanted a proper wooing of several months, as any gently bred young woman might, it would buy her some time . . .

"Camille."

Susanna met Adam's restless gaze. "I'm sorry, Mr. Thornton. As you said, this is all so . . . sudden."

"Adam. Call me Adam."

She offered him a smile, and was rewarded when the flicker of doubt in his eyes was replaced by renewed confidence. She had expected his reaction, but it made her all the angrier. It was a good thing he was still holding her hands; otherwise she would have slapped him!

"Very well. Adam."

His name was barely off her lips when he leaned toward her and for a fleeting instant, her heart pounding, Susanna thought he was going to kiss her. When he didn't, she actually felt disappointed, but she quickly regained her composure as his expression became intense, his gaze searching.

She was damned and determined to deceive him, which, now that she thought about it might even be fun. Why not lead him on with all her other suitors until she settled upon her choice, then send him crashing back down to earth when she finally told him the truth? He deserved nothing less!

"Since you haven't denied me, I take it that you accept my wish to court you."

Holding his breath, Adam thought he might burst as he scrutinized her face for signs of her decision. He had had a slight scare when she didn't answer him for so long, but he should have known a shy mouse like Camille would be initially taken aback by such an ardent proposal. He gazed into her beautiful green eyes, wondering anew how a woman so damnably lovely could be so retiring, meanwhile inwardly cursing that still she did not answer him—

"Yes, I accept . . . but . . ."

Adam's heady exultation, instantaneous and overwhelming, was just as suddenly checked by her last word.

"What is it, Camille?" he urged, trying to keep his agitation from his voice. "Tell me what you're thinking."

She chewed her bottom lip before answering hesitantly, "It's just that I've never been courted before,

Mr. Thorn—Adam. It's . . . well, it's what every girl dreams about . . . a proper courting, I mean.''

Adam was momentarily stumped. He had no idea what she was trying to say.

''A proper courting?''

Nodding, she glanced up at him through lashes he imagined would feel like the soft flutter of feathers upon his skin.

''There's no need for us to rush, is there, Adam? You seem in such a hurry, yet from what I know, a proper courting takes time. A man must woo a woman gently, am I not right? At least that is how I always imagined it would be . . .''

Realization swamped him as she flushed prettily, and he wanted to throw back his head and laugh. Yet he restrained himself, not wanting her to think he was making light of her girlish fantasies.

So this timid beauty was a romantic at heart! Then his instincts about a passionate nature simmering beneath her bashful exterior must also be right. No doubt she had read plenty of sentimental stories which had filled her head with all sorts of notions about how a man should court a woman. Well, he would gladly oblige her, and in ways that before long would send her scurrying into his arms.

''We have time, my love,'' he murmured, reaching up to stroke her hair. It was soft to his touch and smooth, like silk. It wasn't difficult to imagine threading his fingers through its honeyed loveliness, or how it might look spread out upon a pillow.

''Oh, I'm so glad, Adam. I'm sure that after a few months—''

''Months?'' he queried sharply, his hand falling still as he met her astonished gaze. He hadn't said anything about waiting a few months.

''I . . . I think it would be best,'' she said in a rush, her expression clouding. ''I've only just returned and . . . well, I know so little about my home. I'm sure my father would have wanted me to be comfortable with my surroundings and my new duties as the mistress of Briarwood before I gave any thought to—to marriage . . .''

Adam pondered her nervous explanation, deciding it was best to humor her. God help him, it looked as if she might cry if he so much as shook his head. That was the last thing he wanted. A woman's tears always left him at a total loss.

He had no intention of waiting that long to marry her, but he doubted he'd have to. He imagined that her excuses merely masked fears about marriage, and about the intimacy between husband and wife, which any innocent young woman would harbor. Yet he knew very well how to allay her concerns. It would be a pleasurable task indeed, awakening her to the desire lying dormant within her, while preserving her innocence for the night when he could call her lawfully his. He doubted she would want to wait long after she tasted passion.

''We'll take as much time as you need,'' he promised, smiling to himself when she seemed pleased with his response.

''There's just one more thing, Adam.''

''Yes?''

''Could we keep our courting a secret? Just between you and me . . . at least until it's time to announce the betrothal? I don't think it would be proper, considering your bedroom is only a few doors from mine.'' She paused, coughing delicately. ''You understand, I'm sure. My reputation . . .''

Adam hadn't expected this request, but again, he decided to humor her. What harm was there anyway? Probably another girlish fancy, a secretive courting replete with stolen kisses and furtive glances. What the hell, he had her consent, which was all that mattered. He would play her virgin's game.

''Done,'' he answered, noting a flicker of relief cross her face, which transposed quickly into a becoming, albeit shy smile. Mesmerized by the ripe, red fullness of her lips and thinking there would be no harm in sealing their agreement with a chaste kiss, he leaned closer. But she coyly dodged him and rose from the bench.

"I think I should go inside, Adam," she said, glancing toward the house. "It's growing dark and there are some things I'd like to do . . . make sure my trunks have been properly unpacked, and perhaps read a little before I retire."

"Of course," he murmured, more disappointed than he would have thought. As he imagined the day when she would find her pleasure not in reading before bedtime, but in far more sensual pursuits, he stood and offered his arm. Pointedly, she refused to take it.

So their secretive game had already begun, he thought with amusement, escorting a silent Camille past the still, shadowed gardens and into the house.

"Good night, Mr. Thornton," she said softly, her eyes pleading with him to answer in kind as a servant walked by them. "I'm sure we'll talk again soon. Perhaps, when you have time, you could show me more of the plantation."

"I'd be delighted, Miss Cary," he replied, realizing that their outward formality would extend to any times other than when they were alone. He didn't exactly like the idea, but if it was the way to win her, he would do it. "Sleep well." And as he watched her ascend the stairs without even a backward glance, her natural grace causing her slender hips to sway provocatively, he found himself looking forward to the coming days with great anticipation indeed.

So he didn't have a betrothal to announce on Saturday, he thought, striding into the library to pour himself a brandy. He would announce it soon enough, though, once he cornered her a few times alone and she discovered exactly what kind of game they were playing.

Raising his glass, Adam silently toasted the revenge that was almost within his grasp, then he tossed down the fiery contents, thinking of the woman who would make it possible.

His beautiful, acquiescent, and oh-so-delectable Camille.

# Chapter 6

Susanna was up to her chin in lavender-scented bubbles, luxuriating in her first full bath since she had left England, when Corliss returned from downstairs with clean towels and an unexpected message from Adam.

"Mr. Thornton says he has time this morning to show you the rest of the plantation, Miss Camille. What do you want me to tell him? He's waiting in the library."

The tranquillity of her bath spoiled by this intrusion, Susanna bit off a tart response as she glanced at the mantel clock.

Only half past eight! He had a lot of gall to bother her so early. Clearly he was eager to begin their courtship, which made her all the more eager to frustrate him. She wanted to spend no more time with him than was absolutely necessary to maintain her illusion of welcoming his advances, no matter what she had said to him last evening about seeing more of the plantation. That statement had been merely for the servant's benefit. She could bloody well explore Briarwood on her own.

"Kindly tell Mr. Thornton that I won't be ready for at least another two hours," Susanna instructed, swept by a heady sense of mischief. "Perhaps we should wait until another day. I know how busy he must be. I don't want to keep him from his work. But please thank him, Corliss, for his gracious offer."

"Yes, Miss Camille."

As the maid set the towels on a low table pulled close to the tub and left the room, Susanna smiled to herself.

Adam had said that they had time for a proper courting, she thought, playfully flicking bubbles with her toes. It was her intention to make this the longest and most secretive courtship on record, at least until she had decided upon the man she really wanted.

The overbearing, overconfident lout! She still couldn't believe how easily she had deceived him and how readily he had accepted her conditions to his preposterous proposal, especially the one about their courtship remaining a secret. She didn't want anyone—especially the servants—to know that there was anything between her and Adam; her reputation truly was at stake. She had no intention of jeopardizing her chances of marrying the right man by having Camille's good name sullied in any way.

In the letters Camille had shared with her, Mr. Cary had claimed Adam was intelligent, but he was a total fool when it came to women, Susanna decided. He truly believed that she would consider him as a potential husband. Had he no sense of what was proper? Why, it would be as if she, a lady's maid, had come to Briarwood with the intention of marrying a wealthy planter's son. Impossible! Absurd! It simply wasn't done!

Susanna shrugged, at a complete loss, and concentrated upon soaping her arm with long, languorous strokes.

If and when Adam realized her true intentions, it would be too late. He would find himself without an heiress and without his bloody job!

"Miss Camille, Mr. Thornton says he'll come back to the house in two hours to fetch you," Corliss relayed, stepping into the room and closing the door behind her. "He said it would be no trouble at all. He left his day free just so he could show you around."

Hearing this, Susanna was tempted to fling the bar of soap across the room, but she let it sink to the bottom of the tub instead. Disgruntled that her plan to avoid him had failed, she leaned her head against the rim and defiantly closed her eyes.

Very well, then, the bastard. If he was going to be so persistent, she would make him wait even longer for her company.

She dawdled in the tub until her skin was thoroughly pink and puckered—explaining to a curious Corliss that she hadn't enjoyed a real bath in ages—then she dallied in her room long after she had dressed in a burgundy riding habit, eaten her breakfast, and sent Corliss away, saying she wanted to read for a while. Instead she re-hid Camille's portrait, taking the rolled canvas from the writing table drawer where she had put it last night— and none too soon since Corliss had come upstairs soon afterward to finish unpacking her trunks—and placing it in a large oval hatbox in which she had fashioned a false bottom. It would have to do until she knew the house well enough to find an even safer place.

Finally, when the clock read exactly eleven-thirty and she was beginning to feel restless, Susanna left her room.

She was not surprised to find Adam waiting for her at the bottom of the stairs, dressed in a black riding coat and snug-fitting buckskin breeches which emphasized the shape of his powerful thighs. His gaze swept her appraisingly from head to toe, then his eyes caught and held hers as she descended. She felt a nervous rush of excitement, unexpected and disturbing. She wished he wasn't so intensely masculine. She would have to keep her wits about her in her dealings with this man. He seemed to have the ability to make her feel very strange inside. Quite unlike herself.

"Please forgive my tardiness, Mr. Thornton," she said with mock sincerity, noting the tightness of his smile. It revealed his impatience, although his posture appeared relaxed, leaning as he was against the polished balustrade with his arms crossed over his chest. She felt a small sense of triumph. "I was reading and . . . well, I lost track of the time."

"Don't trouble yourself, Miss Cary," he replied with

a husky emphasis on her name. "All that matters now is that you are here. I trust you slept well last night?"

"Yes, I did." In truth, she hadn't, her slumber disrupted by a vivid and familiar nightmare that had left her sweat-soaked and shaken, but she wasn't about to tell him that. "And you?"

"Actually, my thoughts would not let me sleep until very late," he said, the words laced with innuendo. "Yesterday was a very momentous day . . . for both of us."

"Please, Mr. Thornton," Susanna whispered, doing her best not to show too much irritation at his thinly disguised breach as her eyes darted to the young footman seated by the door. "We agreed . . ."

"I haven't forgotten, Miss Cary," Adam said quietly. "I haven't forgotten." As if to reinforce his words, he didn't offer to take her arm as he had the night before, but merely inclined his head. "I have a great deal to show you today, and it's almost noon. Shall we get started?"

Nodding, Susanna said nothing more except for a soft greeting to the footman, a mere boy, who grinned broadly as he jumped up from his chair and opened the door for them. Her irritation was quickly replaced by enthusiasm at the bright sunny day which greeted her, and again she reveled in the fact that she was no longer aboard a confining ship but possessed the freedom to roam where she pleased.

As she walked with Adam to the circular drive where stable hands waited with two spirited mounts, one of them the same chestnut stallion she had seen yesterday, she was glad that Lady Redmayne had allowed her to learn to ride so that she might accompany Camille on occasional jaunts around the estate. Competent, assured horsemanship would have been nearly impossible to feign.

"What a beautiful animal," she murmured, stepping closer to pat the mare's snow-white neck.

"Yes, Arabian bloodlines. The Cary stable has some of the finest steeds in Virginia."

As if in firm agreement with Adam's remark, the pretty mare nickered and tossed its finely shaped head, then stamped its hoof impatiently.

"She seems most eager for us to be on our way."

"Has been for an hour now," Adam said lightly, his face inscrutable. "If you would allow me . . ."

Susanna gasped softly as his strong hands encompassed her waist and he lifted her as easily into the sidesaddle as if she weighed no more than a child. He did not readily release her; instead, his fingers gently caressed her back.

"Are you well-settled, Miss Cary?" he inquired, a slow smile tugging at his lips.

"I am, thank you," she replied, unnerved by both his touch and the almost conspiratorial look in his eyes, which seemed to say that yes indeed, they shared a wonderful little secret.

Despite her response, Adam held her for an instant longer, which further flustered Susanna, her skin feeling very warm beneath the weight of his hands. Then he abruptly let go of her and mounted his stallion. She was not pleased to discover that her fingers were shaking as she tied the ribbons on her wide-brimmed riding hat beneath her chin.

"I'll show you the outbuildings first, then we'll ride out to the fields," Adam said, his tone becoming suitably deferential, as if to reassure her that their secret was safe with him. "If you have any questions, Miss Cary, please don't hesitate to ask." He fastened the large buckle on the full saddlebag behind his left thigh, then added, "I hope you don't mind, but I took the liberty of canceling dinner. We won't be back by three." He patted the saddlebag. "Prue packed us some food, so have no fear that you'll go hungry."

Susanna didn't reply, but nudged the frisky mare into a trot beside his much larger mount.

Just you wait, Mr. Adam Thornton, she fumed, thinking ahead to that happy day when she could tell him exactly what she thought about him and his courtship and his ordering of her life. Just you wait!

They had ridden a short distance from the house when Adam pulled up on the reins and waited for her to halt beside him. He pointed to a large one-story building not far from the river which was almost hidden by towering trees.

"The laundry," he explained. "There are three other main buildings beside this one, each standing ninety yards from a corner of the house to form a square. The guest house"—he indicated the brick building opposite, a smaller version of the mansion yet with a one-story addition in the rear that had a white-painted roof—"with the new schoolhouse behind it, while on the other side of the house you'll find the coach house and stable."

"Schoolhouse?" she asked.

"It was to have been a surprise. Your father had it built last summer for his future grandchildren."

"Oh." Susanna didn't appreciate the way he was looking at her, her cheeks growing warm as she imagined the unseemly thoughts passing through his mind. She was glad that there were servants bustling about on their various tasks, so he wouldn't dare voice any of them. Wishing to change the uncomfortable subject altogether, she turned her attention to the cluster of smaller outbuildings standing within the triangle formed by the guest house and laundry. "And those?"

"Bake house, some storehouses, the dairy, well house, spinning house, smokehouse, kitchen, house servants' quarters—"

"A kitchen?" How unusual, Susanna thought, realizing that she had assumed the kitchen was attached to the house, as at the Redmaynes'. "In England, it's part of the house."

"As I told you yesterday, things are done differently in Virginia," Adam replied. "Planters design their homes for elegance and beauty, which is what your grandfather did when he built Briarwood. The interior is devoted to rooms where the planter and his family engage in pursuits that are proper to their station. Cooking is not among them. Prue and her kitchen maids carry all the food to the house."

No wonder Lady Redmayne had often told Camille that when she arrived in Virginia, her main purpose would be to serve as a decoration for society, Susanna thought as they set out again, walking the horses carefully through the riverfront garden. With all the rooms dedicated to leisure, there wasn't anything practical for the mistress of the house to do . . . well, other than have babies. That would keep her busy for a while, but of course, a nurse or two would doubtless be employed to help out.

Suddenly disliking the picture of life she conjured in her mind, Susanna decided then and there that she would change things to better suit her. She wouldn't be able to stand such an idle existence for long, especially since she would never be one to while away the hours doing needlepoint or practicing an instrument in the music room. After she was married, she would take an active part in the life at Briarwood, even if it meant she must usurp some of Ertha's managerial tasks. Surely she could maintain the appearance of leisure required of planters' wives yet keep busy.

"As you can see on this side of the house," Adam continued, "there are a number of buildings between the coach house and stable—the wheelwright, blacksmith shop, a carpenter shop, shoemaker, distillery, and so on, while located further back are quarters for the servants who perform these jobs and other outdoor tasks. There's also a barn behind the stable, and upriver a short way, the Cary mill."

"There's so much here," Susanna said, astounded. "In England, we would just go into town for many of these things."

"The towns in Virginia are too far apart and even if they weren't, planters tend to be self-sufficient. They'd rather have their own craftsmen than rely on outsiders for what they need."

"Papa was like that," she replied, looking down at the braided reins in her hands. It was still difficult for her to call Mr. Cary by such a familiar name. "Independent, I mean."

"Yes, he was," Adam said, his voice sounding so hollow and distant that Susanna, startled, glanced at him. He was staring toward a thick copse of elm trees that stood well beyond the coach house close to the river.

"What's down there?" she asked, wondering at his sudden change of mood. She could tell he was upset, but why? She drew in her breath when he turned to look at her, his face set as in stone, his expressive brown eyes revealing turmoil . . . and something else. Pain.

"The Cary family graveyard."

Susanna's widened gaze flew to the circle of trees, then back to Adam.

"You know," he continued, "it's easy to see that you remember next to nothing about this place. Yet for some reason, I would have thought you knew where the graveyard was located."

He was right, Susanna thought, stunned by his statement and even more by the naked emotion in his eyes. Camille probably would have known about the graveyard, but it wasn't something they had ever discussed. She fumbled for a convincing reply.

"Captain Keyes told me Papa was buried next to my mother in the family cemetery, but that was all. He said nothing about it being near the York, or within sight of the house, and . . . and Papa never really spoke of the graveyard, probably because he lost my mother so young—"

"Camille, you don't owe me an explanation," Adam broke in quietly, his expression somber as he studied her flushed face. She could see that whatever had so troubled him only a moment ago had subsided, his emotions once again tightly under control. "It was an inconsiderate thing for me to say. I'm sorry." He paused, a heavy silence falling between them, then asked gently, "Do you want to go down there?"

"No . . . not right now," she said, her heart thudding against her breast. She had never felt less like Camille and more like an impostor than in that moment. "Maybe later. When I'm alone."

He nodded, understanding in his gaze. "Come on, then. I've a lot more to show you. If you think the grounds around the house are impressive, wait until you see the rest of Briarwood."

Following his lead, Susanna kicked her mount into a gallop, thinking a good, hard ride was exactly what she needed. Anything to escape how miserable she felt right now.

Susanna was relieved when they finally slowed their pace a few hours later, not so much because she was tired but because she was hungry.

She had become embarrassed no more than twenty minutes ago when, as she was being introduced to Josiah Skinner, one of Briarwood's head overseers, a discernible grumbling had sounded from her stomach. Adam and Josiah had both pretended they heard nothing, continuing their discussion about the overseer who had been fired the day before, but she knew that Adam had heard when he smilingly suggested a few moments later that they find a comfortable spot to have dinner. Now, as they approached a small freshwater pond lined with enchanting weeping willows, Adam slowing his stallion's powerful stride to a trot, she guessed he had finally found that special site.

"How does this look?" he asked, surprising her that he would seek her approval when he seemed to have already made up his mind. She was tempted to say that she hated willow trees, which she really didn't, just to see if he was willing to act the gentleman and take her elsewhere, but she decided she was too hungry to test him.

"Lovely."

"I thought you would think so. It's a favorite place of mine."

Now she wished that she *had* said it, Susanna thought with renewed irritation as she halted her mare a few yards from the pond in the cool shade of a giant willow. He seemed so bloody sure of her and her reactions.

"Let me help you," Adam said, dismounting quickly

and reaching up to lift her to the ground, as he had done all day during their tour of various sites on the plantation. She had decided earlier to allow him to play his game of gallant instead of jumping down by herself, as she was accustomed to doing, but this time was different as he finished his offer by adding ". . . my love."

Liar! You don't love me, Susanna fumed silently as his strong hands easily spanned her waist. All you love is my wealth. Camille's wealth. You don't care about anything but your own ambition. Your own greed.

Yet her agitation quickly turned to alarm when he slowly slid her down the hard, muscular length of his body before setting her upon the ground. He held her closely, too close, staring deeply into her eyes, and she tensed, again afraid that he was going to kiss her. When she cast down her eyes to thwart him, he gently nudged up her chin, his other hand stroking her lower back.

"You're trembling, Camille. Why? No one will see us here. We're finally alone."

Susanna tried to control her racing senses. That's exactly what she was afraid of!

"You don't have to be so shy with me, my love," Adam continued, his tone husky and soothing. "We're courting now, remember? Men and women usually embrace when they like each other. When they want to be near each other. You can't tell me you didn't read about such things in those romantic books of yours."

I don't like you! Susanna screamed in her mind, though from the strange feelings enveloping her it seemed her body possessed an entirely different viewpoint. Reason told her to pull away, to feign insult and dismay, as any gently bred young woman would do if entrapped by an overzealous suitor. But her senses cried out for her to draw even closer to his compelling warmth, to enjoy the stirring sensations his touch aroused in her.

"Have you nothing to say?" he queried softly, tracing the full curve of her mouth with his fingertip as he wound his arm more tightly around her. "I long to hear my name upon your lips again, Camille."

"Please . . . Adam. This is so much, so soon," Susanna blurted nervously, her better judgment finally gaining some small advantage over her bewildering feelings. "We've hardly had a chance to become acquainted . . . and—and you said we had time. You're rushing me"—she twisted slightly in his arms, bracing her hands upon his chest—"rushing this, yet you said you wouldn't!"

"Forgive me," he said, her words piercing the mounting desire clouding his brain. With great reluctance, he gradually began to release his hold upon her, although his body was demanding that he begin a far more sensual assault.

Dammit, man, you've got to move more slowly with her! he berated himself, drawing a deep, ragged breath. She was quaking like a leaf in autumn, her brilliant sea-green eyes so wide he felt as if he could plunge right into them.

Shaken by another streak of hot desire, Adam had to steel himself again from the reckless course his body wanted to take.

God help him, if only she wasn't so soft and warm. If only her lush body didn't mold so perfectly to his! She would tempt any man's baser nature to hold her as closely as he had just done. But he wasn't any man. He was the man she was going to marry. And he had promised to give her as much time as she needed, promised to court her gently. Well, by God, he would court her so gently that one day soon, instead of shaking like a nervous virgin in his arms, she would melt like butter and bend eagerly, even wantonly, to his will.

"You might not think it much of an excuse, but if I seem overly eager, it is because you are so beautiful," Adam admitted honestly, holding only her hand now. "I don't want you to think that I'm rushing you, Camille. I promise on my honor that you won't have reason to accuse me of that again. Now, come with me." Drawing her with him, he paused beside his grazing mount to grab the saddlebag, then said, "How about if we sit by the water? We'll have our dinner and become better acquainted. I think that's something we both want.''

A nod was her only reply, but he wasn't concerned, surmising she was still shaken by his ardor. Yet once she saw that he fully intended to woo her gently, he was certain she would trust him and be comfortable enough in his presence to abandon her shyness. Already she seemed to be sharing more of her feelings with him. Her timely emotional outburst had proved that.

"I forgot to bring a blanket," he apologized, releasing her hand to shrug out of his coat. He laid it upon the sweet-scented grass, then gestured with a flourish. "For you, my lady fair."

As she grudgingly sat upon his coat, Susanna could not help thinking how such a gentlemanly display might have easily charmed another woman, perhaps even Camille, but she wasn't fooled. Just as she wasn't fooled by his honorable promise.

Men like Adam Thornton didn't have any honor, and she would do well to remember it. She didn't trust him, especially not after what had just happened. Yet she had to admit that she didn't trust her feelings right now, either. Looking at the way his sweat-dampened shirt clung to his wide shoulders and accentuated his powerful biceps was enough to make her feel strange . . .

Bloody hell! Susanna cursed to herself, glancing away just as Adam caught her staring at him. What the devil was coming over her?

Disconcerted, she did her best to concentrate upon the array of food Adam was placing between them: a crusty loaf of bread, thick slices of ham, a small wheel of cheese, and plump apple tarts, all the while thinking determinedly that she would have to learn to keep a tight rein on her emotions whenever she was around him. She hoped that, after today, that wouldn't be often. In fact, she would see to it.

"Wine?"

"Yes, thank you." She took the silver goblet, amazed that Prue would have thought to pack such fine service for a picnic dinner. There were also white linen napkins; holding her wine, she laid one neatly across her lap. She watched silently as Adam cut her a thick slice of bread, topped it with ham and crumbled cheese, then set it upon a small silver plate and handed it to her.

"Have you ever tasted our famed smoked Virginia ham?"

"No," she replied, the smell of food making her stomach growl with added ferocity.

"I'd say you'd better try it. You sound pretty hungry. I'm not surprised, since I heard from Prue that you didn't eat much yesterday." His gaze flickered to her slender waist. "I would think you have more room in that riding habit than in the gown you wore yesterday. Stays aren't laced so tightly."

"How . . . ?" The minute the question popped out, Susanna felt like a naive fool. Of course a rogue like him would know about such things. No doubt he had unfastened his fair share of women's laces. Probably a randy lion's share, from the looks of him.

"Suffice it to say, my love, I've had some experience with women's clothing, which I hope doesn't shock you. Any young woman should be pleased when the man she chooses for her husband has the . . . skills to satisfy her."

You can wager that I'll never choose you, Susanna thought defiantly, although she felt an unbidden and rather wanton niggling of curiosity about the skills he might possess. Her unladylike interest irked her all the more, and she bit with a vengeance into her food. She did not look at him again until she had eaten every morsel and drained her red wine, but when she did raise her eyes, she found he was smiling broadly at her.

"You were hungry. Can I cut you some more bread? Ham?"

"No, but I will take an apple tart."

Adam threw his head back and laughed, a deep, rich sound that Susanna had to admit was very pleasant. Yet she had no idea what he found so funny.

"By all means have a tart. Take two," he said, his

eyes dancing. "My God, Camille, you're such a sweet innocent. If I'd known my comment about women's clothing would upset you so, making you wolf down your food, I wouldn't have said it. I see that I'll have to keep such comments to myself until . . ." He didn't finish but took a long, slow draught of wine, his gaze never leaving her face.

Embarrassed for obviously making a pig of herself, Susanna kept her eyes upon the lush grass at her feet as she nibbled the tart. She was wholly amazed that Adam had so misread her, but it was just as well. It wouldn't do for him to know what she really thought of him. Not yet. She needed his services at Briarwood, especially after what she had seen today.

She had never imagined the plantation would be so vast, the laborers so many, the responsibilities so great. One hundred thousand tobacco plants in rows across countless fields! Add to that secondary crops of wheat and Indian corn, and it was easy to see why she could never direct such an operation by herself. Just hearing how Adam had thrown that cruel overseer off Cary lands had proved to her that managing a plantation could be a very rough business. Until she was betrothed to a man who could take on these duties, she needed Adam. For Briarwood's sake, she would have to bear his unwanted advances.

"Tell me, Camille," he said, his rich voice nudging her from her musings. He leaned forward and poured her more wine, then drew up one knee and leaned his arms upon it. "What do you think of the plantation?"

"Impressive. I never realized it was so big."

"You haven't seen even half of it yet."

Susanna gaped in astonishment. "Really?"

"Briarwood is the largest plantation on the York . . . well, other than . . ." Adam didn't finish, a sudden scowl on his brow, and shook his head, as if he was berating himself for something he had almost said. He glanced out across the placid pond for a brief moment, then met her eyes. His scowl was gone, but so was the good-natured ease in his voice. "What about Fairford? Did you enjoy living there?"

Susanna had no intention of discussing Fairford, at least not now. She was curious to know what had brought on his sudden shift of mood, much like what had happened earlier that day when he had told her about the Cary graveyard. This man was such a puzzle!

"What plantation rivals Briarwood?" she asked, and was not surprised to see his frown return.

"Raven's Point."

From the manner in which he bit off the words, Susanna could tell it was a topic he didn't want to pursue, but she couldn't help herself.

"I don't recall my father ever mentioning that plantation," she said, watching him closely. "Who does it belong to?"

"Dominick Spencer."

"Oh, yes, Corliss told me about him," Susanna replied innocently, wondering why the mention of Adam's former employer would upset him so. His eyes had darkened to a deep, stormy hue, and she could almost feel the tension gathering within him. His grip on his goblet was so tight that his knuckles were taut and pale.

"And what did Corliss say about Mr. Spencer?" he asked, the steadiness of his voice belying his stiffened posture.

"Not much, really. Just that he lived upriver from Briarwood and that he was well-respected and very wealthy."

"Well-respected, perhaps, but not as wealthy as he may seem," Adam muttered, furious with himself for even bringing up the subject. The last thing he wanted right now was to discuss that son of a bitch!

"I'm sorry, Adam. I didn't hear you."

"I said did Corliss say anything else?"

"Well, she told me that you once worked for Mr. Spencer . . . as an indentured servant. Is that true? She said you used to work in the fields hoeing tobacco."

Adam knew he shouldn't be upset by such a question. His background was common knowledge in the Tidewater. Yet the details of his life at Raven's Point were not, and he didn't intend to share them with anyone, least of all Camille. That existence was behind him now; all that lay in front of him was sweet revenge.

She would never know about those bitter years, or that she was the instrument of his vengeance. He fully expected that she would have questions once she saw his back and what remained of his right foot, but he would make up convincing lies, if only to spare her the knowledge that he had used her to satisfy his own ends. He was driven, but he wasn't cruel. He would not hurt her if he could prevent it; they would be sharing their lives together, after all. He did not want a bitter rift between them, as such a revelation would surely cause.

"Yes, it's true, but that was a long time ago," he finally replied, though in truth, he could remember the stinging bite of the lash across his back as if it had been yesterday. And the incident with his foot . . .

Adam swallowed hard against the bile burning his throat, and sweat broke out on his forehead. If he didn't get up and move now, he wouldn't be able to shake the many images, the terrible memories, the nightmare sounds locked forever in his mind: his mother screaming, screaming . . . his own screams after the indescribable flash of pain, and the bright red blood spurting—

"I think we should head back," he said abruptly, rising to his feet in one agile movement and extending his hand. "We've a long ride ahead of us and, as you said, we must think of your reputation. It wouldn't do for us to arrive at the house after dark."

As Susanna stared up at him in astonishment, she was struck by the wildness, almost a desperation, in his eyes.

Whatever was the matter with him? she wondered, thinking back on their conversation. Could their talk about Raven's Point and Dominick Spencer account for this strange behavior, or had he simply, suddenly, realized the lateness of the hour?

"Camille . . ."

# Chapter 7

D usk was settling as Adam escorted Susanna to the mansion's front door, but instead of accompanying her inside, he excused himself by saying he had some urgent business. He strode off toward the coach house—where, she was later told by Ertha, he had a small office—while the stable hands led their exhausted and lathered horses away. He never came in for supper, and she went to bed early, as puzzled as ever.

Nor did she have even the briefest chance to talk to him over the next three days. She never saw him.

Sometime during the night a furious summer storm erupted, accompanied by wicked lightning, deafening thunder, and torrential rains which didn't let up for much of the week. She didn't see Adam at all the following day, occupied as she was by a disconcerting visit from William Booth, the Cary family attorney, who read her James Cary's will: It named her as the sole heir of Briarwood. That evening, when she queried Ertha about Adam's possible whereabouts, the housekeeper informed her that the ripening tobacco was being threatened by the unusual rainfall. He was in the fields, supervising the workers as they did everything they could to save the plants from flooding. He would probably be there day and night until the downpour ended.

By Friday morning, which dawned sunny and clear, Susanna was anxious to escape outside after being cooped up in the house for so long, and to see for herself how Cary's Finest had fared.

When Corliss declined to accompany her on her ride, saying she was afraid of horses, Susanna decided to go alone. She only wanted to see the closest fields; if their condition was good she imagined the others would be much the same. She had no intention of riding out as far as she and Adam had gone a few days ago, and she didn't want to go near that pond. Just thinking about it brought back memories of his embrace, a troubling recollection that had plagued her during the day. Yet even more disturbing was how her memory became altered at night.

In her dreams, Adam kissed her slowly, lingeringly, his mouth warm and tender at first, but then becoming passionately demanding, his strong hands roaming at will over her body as she kissed him back—

"Here she is, Miss Camille. All saddled and ready to go."

Susanna blinked, startled. Her face felt warm as she smiled at the spry older man who was leading the same spirited mare toward her that she had ridden before.

"Thank you . . . uh . . ."

"Zachary Roe, ma'am. I'm the stable manager." He threw his shoulders back proudly, his smile broadening. "A free man, thanks to your fine papa."

"It's a pleasure to meet you, Zachary." As he gave her a boost into the saddle, Susanna fought to control her jumbled thoughts.

"Would you like one of the hands to accompany you, Miss Camille? I'd hate for you to get lost—"

"No, I'll be fine," she insisted. "Adam"—she drew a quick breath, angry at herself for calling him by his first name—"Mr. Thornton was an excellent guide the other day. He showed me how to get across the fields."

"If you say so, Miss Camille. Have a good ride."

She drew up on the reins, expertly wheeling the animal around, then asked as an afterthought, "Have you seen Mr. Thornton this morning, Zachary?"

"No, ma'am. His horse is gone, so he must still be

out checking the tobo. The rains were pretty bad these past few days."

"Yes," she agreed. "I want to check on the plants, too."

"Oh, you don't have to worry none, Miss Camille. With Mr. Thornton watching over 'em, I'm sure they came out of it just fine."

She smiled tightly, nudging the mare into a trot with her boot.

Didn't anyone but herself have a bad word to say about Adam? she wondered, her irritation piqued. Were these people blind to what manner of man he really was?

Within a few minutes, Susanna had cleared the main grounds, and she urged the mare into a gallop. The first fields she came to were empty, no laborers or overseers in sight, but the large-leafed plants looked healthy, each sitting upon a small hill of earth. The ground was very muddy and in the warm sunshine steam rose up from the moist dirt. It appeared that narrow troughs had been dug around each tobacco hill, but other than that, things seemed much as they had been the other day.

She rode on, wanting to hear some sort of assessment from an overseer if she couldn't find Adam. She was glad when she finally spied Josiah Skinner riding toward the neat cluster of houses where the overseers lived, either alone or with their families. He changed his course and met her halfway.

"What brings you out here this morning, Miss Cary?" he asked, sweeping off his tricorn and clutching it beneath his arm. His brown coat was damp, and his long, lean face looked worn and tired. His breeches and jackboots were caked with mud.

"I wanted to see how the plants held up through the storm. As far as I can tell, they seem all right, though I don't know much about tobacco . . ."

"Everything's just fine," the overseer said, reassurance in his gravelly voice. "I admit, it was going a bit rough for a while, but Adam came up with the notion of digging troughs around the plants so the water could run off. That's what saved us.''

So that was Adam's idea, she thought, relieved to hear that all was well with this year's crop. She should have known.

''You must have just missed him, Miss Cary. He rode back to the house only a short while ago after telling everyone to get some rest now that the weather has cleared. We were up all night, and the other two nights we slept in short shifts. I was just heading home myself.''

''Of course, Mr. Skinner,'' Susanna said. ''I won't keep you. I'm sure Mr. Thornton will give me his own report when I see him.''

''He said that very same thing, but that it wouldn't be until dinnertime.''

''Dinner?''

The overseer eyed her curiously, though his weary expression didn't change. ''I think he wanted to get himself some rest first, Miss Cary. He was up longer than any of us, digging side by side with the field hands. He probably figured you'd trust his judgment just like your father used to, and know that everything was all right unless he made it a point to tell you different.''

And leave her wondering all day if Cary's Finest was ruined or not? Susanna fumed, veering her horse around after thanking the overseer for his hard work and bidding him also to get some sleep.

She rode back toward the house, imagining how wonderful it would feel to storm into Adam's bedroom and demand he give her a full accounting of the past days' events, but she knew Camille would never have done such a thing. Instead, as the coach house came into view, she decided to cool her temper by exploring a little, her natural curiosity spurring her on.

She wanted to see his office. She had seen practically everything else on the plantation, and she had no wish to while away the hours in the library or in the game room playing solitary rounds of cards as she had done since Tuesday. Maybe she would be able to gain a little more insight into Adam's character by inspecting the place where, according to Ertha, he spent a fair amount of time. Perhaps she might even find some information she could use against him, in addition to his cocksure and improper advances toward her, when the time came to fire him. The housekeeper had said the office had a private door near the back of the coach house . . .

As she approached the large two-story building, Susanna immediately spied the door. She dismounted and tethered the mare to a tree. She was surprised to discover that the door led not into a room, but to a narrow flight of stairs.

The wooden steps creaked as she ascended them, but no one would dare question her if she was discovered here. She was the mistress of Briarwood. She could do anything she wanted on this plantation.

Susanna opened another door at the top of the stairs and, holding her breath in anticipation, stepped inside a small, sunlit room that was furnished with a writing desk, bookcases, and a narrow bed pushed up against one wall that took up much of the floor space. Other than the tall stool behind the desk and a threadbare stuffed chair with an accompanying side table placed near one of the two windows, there were no other furnishings, and the bare, whitewashed walls gave the room a spartan appearance. The air was tinged with the smell of leather and polish, drifting up from the coach house below.

As she quickly scanned the crowded, well-dusted bookshelves—his own private collection? she wondered—she noted books on the growing of tobacco and horticulture—no surprise there—and others which did surprise her. She had grudgingly sensed in Adam a keen intelligence, but from the variety of subjects presented here—history, mathematics, religion, philosophy, poetry, navigation, law, architecture, and many others—it was clear his intellectual interests were diverse and admittedly more advanced than her own.

There were even well-thumbed volumes on English grammar and a copy of *The Art of Fair Writing,* which led her to think Adam might be a self-educated man. She also surmised from the thick pools of dried wax beneath the pewter candleholders on the desk and side table that he spent most of his evenings here. A half-empty glass of some liquid—spirits, no doubt, judging from the tall crystal decanter which appeared to be the only luxury in the room—had been left there, and a padded footstool was placed an outstretched-leg's distance from the chair, giving her the impression that he was one to relax and enjoy his reading time.

Susanna's gaze skipped to the writing desk. Some sort of journal lay open, and she decided to take a closer look. She normally wasn't one to pry into someone's personal diary, but in this case, she felt her curiosity justified.

She was disappointed to discover that the journal held only a day-to-day account of plantation business, written in a stilted scrawl.

How strange, she thought, perusing the spare, matter-of-fact entries which made only slight mention of her: *Miss Cary arrived today . . . Tour of Briarwood with Miss Cary.* Hadn't Adam received any schooling when he was younger, in England before he came to Virginia or under Dominick Spencer's employ? From the scratched-out words and occasional ink blots, it appeared not. But then, she hadn't had her first writing lesson until she was thirteen, so their backgrounds weren't so dissimilar.

Susanna's gaze fixed upon the last entry which to her surprise held that day's date. Adam had clearly come here before he went to the house, writing simply that Cary's Finest had survived the heavy rains. Bastard! If he had had the energy to do this, why couldn't he have made an effort to give her some kind of report before—

She jumped up from the stool with a gasp as heavy footsteps sounded upon the stairs. Grabbing the nearest book from the shelf, she plopped into the stuffed chair just as the door opened. Her heart pounding, she stared blindly at the pages in front of her.

"I thought I might find you here, my love. I saw your horse outside."

Thrilled more than she would ever admit by Adam's husky voice, and chagrined that she had been caught snooping again, Susanna did not have to feign her discomfort as she glanced up to find him walking toward her.

Her breath caught sharply, and she marveled anew at his dark good looks. After not seeing him for three days, she had forgotten how intensely handsome he was, despite that his face was deeply lined with fatigue and that mud was spattered from his head to the toes of his thigh-high jackboots. He was smiling at her, making her heart thump all the harder.

"I'm sorry, Adam. I should have asked your permission first . . . but I was riding by the coach house and since Ertha said you had an office here, I thought I'd take a look—"

"There's no need to be embarrassed, Camille. I don't mind you coming up here, but I do question your choice of literature. Chaucer's *Canterbury Tales?* I would think that story too bawdy for a young lady, but I guess it does have its touch of romanticism. And do you always read books upside down?"

Susanna realized to her dismay that it was indeed Chaucer, a lusty tale long banned in Lady Redmayne's home, and yes, it was upside down. Her cheeks fired with warmth. She really didn't know what to say to explain herself, so she decided to ignore his observation altogether.

"You were looking for me?" she asked, setting the book aside with studied nonchalance. Her obvious skirting of the issue must have amused him, for he chuckled, nodding.

"Corliss told me you had gone for a ride out to the fields, so I decided to follow you and give you the good news about the crop. Then I spied your horse . . ." He paused, his gaze moving appraisingly over her mauve riding dress. "You look very charming this morning, my love. That color suits you. It heightens the beauty of your eyes.''

His compliment warming her further, Susanna guiltily chided herself for her harsh judgment of him. So he *had* made an effort to find her despite his apparent exhaustion. Yet she wished he wouldn't use that term of endearment. He obviously believed she was a romantic ninny and easily swayed by pretty words. Familiar aggravation bubbled inside her at his confident presumption, quickly overshadowing her remorse.

"So you say that everything is fine with the tobacco crop, Adam?" she asked, suddenly uncomfortable in such close confines with him. His sheer physical size seemed to dwarf the small room, and it didn't help that he smelled so overpoweringly masculine, a musky combination of sweat, dirt, and horses which to her surprise she found quite appealing. "Mr. Skinner told me that, too, but I wanted to hear it from you. I've been worried—''

"Camille, you must learn not to worry unless I give you reason to do so," he interrupted her gently, his smile fading as his expression grew serious. "If there had been any critical problems, I would have told you long before this morning. I wouldn't purposely leave you in the dark, especially about something so important. You must trust me in this, as your father did.''

Trust you? she thought incredulously. How can I trust you when I know exactly what kind of man you are? Greedy, ambitious, opportunistic. Why, the list could go on and on!

"I care about this plantation as much as you do," Adam continued, shrugging out of his filthy coat and tossing it on the floor. "I've worked this land for five years, Camille. I've done everything I know to make it what it is today." He began to unfasten the buttons on his vest. "There were many times during the past three days when I wanted to leave the fields to reassure you, but I decided against it, thinking that if I turned my back for a minute, the rain might win the battle we were waging. So I stayed. If this caused you undue concern, then I apologize. But I did what I thought was best.''

Susanna, staring at him wide-eyed as he flung his sweat-stained vest on top of his coat, scarcely heard what he was saying. Then he began to undo the top buttons of his shirt, baring an upper chest that was sleek and powerfully defined with muscle.

What in bloody hell was he doing? Was he going to continue to undress right in front of her? Perhaps he was thinking he was going to undress her, too! At the unseemly flash of excitement that raced through her, she wanted to curse aloud. Sweet Lord, she had to get out of here!

"I—I should go, Adam," she stammered, rising abruptly and hurrying past him to the door, so close that her arm brushed against his. She pulled away as if stung and, spinning around to walk backward now, crossed her arms tightly over her chest as she gazed apprehensively at him. "I don't know why you're taking off your clothes, but—"

"Camille, I'm going to sleep here," he interjected, humor lighting his eyes, although he suddenly looked twice as weary.

"What?"

"Sleep," he repeated, nodding at the narrow bed. 'Here. There's too much commotion at the house today, what with the preparations for the ball, the cleaning, Ertha fussing . . .'' He shook his head. "I knew the minute I walked in there this morning that I'd never get any rest."

"Oh, yes, the ball," Susanna mumbled, feeling her cheeks redden. She would never understand why this man could so easily fluster her, yet it was clear that this time she had brought it upon herself.

Adam's hands fell from his half-unbuttoned shirt and he sat down heavily on the bed, his fatigue obviously catching up with him. "I'll meet you for dinner, my love. Looking forward to it. One more evening to be alone before all the guests arrive in the morning. I just need to sleep for a while . . ."

Susanna watched as, wholly exhausted, he closed his eyes and sank back upon the mattress, muddy boots and all. It suddenly occurred to her that she hadn't thanked him for everything he'd done to save this year's tobacco crop, but she was clearly too late. Already he was asleep, his breathing deep and even, his muscular body totally relaxed.

She stood there for a long moment, listening to him breathe, watching the slow rise and fall of his chest, and not quite knowing why she did so. Then she quietly opened the door. Yet she didn't leave until she had first tiptoed over to the bed and drawn the wool blanket up to his shoulders, scarcely breathing herself for fear she might wake him.

As she stared down at his face, Susanna had the strangest impulse to touch his stubbled cheek, just to see how his skin felt beneath her fingertips. Instead, her heart beating hard, she hurried from the room and closed the door softly behind her.

# Chapter 8

A dam hastily tied the white linen cravat at his throat, cursing himself again because he hadn't arranged with Ertha for a servant to come to his office at two o'clock and wake him.

He had been so exhausted, he hadn't been thinking clearly when he'd left the house to look for Camille. All he had wanted to do was find her quickly, give her the news, and then get some rest. Well, he had found her easily enough, but he still couldn't believe he had fallen asleep right in front of her, as he vaguely remembered doing. And not before frightening her, which he hadn't meant to do either. It seemed the whole blasted week had gone like that.

First he had become angry at her when she had discovered that his bedroom was just down the hall from her own; he had unfairly criticized her about the Cary graveyard; and he had almost ravaged her at the pond. Then he had shocked her virginal sensibilities that morning by undressing while she was in the room, and now this, sleeping right through dinner. Damn if he wasn't frustrating his own plan by his careless actions!

"Tonight's going to be different," Adam vowed under his breath, glancing at the grandfather clock's ornate face, which read twenty minutes past six. His eagerness mounting, he pulled on a tailored forest-green coat. He wouldn't let anything spoil the evening, least of all his own behavior.

This would be their last night alone before the Tidewater gentry swarmed down upon them, and he wanted it to be special. He wanted to charm her, to woo her, to make her laugh and reveal more about herself.

He wanted to make sure that if she harbored any doubts or insecurities about his courting of her, these feelings would be gone by the time they said good night. It was important that she know how much he wanted her, how much her father had wanted them to be together, and for him to hear from her lips again that she welcomed his courtship. Especially since tomorrow would bring to Briarwood every fortune hunter in the region, each one anxious to meet Camille. *His* beautiful, shy Camille.

Irritation seized him just thinking about how she would have to endure her guest's fawning attentions for the entire weekend. Tidewater plantations were so far apart that people living more than ten miles away usually stayed overnight. Every bed would be filled, including his own. Ertha had asked him to sleep in his office, and she had been so worried about having enough room for everybody that he had grudgingly agreed.

Shoving his unpleasant thoughts from his mind, Adam took a last bite of the rich vension stew Prue had sent up for him, and then, after a draught of wine, he headed for the door.

He felt like a new man after his bath, a shave, and a hot meal, and he had dressed carefully for this evening. He wanted to show Camille that he could hold his own against any wealthy gentleman. At least he could say he had earned the money to pay for the clothes on his back. To him, that made all the difference.

"Have you seen Miss Cary?" Adam queried the chambermaid who was hurrying toward the dining room with her arms full of freshly ironed table linens. Growing annoyed that the house was still such a bustle of activity, he hoped that he and Camille would be able to find some privacy tonight.

"No, sir, Mr. Thornton. I've just come from the laundry."

"Damn," he muttered to himself as the maid hustled away. He was so anxious to find Camille, to be with her, and he couldn't help thinking that such urgency was wholly unlike him.

Funny that he should feel this way about any woman. He never had before. It wasn't as if he loved her, though he did feel some affection melded with an extreme protectiveness toward the woman who would soon become his wife. She was so endearing, so enticingly innocent, and God knew he desired her—had from the first moment he had seen her at the Yorktown dock. The episode at the pond had only whetted his appetite for more such embraces, and especially for the day when she would share his bed.

Struck by fierce longing, Adam began searching the house, first the drawing room and then the library, but they were empty. The music room and game room were occupied by maids doing some last-minute dusting, and he knew Camille wouldn't still be across the hall in the dining room. Dinner had been over almost three hours ago. He was about to head for the garden when he caught a whiff of lavender scent wafting from the ballroom. Smiling triumphantly, he opened the door and peered inside.

Adam exhaled slowly, enchanted by the sight of Camille slowly swirling round and round at the far end of the ballroom, her voluminous apricot silk gown picking up the last golden rays of sunlight flooding through the tall arched windows. She looked so lovely with her eyes closed, her head tilted becomingly as she softly hummed an unfamiliar melody—slightly off pitch, he thought, charmed all the more—her honey-blonde curls cascading down her back like a glistening waterfall, her gown rustling and swaying. For long, long moments he could only stare at her, entranced. Yet finally his overwhelming desire to be close to her, to touch even just her hand, overcame him, and he slipped into the room.

So his sweet, romantic innocent secretly liked to

dance, he mused, marveling at the fluid grace of her movements as he edged closer. That surprised him, considering that she had reputedly avoided balls, but perhaps she had simply disliked the crush of people and commotion that typified such events.

She stopped twirling, her slender back to him, and rather awkwardly attempted some dance steps. It was plain that she didn't know what to do, which also surprised him. From what he had heard about Lady Redmayne, he found it difficult to imagine that the domineering baroness would have allowed Camille to forgo her dancing lessons.

Then again, maybe she just wasn't very good at dancing. He wasn't the best dancer in the Tidewater, but he had attended enough balls to know the steps. He would have to teach her a few things before the ball; Grymes had probably hired musicians. He didn't want her to be embarrassed by her lack of proficiency, or see her hurt by callous tittering behind raised fans.

"Could I be of some assistance?" he asked softly, feeling his breath jam in his chest as she swirled to face him. Though he had spoken with her that morning, he had been so exhausted he felt now as if he was seeing her for the first time in days. God, but she was beautiful!

"What . . . how long have you . . . ?" Susanna's voice trailed off as she gaped at him, stunned by his unexpected presence. She immediately fought to regain her composure while her thoughts raced wildly.

He had seen her dancing. Oh, bloody hell, she could just imagine what he must be thinking. How was she going to explain herself this time?

"You've revealed a little secret of yours, my love. One doesn't necessarily have to like balls to enjoy dancing." He bowed gallantly, offering his hand. "Yet from watching you, and I mean this as no insult, it appears that you need a little practice. Any lack of ability can certainly be amended by one's desire to learn."

Overwhelmed with relief, Susanna knew she couldn't have explained herself any better than Adam just had.

For once she was glad that he assumed to know so much about her, the overconfident blackguard!

If she had hoped by some miracle to learn how to dance before tomorrow, having never been allowed any lessons when she was a waiting-maid other than the few steps Camille had taught her, then she had just found such a miracle in Adam Thornton. Now she wouldn't have to decline demurely when she was asked to dance!

"What would you like to practice first? Some steps from a country dance or a minuet?" he asked.

"A minuet, please," she said with a grateful smile as she took his hand. She shivered at the warmth of his palm, and as he led her to the middle of the ballroom, he gently caressed her fingers with his thumb, a most disconcerting sensation. Trying to distract herself from what he was doing, she observed lightly, "I suppose it will be difficult since we have no music."

"No trouble at all." In a rich baritone he began to hum several measures of a minuet, then he stopped, smiling roguishly. "Music, my love. Now, since I'm sure you already know the basic steps—"

"Could we review them?" Susanna blurted, immediately glancing down at the parquet floor, fearing she had given herself away. "It's been so long . . . since my last lesson, I mean. And considering I never was any good . . ."

"Nonsense, Camille," Adam objected, lifting her chin to stare deeply into her eyes. "You've a natural grace that any woman would wish to possess. I promise you'll be the envy of any Tidewater belle who sees you dance tomorrow night." He stroked her cheek lightly, as if to reassure her. "Come now. Let's begin. First, place your hand on top of mine, like so, and remember the steps are small . . ."

Susanna listened carefully to his instructions, though her body was alive with a bewildering excitement. She couldn't tell if it was because she was finally learning to dance or because of his closeness, a troubling possibility she didn't even want to consider.

As they began to move in stately three-four time

through the elegant figures of the minuet, Adam's voice astounding her with its deep richness, she wondered if any of the young men who would be coming to the ball were as strikingly handsome. She had to admit Adam looked dashing this evening in his dark-green coat and brocade vest, and capable of taking any woman's breath away.

She liked that he didn't bother with wigs, which to her seemed effeminate in men. His thick mahogany hair, tied casually in a queue with a black satin ribbon, shone with burnished highlights in the waning sunlight. Strangely, she found herself imagining what his hair would feel like if she dared to touch it. Soft and silky, or perhaps somewhat rough, like the man himself?

"You catch on quickly," he complimented her, releasing her hand and passing by her so closely that his arm brushed her shoulder, making her flesh tingle. He circled her, then they faced each other again, and she placed her much smaller hand upon his. As they stepped toward each other in a single motion, separated, then came together again, his admiring gaze never left hers. "Wonderful, Camille. Just have some confidence in yourself and you'll do very well."

She blushed warmly, not so much at his words or the way he was looking at her as at the incredible absurdity of her thoughts. Run her fingers through his hair? Why would she ever want to do that? She was relieved when he began to instruct her in some country dances and lively reels, which demanded all of her attention and energy just to keep up with him.

"Excellent. You've mastered those steps," he praised her a short while later, clearly pleased with her progress. "I'm beginning to think you must have had a poor teacher at Fairford. The fault certainly does not lie with you. Now let's put your new expertise into practice."

Before Susanna could respond, Adam swept her from one end of the ballroom to the other in a spirited country dance. Round and round they flew, pausing only now and then to stand in one place and perform the required steps in a fast tempo. Soon she was breathlessly laughing, Adam joining her, their mirth resounding in the room. When she didn't think she could go another step further, he urged her on, spinning her around in a circle so fast that the mirrored walls and gilt chandeliers became a blur, and she felt for sure that she would collapse from dizziness.

She finally did, in his arms, her laughter muffled in his coat as she fought to catch her breath, his clean, musky scent enveloping her. Yet when she felt his embrace tighten around her as they circled slowly to a stop, she abruptly ceased giggling and looked up at him in surprise, still light-headed from their exertion. He was gazing at her with a look of such burning intensity that if she had not already been breathless, she would have become so.

"You dance . . . wondrously, my love," he said huskily, his arms like steel around her.

As his gaze fell to her lips and he bent his head, Susanna thought fleetingly that she should struggle, protest, coyly turn away . . . something! But then she felt the warm pressure of his mouth on hers, and all reason fled. Almost in wonder she parted her lips to him, his breath melding with hers, her knees turning to jelly as his kiss slowly deepened. In some far recess of her mind she faintly heard a knock upon the door, but she was so lost in the wonderful sensations sweeping over her that she gave no heed to the sound. Then Adam's warm mouth was gone and she opened her eyes, dazed.

"What . . . ?"

"Ertha. At the door."

Reality came back into sharp focus and Susanna gasped, stepping away from Adam so abruptly that she almost fell. He caught her around the waist just in time, waiting a fleeting instant until he seemed convinced that she could stand on her own before he released her. Then he called out, "Come in, Ertha."

Susanna took another few steps away from Adam as the door opened, wondering anxiously if her hair was mussed, her gown rumpled, her lips too red, her eyes too wide. What had happened to her wits? How could she have so easily lost control of herself? She didn't want anyone to know that she and Adam . . .

"I'm sorry to bother you, Mr. Thornton . . . Miss Camille," the housekeeper began, appearing curious as she looked from one to the other.

"It's all right, Ertha," Adam said, apparently willing to speak for both of them. He gave Susanna a slight wink, as if to say their secret was still safe with him. "I was just helping Miss Cary practice her dancing in anticipation of tomorrow night. She needed a partner, and I seemed to be the only one available." He smiled at Susanna, then added, "Now, what can either I or Miss Cary do for you?"

"Actually, I wanted to speak with Miss Camille," Ertha said. "If you don't mind, I thought the girls could give the floor another polishing. You know how I want everything to look just right for your guests."

"Of course," Susanna replied, finally finding her voice. "I don't mind at all. Mr. Thornton and I were already finished dancing . . . and we were just discussing a possible game of billiards before I retire for the evening. Mr. Thornton has faced so many pressures these past few days, I thought a small contest would cheer him." She glanced pointedly at Adam. "Don't you agree?"

"Absolutely," he said, amused.

"Well, the girls are done cleaning in the game room now, and I'll make sure they keep quiet in here so they don't bother you," Ertha said, bustling over to the door which opened into the adjoining game room. "Forgive me for rushing you, Miss Camille, but we've got so much to do yet . . ."

As she left the room, Susanna didn't have to look over her shoulder to know that Adam was right behind her. She could sense his presence in a disturbing and, though she hated to admit it, compelling way.

"Would you like anything from the kitchen?" Ertha asked as three housemaids equipped with buckets and mops trooped wearily into the ballroom. "Something to drink?"

"Wine would be nice," Adam said, speaking for them again. "Is that all right with you, Miss Cary?"

"Yes. Fine."

"If you're hungry—"

"I'm not hungry."

"Just wine, then, Ertha. Thank you."

The housekeeper nodded and shut the door, leaving them alone.

"Poor woman," Adam commented with a deep laugh. "I think she's forgotten how much work a ball can be. Of course it doesn't help matters when she has the same tasks done two and three times. That floor will be so polished that your guests might very well be risking their necks to dance upon it."

Susanna scarcely heard him as she moved to a window, gathering her frayed thoughts. It was almost dusk and the game room, with its heavy velvet draperies, was growing dark. Yet she made no move to light the candles. She had no intention of remaining here for more than a few minutes. After what had happened between her and Adam, she could hardly wait to seek the blessed solace of her room. She had given him quite enough encouragement for one night, and so unexpectedly—

The sharp flaring of tinder startled her and she turned to find Adam watching her, the flame from the candle he had just lit illuminating his face. From the possessive glitter in his eyes, Susanna sensed with increasing exasperation that he was becoming even more sure of himself and his ability to win her.

Did he think her such a naive, impressionable girl that she wouldn't see exactly what he was doing? she fumed as he lit more candles around the room. That he was trying to seduce her with lies and gallant actions, appearing the gentleman when clearly he was not? No doubt he even imagined that after a few more kisses, she would eagerly give him leave to announce their betrothal. Bastard! Like bloody hell she would!

Infuriated, she decided then and there that she

wouldn't hasten up to her room like some flustered rabbit. She was going to stay right here and lead him on, just as she had originally planned.

In fact, she wanted to stay! She wanted to tease him and deceive him, to do everything she could to heighten the illusion that she had every intention of marrying him. What a shock it would be to him when she finally told him the truth. She could just imagine the look on his face. Why, she couldn't wait!

"You know, I just realized I haven't yet apologized for missing dinner," Adam said, appreciating how large and lovely Camille's eyes were in the candlelight and how startlingly green, like bright emeralds. "I'm afraid I overslept."

"Don't trouble yourself about it, Adam," she said softly. "You have a very good excuse."

Her direct gaze surprised him, considering what had just transpired in the ballroom. He would have thought she'd still be blushing and embarrassed, perhaps even begging early leave for the night. Instead she appeared composed and in no hurry to retire, which pleased him. Perhaps she had enjoyed his kiss . . . no, he knew she had. He had felt her soft lips part eagerly beneath his and her body become like liquid in his arms. Damn, if only Ertha hadn't come to the door. Who knew what might have happened?

Adam leaned his hip against the oaken billiards table. "Nonetheless, I hope you can forgive me."

"No apology is necessary," she insisted, her slim fingers toying with the gold drapery fringe. "I know how tired you were. I saw you, remember?"

"Yes, I do," Adam murmured, enjoying the provocative swish of her gown as she walked to the opposite side of the table.

"In fact, I told Ertha not to send anyone for you so you might get enough rest. I didn't expect to see you until tomorrow." At his raised eyebrow, she added, "I hope that was all right. I was so worried about you . . . you'd gotten so little sleep over the last few days . . ."

Worried about him? Adam thought with keen triumph. Obviously he had had no reason to be concerned about his ill-mannered behavior this past week. If she had been worried, that must mean she was beginning to care. By God, this courtship was proving easier than he had ever imagined!

"Then I owe you my thanks and not an apology," he said, gratified by her smile. "I am flattered that you would consider my welfare. Very much so."

She didn't readily reply, but glanced at the cues hanging in a walnut holder on the wall. "Adam . . ."

"Yes?"

"I—I have a confession to make."

His heart seemed to skip a beat, his mind racing over what she might divulge to him. He waited, then, growing impatient, finally had to urge her, "Tell me what's on your mind, Camille."

Her expression was solemn, which only heightened the unusual beauty of her features.

"I don't know the first thing about billiards. I only said that as an explanation to Ertha. It must have been so quiet in the ballroom when she knocked on the door . . . well, since we were . . ." She shrugged prettily. "I didn't want her to think—"

"I know," Adam said just as solemnly, although he had an incredible urge to laugh—not at her discomfiture, but because she had admitted her clever lie so charmingly.

He had already sensed an innate intelligence in her from how easily she had absorbed everything he had told her about Briarwood, but now it was obvious from her confession that she was quick-witted as well, a discovery that pleased him. He didn't need a bluestocking for a wife, but if she could hold her own in intellectual conversations, he wouldn't complain. Yet it was also clear that she still wanted to play their secret game of courtship. Well, why not, if things were going so well?

He gave her a conspiratorial wink. "I haven't forgotten our secret."

She brightened immediately, offering him a becoming smile. "Thank you for understanding, Adam."

"Anything to please a lady," he said, walking around the table to be closer to her. "A most beautiful lady." It was so strange, this feeling inside him. He seemed to be inexplicably drawn to her, in ways that had nothing to do with the revenge that drove him. "Perhaps you'd like to learn how to play billiards, my love. If you do, however, I must ask you for something in return."

"And what might that be?" she asked coquettishly, her light tone surprising him. Could it be that his shy mouse was finally opening up to him? And in a seductive manner he could easily become accustomed to . . .

"I want to hear about your life in Fairford. How you spent your time. The things you liked to do. I want you to tell me all about yourself, Camille. The things any woman would tell the man she intends to marry."

"I shall surely bore you, Mr. Thornton."

"Not at all," he objected, delighting again in her playful tone. "You could never bore me."

When she didn't answer, a soft rose blush suffusing her cheeks, he urged her huskily, "Are we agreed, then? Billiards in exchange for as much as you wish to tell me . . . tonight."

She hesitated another moment longer, then murmured, "Agreed."

The house was dark and quiet when they finally left the game room, Adam lighting the way with a silver candlelabra.

Susanna held on to his hand—only so he might guide her, she assured herself—taking care with her footing as they passed through the music room and then into the hall. Two candles had been left burning in wall sconces near the front door, dimly illuminating the sleepy form of a footman stretched out upon a pallet. She had learned there was always someone by the door, day or night, in case of unexpected guests, and she tread even more lightly for fear she might wake him.

Their billiards match had lasted longer than she had intended, but all in all, she believed the evening had gone well. She had achieved her purpose, which was all that mattered. She had fooled Adam completely and had enjoyed herself while doing so.

The only thing she had failed to do was discover more about Adam's background. She had told him a lot about life at Fairford, an unsettling combination of her own personal likes and dislikes and memories with what she knew of Camille's. But whenever she had asked him any questions about his own past he had veered their discussion right back to her. It was obvious he didn't want to reveal much of himself.

At last she had given up. It didn't matter if she knew anything about him or not. He would be out of her life soon enough. She had resolved not to bother him with such questions again.

"Careful on the stairs," Adam said, holding the candlelabra higher. "I don't want you to twist an ankle before you can show off the dance steps you learned today."

You can wager I won't twist my ankle, Susanna thought rebelliously, although you'll wish I had when you see all my handsome dance partners. Anticipation rippled through her, the kind she knew would prevent her from getting much sleep tonight.

She could hardly wait to meet everybody, though she knew she mustn't appear too eager. At least not at first, and not with Adam around. But when she began attending social gatherings throughout the Tidewater, it wouldn't be long before she could act like herself again.

Would she meet her future husband tomorrow? she wondered as they moved down the hall to her room. Oh, please, she hoped so. She wanted things to be settled, to be able to get on with her life and be free of this intolerable man—

"Here you are, my love," Adam said, his voice low as he pushed open her door.

Susanna waited impatiently just outside the threshold as he stepped into her room and set the candlelabra on the bedside table. She had no intention of entering until he was in the hall again, and she doubted that he expected her to. They had her reputation to think about, after all.

She wanted to get their good nights over with as quickly as possible so she could shut her door and bolt it. He'd made no advances toward her since the kiss in the ballroom . . . well, except for standing rather close to her when showing her how to play billiards, his hands over hers as he demonstrated how to hold the cue. But she didn't trust him. Not with him sleeping only a few doors away from her.

"Thank you, Adam," she murmured when he returned to the hall. The light was so dim this far from her bed that she could barely see him, but from the soft rustling of his clothing she knew he was very close. She could smell him, too, that heavy, masculine scent that always had such a strange effect on her. Becoming disconcerted by his nearness and the enveloping darkness, she moved abruptly to the door. "I had a very nice evening. I hope we can play billiards again soon—"

Susanna gasped sharply as he grabbed her arm, not roughly but firmly, and drew her back to him.

"You're in such a hurry, Camille," he whispered in her ear, his warm breath fanning her neck as he enfolded her in his embrace. "I've taught you so many things today, I thought you might want to learn how a man courting a woman says good night."

"V-very well, Adam," she replied, desperately wanting to scream out "No!" yet knowing that if she refused she would negate all the progress she had made in misleading him tonight. Her mind raced as he gently nibbled her earlobe, her thoughts somersaulting.

She could manage this, she assured herself, feeling shivers of sensation radiate from the ticklish point just beneath her ear where his mouth was wandering. She was the one teasing him. She was in control here, not him. She was in control . . . oh, dear God, why was he nibbling her ear again? She clutched his coat, unable to deny how wonderful it felt.

"When a man bids his beloved good night, he kisses

her on the lips," Adam murmured, his breath a feather-light whisper on her flushed cheek. "Like this . . . very gently at first, so he doesn't startle her."

Susanna tensed when his mouth moved over hers, warm and fragrant with wine, yet with such a light pressure she unwittingly ached for more. She relaxed in his arms, liking very much what he was doing to her mouth yet knowing she should stop him. Why, then, couldn't she find the words with which to speak?

"If he thinks she's pleased with his kiss," Adam whispered against her slightly parted lips, "then maybe he'll make it a little rougher . . . a little deeper . . ."

A low moan broke from her throat when his mouth became heavier upon hers, growing more insistent, more demanding, and she wound her arms around his neck as she leaned into his hard body. She felt a frightening wildness brewing inside her, like the time that boy had kissed her in the coach house, but now it was so much stronger that she was shaken all the way to her toes by its gathering intensity. She sensed there was more he could give her and she wanted it . . . oh, she wanted it terribly.

With a wantonness she didn't know she possessed, she opened her mouth to him as his tongue slowly wet her lips then plunged inside to seek her softness, his arms tightening around her like bands of iron. She tasted his mouth as boldly as he ravaged hers, his husky groan exciting her all the more. Then, just as suddenly, she was standing dazed and disoriented against the wall with only his hands supporting her waist.

"And if a man knows what's best for the woman concerned," she heard Adam say, his fingers tracing her swollen lips in the dark, "though he would like nothing more than to stay . . . Oh, God, Camille . . ."

He didn't finish but guided her quickly into her room and shut the door firmly between them. Trembling and breathless, she leaned her forehead upon the wood, her hand to her throat, her pulse racing beneath her finger-tips.

"Draw the bolt, Camille," came his voice through

the door, ragged yet resolute. ''I want to know that you're . . . safe.''

As she did what he commanded, her fumbling fingers at last managing to hold onto the lock, the jarring sound of the bolt sliding into place shattered the spell that gripped her.

Tears stung her eyes, her emotions in chaos. She waited until his footsteps receded down the hall, then she silently cursed him for how he was making her feel . . . wishing futilely, incredibly, that she was still just a lady's maid and that he wanted *her,* Susanna Jane Guthrie, not Camille.

# Chapter 9

A dam leaned his shoulder against a tree and watched with barely concealed irritation as the absurd scene was played out not far from him on the mansion's side lawn.

Camille was seated in the shade of a giant spreading oak, looking lovelier than any woman ought to in a sky-blue frock and matching straw hat, while sitting on the bench next to her, standing behind her, and kneeling on the ground at her feet were well over a dozen young men, planters' sons every one. The only redeeming factor in the picture that so frustrated Adam was that several women were there, too, clutching tightly to their sweethearts' arms and appearing none too happy about the sudden appearance of this new rival in the Tidewater.

Too bad he couldn't tell those nervous belles that their fears were misplaced, Adam thought, and tell Camille's fawning entourage that their hopes were for naught. He certainly had been tempted to do just that many times already, and there was still the long evening ahead of him.

She had been surrounded like this since the carriages had first begun arriving at Briarwood shortly before noon, starting first in the main hall where she had greeted her guests, then in the drawing room and adjoining dining room where light refreshments had been served while a sumptuous picnic dinner was being set up outside. Adam hadn't been able to speak with her yet due to an inspection of the fields which had occupied him much of the morning, and now with this admiring audience, he didn't know when he would find a chance to be alone with her. Everywhere she went she was being hounded by these persistent pups, some of them barely out of their teens, their faces still spotted.

It made him sick to watch the ridiculous spectacle they were making of themselves, posturing and preening in their attempts to outmaneuver each other in hopes of gaining her notice, yet thankfully Camille appeared to be holding up well. So far she hadn't burst into tears or hidden herself in her room; actually, she seemed to be making a very brave attempt to enjoy herself and become acquainted with her guests. He could tell from her shy responses to their eager queries, however, that she must be overwhelmed by all the attention.

"Could I bring you something more to eat, Miss Cary? Another piece of barbequed chicken or a slice of veal pie?"

"No, thank you."

"How about more lemon punch?" another piped up.

"I still have some in my glass, thank you."

"Would you like dessert, Miss Cary? I saw a tempting peach cobbler on the table—"

"No, not yet, but maybe in a little while."

"I could bring a cushion for your feet. Would you like that, Miss Cary?"

"Thank you, Matthew, but I'm fine. Really."

The bastard, Adam thought, his narrowed gaze settling upon Robert Grymes's eldest son.

Already as portly as his father, with soft, rounded shoulders that had never seen a day's hard work, Matthew Grymes had been pestering Camille since he had clumsily dismounted from his horse and offered her an enthusiastic bow so low to the ground he had practically lost his powdered wig. Somehow he had weasled the seat next to her on the bench, his fat, pug-nosed face sickeningly adoring as he stared at her as if she was the answer to his prayers. By God, what Adam would give to collar that rascal, all of them for that matter, and toss them into the river to cool their ardor.

"Lovely day for a welcome ball, wouldn't you say, Adam? Shade on the warm side, but that's to be expected for early August, I suppose."

Adam glanced at Robert Grymes, who was sopping up the sweat on his forehead with an already stained handkerchief. Adam offered the planter only a curt nod before veering his gaze back to Camille.

"The heat doesn't appear to be affecting Miss Cary, I'm happy to see," Robert added. "She looks as pretty as a flower and quite fully recovered from her journey. I would even venture to say that she seems to be having a good time for someone who supposedly doesn't like parties, which is just what I expected. When she sees how much fun we Virginians have at our gatherings, she'll forget all this nonsense about being shy and join right in. That's what my Celeste did."

Adam wanted to reply that Grymes didn't know what the hell he was talking about, that Camille was simply enduring her neighbors' attentions for her father's sake, but he refrained when the sound of laughter carried to him. Camille was smiling at someone's comment, which annoyed him, but he had missed whatever had been said due to the planter's asinine babbling.

Wondering with a twinge of jealousy what had so amused her, Adam recalled the countless smiles she had bestowed upon him last night. There were so many incredible things for him to remember about their evening together, the kinds of memories that had made sleep almost impossible: the throaty warmth of her laughter, the way her eyes glowed in the candlelight, her delightfully flirtatious manner, the delicate lavender scent of her perfume, her kiss, the astonishing depth of her passion . . . Dammit, he didn't want her smiling at anyone but him!

"They're starting up some card games in the house," Robert continued, undaunted by Adam's reticence. "Have any inclination to play? With this crowd of planters, I'll wager the stakes will be high. I know how free my boys are with their money—"

"I don't gamble," Adam said, cutting him off.

"Oh, that's right. I'd heard that . . . Guess I simply forgot. Forgive me for asking, my boy."

Silence settled between them, and Adam was just about to excuse himself and move closer to where Camille was sitting when Robert suddenly blurted, "Ah, there's Celeste now, just come from the house with her mother. It's been a while since you've seen my darling girl, hasn't it, Adam? Why, I believe the last time was at the Carters' ball in May. If I remember correctly, you and she even danced a time or two. What a fine pair you made!"

Adam groaned inwardly, surmising exactly what Grymes was up to as he waved over his wife and daughter.

The planter had foisted the pretty redhead upon him on several occasions since James Cary had died, and although Grymes hadn't come right out and said it, he seemed eager for Adam to spend time with her. No doubt he wanted him to ask for permission to court Celeste, much as a half dozen other planters wanted him to make the same request for their daughters. They all seemed to believe that a crop master marrying into the family was the same thing as gold jangling in their pockets.

True enough, Adam thought, watching as Celeste smilingly approached with a cheerful-faced Mrs. Grymes, but he didn't want any of their daughters. Nor did it matter to him that most of these young women were beauties in their own right, with sizable dowries to match.

The only dowry he wanted was Briarwood. The only woman, Camille. Especially now.

All he had to do was recall the raging heat in his loins last night to know that his need to possess her was reaching new and altogether unexpected proportions. It was coming to the point where he wasn't sure anymore if revenge was driving him or desire. He was only certain that he wanted her, more than he had ever wanted any woman, and that soon she would become his wife. That knowledge was the one thing that made it possible to tolerate this insufferable gathering.

Adam glanced again toward the gigantic oak and cursed under his breath when he saw that she was now walking toward the garden with her burgeoning entourage in tow. Damn, he would follow her if only—

"How nice to see you again, Mr. Thornton," said Charity Grymes, her pleasant voice only irritating him further. Reluctantly he forced his attention back to their little group.

"Mrs. Grymes. Miss Grymes."

"It's indeed a pleasure," Celeste added saucily, fluttering her fan, "although I do wish you'd call me by my first name, as I asked you to the last time we met, Mr. Thornton. 'Miss Grymes' sounds so stiff. And would you mind if I called you Adam? It seems only right, considering we're such close neighbors. And we have danced together before . . ."

"As you wish," Adam replied, dryly amused by her boldness. He couldn't imagine this young woman ever having been shy, no matter what her father had said about her. Though her freckled cheeks were flushed pink under his scrutiny, he could tell by the lively sparkle in her china-blue eyes that she was enjoying the attention. Clearly she welcomed her father's plans for her.

"My, it is warm out here, don't you agree?" Robert asked his wife, mopping the back of his neck. "Why don't you and I retire to that refreshing punch bowl while Adam escorts our Celeste through the garden." He smiled at his daughter like a true co-conspirator. "You'd like that, wouldn't you, my dear?"

Appearing not at all embarrassed by her father's obvious ruse to get them alone, Celeste replied, "I'd adore a walk in the garden."

"By all means, then," Adam said, knowing from their surprised expressions that they were somewhat taken aback by his ready agreement. He was aware that he had a reputation throughout the Tidewater for being aloof and brusque, a facade he had assumed to protect himself from just this sort of situation. But Grymes's opportune suggestion was the perfect way to keep an eye on Camille. "I would hate to disappoint so pretty a young lady."

"Harrumph . . . uh, yes," Robert said, his expression still tinged with disbelief as he looped his arm through his wife's. "Well, enjoy yourselves."

Adam put his hand lightly beneath Celeste's elbow, then wished he hadn't when she smiled flirtatiously up at him through her long russet lashes. As they strolled toward the garden, he knew they were turning some heads, which also annoyed him. Damm if two people couldn't be seen innocently together without starting up the rumor mill!

"The Carys have always had the loveliest garden," Celeste commented, pausing to smell a scarlet rose.

Adam scanned the grounds as she bent her head. His heart raced as he spied Camille, seated by the river at the same point where he had first revealed his intention to marry her.

Was she sending him a private message? he wondered. That despite the many young men surrounding her, she was thinking of him? He would like to believe that was the case. He wished there was some way he could hurry Celeste, but she seemed determined to smell every flower along the path.

"Have you met Miss Cary?" he asked, hoping there was a remote chance she hadn't. That would certainly make a good excuse for hastening her toward the river.

"Yes, when we arrived," Celeste replied, smiling as she glanced at him over her shoulder. "Lovely girl. A bit reserved, just like Papa told us she might be, but I'm sure that will change once she becomes better acquainted with everyone." She turned back to the roses, inhaling deeply. "In fact, I think Camille and I might become good friends. We had a nice chat in the drawing room."

"Really?" Adam queried, his casual tone belying his

vexation that her assessment of Camille's character matched her father's.

Did they seriously believe a few outings would permanently alter Camille's personality? So the woman was shy! Why did everyone feel the need to change her? He liked her exactly the way she was—well, he had to admit her coquettish behavior last night had captivated him. But that was different. Of course she would feel free to behave like that around him. She trusted him, and they were going to be married, for God's sake.

"Yes, a lovely chat," Celeste said, twirling the yellow rose she had just plucked as they proceeded down the path. "I told her about all the exciting events coming up—Amy Johnson's birthday picnic, dinner parties here and there, the horse races at the Tate plantation near Williamsburg, the Byrds' annual summer ball at Westover near the end of the month. Oh, so many more, and I insisted she must attend them all. She balked a little, but when I said she could accompany me and my brothers, she agreed. Such a silly goose! I think she imagined at first that she might have to go alone, which I suppose would be a daunting prospect for any newcomer."

If Adam had ever come close to strangling anyone, it was in that moment.

First Robert Grymes had coerced Camille into having this ball, and now his social butterfly of a daughter was demanding that she traipse all over the Tidewater with her. He didn't believe for an instant that Camille had agreed to such a proposition. Knowing her as he did, he'd wager his last dollar that she had simply said she might go along even though she hadn't really meant it. That would have been the courteous thing to do, and from what he had seen, Camille was unfailingly polite.

"Matthew was elated when he heard the news, of course," Celeste continued, oblivious to Adam's growing anger. "He's smitten with her and actually begged her to call him by his first name, though he wouldn't dare presume to address her as anything but Miss Cary, at least for now. He's very concerned with propriety, especially when it comes to courting a woman—''

"Courting?" Adam said abruptly.

"Why, yes," she answered, pausing to study him. "It's been common knowledge for months that Camille came home to Virginia to find herself a husband. The only question is when. Don't tell me you didn't know this, Adam."

He was so tempted to tell her that he was already courting Camille, with the full expectation that they would marry, that he could barely choke down the words. Silently cursing his agreement to keep their courtship secret, he said tightly, "James Cary informed me last autumn that he was sending for his daughter, and why."

"Well then, why do you seem so surprised?" Celeste asked, giggling as she gestured to the animated group by the riverbank, which was made up of twice as many young men as women. "Most of those gentlemen are interested in courting Camille, and the ones already spoken for probably wish they hadn't been cornered before she arrived."

Adam's gaze was focused not on the crowd but upon a wide-brimmed sky-blue hat and the beautiful face beneath it. It seemed as if she was looking at him across the garden, though he couldn't be sure. Yet the thought that she might be made him ache to be near her.

"Matthew is going to have an uphill fight on his hands with so much competition. That's why I decided to take it upon myself to help him out. Perhaps her spending time with us will give him the edge he needs to win her. She's the prize catch of the Tidewater, you know." Celeste turned back to Adam, the rose falling still in her fingers. Her eyes were as inquisitive as her expression was guarded. "I don't suppose you've considered courting her yourself, have you, Adam? I know it's presumptuous for me to ask, but there are those who would find such news . . . distressing."

"Hasn't crossed my mind," he lied smoothly, a fierce protectiveness rising in him as he watched the rose begin to twirl again. He had not missed the dark innuendo in her voice, and had taken it as an immediate warning.

He sensed in Celeste a young woman who didn't like to be crossed, one who could prove malicious if it so pleased her. With Celeste's sort around, Camille had every right to be concerned about her reputation. He would have to curb his reckless impatience and wait for the day when she agreed they could announce their betrothal. He would do anything to spare her the distress this pretty viper might cause her.

"I'm so glad to hear that," Celeste practically purred, a well-practiced smile upon her heart-shaped face. "Then I won't hesitate to invite you along on our outings. Perhaps as Matthew and Camille become better acquainted, we can, too."

"I have no doubt we will," Adam replied, imagining the tantrum this little tart would throw when she discovered that Camille had no intention of accompanying either her or her fat brother to social events around the Tidewater. And he certainly didn't want to have anything to do with Celeste. Manipulative, calculating women disgusted him.

"Shall we join them and see how Matthew is coming along?" Celeste suggested, shading her eyes from the late-afternoon sun as she gazed toward the river. "I see he has lost his seat on the bench, and—oh, dear, he appears to be sulking. Perhaps he needs my assistance."

"I'm sure your brother can manage quite well on his own," Adam said, resisting the impulse to look again in Camille's direction. "Let's walk over this way."

Celeste's expression was one of complete acquiescence, though her eyes held triumph. "Why, of course, Adam. Anything you say."

Taking her arm, he guided her purposely along a path that led away from the riverbank. After not speaking to Camille since last night, he didn't trust himself to be so near her and not reveal his true feelings. Cunning women like Celeste had a gift for sniffing out such things, and right now, he didn't need that added irritation. It was enough that this day had already been full of them.


The spirited conversation around Susanna seemed to fade away as she watched Adam and Celeste Grymes turn their backs on the river and stroll arm in arm in the opposite direction.

Bastard! she seethed. He hadn't said a word to her all day—not that she wanted him to—and now he was squiring one of the nicest girls she had met so far. Did he think her so naive that she wouldn't know exactly what he was doing? He was nothing but a rogue and a rake! It was obvious that womanizing came to him as easily as breathing. Since he was so certain he had her practically wedded and bedded, why not pursue another young innocent to pass the time?

Casting occasional glances in their direction, she had seen how deep in discussion they had been for the past ten minutes. Talking about what? Probably he had grilled Celeste on her likes and dislikes, as he had done to her last night. And what of that yellow rose he must have given that poor, unsuspecting girl? How dare he pluck flowers from her garden—

"Miss Cary?"

Susanna swung her gaze to the lanky gentleman seated on the bench beside her. She imagined her cheeks must be very red. Her face actually burned from the vehemence of her thoughts.

"Yes, Mr. Dandridge?"

"You look flushed, Miss Cary, and it's such a warm day. Are you sure I can't fetch you more lemon punch?"

She licked her lips, deciding she could use some cool refreshment, if only to soothe her temper. "That would be very nice, Mr. Dandridge. Thank you."

Beaming from ear to ear, the attractive, long-legged young man almost tripped over several gentlemen lounging on the grass in his haste to answer her needs. His place was quickly taken up by Matthew Grymes, who had been hovering behind the bench, clearly waiting for such a moment.

"I could have gotten the punch for you, Miss Cary," he said, his heavily lidded eyes and disappointed expression reminding Susanna of a doleful spaniel.

"Perhaps next time," she murmured, throwing another glance toward the house, only to discover with keen irritation that Adam and Celeste were no longer in sight.

She was grateful when Matthew, having brightened at her response, launched into another long-winded description of his prowess during a recent fox hunt, his favorite sport, which enabled her to listen with half an ear and once again retreat into her thoughts. As the other gentlemen eagerly joined in with their own experiences, each seeking to outdo the other with their prideful boasting, she could not help but wonder if all the gentry ever talked about was themselves and their amusements. It seemed so. How unlike Adam, who didn't want to talk about himself at all.

Of course he *wasn't* gentry, Susanna reminded herself, her anger pricked anew. He was nothing but a hired man, a born liar, and an opportunistic blackguard.

She knew she wasn't jealous about him walking through the garden with Celeste, but simply disgusted that he might have been the man to marry Camille if things hadn't turned out as they had. Then her gentle, trusting friend would have had to suffer through life with a man who wanted her only for her wealth, and who, when he could finally afford it, was certain to keep a dozen beautiful mistresses to satisfy his base and lustful nature.

Dear God, she hoped Celeste wouldn't fall for his pretty words. She knew from unwanted experience how good he was at exploiting a woman's sensibilities. Perhaps it was Adam's plan to nurture a relationship between himself and Celeste in hopes of one day enticing her into his bed. It probably didn't matter to him that she was yet unmarried and that he could so easily ruin her reputation . . .

Susanna was astounded by how her mind was racing on and on about Adam. Why couldn't she stop thinking about him and enjoy herself? She had waited so eagerly for this day, but now that it was here, she had to admit she was disappointed.

Her gaze skipped from one gentleman's face to another. They all seemed so young, and though several of them were handsome, no one man stood out. Yet these were her suitors, and from men such as these she must choose a husband. Oh, they were nice enough, eager to please, fun-loving and witty. Yet she couldn't imagine kissing but a few of them—she glanced at Matthew's pudgy face with its sweating upper lip and shuddered slightly—and even if she did, they couldn't possibly make her feel as Adam had last night—

Stunned that she would even think such a thing, Susanna barely saw the brimming crystal cup hovering in front of her. She rose from the bench so suddenly that lemon punch flew everywhere, but mostly down the front of her gown, completely soaking the ruffled bodice.

"Oh, God, Miss Cary, forgive me! I've ruined your pretty dress."

"No, no, it's all right," she said, trying to reassure a stricken Mr. Dandridge as everyone gathered around her, appearing uncertain how best to help. "I'll . . . I'll just go inside and change."

"Let me escort you—"

"There's no need, Matthew. I'll be fine," she insisted. Dropping her fan on the bench, she held her spattered skirt slightly away from her body so as not to wet the hoop-petticoat underneath. "It was about time for me to change into something more formal anyway. I'm sure the dancing will start soon . . ." She paused, her eyes sweeping her anxious guests. She felt terrible about the ruckus she had caused, and all because of . . . Oh, she didn't want to think about it!

"Please, help yourselves to more food and drink," she added graciously. "Prue will be so disappointed if her good cooking goes to waste. And don't worry about me. This is such a small mishap, it's truly not worth your concern.''

Before anyone could say another word, she hurried toward the house. She had almost reached the French doors when she spied Adam rounding the corner with a smiling Celeste clinging to his arm.

Susanna shivered as his questioning gaze met hers, his eyes intensely brown and piercing. She stepped inside quickly, trying not to slam the doors behind her.

# Chapter 10

❦❦**"O**h, do you ever look pretty, Miss Camille,"
Corliss said, her hands clasped in front of
her. "Prettier than any other woman I've seen in these
parts, I do swear. And it's only fitting that you should
be the belle of the ball tonight. It's your house party,
after all."

Studying her reflection in the full-length mirror, Susanna didn't fully agree with her maid's flattering pronouncement, but she did feel wonderful in this gown.
The shimmering pearl-gray satin felt cool and silky
upon her skin, and it was nice to be out of that damp
one. The rounded neckline was a bit low and certainly
like nothing she had ever worn before, with her breasts
swelling seductively above the glittery lace edging, but
she knew it was fashionable for formal gowns to reveal
more of a woman's assets than day wear.

"Don't worry none about these stains on your blue
dress," Corliss added, picking up the soiled gown and
draping it over her arm. "I'll take it over to the laundry
right now, before the spots have a chance to dry." She
shook her head disapprovingly. "I can't understand why
that Thomas Dandridge was so clumsy—"

"It was my fault," Susanna said, sighing with exasperation. "I didn't see him handing the punch cup to
me and when I rose, I upset it. It was a silly accident,
nothing more."

"Well, he should have been more careful, just the
same," the maid insisted, then her comely face broke

136

into a grin. " 'Course I can understand why he was so nervous, there being those other fine gentlemen around him and all of them wanting your undivided attention. Have any of those young bucks tickled your fancy, Miss Camille?''

Susanna couldn't suppress a smile at Corliss's description of her suitors, but it quickly faded when she recalled her thoughts just before her little mishap.

"No," she answered, deeply troubled and equally angry with herself. It seemed only one man had struck her fancy thus far. The wrong one.

"Well, don't you worry about that either. They'll be plenty more parties coming up and more menfolk who'll be wanting to meet you. You'll find that husband of yours. Just keep your eyes wide open."

She fully intended to, Susanna silently agreed as Corliss bustled to the door. Especially now. As soon as she gathered herself together, she was going to plunge right back into the frivolity and give the young gentlemen present another chance to prove themselves. Surely there had to be at least one among them who was worthy of being a serious suitor, one who could kiss as well as Adam Thornton!

"Are you coming down now, Miss Camille?" the maid asked over her shoulder.

"Shortly. I'd like to stay here for a little while and enjoy some peace and quiet. There's been so much commotion, so many people around. It's been overwhelming."

"Yes, these gentry sure take their fun seriously. I 'spect the house will be jumping till early morning, what with all the card playing, drinking, and dancing." Corliss opened the door, then seemed to start as she began to close it behind her. "Oh, Mr. Thornton. I didn't see you standing there."

Susanna froze, staring blindly at her shimmering reflection.

"I have some important business to discuss with Miss Cary. Would you ask her if she'll see me?"

"Miss Camille—"

"Thank you, Corliss. I heard him. Mr. Thornton may come in."

Susanna's gaze broke away from the mirror and she inclined her head, listening breathlessly as the door closed behind the maid with a soft click. Her body tensed at the sound of Adam's footfalls slowly approaching, although when they stopped, she couldn't tell how far away from her he was standing. Nor did she want to peek in the mirror. She was afraid she might discover he was right behind her.

Oh, dear God, they were alone for the first time since last night, she thought, her emotions in an uproar. Buffeted by anger, excitement, and an inexplicable longing, she knew she should turn around and face him, yet for some reason she couldn't. Her silver shoes seemed rooted to the floor.

"I heard what happened, Camille. Why didn't you stop when Miss Grymes and I saw you earlier?"

"I wanted to change as quickly as possible," she said in hasty explanation, her heart thudding at the deep resonance in his voice. "I was practically soaked to the skin."

"Well, I very much like the gown you've chosen for tonight. Turn around so I can see you better. Slowly."

As Susanna did as he bade her, the wide, bell-shaped skirt lilting gently around her feet, she told herself that she must continue to mislead him just as she had done the night before. She had no choice. She needed him here at Briarwood for as long as it took her to find a husband.

Yet, after her disappointing day, she wondered with no small amount of apprehension just when that might be. She was not one to deceive herself. She could not deny that matters between her and Adam had taken a decidedly dangerous and perplexing turn, at least as far as she was concerned. She could sense a new urgency in herself, almost fear of what might happen if she didn't meet the right man soon. Oh, please, please, may it not be too long from now!

By the time Susanna was facing him, her gaze direct

and her chin raised, she had somehow found the courage to continue with her plan even as her legs felt oddly weak. His eyes were raking over her in a manner that made her feel as if he could see right through her clothing, and when his gaze lingered overlong upon her breasts, it was all she could do to ask him lightly, "Do I meet with your approval?"

"Completely." It took her breath away to see desire written so plainly in the smoldering mahogany depths of his eyes. She hoped he couldn't read it so easily in hers.

How long they stood there looking at each other Susanna couldn't say, but she finally regained enough presence of mind to notice he held the delicate silk fan she had left outside on the bench.

"My fan."

He nodded, a smile on his lips as he held it out to her, although his eyes were serious.

"Matthew Grymes wanted to bring it to you, but when I informed him that you and I had some plantation business to discuss, he agreed that I might return it for him. Yet he wanted me to tell you that he will happily buy you another as a gift if you find this one marred in any way."

"I'm sure it's fine," she said, walking past him to set the fan upon her dressing table. She had no wish to inspect it right now, especially not in front of Adam. Fans were one thing she had as yet failed to master, unlike hoop-petticoats, high heels, and dancing. There was a flirtatious artistry in the use of the accessory that left her all thumbs.

Susanna moved to the separate sitting area near the fireplace and, taking a seat in one of the comfortable stuffed chairs, gestured for Adam to join her.

"You mentioned some important business," she said in an attempt to draw their conversation away from herself. As he sat across from her and stretched out his heavily muscled legs, she found herself thinking how handsome he looked in his royal-blue coat, damask waistcoat, and black breeches. He certainly didn't lack for fine clothing; everything he wore was expertly tailored to fit his powerful body and appeared not foppish or overdone, but profoundly masculine. With effort, she forced her mind back to the matter at hand. "I hope it's nothing serious."

"That depends," Adam replied, searching her face, "although it doesn't concern Briarwood. I only said that to deceive any curious souls who might wonder why we're alone in your room, my love. A plantation manager speaking to his employer is one thing, but a man and the woman he's courting . . . We've our little secret to maintain, remember?"

She didn't answer, sensing tension beneath his words. He suddenly seemed annoyed with her, but why?

"Our business is of a private nature, Camille. It concerns the young woman you saw with me in the garden, Celeste Grymes. I believe you met her earlier?"

"Yes, we've met," Susanna said tightly. "She's very pleasant—"

"And very talkative and very, very cunning."

She was startled by his biting tone. That certainly wasn't the way a man spoke of someone with whom he might be enamored.

"Celeste told me that you agreed to accompany her on some outings. Is this true?"

Oh, dear, she hadn't expected to have to deal with this question so soon, Susanna thought, her mind racing. She had hoped he wouldn't discover her plans until the Grymes's carriage came to take her away next Tuesday, the day of Amy Johnson's birthday party. How was she going to explain herself? Camille wasn't supposed to like outings.

"Y-yes," she answered hesitantly, but before she could continue he cut her off.

"You mustn't let her force you into anything you don't want to do," he said, leaning forward in his chair. "She's not to be trusted, Camille. She only wants you to accompany her so that her pompous idiot of a brother can spend more time with you . . ." He paused, sighing heavily. "Forgive me. I know that you have no intention of going anywhere with them—"

"But I do," she interrupted softly, flinching at his sharp look.

"What?"

"I've decided to attend a birthday picnic with Celeste and her brothers on Tuesday, and I'll probably go to other events with them as well."

"Are you serious?" he asked, appearing both stunned and confused for a man who was usually so confident. "You yourself admitted to me that you prefer to stay at home, that you want a quiet life."

"I'm not so sure anymore, Adam," she began, trying to sound uncertain as she spun her hastily concocted explanation. "I've spent a lot of time thinking about it, during the voyage and then over this past week. I just hadn't found the right moment to talk about it with you yet . . ."

When she made a pretense of faltering, his voice became gentle despite his palpable impatience. "Go on," he encouraged her, his gaze intent.

"When I lived at Fairford, I had no desire to go out because it wasn't my home. The people there were Aunt Melicent's friends, not mine. It all seemed so pointless, their constant card parties and balls. I always knew I'd return to Virginia one day, and now that I'm here, I'd like to see more of the Tidewater and meet the people who knew my father. I don't see any harm in it, Adam. Papa would have wanted me to be happy here. To make friends. He wouldn't have liked me to shut myself away from everybody."

Susanna sighed softly, thinking how in truth, Camille might have said those words. Feeling suddenly very much an impostor, she looked down at her hands. Her next words, something Camille had shared with her, she doubted she could tell Adam to his face without giving herself away.

"Actually, I'd like to be more like my mother. Papa didn't speak of her often, I think it was too painful for him, but he once told me that she was as vivacious as a spring morning, and that she loved to dance. Everybody liked her, and they used to have parties here a lot, before she and my brothers . . .''

Susanna was unable to continue for the tightness in her throat. Long moments passed during which she still couldn't bring herself to look at him, but she knew from his silence that he was carefully pondering what she had said. Finally, when she heard him lean back in the chair, his movement carrying with it a sense of resignation, she knew she had convinced him. She met his eyes.

''All right, Camille, all right. God knows, I want you to be happy and to do whatever you think will make you feel more at home here. I guess I should be thankful that at least I'll be able to accompany you, unless something occurs here that needs my attention.''

Her immense relief that she could finally shed her oppressive shyness and act more like herself was immediately checked by surprise. ''You will?'' she asked, his response not at all what she had anticipated. Bloody hell! How was she ever going to encourage other suitors with Adam dogging her every step? ''Th-that's wonderful, Adam.''

''Yes, though there's another thing you should know about your friend Celeste. She believes I'm interested in courting her . . . in fact, she welcomes it. It wasn't my idea to walk with her in the garden this afternoon, but her father's. I think he wants a crop master for a son-in-law.''

Susanna felt unexpected and wholly preposterous jealousy. Celeste was interested in marrying Adam? Surely that had to be another one of his lies.

''She invited me to accompany all of you on your outings, but only after I assured her that I had no interest in courting you myself.'' Adam rose from the chair, clearly exasperated, and began to pace the floor, his limp more pronounced now that he had been sitting for a while. He seemed to be wrestling with some issue when he stopped and faced her squarely.

''Camille, I know you don't want to be rushed and

I have no wish to pressure you, but the secretive nature of our courtship must end! I won't have Celeste fawning all over me while I watch you being hounded by her brother . . . or any other man for that matter. Dammit, I'll move into my office, if that's what it takes to prevent any malicious rumors. I'll do anything to protect you and your reputation, but I won't stand for this charade any longer!''

Susanna was stunned by his outburst. All she knew was that her plan to keep him at Briarwood for as long as necessary was about to crash down around her like a flimsy house of cards, unless she thought of something fast.

"I-I don't want you to move out," she stammered, rising shakily to her feet. "I want you to stay near me, Adam. I like having you so close, and I don't want to be in this big house alone. Please . . . can't we go on as we have been for a few more weeks? Then I promise you we'll announce our betrothal. It's been so lovely . . . so romantic having our own little secret, just like in the books I used to read. Please, just for a little while longer . . .''

Adam was tempted to sweep her into his arms, the plea in her beautiful eyes enough to make him relent, but it wasn't just the two of them involved anymore.

"What of Matthew and Celeste Grymes?" he asked. "And what of those other gentlemen who've been surrounding you all day? Is it fair to so mislead everyone?"

She appeared to choose her words carefully. "I suppose . . . it depends on whose interests you have at heart, Adam," she finally said softly, a playful tone creeping into her voice. "Theirs . . . or mine.''

He regarded her quizzically. "You know my answer to that.''

"Then I don't see that there's any problem, do you? It could actually be fun . . . our deception.''

Adam exhaled slowly, thinking with amusement that he didn't know this woman very well. It seemed that there was a mischievous vixen hiding within his timid mouse, a spirited and naughty side to her that might prove most entertaining once they were wed.

Adam smiled with keen anticipation.

He had sensed early on that she possessed a passionate nature, but last night her wanton response to his kiss had almost made him forget he was a gentleman, and he could have sworn that her fiery passion had startled even her. Nor would he have ever guessed she had an impish streak in her, but it was clear that she was trusting him more and more to reveal such a facet of herself. Damn, if it wasn't amazing what a little gentle wooing could do; everything was progressing just as he had expected! She was no longer asking for months of courtship, but mere days.

"A few weeks?" he asked huskily, reaching out and drawing her slowly toward him.

"Yes," Susanna murmured, her heart pounding as his strong arms went around her in a possessive embrace. "Only a few more weeks."

"Done."

Although she was swept by overwhelming relief that once again she had so easily deceived him, Susanna was equally aware of how difficult her search for the proper husband had suddenly become and how little time she had to accomplish it. Then his lips brushed hers, his breath whispering past her parted lips, and she thought no more of her perilous situation, only how warm his mouth was and how good it felt for him to kiss her.

She melted within his arms, somewhere in her passionate haze hearing the soft swoosh of satin and the crisp rustle of damask as he hugged her more closely. She scarcely knew when he lifted his mouth from hers and trailed a fiery path down her throat, but she started when his lips found the deep hollow between her breasts and he kissed her there, his tongue flicking a soft, rounded curve. It was a sensation wholly unlike any other, and she could not deny she liked it . . . very much.

"You are perfection, my love," he whispered against

her skin, the warmth of his breath heating her lavender perfume so that it drifted around them. "Sweet, wondrous perfection." He kissed her breasts again, lingering over each in turn until she was softly moaning, then he raised his head and stared into her half-closed eyes. "A few weeks?" he teased.

Susanna couldn't speak, her reason shattered. Only her senses were wildly alive to the sensual wonders of the man who held her: the iron strength of his arms; the hard, solid feel of his body pressing against hers; the incredible depth of his eyes which made her feel as if she was drowning. She had never before felt such an acute disappointment as when a soft rap came at the door and Corliss's voice called out to her.

"Miss Camille, your guests have been asking for you. Shall I tell them you'll be coming down soon? And I've a message here from a gentleman who just arrived. He said for me to deliver it to you straightaway."

"Damn. Saved again, my love," Adam murmured, releasing her as reluctantly as Susanna, still dazed, wanted to be free of his arms.

But when Corliss knocked more loudly a second time, Susanna disengaged herself from his embrace. Walking shakily to the door, her skin still feeling as if it burned from his touch, she hoped her voice didn't sound too breathless or strange.

"I'll be right down, Corliss. Mr. Thornton and I were just finishing our"—she glanced at him, thankful for her sudden irritation at the conspiratorial smile on his handsome face—"business discussion."

"All right, Miss Camille, but I don't dare return to the hall without giving you this message first."

Annoyed that anyone would order her maid around, Susanna quickly smoothed her skirt, flipped a slightly mussed curl over her shoulder, and opened the door.

"Who is it from, Corliss?"

The maid shrugged, though she smiled secretively. From her excited expression, she didn't appear to be upset that one of the guests had sent her on such an odd mission.

Susanna quickly broke the blood-red wax seal and read the carefully inscribed note:

My dearest Miss Cary,
  If you will kindly grace the balcony with your presence, you will see the gift I have brought for you, which I hope will be only the first of many tokens of my esteem and affection.
                                          Yours,
                                          An ardent admirer

Susanna folded the fine cream paper, curiosity and excitement building within her. Who could have sent this?

"Well?" asked Adam.

Susanna glanced at him. He seemed to be glaring at the letter in her hand. "It says to step out onto the balcony. Someone has brought me a gift," she said, not sure why she felt the need to offer him an explanation and wishing she hadn't when his expression darkened. It angered her that he would show his resentment so openly. Their agreement to keep their courtship a secret was still very much in effect.

"Come on, Miss Camille," Corliss urged, paying no heed to Adam as she flung open the latticed doors to the balcony. "Oh, will you just look at that . . ."

As Susanna stepped outside and leaned on the wooden banister, her breath caught at the sight of the most beautiful thoroughbred mare she had ever seen, prancing friskily in place almost directly below her. A bewigged black man in splendid silver brocade livery held the reins, while encircling him and the restless animal was a crowd of her guests. From the curious, expectant looks on their faces, everyone was enjoying the unusual spectacle.

"Miss Cary, I present this filly to you on behalf of my master, Mr. Dominick Spencer," the groom announced. "Her name is Sheba, and she bears the finest quarter-horse blood to be found in the Tidewater."

"Dominick Spencer?" Susanna breathed. "Of Raven's Point?"

Corliss nodded excitedly. "That's right, Miss Camille. I told you he had the finest racehorses around. That Sheba's just one of them."

"Which gentleman is he?" she asked, scanning the crowd.

"Oh, Mr. Spencer's not down there. He's waiting for you in the ballroom. He said to tell you he didn't want no thanks for the mare. All he wanted was the first and last dances of the evening."

How intriguing, Susanna thought, impressed by the planter's extravagant gift and its grand presentation.

"Well then, I suppose I should go downstairs and meet my ardent admirer," she said, turning eagerly back into the room. She was surprised to see that Adam was gone, the door to her room left open.

Then again, he had said earlier that he didn't want any other man hounding her, and if her woman's intuition was any gauge, she imagined Mr. Spencer intended on doing just that, and maybe more. Corliss had told her that the rich widower was looking for a wife.

Adam had shown he was jealous just by hearing that someone had brought her a present, and it had probably made him even more resentful to hear that his latest rival was his former employer. From the one time they had discussed Dominick Spencer, followed by Adam's stubborn reluctance to answer any of her questions about his former life at Raven's Point, she was certain that there was bad blood between them.

But whatever that might be, it didn't matter to her, Susanna thought defiantly as she took a last look at herself in the mirror, determined to forget the scorching memory of Adam's lips upon her breasts. All that mattered was that she meet this gentleman who had gone so out of his way to impress her. Adam might soon discover that he had good reason to be jealous.

# Chapter 11

When Susanna entered the ballroom, she found it ablaze with hundreds of white candles adorning the crystal chandeliers. Many of her guests had already assembled, eager for the dancing to begin, and the air was charged with excitement. Gay laughter and the animated buzz of conversation rang all around.

The double doors to the adjoining music room had been thrown open and the harpsichord repositioned just outside them; a musician was practicing lightly on the keys. A trio of violinists tuned their instruments nearby, while a fifth musician tooted upon his French horn and another performed trills on a silver flute. Robert Grymes had outdone himself in providing music for the evening, and Susanna made a mental note to thank him. Everything looked and sounded so festive!

A quick scan of the room told her that Adam was not present, an easy thing to discern since most of the men were wearing wigs while he did not, and she was surprised by her sudden disappointment. Telling herself that she didn't need his furtive attentions or interference right now, she searched the crowd for a gentleman who might fit Corliss's description of Dominick Spencer: handsome, distinguished, and about forty-five years old. She was surprised he had not greeted her at the entrance to the ballroom, considering that Corliss had said he would be waiting for her—

"Miss Cary?"

Susanna whirled around and came face-to-face with

one of the most aristocratic-looking men she had ever seen. "Yes?"

"Forgive me, but I stepped into the game room for a moment and missed your arrival. If I may introduce myself . . . Dominick Spencer." He bowed gallantly, with a practiced flourish, then straightened and met her eyes with a gaze of ice-blue intensity. "I am delighted to finally make your acquaintance."

"Mr. Spencer," she said softly, inclining her head in the polite fashion she had seen women doing all day.

"You saw my gift, I take it . . ."

"Oh, yes. Yes, I did," she blurted, thinking how ungrateful she must appear that she hadn't thought to thank him. "It was so unexpected. Such a beautiful creature—"

"No more so than the lovely vision you make, Miss Cary, if you don't mind me complimenting you so boldly. Simply put, you take my breath away."

In truth, Susanna did find his praise rather fulsome. He had delivered it in so smooth a manner she could not help thinking that however out of breath he might claim to be, he looked as cool and unruffled as a judge. Yet her cheeks grew warm under his admiring appraisal.

If she had been asked to pick someone among her guests who appeared the perfect embodiment of a Tidewater gentleman, it was Dominick Spencer. Everything about his attire proclaimed his wealth and prominence, from his full campaign wig, gold brocade coat and blue satin waistcoat, white silk stockings and diamond-studded buckles on his red-heeled shoes, to the gold sword hilt encrusted with jewels which protruded through the side vent of his coat.

He was tall—though perhaps surpassing Adam by only an inch—and his demeanor was proud. He had a decided air of arrogance about him, but she quickly reasoned that any man of his caliber would possess the same. And Corliss had certainly been right about his looks.

His features were patrician and symmetrical in a

long, angular face which appeared surprisingly unlined and youthful for his age. His countenance was almost too perfect, in fact, and to Susanna it seemed much less compelling than Adam's rugged good looks. He wasn't as broad-shouldered or as powerfully built as Adam either, but somewhat on the lean side—

Oh, Adam, Adam, Adam! she fumed in frustration. Why could she never get him out of her mind?

"I believe your guests are waiting for you to lead them in the first dance," Dominick said, his hard, thin lips curved into a quizzical smile, as if he was amused by her open scrutiny. "Did your maid remember to give you my full message . . . the first dance and the last?"

"Why, yes. She did," Susanna replied, embarrassed that she had been staring at him so blatantly, and equally flustered by her persistent thoughts of Adam. She hoped that Dominick had also heard Camille Cary was shy, which would serve as a plausible explanation for much of her discomfiture.

"I shall only demand them, Miss Cary, if you are well-pleased with your gift . . ."

"Oh, I'm very pleased, Mr. Spencer—"

"Call me Dominick. Last names are so formal for two people who I predict are going to become very good friends." He took her arm solicitously. "Our minuet, Camille."

Susanna barely had a chance to nod her assent before he was leading her onto the dance floor, the other guests forming several long lines of paired couples both in front of them and behind. She was stunned by how suavely he had taken charge of the proceedings; something, she realized as he bowed deeply and she curtsied, that he must be accustomed to doing. Then the music began, and they were dancing to the strains of a courtly minuet, Dominick holding her gaze as he continued to converse with her in low, precise tones meant for her ears alone.

"This is quite an impressive event, Camille. Your father would have been proud of you."

"Thank you . . . Dominick," she replied, thinking

it strange to be addressing him with such familiarity when they had just met. Then again, Adam had done the same thing, perhaps waiting only a little bit longer. It seemed neither man wanted to waste any time, but of course, she didn't care what Adam wanted. She was, however, very interested in what this particular gentleman had in mind. "I'm glad you could attend. I've heard so much about you."

"Really? From whom?"

Susanna felt a moment's unease, wishing she could retract her statement. She didn't know if he would be pleased or not to discover he was the subject of gossip among her servants.

"Actually, my waiting-maid Corliss. She brought me your message."

"Oh, yes. A well-mannered, obliging girl, though a little talkative for my taste. You might want to rein her in a notch. It's always a good thing for slaves to know their places. They can become uppity, which must then be corrected with a very firm hand . . ."

"I'm sorry," Susanna asked, not sure what he had just intimated. "I don't understand—"

"It was nothing. Don't trouble yourself," he interrupted as smoothly as silk when they stepped toward each other. "Beautiful young women leave such details to their husbands. In your case"—he smiled meaningfully at her—"to your future husband." They parted, then drew together again, although now his expression was serious. "Bluntly speaking, I want to be that man, Camille."

Susanna drew in her breath sharply, astonished and cautiously elated by his bold admission.

Now that she knew exactly what Dominick's intentions were toward her, she would have to move with some restraint. She had to make an important decision, after all, one which would affect not only her future but Briarwood's as well. She wanted to become better acquainted with him and to see his home, Raven's Point. She already sensed that he was the kind of man she had vowed to wed—rich, prominent, and eligible—but she wanted to be sure he met with all of Lady Redmayne's criteria. Camille had charged her to marry wisely, and so she would.

Of course she would also have to consider Adam, Susanna thought resentfully, spying him out of the corner of her eye. He was leaning against the doorjamb, glaring not so much at her as at Dominick. Oh, if only he wouldn't scowl so! Someone would surely guess why he was upset.

"Has my confession pleased or dismayed you?" Dominick asked, catching her furtive glance in Adam's direction. "You seem troubled, Camille."

"It is only that this is so sudden," she answered hastily, gifting him with a smile that she hoped would divert him. "Perhaps when we know each other better . . ."

"That is my desire, to know you better," he murmured, his cool fingers caressing her hand as they circled each other. "If I may, I would like to call upon you in the coming days—"

"Well, actually I've been invited to a host of social events which will take me away from Briarwood much of the time," Susanna said, doing her best to sway him from any thoughts of visiting the plantation during the next few weeks. Adam would know at once that Dominick was paying her court, and until she was sure she wanted to marry this man, she didn't dare risk losing Adam as her plantation manager.

"Then perhaps you can tell me where I might find you," Dominick suggested. "We could meet here and there and become better acquainted." He glanced pointedly at the half dozen or so young men who weren't yet dancing, a cow-eyed Matthew Grymes among them. "I fear that tonight we'll have little chance to speak further, my dear. You have a wealth of eager partners seeking your hand, and it is only fair that I relinquish you to them, since it is your welcome ball. In the future, however, I promise that you won't find me so charitable."

Susanna shivered at the forceful intent behind his

words, although he still spoke in low tones. Dominick Spencer was clearly a man who was accustomed to getting what he wanted. Obliging him, she enumerated her plans for the days ahead, at least as far as she knew them, adding softly, "If I decide to attend any other functions, I could always send you a message . . ."

"Splendid," he murmured with an almost smug smile as the minuet began to draw to a close. "By the way, beautiful lady, I must tell you that you dance exquisitely. You must have had an excellent teacher in England. I would say your grace and skill surpass most of the ladies present."

She nearly choked, gratified by his compliment yet flushing uncomfortably as she recalled her lesson with Adam and its passionate conclusion. "Thank you," she replied simply, not trusting herself to say more.

"Remember," Dominick reminded her when the music ceased, the guests' conversations and enthusiastic applause swelling around them, "I claim the last dance, Camille."

Before she could respond, he bowed with the same practiced flourish and left her, his back stiff and straight as he walked toward the game room, his voice authoritative as he acknowledged greetings and comments from other guests. Yet Susanna had little time to reflect upon how well-respected he seemed to be, before Matthew Grymes practically ran across the dance floor in his unabashed haste to beat the other gentlemen to her side.

"We're going to dance the Sir Roger de Coverley," he said excitedly, his round face already mottled and sweaty despite the fresh breeze wafting through the open windows. "Do you know it, Miss Cary?"

"I think so," she replied, vaguely recalling Adam telling her it was the name for a lively reel.

"Well, don't worry, I'll show you. It's great fun!"

As Matthew took her hands in his clammy palms, she forced a smile while wishing that Dominick had insisted upon being her partner for the entire evening. She expected he would now have to amuse himself in that smoky game room, playing cards and shooting billiards while most everybody else danced the hours away. What a sad reward for his thoughtful gallantry.

The music began and Susanna was swept into the dance by her enthusiastic yet clumsy partner. It turned out to be the same dance she and Adam had enjoyed the night before, which had ended when she had collapsed breathlessly into his arms. She had no intention of doing that with Matthew. She was delighted when he told her that at intervals everyone exchanged partners, although when she suddenly spied a giggling Celeste being whirled along by Adam, she hoped she wouldn't end up paired with him.

To her surprise Adam actually seemed to be having a good time now that she wasn't dancing with Dominick, or else he was putting up a very good front. Occasionally she heard his low, husky laughter, which irked her. She had told him to deceive Celeste, but he didn't have to charm her so thoroughly—

What the devil's the matter with you? Susanna scolded herself, wincing as she failed to avoid Matthew's stomping feet. What did she care if Adam was paying attention to Celeste? No doubt he would end up marrying the vivacious redhead when she herself chose someone else.

"We're about to . . . change partners, Miss Cary," Matthew said, huffing, sweat trickling from beneath his powdered tie-wig. "But I'll have you back . . . by the end of the dance."

It was on Susanna's tongue to utter a gracious reply, but when he trounced again upon her toe she hissed in exasperation, "Watch your bloody feet, Matthew!"

Gaping at her in astonishment, he spun her into the next gentleman's arms. Susanna, regretting her unthinking remark and knowing she must apologize later, was relieved to discover her new partner was Adam, but only for the respite she knew he would offer her bruised toes.

"I've missed you, my love," he said, loud enough for only her to hear as they followed the spirited line of couples across the dance floor. His eyes glittered at her possessively, the tiny flecks of gold in his gaze heightened by the blazing candlelight overhead, and she felt a heady rush of warmth.

"And I, you," she lied, although she suspected from her strange giddiness in holding his hands that she *had* missed him, if only a little. Fleetingly she marveled at how warm his skin felt while Dominick's had been so cool, then she added, "You and Celeste seem to be enjoying yourselves. I heard you laughing."

"Jealous?"

Susanna attempted a flippant smile, realizing in that moment how deeply his query had cut her and that she might very well be jealous. "Not at all," she replied, keeping her voice light. "And you?"

He sobered, his expression becoming hard, although his eyes held a tormented and poignant vulnerability she had never seen before. "Should I be?" he asked as he prepared to hand her over to her next partner.

"Of course not, Adam," she lied again, feeling guilty when relief flickered over his handsome features. Then she was whisked from his arms and halfway across the floor before she caught another glimpse of him, his gaze hungrily capturing hers through the swirl of laughing dancers.

For one heart-stopping instant she had the oddest sensation that they were alone in the room, just the two of them, dancing together despite that she held another man's hands and he, another woman's. Unwittingly, again she found herself wishing that she wasn't living a lie with its rigid obligations . . . wishing he didn't have his every hope set upon marrying a rich heiress . . . oh, God, wishing . . . wishing . . .

"There! I told you I'd get you back!" enthused Matthew, his breathless voice shattering her thoughts into shards of hopeless fantasy. Seemingly undaunted by her earlier rudeness to him, he added earnestly, "I'll try to be more careful, Miss Cary, I promise. I didn't mean to step on your feet."

Susanna smiled, but there was no pleasure behind it,

even as the dance ended and Thomas Dandridge, despite Matthew's protests, swept her into another minuet.

For her, the sparkling excitement of the evening was gone. All she could think of was the tortured look in Adam's eyes which had revealed not only that he was jealous, painfully so, but also that he might be falling in love.

With Camille.

Not with Susanna Jane Guthrie.

And, heaven help her for being a fool, there was a chance she might be falling in love with him, too.

"If you'll excuse me, gentlemen," Dominick said, maintaining a congenial tone despite the irritation that gnawed like a thousand maggots at his gut. As he rose he attempted not to dwell on the large sum of money he had lost so far this evening. "I'd like to see how the ball is progressing. But rest assured, my friends, I will be back."

As he swallowed the last of his ruby port and moved to the door, the grandfather clock chimed a quarter past eleven.

It was early yet. He still had plenty of time to recoup his losses before the last dance of the evening, and no doubt the card playing would continue even after the rest of the house grew quiet. He had seen many a sunrise from gaming tables, as had other gentlemen of his acquaintance for whom gambling was as essential as breathing.

Hell, he wouldn't be surprised if he and his half dozen or so compatriots heralded the dawn with a rousing and bloody cockfight. He knew he wasn't the only planter who had brought along his prize bird for just such a possibility. He usually fared better wagering on cockfights and horse races anyway, although not so well that he didn't suffer some financial loss. He had been on one long losing streak for the past eight years, the good days when he chanced to break even becoming fewer and farther between.

As an acute pain twisted his stomach again, Dominick cursed under his breath. Closing the game room door behind him, he surveyed the crowded ballroom.

Where was that little chit? he wondered with annoyance, his narrowed gaze skimming over the many couples engaged in a lively saraband. Where was Miss Camille Cary, the mistress of Briarwood and the answer to his prayers?

She was a pretty piece, though she could have been as ugly as a field toad for all he cared. All he wanted was her vast fortune, which would save him from bankruptcy—and he would have it, too. She had been like butter in his hands earlier tonight, as acquiescent as a lamb going to the slaughter. He had seen in her eyes how impressed she was with him. For the way she had stared after he introduced himself, he might as well have been King George II of England!

If there was one thing he knew how to do well, it was to keep up the appearance of wealth no matter how bad things were getting at Raven's Point. Even his immediate neighbors and gambling associates didn't know how deeply into debt he had fallen, a further testament to his ability to deceive the world. Fooling a naive slip of a girl would pose him no difficulty. He had every expectation that after a few more pleasant meetings, a good sprinkling of compliments, and another costly gift or two—all of which would revert back to his possession once they were married—she would play right into his hands.

It seemed that the hardest part had been getting her father out of the way so he had the freedom to court her, and even that he had accomplished easily enough. Making it appear that James Cary had accidentally shot himself with his own loaded hunting musket while climbing over a low fieldstone wall had truly been an inspired touch—

"Enjoying the ball, Dominick?" Robert Grymes blustered jovially as he ambled up, his bulbous nose and fat cheeks red from drinking.

"Well enough," Dominick replied, paying the

drunken planter little heed as his gaze again swept the ballroom. "What of our beautiful hostess? I don't see her."

"Miss Cary retired to her chamber over a half hour ago," Robert informed him, shrugging. "My son Matthew was dancing with her when she suddenly complained of a headache and bade him good night. She must still be recovering from her journey after all."

"I suppose," Dominick murmured, thinking it strange.

Camille had seemed radiant and happy enough while they were dancing, except for that brief moment when he had caught her glancing at Adam Thornton. Now there was one insolent bastard he should have whipped to death when he had the chance. He wouldn't be surprised if her sudden unease had been due to his unwelcome appearance in her ballroom.

It must have been a rude shock for her to discover the license her father had granted that base, illiterate son of a miner who had somehow managed over the years to distinguish himself as a crop master. It made Dominick sick to think that his former indentured servant, the surliest, most mutinous he'd ever come across, was living in this house and managing one of the richest plantations in the Tidewater. He certainly wouldn't tolerate Adam's loathesome presence once he was the master of Briarwood. He would have him horsewhipped right off his property.

"She did look a bit pale to me, I must admit," Robert added with a loud hiccough, then he grimaced. "Nine weeks at sea aboard a disease-ridden vessel . . ."

Banishing Adam from his mind, Dominick reasoned that it did make sense that Camille might still be fatigued from such a long and arduous voyage. He would have to be extra solicitous of her at the Johnson girl's birthday party on Tuesday, which would be the next time he saw her. He intended to leave Briarwood shortly after daybreak tomorrow. He always spent Sunday afternoons in bed with his mistress, Cleo, the only woman he had ever come close to loving.

"Pity, though. Miss Cary's missing a splendid good time." Robert belched loudly, reeling a little to the left. "Too bad about the last dance she promised you, eh, Dominick? Heard all about it from Matthew, who hoped he'd be the one honored. You're not thinking of throwing a bid for her into the hat with all the younger boys, are you? Good God, man, you could be her father!"

Dominick didn't deem the slurred comment worthy of an answer, nor would he waste more of his time on this fat, babbling fool. If Camille had gone to bed, there was no point in remaining in this noisy ballroom.

Without even a nod of farewell, he disappeared into the dim, smoke-filled game room, his palms itching to once again pick up the cards.

Adam stood just outside the yellow spill of light from the ballroom's high arched windows, the shadows of the humid summer night enveloping him, and watched grimly as Dominick closed the game room door in Robert Grymes's face.

"Go on, you bastard," he muttered, his fingers tightening around his snifter of brandy. "Murdering devil. Go gamble away what little money you have left. You'll only make my revenge that much easier, and that much sweeter."

He lifted the glass and drank deeply, the dark amber liquid burning his throat like the fiery hatred coursing through his body.

The intensity of his feeling echoed the jealous fury he had felt earlier when he had entered the ballroom to find Dominick dancing with Camille, smiling at her, conversing quietly with her, holding her hand. His beautiful Camille! If not for her assurances that they would announce their betrothal in a few weeks' time, he would have ended their secret courtship then and there by throwing that fiendish spawn of Satan right out the front door, along with the rest of her slathering suitors.

Drawing a deep, ragged breath, Adam's gaze shot to the second-story window high above him, the soft candlelight that streaked the delicate lace curtains proof that she was still awake. She had disappeared from the ballroom so suddenly while he had been dancing a gavotte with Celeste that he hadn't had a chance to bid her good night. He had left immediately thereafter himself, despite his partner's pretty sulking. He had been standing beneath Camille's window for almost an hour now, hoping to catch a last glimpse of her before he, too, went to bed.

It was not to be. Suddenly the dim light was doused, her room falling dark.

"Damn." Adam turned on his heel and strode toward the coach house, growing angry with himself.

He could have gone to her and inquired as to how she was feeling, if he hadn't so readily agreed to sleep in his office. Matthew had told him she had complained of a headache and fatigue, which told him that the commotion of the evening had been too much for her. Now he would have to wait until morning to see her while someone else slept in his bed, in his room, only two doors away from his beloved.

He stopped, stunned, and glanced back at her darkened windows.

*His beloved.* Was that what Camille was becoming to him? He had never expected that he might fall in love with her, but it was happening, he admitted, and almost without his awareness of her evolution from the mere instrument of his revenge into the fascinating woman who was capturing his heart.

If anything, this long, frustrating day had driven home his powerful feelings with resounding force. He didn't want any other man near her. He didn't want any other man touching her. He didn't want anyone sharing her beautiful smiles, her laughter, or her playful glances. Dammit, then why had he agreed to continue their secret courtship? Why had he agreed to play her deceptive little game, which would only draw more men to her like buzzing bees around the sweetest, most fragrant wildflower in the field?

Remembering the plea in her incredible green eyes, Adam shook his head as he resumed his stride. It was amazing what a man would do for the love of a woman.

He mounted the steps to his office and, once inside the moonlit room, sat down heavily on the bed.

One thing was perfectly clear to him. Camille might think their "little deception" as she called it, was going to be fun and romantic and slightly naughty, but he knew better.

For him, at least, the next few weeks would be pure hell.

# Chapter 12

"**M**y, we've certainly made the rounds in the last two weeks, haven't we?" Celeste commented to no one in particular inside the swaying coach. She began to count on her slim white fingers. "First, of course, was Camille's lovely welcome ball, which was a huge success by any standards, then Amy's birthday picnic on Tuesday, followed by several dinner parties and overnight stays at the homes of some of the finest families in the Tidewater . . ." She paused and pointedly regarded her brother, who was seated directly across from her ogling Susanna. "Help me, Matthew dear. What else?"

He shot her a look of chagrin. "There was the all-day musicale last Monday at the Wormeleys'—"

"Oh, yes, the one event Adam couldn't attend because he had to catch up on his work at Briarwood," Celeste said in a petulant voice, placing her hand possessively on Adam's forearm. When he continued to stare out the window without replying, she focused her attention upon Susanna, who was seated across from him, uncomfortably close to Matthew.

"I still can't believe you refused to play the pianoforte for us, Camille, especially after how your father once boasted to my papa that you played like an angel. And don't tell me that you're just too shy to perform in public. You've blossomed into the belle of the Tidewater since your ball, so that excuse doesn't count any longer."

Exasperated because she had already explained herself to Celeste several times, Susanna nonetheless kept her voice light as she repeated her excuse. "Papa highly exaggerated my skills. I'm really not very good, despite what he must have said."

Not good was an understatement, she thought, trying to ignore how Celeste was caressing Adam's sleeve. She couldn't play a note. Recalling how unpleasant it had felt to be pressured in front of so many people, she resolved again never to attend any more musicales.

"Well, I don't know if I believe you," Celeste replied airily, snaking her arm through Adam's as she said to him in a playful aside, "Do you?"

"If Miss Cary says she doesn't play well, then I believe her," he answered, the tightness along his jaw showing that he wasn't happy with Celeste's increasingly frequent gestures of familiarity.

"Oh, you *would*, seeing as Camille's your employer," the redhead retorted, then she blithely changed the subject, counting once more upon her fingers. "Let's see, after the musicale there was the card party Wednesday at the Dandridges', a boat ride on the James and that wonderful two-night stay with the Fitzhughs', a barbeque at our house on Saturday, services yesterday at the parish church, and now today, a trip into Yorktown to visit the shops." She meaningfully kneed her brother, who was staring at Susanna with a look of rapt admiration. "Do you have any suggestions as to what we might do tomorrow, Matthew? We have several events to choose from or we could find our own amusement."

"Well—"

"Actually, I'd like to spend the day at home," Susanna interrupted him, more weary of Matthew's incessant company and moon-eyed, worshipful glances than she could ever say. When Celeste and her brother looked equally surprised and crestfallen, she hastily added, "I'll see you again on Wednesday. That is, Mr. Thornton and I"—she glanced at Adam, who was smiling his approval in that warm, intimate fashion that never failed to fluster her, then she skipped her gaze back to Celeste—"since we're all attending the horse races together at the Tates'. I need some time to rest. We've been so busy, traveling so much . . ."

"No, you just want some time to decide which of your suitors you're going to take seriously, isn't that right, Camille?" Celeste said, arching a slim russet brow. "You certainly have enough of them."

"I don't know what you mean," Susanna answered, acutely aware that Adam's smile had suddenly faded.

"Oh, come now, you don't fool me. You know that you'll have a riot on your hands if you don't make up your mind soon. Why, you're making all the unmarried girls in the Tidewater as jealous as peahens." She gave Adam's arm a light squeeze, smiling up at him. "Except me, of course." She sobered a little, darting a sympathetic glance at her brother. "I think you're making Matthew a little jealous, too."

"Celeste . . ."

She ignored her brother's embarrassed entreaty and rushed on. "I do believe today was the first time he didn't have to compete with anyone else for your attention, and especially not the honorable Mr. Spencer. Yorktown must have been a bit too far of a drive for him from Raven's Point." Her forehead crinkled into a frown. "I really don't know what attracts you to him, Camille. Oh, he might be rich and handsome and have a seat on the governor's council, but he's so old!"

As Adam noticeably tensed, his expression growing thunderous, Susanna wished Celeste would swallow a fly or choke on her foolish tongue, anything to cease her endless chatter.

How much longer would she be able to stall Adam's desire to publicly announce his courtship of her, when Celeste continually made it a point to comment upon Dominick's presence at most of their outings? She could sense Adam's frustration growing with each passing day, and these little barbs didn't help. She couldn't have been more relieved when the Grymes's coach turned onto her drive, and the Cary mansion appeared through the trees.

"Are you sure we can't persuade you to join us tomorrow?" Celeste asked, directing her pouty question more at Adam than at Susanna. "Perhaps just you and I could meet—"

"Sorry, Celeste. There's a lot of work I have to get done before Wednesday," he said, cutting her off brusquely, then climbing from the carriage as soon as it jolted to a halt. As he assisted Susanna to the ground and unloaded her few packages, Matthew jumped down, too, and stood awkwardly next to her.

"I had a wonderful time today, Miss Cary. I'm glad you liked the music box I bought for you."

"It was too generous a gift," Susanna said, holding the prettily wrapped box. "You shouldn't have."

Matthew shrugged self-consciously, a blush creeping over his chubby cheeks. "I wanted to."

"I'll treasure it, then. Thank you, Matthew."

His neck turned bright red against the abundant white frills at his throat. "Yes . . . uh, well, good-bye, Miss Cary. We'll see you on Wednesday morning. Would nine o'clock be too early?"

"No, that will be fine."

Adam's voice held barely concealed irritation. "Good-bye, Matthew. You two had better head home. There's only an hour left before dark."

Nodding, the young planter reboarded the carriage. Both he and his sister waved from the windows as it clattered around the drive.

"Good-bye, Adam!" Celeste called out, boldly throwing him a kiss. "I can hardly wait until Wednesday!"

"Nor can I," he muttered sarcastically.

Deciding it was best to pretend not to hear him, Susanna picked up the largest package, which contained a new straw hat she planned to wear at the horse races.

"I'll carry that for you," Adam said, their hands brushing as he took the round box from her and gathered up her two smaller parcels.

"Thank you," she murmured, unsettled by even the slightest physical contact with him. He hadn't touched her since his good-night kiss yesterday, which was quite enough temptation for her weakening defenses.

She had come to dread that intimate ritual when he escorted her to her room on the evenings they spent alone at Briarwood. His embraces, sometimes passionate, sometimes achingly tender, never failed to unleash within her desires she had been desperately trying to keep under control. She had told herself a thousand times she wasn't falling in love with him, nor he with her, but when he held her in his arms, nothing made sense anymore.

Thank God she had made up her mind to marry Dominick Spencer, Susanna thought as they walked to the house, Adam strangely silent beside her. She wanted this increasingly disturbing relationship to end. She had yet to visit Raven's Point, but now she considered that a mere formality. During the past two weeks Dominick had more than shown her that he was the kind of gentleman of whom Lady Redmayne would have approved.

He had been very well received by all of her hosts, indicating to her that he was highly respected. Everything she had heard from him and others about Raven's Point had convinced her that he would be able to support her without any assistance from her own inheritance, and her marriage to one of the governor's close advisors certainly wouldn't damage the Cary reputation.

She wasn't in love with him, but that had never been an issue. And she didn't mind that he was much older than she was, despite what Celeste might think. Dominick possessed a mature and elegant manner that was altogether lacking in the younger planters she had met. He was so attractive and charming and generous, she couldn't help but believe she would be content with him, just as Lady Redmayne had said—

"Did you have a nice time in Yorktown, Miss Camille?"

Nudged from her reverie by Ertha's friendly question, Susanna smiled at the housekeeper, who was holding open the front door for them. "Yes, I did," she replied, although it was a half-truth. Having Matthew follow her around all day like a besotted puppy hadn't been pleasant, and Celeste's constant flirting with Adam had defied Susanna's best efforts to remain unaffected by her niggling, irrational jealousy. Still, she had enjoyed the shopping.

It had been a new and unsettling experience to have so much money to spend. She couldn't wait to use the hard-milled soap, bath oil, powder, and perfume she had bought, all of which had the same heady fragrance, yellow jasmine. She liked it much better than lavender, which only brought her sad reminders of Camille.

"What's this?" Ertha asked, eyeing the beribboned package Susanna held in her hands. "Another gift?"

"Yes, from Matthew Grymes. A porcelain music box."

"My goodness, child, you're surely collecting a host of lovely things from your admirers, but I think Mr. Spencer has them beat with that fine racehorse he gave you and that beautiful emerald necklace. You must be considering him seriously to accept such expensive things from him."

Susanna jumped as Adam fairly slammed her packages down on the hall table behind her.

"Forgive me," he said tersely, his eyes a dark, turbulent hue as he leveled his gaze upon her. "They slipped."

"Th-that's all right," she said, throwing a nervous smile at Ertha, who was regarding them curiously.

"Could we step into the library, Miss Cary? There is some business I've been meaning to discuss with you, and now that Mr. and Miss Grymes have left, I think it's a good time—"

"Can't it wait until later, Mr. Thornton?" she interrupted, surmising exactly what he wanted to talk about and hoping to avoid for as long as possible what she imagined would be a disagreeable discussion. "Perhaps until morning? It's been such a long day."

"No."

She swallowed hard, knowing from his curt answer

that she had lost this battle. Not wanting to make any more of a scene in front of Ertha, she acquiesced. "Very well, Mr. Thornton. If your business is that urgent."

"I assure you, it is."

"If you'd like, Miss Camille, I could take your things upstairs for you," the housekeeper offered, appearing more confused.

"Thank you, Ertha. There are some toiletries in that small package"—hopefully not shattered, she thought with vexation, glancing at Adam—"several pairs of dress gloves in the other one and a new hat in the large box. Could you see that everything is put away?"

"Of course."

Susanna handed the housekeeper the gift from Matthew, then she followed Adam into the library.

"Sit down," he ordered, closing the door firmly.

She obliged him, feeling nervous yet angry that he would treat her like a disobedient child. He walked to a window and stared outside for a long moment, as if not readily trusting himself to speak, then he turned and met her eyes. She had never seen him look more deadly serious, or more devastatingly handsome.

"I will not tolerate any more of this charade, Camille. I've kept silent and played along for two weeks now, but that's it. On Wednesday, I plan to announce our betrothal at the Tates'."

Susanna gaped at him, a strange, trapped feeling rising inside her chest. She had expected him to be upset, to perhaps express some reservations about continuing as they had been, but not this! He looked so resolute, his very stance screaming to her that he had firmly made up his mind, that she didn't know what she could possibly say to persuade him to wait just a little while longer.

"Adam, if it was Matthew's gift—" she began lamely.

"A trinket, Camille! I don't care about that damn music box or the bumpkin who gave it to you. It's the racehorse and jeweled necklace that you've so naively accepted which concern me. Don't you realize the false impression you're giving that bast—" He fell abruptly silent, as if catching himself, then sighed heavily. "Our deception isn't a game anymore, my love. You may have derived some innocent pleasure from it and found it romantic and perhaps even exciting, but these few weeks have been nothing but torture for me."

Her heart pounding, Susanna watched as he sat down almost wearily on the arm of a stuffed chair. She sensed truth behind his words, and felt fresh guilt for the devious chase on which she was leading him. But she wouldn't be doing so if he hadn't overstepped the bounds of propriety with her in the first place! It was his own fault that he would soon find himself so rudely disappointed.

"Adam," she tried again, desperately trying to think of some way to mollify him. "I never expected that I'd be receiving presents from those gentlemen, and I never intended to keep any of them. They don't mean anything to me."

"Then you can return them on Wednesday."

When he paused, studying her face, Susanna feared he might detect her lie. She almost sighed in relief when he continued with quiet vehemence.

"Your secret glances and furtive smiles, however beautiful, are not enough for me, Camille. Our rare, stolen moments of conversation will no longer suffice. I want to court you in public where everyone can see us; to talk to you openly; to hold your hand, embrace you, and kiss you as I've been tempted to do countless times. I want *everyone*," he emphasized, his voice growing harsh, "especially those who've held any hope of having you for themselves, to know that you belong to me."

Susanna inhaled in surprise as Adam came to her, pulling her up almost roughly to stand in front of him.

"Tell me that you want this, Camille," he demanded softly. "Please. Tell me."

Panicking, Susanna could think of nothing to sway him.

What was she going to do? Wednesday was too soon.
Adam would ruin everything . . . her reputation, her
chance to wed the proper husband! Oh, if only she could
somehow speak to Dominick, somehow see him before
the races and let him know that she wanted to become
his wife. If only there was some way she could make
Adam promise he wouldn't say anything until after
Wednesday, buying her a little more time—

The idea, a feminine, manipulative ploy as old as
time, came to her at the same instant Adam lowered
his head to kiss her. Tears sprang to her eyes as she
forced herself to think of the only thing that had made
her weep in years, Camille's death, and she began to
cry in earnest, hating herself for exploiting her painful
memories but believing she had no other choice. She
was doing it for Camille's sake, after all.

Adam felt her shoulders trembling an instant before
he tasted a salty, telltale wetness on her lips. Drawing
back as if stung, he regarded her in astonishment.

"Camille. What the devil . . . ?"

"I—I'm sorry, Adam," she sobbed, her eyes like huge
green pools as tears tumbled down her cheeks. "I . . . I
don't know why I'm crying . . ."

Now you've gone and done it, he thought angrily,
thoroughly exasperated with himself. Pushed her too
damn hard. Forced his will on her when he had promised that he never would. As she sank into her chair
and wept harder, burying her face in her hands, his
self-disgust mounted.

Why did he have to be so blasted impatient anyway?
She hadn't deliberately done anything to displease him.
It wasn't her fault that his jealousy and frustration were
practically eating him alive. He knew she was playing
a harmless virgin's game, harmless but for the bruised
male pride her hapless suitors would be nursing when
she announced who she intended to marry. Why
couldn't he allow her to satisfy her girlish fantasies?

"Camille, it's all right," he said, at a total loss as
how best to comfort her. What man wasn't stumped
when faced with a woman's tears? He made a quick

search of his pockets and, finding a cambric handkerchief, went down on one knee beside her.

"Look at me," he bade her gently. When she lifted
her head, he cradled her softly rounded chin in his palm
and wiped the moisture from her flushed face. "Shhh,
love," he murmured, attempting to calm her. "Forgive
me. I shouldn't have been so harsh with you, so impatient. Shhh, there's no need to cry."

"Oh, Adam . . . I'd like to announce our betrothal,
too," she managed shakily, gazing at him so beseech-
ingly that he felt like kicking himself. "But not . . . at
the Tates'."

"Where then, love?" he asked.

"I thought we might have a small engagement party,
not too many people . . . here at Briarwood. At home.
Papa would have liked that." She took the handkerchief
from him with trembling fingers and delicately blew her
nose. "Do you think that would be all right?"

Elation momentarily clogging his throat, Adam knew
he could refuse her nothing. He gathered her into his
arms and stroked her honey-colored hair, reveling in its
silkiness. Only when she lifted her head from his shoulder to look at him did he murmur, "Of course, love.
Anything, if it will please you. When would you like
to have your party?"

"I—was thinking a week from this Saturday, just so
Ertha and Prue would have enough time to prepare everything." She hesitated, "Unless you would like it to
be sooner . . ."

"Next Saturday will be fine," Adam said, finding it
difficult to believe that they had finally picked a day to
announce their betrothal. He would have to play their
charade a little longer, but at least now there was an
end in sight.

He hugged her more tightly, feeling as if he would
never let her go. He hadn't told her yet how much he
had come to care for her, wanting to find that perfect
moment, and he quickly decided that now was not the
time. Not when he had just caused her unhappiness;
her face was still slightly damp with tears brought on

by his own callousness. No, he would wait until everything felt right between them.

"Adam . . ."

"Yes, love?"

"Would you mind if we waited a few more days before telling Ertha or any of the other servants? Say . . . until Friday? I want to enjoy our secret just a little while longer."

"Whatever you wish."

She seemed to relax fully in his arms then, and he felt a sweeping relief that he had consoled and pleased her. Curling his forefinger beneath her chin, he raised her face to him again, entranced anew by the stunning radiance of her eyes. In that moment he was certain as surely as he was breathing that if for some reason he could not gain his revenge, he would be content just to have this captivating woman beside him for the rest of his life.

With infinite tenderness, he moved his mouth over her soft lips, exulting in the sweet taste of her, still lightly tinged with salt. Then he deepened his kiss, swearing in his heart as she parted her lips that he would do his utmost to never again be the source of her unhappy tears. Never.

# Chapter 13

⌒~⌒

**T**he mantel clock softly chimed the early morning hour of two across the moonlit room, but it did not awaken Susanna. Held captive by a vivid nightmare, she moaned and tossed fitfully in the canopied bed, her legs and arms ensnared by white sheets that in her unconscious mind had become the huge, grasping hands of a man long dead come back to life.

"No, Papa . . . no," she rasped, her features contorted with stark terror in the silvery wash of moonlight spilling across the mattress. She twisted hopelessly as phantom ropes were tightening cruelly around her wrists and ankles, tying her face-down to a filthy, putrid-smelling cot. She jerked spasmodically as her threadbare dress was torn from her back, and she began to whimper afresh.

"Papa . . . Papa, please don't hit me. I'll do what you want. I'll go to him, Papa . . . I promise. I'll go to him!"

"Ye lyin' bitch!" slurred a gruff phantom voice. "I'll teach ye t' run away from yer Daniel Guthrie! Ye'll do what I say and like it well enough, ye 'ear me, chit? Ye'll spread yer legs fer Keefer Dunn and like it! Ye'll not make a liar out o' me. I sold ye t' 'im, damn ye! He paid me good 'ard coin fer yer favors!"

Another voice, coarse and loud, came flying at her from the darkness, and she was suddenly surrounded by crude laughter. She gasped in fright at the sneering, disembodied, pockmarked face hovering in front of her, and she felt near to retching when the sour smell of stale ale filled her nostrils.

"Beat 'er well, Guthrie, but mind ye don't mar 'er pretty puss. I'll not want 'er in bed if she's no longer fair t' look upon. Aye, and maybe when yer done wi' her, I'll give 'er a few blows m'self fer good measure. Do ye 'ear me, girl? I'll teach ye t' run away from Keefer Dunn!"

"No . . . please, God . . . no!"

Susanna screwed her eyes shut and turned her face into the stinking straw as the menacing shadow of a hand clenching a leather strap fell across her bare, quaking shoulders. She began to mumble incoherently, her futile tears nearly choking her. Thrashing in vain, she could only wait in raw panic for the terrible fall of the lash, wait for the slicing pain . . . the sting . . . the horror . . .

Reclining in bed with the covers drawn to his waist and his hands folded behind his head, Adam stared out the window at the round summer moon dangling like a bright orb in the pitch-black sky. Sleep was evading him again, but thankfully he was not suffering the wretched torments that had plagued him for the past two weeks. Tonight was blessedly, peacefully different.

He kept running through his mind the delights of the evening, savoring them, reliving them; the unexpected understanding he and Camille had reached in the library, their supper which had been filled with laughter and gentle teasing, a walk in the garden and then a light-hearted game of billiards just before bed. Her soft-spoken promise as he escorted her to her chamber that, although he would be out in the tobacco fields much of the day tomorrow, they would share supper again in the evening. Alone. Together.

Adam rolled restlessly onto his side. As he recalled the good-night kiss they had shared outside her door, he felt a familiar stirring, a burning ache he hoped before long to ease in the lush softness of her body.

It was a sweet torture being so close to her, only two

doors away, yet he relished it, his anticipation becoming that much more keen. Soon he would be sharing with her that master suite down the hall, their wedding night perhaps only a few more weeks away—

Adam sat bolt upright as a scream rent the air, a sound so tormented that it raised the hair on the back of his neck.

"Oh, God. *Camille.*"

Hurling back the covers, he lunged from the bed and, grabbing his breeches from a nearby chair, quickly pulled them on. He was already racing down the hall, cursing the limp that was even now hindering him, when another scream, more terrified than the last, hurled through her closed door. Cursing again when he found it bolted—at his bidding, he feverishly recalled—he jammed his shoulder against the door. He pushed with all his might until it splintered near the lock and swung open, slamming against the wall.

"Camille!"

Across the dimly lit room he saw her flailing wildly, and when she screamed again he guessed at once that she was locked in a terrible nightmare. Reaching the bed, he swept her into his arms, sheets and all, and held her close, although she beat at him desperately with her fists and tried to twist free.

"No . . . no! God help me, please don't let them beat me anymore! Oh, Papa, Papa, please don't let Keefer Dunn hurt me! No! No . . . oh, Papaaa!"

"Camille, wake up! Wake up! It's me, Adam!" Seeking to still her battering fists, he enfolded her so closely in his arms that she could barely struggle. "It's Adam! No one is beating you. No one is hurting you. I'm here with you, Camille. You're safe, love. You're safe!"

As her eyes suddenly flickered open, he exhaled sharply with relief. But when her slender body stiffened, he knew she was so disoriented from her dream that she hadn't yet recognized him.

"Camille," he said, shaking her gently. "Look at me, sweetheart. Look at me . . . I'm Adam."

She blinked, for the first time focusing her wide, frightened eyes on his face. "Adam?"

"Yes, love, it's me." As she went nearly limp in his arms, he sank down on the bed, cradling her to his chest. He stroked her tousled hair, her tearstained cheeks, the silky-smooth skin of her bare upper arm, speaking to her in low, soothing tones. "You had a bad dream, that's all. Just a bad dream. No one's going to hurt you. I wouldn't let them."

"It was horrible . . . awful," she whispered, trembling.

"I know, love, but it's over now. You're safe."

A sharp knock on the doorjamb caused her to gasp in fright and grow rigid again, and Adam swore under his breath.

"Who is it?"

"The footman, Mr. Thornton. Daniel. I heard Miss Camille scream. Is she all right?"

"Daniel . . . no . . ." she breathed in the voice of a child, scrambling from Adam's arms and over to the headboard, where she curled into a ball, hugging her knees. "Make him go away . . . please. Tell him to go away!"

Adam stared at her in surprise, wondering if someone named Daniel had been in her nightmare. Whoever he was, whether real or imagined, she was obviously terrified of him.

And who was Keefer Dunn? Had these two men perhaps been servants in her aunt's home? Had Camille met them on the *Charming Nancy?* God help him, if he discovered that a sailor or passenger had hurt her in any way aboard that ship, he would track the bastard down if the fever hadn't claimed him and finish the job himself!

Adam rose in anger from the bed, his gaze fixed on the servant's tall, broad-shouldered form standing just inside the door. "Miss Cary is fine. She had a bad nightmare, but she's over it now."

"Are you sure, Mr. Thornton? Maybe I should fetch Corliss to come and stay with her."

"That won't be necessary, Dan—" He stopped himself just in time, glancing at Camille huddled so pitifully against the headboard. He didn't want to utter that name again if it upset her so much. "Go back to your post by the front door. I'll stay with her for a few more minutes, just until I'm sure she's asleep. She'll be fine."

"If you say so, Mr. Thornton," the servant replied, closing the door with its shattered lock behind him. "But if you change your mind, I'll fetch Corliss up here straightaway."

Adam turned back to the bed, knowing it wasn't appropriate for him to remain alone in this room with her, but not wanting to leave her so soon after she had suffered such a scare. He decided to speak with Daniel later, to explain the need to keep silent about his presence here. The servant might think the worst of him for a few days, but when their betrothal was announced, all doubts would be dispelled.

"Is he gone?" came a small voice.

"Yes, love, he's gone." Adam sat down next to her and eased her into his arms again, rocking her gently. He sensed that the last remnants of her nightmare were loosening their grip when she gradually relaxed, her body slipping back against his chest.

If he had noticed earlier that she was clad only in a thin nightrail, now that things were calmer he was acutely aware of it. As he tucked his hand around her narrow waist, he could almost feel the smoothness of her skin through the light, pastel-colored silk. Her hair was soft where her head rested against his cheek and she smelled intoxicatingly sweet, a fragrance she had never worn before. He recognized it as yellow jasmine, a flower native to the southern colonies. He immediately decided its haunting complexity suited her far better than simple lavender.

"Thank you for waking me, Adam," she said after long moments. She leaned her head against his shoulder and sighed softly. "I . . . I think I'll be able to go back to sleep soon."

"Let me know when, and I'll leave you," he an-

swered, lightly kissing her temple, although in truth he
was loath to move an inch from her side. Nor was he
inclined to ask her any questions about her nightmare.
That could wait until tomorrow; he didn't want to upset
her again. It was simply too pleasant to hold her close
against him, feeling her draw breath within his embrace, and inhaling her scent, half perfume, half a
sweetness that was uniquely her own.

She shifted slightly, her hand innocently grazing that
sensitive part of him in which a low burning fire had
already been kindled. As his desire flared bright and
hot, he stifled a groan. For a young woman who had
been so concerned about preserving her reputation, she
certainly seemed comfortable in the arms of a man who
was naked but for his breeches.

Could it be that her normal fears of intimacy had
been eased by the kisses they had shared? he wondered
as the minutes flew by and still she did not ask him to
leave. It seemed so. He knew she hadn't fallen back
asleep. Was it possible, then, that she was hoping he
would make some advance toward her?

His desire blazed hotter at the thought, its searing
heat coming dangerously close to overwhelming him.
How he longed to claim her, to bury himself inside her
and quench the fire that her very nearness had ignited!
But he forced himself to think rationally, to consider
her sensibilities and propriety.

He doubted she would surrender fully without first
sharing marriage vows. Yet perhaps she might welcome
a small taste of the passion they would know on their
wedding night. His own pleasure would have to wait,
but for now it would be enough to arouse the fiery
desire he had glimpsed in her.

Almost enough, Adam amended honestly, the burning tightness in his lower body increasing as he slowly
drew his hands along her bare arms, his knuckles skimming the full outer curves of her breasts. Steeling himself to focus only on her pleasure, he gently nuzzled
her neck and slid his palms back down her arms.

A smile curved his mouth when he felt goose bumps

pucker her flesh. Eager to see how responsive she might be to a far more intimate touch, he quickly brought his splayed hands inward, skimming them along her flat abdomen and over her ribs to the soft undersides of her breasts. As she tensed, gasping in surprise, his thumbs each circled a roused nipple through her silken shift.

"Adam, what . . . what are you doing?"

"Holding you," he teased in a husky whisper, enjoying the sensual weight of her firm breasts in his hands. He had known they would fit his palms perfectly. He also knew she might offer some protest, if only not to appear too eager to enjoy his caresses. A little gentle persuasion would silence her feigned opposition easily enough and free that wonderfully wanton side of her nature.

"But you can't!" Susanna objected, his touch exciting in her the most incredible sensations. If she was still dazed from her nightmare, Adam's light squeezing of her breasts brought her sharply back to reality. She silently cursed her foolishness for being lulled by his comforting presence rather than sending him at once from her room. "We can't! We're not married—"

"We will be, my love," he interrupted her, flicking the ticklish shell of her ear with his tongue. "Very soon."

Susanna gasped again as he shifted both their weights, gently rolling them over. The next thing she knew she was lying flat on her back staring up at him, his eyes gleaming and his rugged features appearing all the more handsome in the moonlight. She also realized for the first time that his powerful shoulders and sleek chest were bare, the warmth of his skin penetrating through her flimsy nightrail. Believing for a terrible, fleeting instant that he must be naked, she was relieved when her fingers caught on some fabric at his waist.

"You trust me, don't you, Camille?" he queried, tracing the lush curve of her lips with a warm fingertip.

She wanted to cry out a vehement denial, to rail at him that he had no right to be doing this to her and to get out of her room, but she knew that to do so would threaten the deception she had so painstakingly crafted. Her heart was beating so hard that she feared it might drown out her tremulous answer. "Yes . . . I trust you."

"And you know that I would never do anything to hurt you or cause you shame."

"Y-yes."

As he stroked the side of her face, his eyes, stained black in the subtle lighting, held hers captive. "Then let me show you how it can be between us, my love. Let me give you a hint of the pleasure we will find in each other's arms—"

"But I'm a virgin, Adam!" she cried, her cheeks on fire that she must reveal such a personal detail about herself to a man who had no right to such knowledge.

"And you will remain so until our wedding night."

"Then what . . . how?"

Adam lowered his head to hers, his mouth hovering only a hairsbreadth above her own. "Trust me, my love," he whispered, brushing her parted lips with his tongue until they were slick and wet. "Kiss me."

As his mouth, tenderly possessive, molded to hers, Susanna thought of protesting further, of using the ploy of tears again . . . anything to stop this madness. Then his hand slid beneath her shift to her breast, and she became aware only of the bewildering sensations sweeping her body. She didn't know whether she found more pleasure in his deepening kiss, from his tongue dueling passionately with hers, or from his fingers taunting her raised nipples. She arched beneath his hand when he flicked the tingling nub lightly with his finger-nails, and she moaned against his lips.

"That's what I want to hear from you, my love," he murmured, tearing his mouth from hers. "Sounds of your passion. Cries of delight. Teach me what you like, Camille. Let me know when I please you."

She shivered when he slipped her nightrail from her body, baring her skin to the balmy breezes stirring the curtains and swirling around them, but her flesh soon grew warm and flushed beneath the seductive weight of his hands. He stroked and savored every inch of her. His palms slid worshipfully down her slim arms, drawn high above her head, over her taut, puckered nipples, her tightening belly, the curve of her hips and her sensitive inner thighs to the delicate arches of her feet, until she could not stop sighing from pleasure.

"That's it, my beautiful, exquisite love, tell me what you like," he urged her, kissing the ticklish hollow beneath her arm before forging a fiery path to her breasts.

A ragged moan broke from her throat when he captured a nipple between his lips and drew upon it hungrily, but she almost screamed when he slipped his hand between her legs, his fingers dipping into that moist, quivering region that had never before felt a man's touch. She jerked in surprise as a jolt of the most incredible sensation shot from some secret, mysterious point and radiated through every fiber of her body. Stunned, she wondered through her passionate haze if anything was wrong with her, and she cried out almost fearfully, "Adam?"

"Shhh, love, you were meant to feel such pleasure," he murmured soothingly, lifting his dark head from her breast to look deeply into her eyes. "Enjoy it, revel in it, but remember, this is only a hint of the ecstasy we will know together." His hips moved emphatically against her outer thigh, a swollen hardness pressing there, and he groaned. "Oh, God, Camille. To think I must wait even another day, another hour to claim you . . . such agony . . ."

His mouth seized hers, his fingers delving again and again into the hot softness of her body until she was writhing beneath him. Each time his fingertips circled and slid over that tingling nether point, she felt as if she was being thrust ever closer to the edge of some lofty precipice, until she was panting for breath, her limbs shaking uncontrollably. He spread her legs wider, applying a little more pressure, and suddenly she was flung over the side, hurtling through shimmering space . . .

"Oh, Adam! *Adam.*"

She couldn't say how long it was before her heavy eyelids fluttered open. Time had lost all meaning for her in the cloud of contentment that blanketed her. All she knew was that she felt warm and safe and protected, and disinclined to leave the strong, solid embrace of the man who held her so tightly.

"How I love you, Camille," came a husky murmur close to her ear. "Love you."

Those were the last words she heard as exhaustion overcame her, her sense of satiation like a potent drug. She slept, not sure if he had spoken the words or if she had merely imagined them.


"Lordy, Miss Camille. I always figured Mr. Thornton was a right powerful man, but just look at this door. I'll bet the carpenters will have to make a new one from the way this whole side is busted up."

"I know, Corliss. I've seen it," Susanna said, trying not to think about what had happened last night. She had awakened at sunrise to find herself thankfully alone in her bed. Now she hastily pulled on her traveling gloves. "Are you ready to go?"

"Yes, I am, but I don't see what the hurry is. It's not even eight o'clock in the morning yet."

Susanna tried to keep her voice calm, although she was wracked by nervousness. She had learned from Ertha, who was the earliest riser among the servants, that Adam had left for the fields well before dawn. She didn't expect him back until that evening, but there was always the chance that he might return to the house for some reason and discover that she was leaving. He would insist on accompanying her, and she couldn't have that. This clandestine journey was part of the urgent plan she had devised after her unsettling exchanges with him yesterday.

"Corliss, I already told you that I want to complete our trip before nightfall. It's a good distance to Raven's Point—"

"Raven's Point, Miss Camille?" Corliss blurted, a smile flashing. "Is that where we're going?"

"Yes," Susanna admitted, not sure she could trust her talkative waiting-maid with such potentially troublesome information. Yet she didn't have much choice. Propriety demanded a chaperone. "We have to start early if I'm going to have enough time for a good visit with Mr. Spencer and then return before it begins to grow dark. We don't want to be out on the roads at night, do we?"

"No, I guess you're right about that," Corliss agreed, the damaged door forgotten as she swept an approving glance over Susanna's apricot-colored gown. "No wonder you dressed so pretty today. Does Mr. Spencer know you're coming to call?"

"Of course he does. We arranged everything at the Grymes's barbeque on Saturday," she lied, looking in the mirror as she tied the ribbons to her matching silk hat under her chin. She thought fleetingly that she appeared a bit pale this morning, but no wonder! She still couldn't believe she had allowed Adam to . . . to . . .

Chasing away the vivid memories that kept leaping into her mind, she whirled to face her maid, adding firmly, "But this is a secret, Corliss. Our secret, and Elias's, who'll be driving the coach. I don't want you to say anything about this journey to anyone. Not to Ertha or Prue or any of the other maids. No one."

"A secret?" the young woman asked, clearly confused.

"Yes. I can't have my other suitors knowing I'm traipsing about the Tidewater paying solitary calls on a rival. From the way all of you gossip around here, any chance visitor might overhear you, and that's how rumors get started. I don't want to crush anyone's hopes, at least not yet."

Understanding crept into Corliss's lively dark eyes. "I 'spect Mr. Grymes is going to find himself mighty disappointed before too long, isn't he, Miss Camille? A host of other young"—she put special stress on the word—"gentlemen, too."

Susanna forced a conspiratorial smile. "Perhaps." After turning around for a last glimpse at herself in the mirror, she picked up her fan and gracefully opened it, giving it an expert flutter. She had been practicing over the past few weeks. Feeling a much-needed boost of confidence, she snapped the fan shut and walked to the door, her wide skirt rustling.

"Now, if anyone asks, Corliss, just say we're going into Yorktown to do some more shopping."

"I hear you, Miss Camille." Glancing at the damaged door as she passed it, the maid shook her head. "You better start drinking some of Prue's special chamomille and peppermint tea before bedtime if you want to stop those nightmares from coming," she suggested, following Susanna into the hallway. "It'll help you sleep nice and peaceful. That way Mr. Thornton won't have to wear out any more doors like he did to that one."

Susanna made no comment, but she did make a mental note to try some of that tea tonight. She certainly didn't want a repeat of last eve—

No, she wasn't going to think about it! It was bad enough that she could almost feel the warm weight of Adam's hands upon her body, his fingers teasing her intimately. And those words she had dreamed he had said . . . *I love you, Camille.* That was the last thing she wanted to hear him say to her! How could she have ever dreamt such nonsense?

Heaving a sigh, Susanna stopped outside his room. "I forgot something, Corliss. Why don't you go on ahead and see that Elias is ready with the coach."

"Yes, ma'am."

Waiting until the maid had disappeared down the stairs, she drew from her bodice a note she had hastily written to Adam in case he came back to the house and she still hadn't returned from Raven's Point. He had become so possessive of her, she imagined he would be upset when he learned she had left without his knowledge. She hoped the short missive explaining that she had enjoyed shopping so much that she had gone into town to do some more would appease him, especially since she had signed it *Yours always, Camille*.

This was the first time she had signed anything with that name. She had been intending to write Lady Redmayne a letter to inform her that all was well, as Camille would have done weeks ago. But she still didn't trust her imitation of Camille's signature. She needed more time to practice, using as a guide a letter Camille had written to her father.

During a visit to Briarwood a few days after Susanna's arrival, William Booth, the family attorney, had given her a key to James Cary's strongbox in which his personal papers were kept. She had immediately destroyed Camille's letters, save for one, and as soon as she felt confident enough writing the signature, she would have to dispose of it, too, however reluctantly.

Sighing, Susanna opened the note and briefly reread it, lingering on the neatly inscribed closing.

*Yours always, Camille.*

Frustrated anew by the same niggling regret that had plagued her since the night she and Adam had first kissed, she defiantly refolded the paper and entered his room. She had no fears that he would discover the ruse. If he had ever seen Camille's letters, he'd hardly remember a signature, and even if he did, it would be passable enough to fool him.

"Now, where shall I put this?" she said to herself, thinking how much neater his chamber was now than the first time she had ventured into it. The room's decidedly masculine appearance hadn't changed, however, with its dark, heavy furnishings and his personal belongings placed here and there.

Idly touching the pages of a book that had been left open upon the bedside table, Homer's *Iliad,* Susanna suddenly had the strangest sensation that she could feel Adam's presence all around her—compelling, warm, and powerful, like the flesh-and-blood man himself. Becoming flustered, she quickly propped the note

# Chapter 14

From Susanna's window, as the carriage rumbled toward the distant brick house along a wide, oak-lined avenue, Raven's Point looked every bit as magnificent as Dominick had described to her. Four huge columns fronted the formal entrance, giving his home an elegant classical appearance, and its size certainly seemed to rival that of Briarwood.

The plantation also appeared to be bustling with activity. She could see slaves—men, women, and even children—toiling in the tobacco fields, which she had been told stretched for hundreds of acres from both sides of the road, and riding on horseback among them were overseers who occasionally cracked their whips high in the air. As the coach turned onto the circular driveway a few moments later, she noted more slaves busily going about their work among the many outbuildings, set a much farther distance away from the house than the arrangement at Briarwood.

"Did you see that, Miss Camille?" Corliss asked, her expression showing shock and dismay as she turned from craning her neck out the opposite window. "They've got little children, no more than six years old, working out in them tobo fields. Babies! And in this hot sun!"

"Yes, I did," Susanna replied, surprised that Dominick would allow such a thing. At Briarwood, children younger than thirteen were given tasks suitable for their

age or left under the watchful eye of motherly atten-
dants to frolic and play near their cabins.

"Those overseers were using whips, too," the maid
added, her tone subdued. "I wonder if they did that
when Mr. Thornton worked here. He never said nothing about it. I 'spect he wouldn't be too happy to see
how things have changed, if that's the case. He doesn't
tolerate no whips at Briarwood."

Recalling Adam's tight-lipped exchange with Josiah
Skinner about the overseer who had dared to raise a
whip against some Cary slaves and been summarily dismissed for it, Susanna could just imagine his response.
As the carriage came to a halt before the front door and
a footman in modest livery rushed out to assist her, she
resolved to discuss these matters with Dominick. She
didn't like slavery in the first place, and there was no
reason to make these people's burden any more difficult
than it already was.

"Corliss, would you mind waiting in the carriage for
just a few moments? I'd like to greet Mr. Spencer
alone."

Susanna was surprised when Corliss failed to tease
her about her interest in the widowed planter. Instead,
the maid appeared willing to remain inside the coach
during the visit, no matter that it was stuffy and warm.
She was clearly upset about what she had just seen out
in the fields.

Thinking that things weren't getting off to the best
start, Susanna disembarked and climbed the broad front
steps to the door. She couldn't ask the footman within
earshot of Corliss if Dominick was at home since this
meeting was supposed to have been prearranged, but
when she was ushered inside the sparsely furnished hall,
she turned to him and said, "My name is Miss Camille
Cary. I've come to pay a call on Mr. Spencer—"

"My dear Camille, this is indeed a pleasant surprise."

Susanna's pulse raced as Dominick, dressed more
plainly than she had ever seen him, in a white full-
sleeved shirt, unadorned waistcoat, and dark breeches,

strode from a room which she could see was the library. Realizing that he must have observed her arrival from the tall windows which looked out onto the front lawn, she wondered why he hadn't come out at once to greet her. As he curtly waved away the footman, she murmured, "Dominick."

"Forgive me for not escorting you myself into my home," he explained as if reading her thoughts, "but I took a moment to ask my housekeeper to prepare us some refreshment. I am delighted to see you, my dear, but I must admit that I'm startled by your unexpected visit. Have you come alone?"

"No, Corliss is with me."

"Ah, yes, your talkative little maid. Where is she?"

"Still in the carriage. I . . . I didn't know if you were home so I asked her to wait until . . ." Susanna sighed, deciding she might as well tell him the truth, or at least some of it. She had no intention of revealing that Adam had played any part in her journey. "Actually, she thinks we arranged at the Grymes's barbeque to meet here today. I told her and the coachman that my coming to Raven's Point was a secret. I didn't think my other suitors should know—"

"I understand," Dominick broke in smoothly. "Propriety."

"Yes," she agreed with a small smile, thankful that she didn't have to explain further.

"Don't trouble yourself, my dear. I'll explain the situation to my housekeeper when she returns from the kitchen and then have her fetch your maid from the carriage. Corliss can wait in the hall while we talk in the drawing room." He took her arm. "Now, enough of that. As you can well imagine, I am most anxious to discover the reason behind your sudden visit. I hadn't expected to see you until the horse races tomorrow at the Tates'."

He led her into an adjoining room which was comfortably furnished, although not in the luxury Susanna might have expected. She was beginning to suspect that Dominick must have simple tastes other than his penchant for wearing very fine clothes whenever he visited his fellow planters. His house might be very grand on the outside, but from what she had seen so far, the interior was almost spartan. Or perhaps it was because he had been a widower for fifteen years, with no wife to decorate the rooms properly and no time to attend to such domestic matters himself.

As she sat in a chair with worn brocade upholstery, Susanna decided that whatever the reason, once they were married she would convince him to furnish this house more in the fashion to which his wealth demanded. She imagined they would divide their time between Briarwood and here, and no doubt they would be entertaining a lot, so both homes would have to be equally splendid. She certainly didn't expect that they might sell one of them, especially when there would one day be children to consider who would need homes of their own—

"So, Camille, to what do I owe the honor of your beautiful presence today?" Dominick queried from where he stood leaning against the bare mantelpiece, his ice-blue eyes moving over her appreciatively.

Embarrassed that her thoughts were running on about having children and they weren't even formally engaged yet, Susanna felt her face grow warm. She didn't know how else to broach the matter for which she had come to Raven's Point other than to get right to the heart of it. She cleared her throat delicately, staring at her hands, clasped nervously in her lap.

"Dominick, you've made it clear to me since my welcome ball that you would like to become my . . ." She paused, concerned by how forward she would surely appear to him.

"Your husband. Yes, I want that very much. I've wanted it since I heard the news last winter that you were returning to Virginia. I knew that we were perfectly suited to each other."

Relieved and grateful that he had been the one to say it first, she met his suddenly intent gaze. Now that the subject was opened, there would be no turning back. She rushed on, eager to have done with it.

"I'm so glad to hear you say that because—well . . . I came to Raven's Point to tell you that you've made a very favorable impression upon me during the past few weeks, more so than any other gentleman I've met." Unwittingly she thought of Adam, but she quickly forced his stirring image from her mind. "And I've decided that I would be willing to consider announcing a . . . announcing a—"

"Betrothal?"

"Yes, between you and me." Blushing at the bluntness of her announcement, Susanna was so overwhelmed by the import of what she had just done that she blurted out, "I know these things aren't usually handled like this . . . it's so bold of me, but I didn't know when we would find the time alone to discuss the matter. I've been rushing here and there, hardly ever at home, and there's always been someone to interrupt us—Matthew Grymes, one of the Carter boys, Thomas Dandridge. I thought if I came to you instead—"

Susanna fell abruptly silent when he cupped her chin, his fingers cool and smooth against her skin. There was tension in his touch, but his expression was not one of displeasure. He looked . . . triumphant.

"I can't tell you how happy you've made me today, Camille," he said, his gaze boring into hers. "Your method may be unconventional, but I respect you for being a young woman who knows what she wants and doesn't hesitate to go after it. We are much alike in that respect." Grasping her hands, he drew her up in front of him but made no move to embrace her. "If I may have your consent, I would like to announce our betrothal as soon as possible. I haven't relished the constant competition, nor will I tolerate it now that we've reached an understanding."

"Whatever you like, Dominick," Susanna heard herself say, numbed by how easily her troubling situation was being resolved.

"Tomorrow at the Tates', then."

Her thoughts flashed to Adam. Dear God, what would he say when he heard the news? What would he do?

"Is something wrong, my dear? If that is too soon, we could wait another day or two—"

"No, no, tomorrow will be fine," she said, feeling strangely sick inside, although by rights she should be overjoyed that everything was working out to her satisfaction. She tried to tell herself that she didn't care one whit about Adam's reaction. She had, after all, been waiting for the chance to set him in his place!

"Excellent. I might even visit some of my neighbors this afternoon just to give them the wonderful news. I expect you'll want to leave here within an hour or so if you wish to be home before dark. In fact, I demand that you do. I don't want my future bride on the road after sunset."

"Yes, I hadn't planned to stay very long," Susanna murmured, her thoughts skittering ahead to the hours she must still spend alone with Adam . . . knowing what she did now. She was scarcely aware that Dominick had drawn her closer until she felt his lips, hard and cool, cover hers.

Amazingly, she felt nothing—no desire, no passion—which surprised her considering that this man was soon to become her husband. His embrace was certainly not like those she had shared with Adam.

No, you will not compare them with each other! she berated herself as Dominick gradually deepened the kiss, his arms almost hurting her as he clasped her tightly to his chest. He parted her lips roughly with his tongue, and his breath began to come in short, ragged spurts as he explored her mouth. Still she felt no excitement, although she did her best to return his kiss, as an inexperienced young woman would.

As his embrace grew more demanding, she kept telling herself that in time she would feel with Dominick the way she had in Adam's arms. In time she would know that same weakness in her limbs, that same wildness welling deep inside her, the same incredible craving for more of his touch.

She almost imagined that she was experiencing the slightest response when Dominick abruptly released her and moved away, yet in her heart she knew she hadn't felt a thing. Discomfited because their first kiss had been so unfulfilling, she was relieved when a soft knock came at the door.

"Come in," Dominick said, his thin, self-assured smile easing her mind. Thankfully he hadn't noticed her lack of response during their embrace.

The door opened, revealing a stunningly beautiful black woman dressed simply in a blue linen gown and apron. Tall and willowy, she had the proud bearing of a queen as she carried in a tray holding a pitcher of lemonade and two glasses, yet her features were strangely expressionless. It was almost as if she had gone through a lifetime of keeping her emotions to herself. Only her dark oval eyes gave any clue as to what she was thinking, and they were filled with pity as she glanced at Susanna while setting the tray upon a table.

"I don't usually introduce my servants to guests," said Dominick, "but I want you to meet Cleo, my housekeeper. She's been at Raven's Point since I bought her as a young girl off a slave ship from Barbados. Cleo, this is the future Mrs. Dominick Spencer, Miss Camille Cary. She'll soon be your new mistress."

"Miss Cary," the woman said with a lilting accent, dropping a slow curtsy.

"It's a pleasure, Cleo," Susanna murmured, wondering why the housekeeper was looking at her so oddly.

"I think you'll be pleased with her work," Dominick continued smoothly. "She manages the house slaves well, and she also knows how to read and write. I had her specially tutored after my wife passed away, since I needed someone who could run the household when I'm not here."

Susanna offered Cleo a kind smile. "I'm sure we'll get along just fine—"

"Yes, now if you'll excuse us for a moment," Dominick broke in, not allowing the housekeeper even a chance to respond. He indicated by a slight touch on Cleo's arm that she was to follow him into the hall. The woman visibly stiffened, but her lovely face remained blank, betraying no emotion, and now neither did her ebony eyes. Without a word, she lowered her head and left the room.

Trying not to eavesdrop, Susanna heard Dominick mention Corliss to the housekeeper, then something about having the cook prepare a light dinner. Then they moved further into the hall and she couldn't hear any more. When Dominick returned, Cleo was gone. He poured them both some lemonade and handed Susanna a glass, then laced his drink with whiskey.

"Cleo will let us know when dinner is ready. It shouldn't be long. We'll talk until then."

"Oh, I was hoping I might see the rest of the house and perhaps the grounds," she said, taking a sip of lemonade.

His frown surprised her. "Another time," he said. "There will be plenty of occasions in the weeks ahead to see everything. Today, my dearest Camille, let us simply enjoy each other's company. Come, a toast to our happiness."

Susanna's disappointment eased as he raised his glass. He was right, after all. From now on, she imagined she would be spending a great deal of time at Raven's Point.

"If she wasn't the strangest bird I've ever seen," Corliss commented as the carriage jostled along the bumpy dirt road toward Briarwood.

"Who?" Susanna asked.

"Mr. Spencer's housekeeper, Cleo."

"Now, why would you say such a thing? I didn't find her strange, only a bit quiet. And she is certainly beautiful."

"She's all of that, Miss Camille, but a whole lot more, too. I don't think she's happy at Raven's Point. I've never seen such empty eyes. I got chills just looking at her. After she brought me into the house, she seemed about to tell me something, then another servant walked by and she got this odd, fearful look on her face. She didn't say another word after that. Not another word.''

"I can't imagine why she wouldn't be happy there,'' Susanna replied, remembering the pity she had seen in the woman's eyes. She shrugged, not understanding. "Dominick is the most charming and generous gentleman I've ever met.''

"Well, I hate to be saying this to you, seeing as you're growing so fond of him and all, but nobody I saw in that house, or outside while I was sitting by myself in the coach looked very happy.'' Corliss shook her head, her pretty face unusually solemn. "There were people working everywhere, but no one was laughing or talking like we do at Briarwood to lighten the day. I saw some poor folk heading to the tobo fields who were dressed in the dirtiest, shabbiest clothes I've ever seen. They looked half-starved too.'' She sighed heavily. "I just don't know what to think, Miss Camille. I always heard such fine things about Mr. Spencer.''

Susanna didn't know either. She hadn't seen any of this, and although she didn't believe Corliss was exaggerating, she wondered if perhaps her maid's impressions had been colored by what they had observed earlier in the tobacco fields.

She had attempted to discuss with Dominick her concerns about the use of young children as field laborers and overseers possessing whips, but he had evaded her questions, saying that they would talk about those issues at a later date. Now she wondered if she should have persisted, at least enough to receive some assurance from him that he would be willing to alter such practices once they were wed. She didn't want her workers at Briarwood worrying that their lives might change for the worse once she became Mrs. Dominick Spencer.

"Corliss, I'm sure things weren't as bad as they might have seemed,'' she said. "Now please cheer up. I can't have you returning to Briarwood with such a sad face. Everyone will think you've been to a funeral instead of shopping in Yorktown. Remember our secret?''

The young woman attempted a smile, but from the uncertainty in her eyes, something was obviously still troubling her. ''You know what else I saw while I was waiting in the carriage, Miss Camille?'' she said, then rushed on before Susanna could reply. ''Convicts.''

''What?''

''Convicts, a whole line of them walking to the fields. They were chained to one another at the ankles, and they weren't dressed no better than those other folk.'' Corliss shuddered. ''They were a sorry-looking bunch, all bearded and dirty. I'd heard before that some planters use such wretches in the fields, working them until they drop, but I never saw any before today.''

So now she had something else to discuss with Dominick, Susanna thought with exasperation, holding tightly onto the strap as the carriage swayed and pitched across a particularly bad patch of road. She didn't like that such desperate and hopeless men were being used as slaves, if only for the danger they presented to everyone else, and she would tell Dominick that she wouldn't allow them at Briarwood. Oh, why was this day turning into more of a frustration than the blessed end to her problems that she had envisioned?

''We're almost home, Miss Camille,'' Elias boomed in his deep baritone above the horses' pounding hooves.

''Just in time,'' she breathed to herself, noting with some apprehension that the sun had already set low behind the trees.

The journey had taken longer than she had anticipated. It must be past six o'clock. She wondered if Adam was back from the fields and hoped he wasn't. She wanted to tear up her note. It had been haunting her all day, along with the knowledge that tomorrow he would receive the shock of his life.

''How long will I have to keep quiet about what we did today?'' Corliss asked, leading Susanna to believe that their secret was already chafing her chatterbox of a waiting-maid.

"Not long," she replied, her breath jamming in her throat when she spied Adam standing at the foot of the walkway, his arms crossed over his broad chest. As the carriage lurched around the drive, her heart began to pound. From the dark frown on his handsome face, she could tell he wasn't pleased.

"Oh bloody hell," she muttered before she could catch herself.

"Miss Camille!" Corliss exclaimed.

Ignoring her maid and forcing a bright smile, Susanna prepared herself for Adam's displeasure.

# Chapter 15

Impatiently watching the carriage come to a halt in front of him, Adam tried to tell himself that he wasn't still angry, ever since an hour ago when he'd returned to the house and discovered that Camille had left early that morning. But dammit, he *was* angry! She could have at least informed him yesterday evening of her plans. He had become wracked by worry, too, especially when the sun had begun to set. He had been on his way to the stable to get his horse when the coach had come into view.

"Why, hello, Mr. Thornton," came a soft, familiar voice from the shadowy coach interior.

"Miss Cary," he said, attempting unsuccessfully not to sound irritated. "How was Yorktown?" He swung open the door, his gaze devouring her. God, she was beautiful. It felt like a lifetime since he had last seen her.

"Oh, we had a lovely time," she said lightly, accepting his outstretched hand as she stepped to the ground, her apricot silk gown billowing around her. When she smiled at him in that sweet, secretive manner she had employed since the beginning of their courtship, he felt much of his anger fade. He squeezed her fingers in warm welcome as she tossed over her shoulder, "Didn't we, Corliss?"

"Yes, sir, Mr. Thornton, we sure did," the maid replied, although her subdued expression struck Adam as odd. Usually so cheerful, Corliss seemed unwilling to meet his eyes as he helped her down from the carriage. "I'll go prepare a bath for you, Miss Camille." The maid hurried toward the house, leaving Adam to wonder.

"What's wrong with Corliss? I've never seen her so quiet."

"I imagine she's just tired, like me. We've been on our feet all day . . . well, except for the ride to town and back."

She glanced up at Elias, who to Adam also seemed strangely silent as he surveyed them from his high driver's seat. Usually the man would have at least offered him a grin of hello. "Thank you for driving us, Elias."

"My pleasure, Miss Camille."

"Just a minute," Adam said as the strapping coachman prepared to give the reins a yank and drive away. "Don't you have any packages, Cam—Miss Cary?"

"Oh, no, I didn't buy anything. Corliss and I just browsed through the shops while Elias waited with the carriage."

"Just browsed? For six hours?"

"Why, yes. Shopping doesn't necessarily mean you must buy something, Mr. Thornton," she replied, her teasing tone chasing away the rest of his irritation. As a chuckle welled deep in his throat, Adam glanced sympathetically at Elias. No wonder the man was subdued after waiting all day for two women engaged in what to his mind must have been a total waste of time.

Waving the somber-faced coachman on his way, Adam was sorely tempted to take Camille's arm as they walked to the house, but he suppressed the impulse. He was afraid that if he so much as touched her, he would crush her in his embrace, no matter how many servants might be watching. God help him, he couldn't wait until Friday, when at least at Briarwood he would no longer have to hide his feelings for her!

"I missed you, my love," he said instead, and was pleased when a pretty pink blush suffused her cheeks. "Terribly. Why didn't you tell me last night that you might go into town today? I would have escorted you."

"I . . . I didn't want to bother you with my plans, Adam. I knew you had a lot of work to do, and I decided I would rather that you accompany me to the horse races tomorrow."

He was startled because her expression had suddenly clouded. It almost appeared that her explanation had caused her some pain, though why that might be he couldn't imagine.

"Is something wrong?" he inquired as they stepped into the hall, a footman closing the door behind them.

She gave him a small, reassuring smile. "No, I'm simply tired. It's been a long day."

"Then why don't you go up and rest for a while?" he suggested with a heightened sense of protectiveness. He stopped with her at the foot of the stairs, repressing another powerful urge to sweep her into his arms. "I'll have Prue hold our supper until a little later—say, half past eight. I hope you haven't forgotten that you promised we would dine together tonight."

"No, I haven't forgotten."

When she reached for the banister, Adam glanced behind him and, seeing that the footman had turned his back, he quickly brushed a kiss against her warm, petal-soft cheek.

"Adam!" she breathed in surprise, her foot freezing on the first step as her gaze darted beyond him to the front door.

He shrugged apologetically, his senses racing from the lush jasmine scent of her perfume, which reminded him all too potently of last night. He lowered his voice to a teasing whisper. "You had better go, my love, or I might be tempted to give you another."

As her beautiful sea-green eyes widened, he could tell that she fully believed his playful threat. She gathered her skirts and, without even a backward glance, quickly ascended the stairs. Yet at the top, she threw him the slightest of smiles before disappearing down the hall.

Chuckling to himself and fingering the note in his pocket, which was to his delight signed *Yours always,*

*Camille,* Adam waited until he heard her door close. It was amazing how relaxed he felt when only a short while ago he had been pacing the library in irrational anger, worry, and frustration.

"Love," he said under his breath, shaking his head as he set out to look for Prue. It was heady, unpredictable stuff.

"Delicious supper, Prue," Susanna said, laying down her napkin. She glanced self-consciously at Adam, who was leaning back in his chair and studying her in the candlelight, just as he had been doing since she had sat down with him at the table. "Didn't you think so, Mr. Thornton?"

"Yes, excellent," he replied, his eyes not leaving her face as he took a draught from his crystal goblet. "Thank you, Prue. I wouldn't hesitate to say that yours is the best roast beef and gravy in the county."

"Oh, go on, Mr. Thornton," the stout cook demurred, although she beamed happily. Clearing the plates while a waiter poured more red wine into Susanna's glass, she inquired, "Would you like some dessert, Miss Camille? I've got a nice berry cobbler warm from the oven . . ."

"No, thank you, Prue," Susanna said, rising gracefully from the table. "Supper was so good and filling I don't think I could eat another bite." She looked at Adam, who appeared about to get up himself. "Oh, there's no hurry, Mr. Thornton. If you'd like some dessert, please stay and help yourself. I really should be getting upstairs—"

"Why so early, Miss Cary?" he queried softly, leaving his chair despite her suggestion. "It's only a little past nine. I know you have a very busy day planned tomorrow, but I would be honored if you could spare me another few moments of your time. There's something I'd like to show you in the library."

Realizing that Prue and the waiter were watching their exchange, Susanna used the most formal tone she could muster, although the teasing challenge in his eyes was making her feel flustered. "Very well, Mr. Thornton. A few minutes more. But then I really must retire."

Smiling as he nodded gallantly, he took their wine goblets from the table and followed her from the dining room.

"You play a pretty game, my love," he said in a hushed voice, which Susanna hoped the housemaid coming down the stairs didn't hear.

Not answering him, she walked quickly down the central hall toward the library, her mind racing. Out of the corner of her eye she could see his shadow, so broad and powerful, projected against the wall directly behind her own, which made her feel all the more uncomfortable. She knew he had nothing to show her. It was just a ruse to get her alone. Oh, why hadn't she simply declined and gone to bed?

For that matter, why hadn't she stayed in her room and not come down to supper at all, pleading fatigue? He would have believed her. What had driven her to spend this last evening with him, when she knew he would probably be cursing her name this same time tomorrow? What had compelled her to fulfill her promise to him when she knew what honoring it might cost her?

This evening had been sheer torture, the lies upon lies she was telling him becoming almost impossible to endure. He had asked her endless questions about her day in Yorktown, forcing her to conjure up stories about shops she hadn't visited, bolts of beautiful fabric she hadn't admired, the seamstress with whom she hadn't discussed sewing some new gowns, and the silversmith over whose jewelry and fine tableware she hadn't oohed and aahed.

She had felt guilty and ill at ease from the moment she had discovered him waiting for her at the bottom of the stairs, looking more devastatingly handsome than any man should, and she didn't like it one bit. It didn't make sense that she should feel this way. She didn't love him. Then why should she imagine that she was betraying him? What utter nonsense!

And he certainly didn't love her, Susanna reminded herself for the hundredth time as he moved in front of her to open the library door and then closed it behind them. He simply wanted her for her money. All of his kisses, cajoling, gallantry, seeming patience and understanding, and his unwanted caresses had been directed toward that end.

Her stays must have been laced too tightly the night of her welcome ball and she'd been suffering from lack of air to think he might be falling in love with her. Not that it would make a difference anyway. She meant nothing to him. Nothing. He was a coldhearted, mercenary bastard—

"Your wine," he said, his husky voice startling her.

She took the goblet, murmuring "Thank you" as he went about the room lighting candles. Feeling suddenly as if she needed extra fortification just to survive the next moments, she raised the glass to her lips and drank deeply, the fragrant red liquid warming her throat. Then, thinking what the hell, she drained the goblet.

"Would you like mine, too?"

Embarrassed, she set down the empty glass and shook her head. To her added discomfort, the wine only heightened the effect of his smile upon her. She felt warmed by it all the way to her toes.

"You've been tense all night, my love," he said, coming to stand in front of her. He reached out to stroke her hair. "Are you sure there isn't something wrong? In fact, you've been like this since you got back from Yorktown."

"No, no, I'm fine," she insisted, fixing her gaze upon the sensual curve of his lips so that he couldn't read the lie in her eyes. She started slightly when he gently touched her cheek, but she didn't look up. She couldn't help thinking that they hadn't been so close together since . . .

"But you're so pale, Camille. That concerns me. Perhaps you've been doing too much lately—too many parties, too many outings. If you'd like, I could send a message to the Tates and tell them you won't be able to make it tomor—''

''No!'' she cried. When his deep brown eyes darkened, she struggled to get a tight grip on her emotions. If she continued like this, he would surely begin to suspect that something was amiss. ''No,'' she repeated softly. ''I want to see the races. I know I've accepted a lot of invitations lately . . . but after tomorrow, I promise I'll stay home and rest.'' She willed herself to smile and ask lightly, ''Would that please you?''

To her relief his expression relaxed. ''And have you all to myself for a while? How could it not please me?''

He appeared about to kiss her then, and not thinking her frazzled, increasingly wine-befuddled wits could bear it, she deftly sidestepped him and added flirtatiously, ''You said you had something to show me, Adam. What is it? A gift, perhaps?''

He turned, following her feigned search about the library as she peeked beneath brocade pillows and behind bric-a-brac. ''No, my love, I have no gift,'' he said with sincere apology. ''I only wanted to get you alone so we might talk.''

''Talk? About what?''

''Last night.''

Susanna stopped, her cheeks firing hotly, cursing the wine she had drank so quickly as she swayed just a little.

''Perhaps you might want to sit down,'' he suggested with a hint of amusement.

She obliged him, sinking gratefully into a comfortable stuffed chair he shoved behind her. As he leaned against the massive mahogany desk that dominated the room, she waited for him to speak. She certainly wasn't going to initiate this conversation, and she would do her best to keep it as short as possible. She began to grow apprehensive when his expression sobered, his eyes searching her face. He seemed almost tense.

''I want you to tell me about your nightmare, Camille.''

"My nightmare?" She was stunned yet relieved that he hadn't brought up what had happened after he woke her from her bad dream.

"Yes. You said some names last night . . . Keefer Dunn, Daniel. Were they people you met aboard the *Charming Nancy?* Or were they acquaintances from Fairford?"

Susanna almost choked, and she wondered if her face had gone chalk-white. Never in a thousand years would she have expected to hear those names mentioned by anyone in the same breath, and certainly not by Adam. If she had said them last night during her nightmare, God only knew what else she had given away about herself.

"You screamed out that this Keefer Dunn was hurting you, beating you," he prodded gently, although his voice was grim. "Did someone hurt you aboard that ship or in England? You must tell me, for if so, I swear those men will be punished."

Understanding dawned upon Susanna, and she breathed a sigh of relief. Thank God she hadn't obviously implicated herself in some way. He didn't seem to have any idea how these people were connected to her real identity, and she would do everything in her power to see that he never did.

"Camille, answer me."

"No, Adam, no one hurt me," she finally replied, her voice sounding shaky to her ears. "I never knew those men."

"But your nightmare, my love—it sounded so vivid. Almost as if you were living it. You were calling on your papa—"

"It wasn't me," she blurted out, perhaps a bit too hastily. When he frowned, she added, "It was a story told me years ago by my waiting-maid . . . the one who died from the fever before we reached Virginia."

"Susanna Guthrie?" he prompted. "Your father never told me much about her, just her name."

"Yes," she replied, unsettled to hear her true name on his lips.

"Go on, I'm listening."

"I've . . . I've had nightmares about that story ever since. I don't know why, maybe because it was so horrible."

"What story?"

Susanna drew a deep breath, realizing she was about to skirt dangerously close to the truth.

"My waiting-maid had a terrible, wretched childhood . . . Aunt Melicent and I saved her from London's slums, you know. Her father, Daniel Guthrie, used to beat her mercilessly. My aunt told me she had the most awful bruises and lash marks upon her skin when we found her." She licked her lips as awful memories flooded her mind, unnerving sights and putrid smells. "One day, Susanna finally admitted to me what had happened on the night she was almost run over by our carriage. Her father sold her to a man named Keefer Dunn." She met Adam's eyes. "She was only twelve, Adam. An innocent young girl. Her father wanted her to . . . to . . ."

"I understand now, Camille," he broke in gently, kneeling in front of her and taking her shaking hands in his large, warm ones. "You don't have to tell me any more if you don't want to."

"She ran away," Susanna continued numbly, unable to stop, "and her father tried to catch her. She ran into the street . . . there was a carriage, my—my Aunt Melicent's carriage. Keefer Dunn pushed her out of the way, rolling with her to the side of the road, but her father was crushed beneath the wheels. That—that gruesome man would have . . . oh, Adam, Keefer Dunn would have taken her with him if my aunt hadn't stopped the carriage . . ."

Tears burning her eyes, Susanna felt his arms go around her as he pulled her close.

"Shhh, love. No wonder you have nightmares," he said soothingly, then his voice fell to a vehement whisper. "God damn to hell's fire all the bastards like that in the world. Damn them. Damn them all!"

A weighty silence fell between them as Susanna

gradually regained her composure, the images that had suddenly become so vividly real retreating once more to a small, locked corner of her mind. Soon she was aware only of the warmth of Adam's embrace and the strong, steady beat of his heart against her breast.

"I'll help you chase those nightmares away, my love," he finally said as he drew back to stare deeply into her eyes. As he cradled her face in his hands, his voice throbbed with fervent intensity. "I would die before I let anything or anyone hurt you. I love you, Camille. Do you hear me? I love you."

Susanna's own heartbeat seemed to stop as she regarded him, dumbstruck. A stirring memory of sweet contentment, a protective embrace, a husky whisper flashed through her mind, and stark realization gripped her.

Last night . . . those words . . . they hadn't been a dream. Adam must have said them . . . he must have said them!

She started when she felt his lips, warm and tender, shape hers in the sweetest kiss she had ever known. For a long, breathless moment she gave back to him what he was giving her, surrendering to the wonder of his mouth upon hers, their breath melding as one. Then something snapped inside her. She was sure it was her heart breaking.

For even if he loved her, and she was beginning to believe that he did, in spite of everything her better judgment was telling her, he was the wrong man.

Even if she loved him, and she knew now that she did, their situation had not changed . . . *could* not change. Adam Thornton was a hired man, a man who owned nothing, a man who would never be what Lady Redmayne and Camille had intended as the master of Briarwood. No matter what lay in Susanna's heart, she could not betray her duty to them. She had sworn to marry wisely! Tomorrow she would become betrothed to the right man, a gentleman who would help her fulfill Camille's dying wish. A man who possessed wealth and prominence. A man she did not love . . .

Adam rose suddenly and, drawing her with him, embraced her for endless moments before pulling away to search her face.

"Are you happy that we're going to be wed, Camille?" he asked huskily, his eyes reflecting the same poignant vulnerability she had seen on the night of her welcome ball. "You accepted our courtship so readily, I know in part to honor your father's wishes, but I believe that you truly care . . . about us, about me. Are you happy, my love?"

Dying inside, Susanna opened her mouth to lie once again when approaching footsteps sounded upon the parquet floor in the entrance hall. Before Adam could stop her, she broke away form him, knowing that he would never again hold her so closely, or kiss her, or say those three words to her. For if he loved her now, tomorrow he would surely hate her. She would be betrothed to another man.

The footsteps stopped and when a soft knock came at the door, she hastened to open it.

"Oh! Forgive me, Miss Camille," Ertha exclaimed in surprise, stepping back and abruptly pulling her right arm behind her back, as if to conceal something. Her wide-eyed gaze skipped to Adam and then back again to Susanna. "I came to talk to Mr. Thornton. Prue told me I'd find him here, but I thought you had already retired for the night. Prue said she heard that you were only going to be in the library for a few moments—"

"I was just leaving, Ertha," Susanna broke in, wondering at the housekeeper's strange behavior. Why was she studying her face so intently, as if seeing her for the first time?

"You don't have to go, Miss Cary," she heard Adam say firmly behind her. "I'd like it very much if we continued our business discussion. I'm sure whatever Ertha has to say can wait until morning."

"Oh, yes, of course it can wait," the housekeeper blurted, looking extremely uncomfortable. "I'm sorry I interrupted you, Miss Camille. Tomorrow morning will be fine . . ."

"That won't be necessary," she insisted, brushing past her into the hall. "I have to rise early if I'm going to be ready by the time Matthew and Celeste Grymes arrive."

As Ertha sharply wheeled around so that her back was to the paneled wall, her arm still twisted behind her, Susanna wondered again what was the matter with the woman. Then her desire to flee Adam's compelling presence overcame her. Bidding them both a hasty good night, she escaped up the stairs.

Adam closed the door to the library, his gaze narrowed as he studied the silent housekeeper. Damn, if he and Camille weren't forever being interrupted in this house!

He moved to the front of the desk, attempting not to sound too irritated. He knew the housekeeper had meant no harm. "All right, Ertha, what did you want to speak to me about?"

"Well, Mr. Thornton, I didn't know if I should bring this to your attention. It might not mean a thing . . ."

"Bring what to my attention?" he demanded, watching as she drew what looked to be a rolled piece of parchment from behind her back.

"This."

As she handed him the cylinder, he saw that it wasn't parchment at all but stiff, fine-grained canvas such as artists used for oil paintings.

"It's a portrait, Mr. Thornton," Ertha added in a nervous rush. "I found it in Miss Camille's closet when I went up there yesterday to put away the things she bought in Yorktown. I was setting her new hat up on the shelf when another hatbox fell to the floor. A straw bonnet tumbled out and along with it came this canvas. I can't say for sure, but I think this painting was hidden beneath a false bottom."

Adam carefully unrolled the canvas, his breath catching as the portrait of a pretty, emerald-eyed woman was revealed.

For a fleeting instant he thought it was Camille, but

on a second look, he doubted his initial judgment. The features were similar but not remarkably so. The main resemblance lay in the color of the eyes and in the hair, which was honey-blonde and worn in the same style, swept back from the forehead and tumbling in ringlets over the woman's shoulders and down her back. Then he wondered if it might indeed be a portrait of Camille, but executed by an artist who had failed to accurately capture her features.

"I don't understand, Ertha. It looks to be Miss Cary, not the best portrait of her, I agree, but it is her."

"That's what I thought, but not anymore. Too many things are different," the housekeeper said, appearing confused herself. "This woman's expression is calm and peaceful, but Miss Camille's is always so lively, even on that first day when she came to the house. And look how this woman holds her hands, so restful-like. I noticed early on that Miss Camille doesn't seem to like to sit still much. Look at the tilt of this woman's chin and that gentle smile. Everything's different, I tell you. Don't you see it, Mr. Thornton?"

"Yes, I suppose I do, but I still don't understand what you're trying to say—"

"This is my baby! I know it! I remember her as clear as the day she left for England. My little Camille was always a quiet, reserved child, and this portrait shows that the years hadn't changed her." Ertha sighed with exasperation, as if knowing she was making little sense. "I didn't realize how completely different Miss Camille was until I saw this picture."

"Ertha . . ." Adam began, his head beginning to hurt. What the hell kind of nonsense was she uttering?

"Please hear me out, Mr. Thornton," she insisted, her deeply lined face anxious. "I don't know what all of this means and, God knows I could be wrong, but I believe there's something strange afoot here at Briarwood. Something in my bones is telling me that the young lady upstairs is not the rightful Miss Camille Cary."

Now Adam's head was actually pounding. He wondered if the frantic preparations for Camille's welcome ball had pushed the housekeeper into hysteria.

"You think I'm crazy, don't you?"

"Not crazy, Ertha. Just overtired." Adam chose his next words carefully. He didn't want to offend her. He knew there wasn't a more faithful servant at Briarwood than this woman.

"We've had a lot of upheaval here during the past months," he continued. "Mr. Cary's death and then Miss Cary's arrival home. I'm not saying you're imagining things, Ertha. You've a right to your feelings. But this idea of yours is impossible. The portrait is a bad one, it's as simple as that. I suggest you have the other maids take on some of your duties for a few weeks so you can get some extra rest."

The housekeeper heaved another sigh, suddenly looking much older than her years as she shrugged wearily. "Lord help me, maybe I am overtired, saying such foolish things," she muttered almost to herself, then she met Adam's eyes. "I'm sorry, Mr. Thornton. Must be my age finally catching up with me." She glanced at the partially rolled canvas in his hands. "I'll put the painting back in the bottom of that hatbox tomorrow morning after you both leave for the Tates'. If Miss Camille wants it there, then it must be for some good reason."

"Leave it in here for the night," Adam suggested gently. "There's no sense in taking it all the way to your cabin and then bringing it back again." He nodded at the desk. "I'll put it in the top left-hand drawer."

"As you say, Mr. Thornton. I'm sorry to have troubled you."

As Ertha left the library, Adam sat down behind the desk and, shaking his head over everything he had just heard, he unrolled the painting again.

After studying it carefully, he came to the same conclusion. Whatever artist had done the work certainly didn't deserve the money he must have been paid for it. Camille's true likeness hadn't been captured at all. He turned over the canvas, looking for the name of the incompetent portraitist since none was visible on the painting itself.

His heart lurched painfully in his chest when he saw an inscription in the lower right corner, written in a skillful, feminine hand. It wasn't the message itself that had caught him by surprise, making him feel a little sick inside. It simply read *To my dearest father, a gift with all my love.*

He traced his finger in disbelief over the closing, *Your beloved daughter, Camille,* then quickly pulled from his coat pocket the note Camille had left for him that morning. Laying the paper next to the inscription, he felt an eerie intuition in the pit of his stomach.

The handwriting was similar, neat and delicate, almost as if taught by the same teacher. But the two signatures were different, one smoothly executed while the other appeared awkward beside it.

Something told him that they could not have been written by the same hand.

# Chapter 16

~~~~~~~~~

**"H**ere's the apple cider you wanted, Miss Cary."

Susanna smiled brightly as Matthew Grymes handed her the brimming cup, although inside she was a bundle of raw nerves. Scarcely listening as he joined with the other young men seated around her in animated conversation about the races that would begin shortly, she glanced out over the crowded side lawn of the Tates' Georgian mansion.

Where was Dominick? she wondered with growing agitation. It had taken the Grymes's carriage only an hour and a half to reach this plantation, situated on the James River a few miles south of Williamsburg. She knew Dominick had a greater distance to travel from his home, but he had said he was also planning to leave at nine o'clock, which should have ensured his arrival by now. It was almost noon.

Could it be that some unexpected business at Raven's Point had prevented him from leaving on time? Maybe he wasn't going to make it at all. That would mean their betrothal announcement must wait until another day. Oh, bloody hell, she hoped not!

She couldn't bear lying again to Adam. Not when things had taken such a drastic and impossible turn between them. His words of love haunted her memory. No, she couldn't bear another night listening to him say such things to her. She just couldn't!

Glimpsing Adam standing beside Celeste not far from

the oval racetrack that lay just beyond the lawn, Susanna felt an incredible rush of warmth when she noticed that he was watching her, and she quickly looked away. Her hand trembled as she lifted the cup to her mouth, and she hardly tasted the cider, knowing his eyes were still upon her. It seemed he was always looking at her, no matter where he was or with whom. Yet today there was a difference in the way he regarded her, although she couldn't define it.

He had been strangely silent during the journey this morning, no matter how Celeste had tried to coax him into joining their conversation. He had scarcely spared a glance for the clinging young woman, keeping his gaze fixed upon either Susanna's face, studying her as if he might somehow divine what she was thinking, or out the carriage window.

At times she even had the oddest sensation that he was angry with her. She imagined he must simply be frustrated with their continuing charade and Celeste's constant attention. Well, thank God, much of her deception would soon be over. That is, if Dominick ever arrived—

"You're so quiet today, Miss Cary," the ever-present Thomas Dandridge said to her. "Is it too warm for you? We could move further into the shade—"

"No, no, it's lovely here," she said, flashing the lanky young man a brilliant smile. Deciding that it would help to keep her mind off Dominick's absence if she focused on her suitors' conversation, she asked him flirtatiously, "Are you going to make any wagers on the first race, Thomas? Perhaps one in my honor?"

"I will, Miss Cary!" Matthew interjected eagerly before Thomas could respond. "I'm going to place a bet for you on each and every race. I'm certain you'll bring me good luck!"

"Well, how do you gentlemen know which horse is likely to win?" she queried, knowing such a question would prompt a lively and hopefully diverting discussion.

As her suitors joined in debating the merits of the

Tidewater's finest horseflesh, each seeking to impress her with their knowledge, Susanna was not surprised to find that she was once more hardly listening to them. Her frustration mounting, she searched the crowd for any sign of Dominick, yet time and again, her gaze strayed back to Adam.

"Isn't it amazing how our shy Camille has blossomed into such a popular belle?" Celeste commented, fluttering her silk fan in front of her generously exposed bosom. "I suppose I always knew it was possible with plenty of outings and masculine attention, and plenty of Virginia sunshine. I just didn't expect it to happen so quickly."

"Yes, amazing," Adam replied dryly, his gut tightening as several more young gentlemen joined the laughing group seated beneath the ancient willow that graced the center of the lawn.

Camille sat at its heart, looking like a beautiful rose of summer in her shell-pink satin gown . . . that is, if she was indeed his Camille. The seeds of doubt had been sown and he couldn't shake them, no matter how many times he had told himself since last night that there must be a reasonable explanation for the difference in signatures on the note and the portrait.

Camille could have written her letter to him in such a hurry that she had signed her name sloppily. Or months ago, before she had learned that her father had been killed, she had been extra careful writing the inscription on the back of the painting for fear of damaging it. That explanation could account for the signature's almost exaggerated neatness. Yet neither rationale rang true to him, and combined with Ertha's intuitive misgivings and the decided facial differences in the portrait, he was beginning to believe—though, God help him, he didn't want to!—that the woman he loved so passionately, the woman he planned to marry, might be a very clever impostor.

"Matthew is certainly in his element today," Celeste added, hugging Adam's arm possessively. "Why, just look at him. He's grinning from ear to ear. He knows he has a much fairer chance around Camille when Dominick Spencer isn't hovering close by."

Adam shot a glance around the bustling lawn and then beyond it to the racetrack, glad to see that the bastard hadn't yet shown his face. The anger he felt at this unsettling turn of events was already boiling like a tempest inside him; he didn't need Dominick adding fuel to the flames. Yet he knew the planter would show up at some point, and he would do well to prepare himself for it. Dominick never missed a horse race. He was drawn to them like a tick to a hound.

"Oh, look, there's Annie Custis! I haven't seen her for the longest time." Celeste smiled up at him, batting her thick russet lashes. "Would you mind getting me a glass of punch while I go and talk to her? I've heard she's absolutely pea-green with envy that Thomas Dandridge hasn't paid her one visit since Camille's ball. I want to reassure her that she has nothing to worry about, not with my brother paying such steady court. I won't be long, Adam dear."

Her endearment grating on his already taut nerves, Adam was grateful when she released his arm and hurried away. Giving her no more thought, he decided this would be the longest trip to the refreshment table he had ever taken. In fact, he probably wouldn't come back.

Camille's lighthearted laughter carried to him as he deliberately skirted the willow tree, and hot, unreasoning jealousy melded with his barely restrained anger.

It wasn't the first time he had wondered during the past weeks, when she was surrounded by her many suitors, if she might be innocently toying with him, teasing him a little as part of their ruse. Yet because he knew they would soon be announcing their betrothal, it had never bothered him except when Dominick Spencer was around.

Now fearing what he did, her actions were suddenly cast in a much darker and wholly unsettling light. He had never felt so wretchedly jealous before. As her voice, raised in a spirited remark, drifted to him, it was all he could do not to yank her from that admiring crowd and demand an explanation for the portrait and the signatures.

Adam willed himself to keep moving toward the refreshment tables, reminding himself of his decision not to confront her until tonight, when they would have time alone to fully discuss the matter. Right now, he could use a drink. Several. Maybe a whole bottle. Two bottles! Anything to kill the pain deep inside him.

"Brandy," he muttered to the bewigged waiter behind the table. Giving the pale amber liquid a brief swirl, he threw back his head and drained the snifter, grimacing as the liquor burned a searing path down his throat. He set the empty glass on the table with a thunk. "Another."

As he lifted the refilled snifter to his mouth, he noticed standing not far from him an ebony-haired young woman dressed in a waiting-maid's gown and apron who looked vaguely familiar. She had obviously been sent to the table for refreshments, for she held two full cups of apple cider. As he tried to place her, she must have felt him staring for she glanced over at him. A wide smile lit her pretty face, her dark eyes dancing with instant recognition.

"Why, yer the fine gentl'man who saved me from takin' a tumble when I come off the *Charmin' Nancy!*" she blurted, setting down the cups so abruptly that cider sloshed onto the white tablecloth. Paying no heed, she rushed over to him. "Don't ye remember me? I'm Polly! Polly Blake."

Recalling the brief incident between himself and the maid—quite a contrived one, he thought wryly—Adam bowed his head in a gallant manner usually reserved for ladies of the gentry. "Of course. Miss Blake. What brings you here to the Tates'?"

"I've come to see the races same as ye, I s'pect," she said, appearing flattered by his courtesy. "Well, that is, with me mistress." She gestured to a fat yet elegantly dressed woman seated at a distant table with a few other dowagers of the Tidewater. "We live in Williamsburg, if y' recall, but me mistress is a second cousin of Mrs. Tate's. They invited us out for the day." She paused, her gaze roaming brazenly over him. "My, y' sure are a handsome one, Mr. . . . uh . . . come to think of it, I don't know yer name."

"Adam Thornton."

"Adam Thornton," she repeated, rolling it on her tongue. "Aye, it suits ye. A fine, strong name for a fine, strong-looking man." Her expression became hopeful, her eyes flirtatious beneath long charcoal lashes as she asked him, "Have ye come here alone, Mr. Thornton?"

"Actually, no," he began, but she cut him off before he could continue, her tone disappointed.

"I should have guessed." Shrugging her slim shoulders, Polly glanced around the lawn. "Which beauty did ye accompany, then? Lord knows, there are enough of 'em here."

Adam made no mention of Celeste, simply inclining his head toward the weeping willow. "That one there, sitting among those gentlemen." His throat tightened around his next words. "Miss Camille Cary."

"Oh, aye, the one y' left me for to follow after on the dock. I remember her from the *Charmin' Nancy*. I spotted that pretty gold hair as soon as I got here. I should have known ye two would be t'gether."

Adam tensed, lowering his half-empty snifter. "You knew Miss Cary?"

"No, just who she was. Me mistress and I never had a chance to meet her. Nobody did, far as I know, 'cept maybe the captain. I saw her comin' aboard ship with him in Bristol, but she had her head down real timid-like. She was a shy bird, hidin' in her cabin with her waitin'-maid from the very start of the voyage. Which was just as well, I s'pose, what with the killin' fever and all. After a few weeks into the trip, we all hid in our cabins, fearin' for our lives." Polly exhaled heavily as uproarious laughter sounded from the group beneath the willow. "That Miss Cary sure has changed since comin' to Virginia. She doesn't look to me like a shy bird now."

"She isn't," Adam muttered, taking a long sip of brandy. "Not anymore."

As silence fell between them, he tried to imagine what might have happened aboard that plagued ship to bring about such an incredible deception.

He already knew that Camille's waiting-maid had caught the typhus fever and died. What if the real Camille Cary had also perished? What if that beautiful young woman sitting beneath the tree, the woman with whom he had fallen in love, was really some extremely clever wench who had seen a golden opportunity and seized it. Yet how? It all seemed so improbable.

Surely the ship's records would have noted both deaths, Camille's and her maid's, so how could anyone have thought they would get by with such a masquerade? And this woman would have had to be acquainted with Camille to have known so much about her. Yet Polly had just said no one ever saw Camille, let alone talked with her, except for her waiting-maid. Dammit, what in blazes was going on? Could it be that the signatures and the portrait were both innocent flukes, that he was torturing himself over nothing?

Adam cursed the sad fact that Captain Keyes had also perished. That old salt would have easily solved this mystery. He had known Camille since she was a child, had gone to England to fetch her home. If only he hadn't died, none of this would be happening—

"Doesn't it make y' jealous, Mr. Thornton, her sittin' there like a princess surrounded by all those fine young gentl'men?" Polly asked, her query breaking into his tormented thoughts.

"Yes," he answered tersely, thinking there was no harm in revealing that much to this young woman. "Very much."

"I can see why. She's sure a pretty thing, and it's funny how she looks kind of like her poor waitin'-maid that died no more than a week before we landed in Yorktown. They both had that same honey hair."

Adam froze, his gaze riveted on the woman in the shell-pink gown, but he said nothing as Polly chattered on.

"I was on deck when they buried the girl, ye know. So was Miss Cary, but she had on a wide-brimmed hat to cover her face. She was weepin' real hard, which made me think the two of them must have been friends. It happens that way sometimes between a lady and her maid," Polly sighed, darting a sidelong glance at her mistress. "The lucky ones, that is. Hmmm . . . Now, what was her name? Sally . . . Sarah . . . Susan . . ."

"Susanna," he said, feeling numb.

"Aye, that was it. I s'pose Miss Cary must have told ye."

Adam didn't answer, asking instead, "Did you know her . . . this Susanna?"

"No, we never talked, and I hardly saw her. She kept pretty much to herself, too. But that long gold hair of hers was hard to miss, and she had green eyes. Does yer Miss Cary have green eyes?"

"Yes," he murmured, the startling pieces falling one by one into place.

"Imagine that. I s'pose if I'd ever seen them side by side and full in the face, they could have passed as sisters. What a shame that poor girl caught the fever and died."

Yes, what a pity, Adam thought, barely able to swallow the last of his brandy for the cold fury gripping him.

What a pity the real Camille Cary, the woman he would have married, lay moldering in a deep, watery grave while her lying, scheming, opportunistic strumpet of a waiting-maid was having the time of her life! No wonder she hadn't even faintly recognized Ertha when she had first arrived at Briarwood, or known the whereabouts of the Cary graveyard, or how to dance! Yet this woman was planning to marry him . . . they would be announcing their betrothal next week—

Cruel intuition shot through him as he heard her vivacious laughter join that of her admirers', and he wondered if her many pretty promises were also part of her cunning deception. God help her, if he had been played the fool . . .

"Oh, no, me mistress is wavin' to me," Polly said. "I've got to run. She'll give me a tongue-lashin' for sure if I don't bring her some cider, and quick." Placing her small hand boldly on his arm, she gave him a meaningful smile. "It's been wonderful to see y' again, Mr. Thornton. If things don't work out between ye and Miss Cary, I'd be more than willin' to help ye forget her. She may not appreciate a fine man like ye, but I surely would. Just remember, y' can find me in Williamsburg."

She grabbed her two cups of cider and hastened away just as Celeste reached his side.

"Who was that little chit?" she asked petulantly, her jealous gaze following Polly's shapely form.

"No one," Adam muttered, tensing as Celeste turned her face to him, her blue eyes flashing.

"Well, for being no one, you certainly were having a fine little talk with her. Here I sent you to fetch me a glass of punch and when I turn around, I see this . . . this common wench fawning all over you. You can imagine how embarrassing it was to me in front of Annie Custis—"

"Drop it, Celeste," he said, in no mood for her babble. He had had enough of playing games, and this one he was going to end. But before he had a chance to say anything, she wound her arm through his and smiled apologetically in a decided effort to placate him.

"Oh, Adam, let's not quarrel," she cooed. "If you say that girl was nobody special, then I believe you." She squeezed his arm, her expression becoming almost conspiratorial. "Besides, I have the most startling news to tell you, although poor Matthew isn't going to be very happy about it. But I suppose all is fair in love—"

"What news?" he queried, his breath snagging in his chest when Celeste glanced toward the willow and then back at him.

"It's a secret yet, Adam, so you have to promise not to tell anyone. The announcement won't be made until Dominick Spencer arrives." When she paused, clearly waiting for him to swear his silence, he considered grabbing her throat and throttling the news out of her. But her eagerness got the better of her as she blurted in a loud whisper, "Camille is going to marry Dominick! It's all been arranged."

Adam was so stunned that he stared at her as if she had just uttered pure gibberish. "What are you talking about?" he finally managed, his voice sounding hoarse.

"Annie Custis told me all about it. You know her family and Dominick are neighbors, don't you? Well, apparently he came by their house last evening to share his good news. It seems Camille spent a good part of yesterday with him at Raven's Point, and they decided to announce the betrothal here at the Tates' before the races get started." Celeste's gaze skimmed the lawn. "Except I don't see him yet . . . Adam! Where are you going? Adam!"

He scarcely heard her cries for the blood pounding in his brain, his narrowed gaze focused upon the pastel splotch of shell pink that was scarcely visible now for the young men blocking it from his view. He strode across the lawn, his every step fueled by emotions that twisted in his gut, his rage at her cruel deception overpowered by an agonizing sense of betrayal.

Why had she done this to him? Why? All he could think of was how he had held her in his arms last night, swearing his love to her, while she must have been laughing inside at him . . . laughing . . . laughing . . .

"Move! Get out of my way," he demanded, shoving aside several young men before coming face-to-face with her. Looking into her wide, questioning eyes, a sparkling green as beautiful as a sunlit sea, he felt such a stab of anguish that he almost doubled over.

"Adam—Mr. Thornton, is something wrong?"

"There's been a fire . . . a fire at Briarwood. I just received word."

As a collective gasp went up from the assembled gentlemen, she jumped up from her chair, her lovely, treacherous face gone white.

"Dear God, no! What are we going to do?"

Adam grabbed her arm and began to pull her through the crowd. "We've got to go. We've got to get there . . ." He glanced over his shoulder at Matthew. "We'll take your carriage, Grymes, but I'll send it back to you as soon as we get to Briarwood."

"All—all right, Mr. Thornton."

"Yes, yes, of course!" she agreed, hastening beside him. "Oh, this is terrible!"

"Yes, it is," he said, knowing his grip was cruelly tight upon her arm.

"Is there anything we can do?" Thomas Dandridge called out, easily catching up to them on his long legs while the other gentlemen were still gathered in shock beneath the willow. "We could ride along—"

"No, that won't be necessary," Adam said, keeping up their frantic pace as they rounded the corner of the house to the driveway, which was lined with carriages. "The fire's been put out, but Miss Cary should be there. Some of her servants were injured—"

"Oh, Adam, no!" she cried. "Who?"

"We'll talk about it on the way. Just get in," he ordered, his loud voice jarring awake the Grymes's coachman, who had apparently been napping inside the carriage. As Adam swung open the door, the sheepish man jumped down with a mumbled apology and scrambled into the driver's seat while she was lifted up into the coach.

"Let's hurry then, Adam. Oh, please, let's hurry!"

"We will," he replied grimly. He wheeled on Thomas, who stood helplessly nearby, while some of the other gentlemen were now rushing around the house toward them, Matthew in the lead and, not surprisingly, an openmouthed Celeste bringing up the rear.

"Tell everyone what I told you, Dandridge. The situation is under control, the fire is out. There's no need for anyone to leave the races. Do you understand?"

"Yes, Mr. Thornton. I'll tell them."

"Good. Please give our regrets to the Tates." He glanced in the shadowed interior of the carriage to find the object of his wrath sitting at the edge of the seat, her face stricken, then added, "And give Miss Cary's regrets to Mr. Dominick Spencer. I believe she might have been expecting him today." Hearing her startled gasp, Adam shouted to the driver as he climbed into the coach and slammed the door shut. "Briarwood! With all haste!"

The coach jolted into motion and he was almost thrown against her, but he regained his balance and took the opposite seat, breathing hard.

"Wh-what did you mean . . . that I was expecting Mr. Spencer?" she asked in alarm.

"Only a rumor, really," he said tightly, even in his fury aware of how truly beautiful she was in her exquisite gown.

"Rumor?"

"Yes, something about a betrothal announcement."

She blanched, and he could see in her strained expression her effort to maintain control. Yet her gaze held more than a glimmer of fear, and he knew then that she suspected he had discovered the truth.

"You . . . you are mistaken, Adam. We're going to announce *our* engagement next Saturday at Briarwood."

"Funny. The rumor I heard was that you and Dominick Spencer were going to announce your plans to marry today. Oh, yes, and something about you spending several hours with him yesterday at Raven's Point to make the arrangements—"

"That's a lie!" she cried. "Surely you don't believe it, Adam. Who told you? Celeste? She *would* fabricate something so absurd."

"Perhaps Elias and Corliss can enlighten us further when we arrive home," he said, knowing he was tormenting her and thinking how much she deserved every bit of it, and more. "No wonder they seemed so unusually quiet after your long day of *shopping* in Yorktown. It's unpleasant when one is forced to lie for another. Of course, you know all about lying, don't you? You seem to be a master of it.''

"Adam, I can explain,'' she said, tears swimming in her eyes. "I can explain!''

"Say what you will, but don't cry for me again,'' he said bitterly, hardening his heart against her. "I promise you, such a ploy will not work with me this time.''

"I—I went to his house to return the emerald necklace, that's all. You must believe me! I knew how much you wanted me to be rid of his gifts, and I thought that that would please you. I just didn't know how to tell you that I had gone there. I know you don't like him.''

"No, I don't like him,'' Adam agreed, "and I might have believed your pretty story if you had told it to me yesterday. But I'll never believe anything you say again . . . Susanna Guthrie.''

Her mouth fell open in stunned surprise. She remained silent for a long time, the carriage wheels rumbling and hooves thundering along the road the only sounds around them. Then she asked him in a small, monotone voice which he barely heard above the din, "Why did you call me that? I'm Camille. Camille Cary.''

"That's the last lie I'll grant you, Susanna. Ever. Now, I'm going to have the driver stop this carriage on a side road off the main thoroughfare and we're going to get out and take a walk. I want to hear every single word you have to tell me, and God help you, woman, it had better be the truth! If not, there's a prison nearby in Williamsburg that would welcome a lying impostor like you with open arms.''

Again she paused, clearly in shock, only to ask after another few interminable moments, "What . . . what of the fire? The servants who were injured?''

"I lied,'' he said, then, in shock himself, he began to laugh. The ragged sound held only raw pain.

# Chapter 17

Susanna hurried with a grimly silent Adam past a densely wooded bend in the road, the Grymes's waiting carriage and the bewildered coachman vanishing from view.

She scarcely noticed the prickly brambles snagging her silk gown, or the birds overhead twittering nervously at their sudden appearance. Nor did she feel the warmth of the early-afternoon sun, which was intense despite the dappled shade and light breeze. All she knew was that her careful deception had suddenly been revealed and she was going to pay.

She had no idea what was to become of her. Would Adam turn her over to the county constable in Williamsburg, as he had threatened in the coach? What would they do to her when they determined her crime? Lock her in the pillory where she would be pelted with sticks, stones, and rotten eggs? Whip her at the post until her back was striped and bleeding? Hang her?

"This is far enough," Adam said, his harsh voice causing her to flinch as he caught her arm and abruptly stopped her. "The coachman can't hear us this far away." His expression was deadly serious, although his arresting brown eyes were filled with torment. "Camille died aboard the *Charming Nancy*, didn't she, Susanna?"

How strange it was not to be addressed as Camille, she thought, remaining dazedly mute. Yet it was almost a relief to be herself again. She had always known deep in her heart that her masquerade had only a slim chance

226

of succeeding, that someone might discover she was an impostor. She had done her best to fulfill her promise to Camille . . . but then again, had she?

How had she given herself away? Everything had been going so perfectly up until this morning, when she had sensed that something was bothering him. Had he known her real identity even before he heard about her and Dominick?

"Dammit, Susanna, answer me! Did Camille die from the fever or did you murder her to suit your own selfish ends?"

"What?" she exclaimed. Fierce indignation swept her at this preposterous charge. "How . . . how dare you ask me such a thing! Camille Cary and I were friends, the best of friends!" Realizing she had just admitted to him that she was an impostor, she clamped her mouth shut. Yet, astonishingly, she didn't regret the revelation. She hadn't felt so much like her true self since she'd arrived in Virginia.

"Friends have killed friends, and scheming servants their hapless employers for much less than what you had to gain," he countered. "The richest tobacco plantation on the York—"

"Is that what you're going to tell the constable?" she demanded, finding it exhilarating that she could finally vent her feelings after weeks of keeping them to herself. Considering the bleakness of her situation, what did it matter? She had nothing left to lose . . .

Except, perhaps, her life.

"I might if you don't start talking, Susanna," he said, his voice dangerously quiet. "Now answer my question."

"Of course I didn't murder her," she replied, her resentment tempered not so much by his threat as by her recollections of those last terrible days aboard the *Charming Nancy*. "Camille died from the fever. She was sick for over two weeks . . . and then she was gone."

"How was the death recorded?"

"I gave them my name, Susanna Jane Guthrie. It's what Camille wanted me to do."

His eyes narrowed. "What do you mean?"

"A few days before she died, she asked me to take her place in Virginia if anything happened to her. She must have known how sick she was . . ." Susanna sighed heavily, remembering their painful conversation as vividly as if it had taken place only yesterday. "She wanted me to become Camille Cary, to inherit Briarwood for her. She insisted we looked so much alike her plan couldn't fail. I tried to tell her that it wouldn't work, but she wouldn't hear of it. She made me swear."

Adam snorted in derision, his expression incredulous. "You expect me to believe that? Why would anyone give such a vast inheritance to someone who wasn't even a family member? You're nothing but a common waiting-maid, for God's sakes!"

So that's all she was now in his eyes, Susanna thought, his callous words cutting deeply. It was obvious his professed love had vanished the instant he realized she was not Camille Cary. Oh, if only her own overwhelming feelings for him would fade so quickly!

No, it was just as well this way, she amended vehemently, berating herself for ever having believed he might care and shoving away any thoughts of love. Bastard! It was about time they started looking at each other from the same level . . . hired man to lady's maid.

"I told you Camille and I were friends, almost like sisters," she insisted, her outrage mounting anew. "Camille truly cared about me, cared about what would happen to me if she didn't make it to Virginia—"

"How touching," Adam broke in sarcastically, trying to forget what Polly had told him about the woman she thought had been Camille weeping so miserably at the burial. "But I don't believe you. When you realized that Camille wasn't going to recover, you saw an opportunity that you couldn't resist and you took it! The chance for a lady's maid to become a real lady."

"That's not true! It wasn't like that at all!"

"It must have been! No one would give away so much wealth to a servant—"

"Camille would, and she did! She was the most gentle, the most kind and generous person I've ever known. She never thought about herself. That's why she got struck down with the fever. One of the rare times she left our cabin, she tried to help a little boy who had taken sick, but then she caught it herself. The boy died, his parents . . . and then Camille."

As Adam briefly pondered Susanna's impassioned words, he had to admit that, however farfetched her story sounded, everything he had heard from James Cary about Camille's sweet and giving nature indicated that she very well might have done such a thing. Then another thought struck him.

"What of Lady Redmayne? She's the rightful heir, the only one remaining. Surely Camille realized that Briarwood would go to her aunt if she died—"

"Of course she did!" Susanna interrupted him, her brilliant eyes flashing emerald fire. "That's the other reason why she wanted me to have her inheritance, probably the most important one. Camille thought she was being selfish, but she wasn't. She came up with such a plan out of love for her father, knowing how hard and long he and her grandfather had worked to build Briarwood out of Virginia's wilderness and how much they had loved the land. She knew that her aunt hated the colonies and would never come here to live. If Lady Redmayne ever inherited Briarwood, the plantation would be sold outright!"

That much was probably true, Adam grudgingly granted her, having heard from James Cary of the deep resentment harbored against the planter and his late father by Lady Redmayne. James had told him that the stubborn baroness had refused his every invitation to visit Briarwood, saying she would rather die than ever set foot in such a vile, uncivilized place.

"I was Camille's only hope to save everything her family had worked and struggled for," Susanna continued, her chin raised defiantly, "but now Lady Redmayne's going to find out the truth, and where will that leave you and your own schemes, Mr. Adam Thornton? You won't have Briarwood, that's for sure—not that I would have let you have it, even if you hadn't discovered who I was. Either way, you'd find yourself soothing your grasping ambition with some lesser planter's daughter, like Celeste Grymes!''

''What are you talking about?'' he demanded, stunned by her vehemence.

''Surely you can imagine! You're an intelligent man to have come so far! Did you really think that I, as Camille Cary, could have ever married *you*, a hired man, a paid worker, a former indentured servant? Perhaps, as a high and mighty crop master, you might be good enough to wed some other planters' daughters, but not one who owned the richest plantation on the York!''

Adam felt as if he had just been slammed hard in the chest, the tide of their heated exchange suddenly turned against him. ''I had James Cary's permission, his wholehearted approval of the match—''

''So you say. But how do I know you didn't seize upon Mr. Cary's death to better your own station in life? A hired man becomes one of the Tidewater's wealthiest planters. What a coup! How do I know that everything you told me wasn't a lie? You have no proof that he gave you his blessing, Adam, as I have no proof that Camille wanted me to have Briarwood. Now, where does that bloody well leave us?''

She was right, Adam thought grimly as a charged silence rose between them, broken by the distant restless neighing from the Grymes's matched bays. He had no proof.

Yet had she really believed that everything he had said to her was a lie? Even that he loved her? No, that couldn't be true! He would have sworn that she cared about him . . . he had seen a softness in her eyes whenever she looked at him. He had felt it in the way she returned his kisses, melted in his embrace, called his name at the height of her passion—

What the hell does it matter now? he railed at himself, attempting to repress his powerful feelings. He had obviously been wrong about her.

This manipulative, calculating wench was incapable of love, incapable of thinking of anyone but herself. He didn't believe her story for a minute. Any woman snobbish enough to reject him just because of his background would be too insensitive to honor the wishes of a dying heiress. Susanna's greed lay at the heart of this charade, and nothing else. She might have been an actress born to the stage, she had deceived him so completely. Well, there were ways to make her pay, to hurt her as much as he was suffering right now. It was time to think of the revenge that might still be within his grasp.

Yet one agonizing question still burned in his mind. He had to know the answer before their discussion went any farther.

"Why didn't you tell me how you felt at the beginning, rather than accept my courtship and play me for a fool? When I think of all the time we spent together . . ." He swallowed hard, his anger almost choking him. "Dammit, woman, you let me kiss you! Hold you! Touch you! You led me to believe that you wanted to marry me, that you might even lov—"

Adam caught himself just in time, knowing he had revealed too much already. He swore in that moment that the last thing he would ever tell her again was that he loved her, even when he knew that he still did. It didn't seem to make any difference to his heart whether she was an heiress or a waiting-maid. God help him, he still wanted her, and not just for his revenge. That made him an even bigger fool.

"Everything you said to me, everything you did was a lie," he went on harshly when she still hadn't answered him, her eyes large in a lovely face grown pale. "Your promises, your kisses, your tears, the other night in your bed . . . Damn you, why did you lead me on? Why?"

Unsettled by the pain in his eyes, Susanna nonethe-

less told herself that it was just his male pride which
had been sorely bruised and nothing more. How could
it be? He had made it clear he didn't care about *her*,
Susanna Jane Guthrie, a common waiting-maid. In fact,
he seemed to hate her for what she had done to him. He
probably had every intention of throwing her in prison
no matter what she said.

"I had no choice," she finally replied. "I didn't
know anything about tobacco or running a plantation,
and until I found the proper husband, I needed someone to manage the place. If you had known the truth,
you would have left Briarwood."

"It's as simple as that?" he asked, his tone incredulous.

"Yes."

He gave a short laugh, but it held no amusement.
"So you chose Dominick Spencer for your *proper*
husband."

"Why not?" she demanded. "He's wealthy and respected. One of the governor's councilors. Lady Redmayne taught Camille that she must marry someone
who would enrich her fortune, and since I was here in
her place, that is what I fully intended to do. Marry
wisely, like Camille asked me to—the richest, most
prominent gentleman I could find. I knew I didn't have
much time, especially when you began to press me.
That's why I went to Raven's Point yesterday and arranged with Dominick to announce our betrothal at the
Tates'. He had already said he wanted to marry me."

"And when did he do that?" Adam queried, a tic
flashing along his jaw.

"At my welcome ball, during the first dance."

"How like him not to waste a moment in pursuit of
his unsuspecting quarry," he muttered.

"I . . . I imagined that hearing the news today might
upset you. I always sensed that you didn't like him,
probably because you used to work for him. But there
wasn't any way to spare you . . ."

"You don't know the half of why I hate that bastard,
Susanna, and I'm certainly not going to explain now,"

he began. "What would you say if I told you that your precious Dominick is not quite the man he makes himself out to be?"

"I don't understand—"

"No, you don't understand. You don't understand anything! What did you see when you went to Raven's Point yesterday? A sumptuous house, yes, but when you went inside, did you find it somewhat lacking in comfort? Did you think it not quite up to the luxury you might have expected from such a rich man?"

"No, I didn't," she responded tartly, not willing to give him the satisfaction of knowing that was exactly what she had thought.

"Really? I'm surprised. And outside, did you see anything strange? No ill-fed, ill-clothed slaves? By the way, Dominick Spencer doesn't have any free laborers at Raven's Point, as we do at Briarwood. His only free slaves are dead slaves, and the few lucky ones like myself who managed to earn back their indentures before he worked us to death. He doesn't employ any more indentured servants for that very reason. He didn't like having to set anyone free, white or black. He imports convicts now, I hear. They make better sport."

"I don't know what you're talking about," she insisted stubbornly, willing Corliss's disturbing observations from her mind. "I didn't see any of the things you've described."

"Well, you would have eventually, but not in time to save you from making the biggest mistake of your life," Adam said tightly, then he abruptly changed the subject. "You said that Lady Redmayne would never come here to the colonies. Do you believe that to be true?"

"If I didn't, I would never have attempted to fulfill my promise to Camille," she said, not sure why he wanted to know. "Whatever you might think of me now, Adam, I am no fool."

"What I think of you . . ." He grabbed her arm and began pulling her along with him toward the carriage.

"What are you doing?" she cried, his cruel grip hurting her. At his hard expression, apprehension flooded her. "Where are we going? Back to Briar-wood?"

"No. Williamsburg."

"Oh, God, you're taking me to prison, aren't you? After I told you the truth? You could at least let me go. I'll leave the colony, go back to England. You'll never see me again—"

"Now why would I want to do that?" He stopped to face her, his eyes ablaze with anger. "Why would I want to spoil something you have so skillfully engi-neered? I'm the only one who knows about your mas-querade, Susanna, and I plan to keep it that way. But I can't do it without your help, so now you must make a very important decision. Either continue on as Camille Cary and become my wife this very afternoon, or I shall convince the constable that you are a murderess and see you hang before the week is out."

"You wouldn't!"

"Try me."

At that moment Susanna became convinced with icy certainty that he had never been in love with her. It was only Briarwood he wanted and he would have it, even if it meant forcing her to marry him against her will. She had been right about him from the very start. He was nothing but a vicious, coldhearted, opportunistic blackguard—

Suddenly she thought she saw uneasiness in his gaze, almost as if he feared from her hesitation that she might choose prison and its terrors over marrying him. But then it was gone, and he was shaking her so hard that her head snapped back.

"Choose, Susanna, for you have tried my patience long enough!"

"I said I was no fool!" she cried, infuriated by his rough treatment of her. "How can I not choose life over death . . . even if it means I must spend my days with a conniving bastard such as you? Maybe to hang would be a better fate!"

For a fleeting instant his expression became so thun-derous that she thought he might strike her, but the poignant anguish in his eyes tempered her fear. Why did he seem to hate her, when at the same time she sensed a hurt deep within him?

"Come on." Yanking her alongside him until they came to the bend in the road, he wound his arm through hers and said in a harsh whisper, "Smile, damn you. We don't want the Grymes's poor coachman to think anything is amiss. He's confused enough already. In fact, I'm sure everyone is bewildered, but I don't doubt you'll come up with some clever excuses for our strange behavior today. I commend you. You're as quick-witted as they come. Your upbringing in London's slums has served you well, *my love.*"

Thinking how hollow his endearment sounded, Susanna reluctantly did as he bade her and pasted a false smile on her face. As the coachman, who appeared relieved to see them again, drove the carriage up to meet them, Adam lifted her inside and ordered, "Take us to the Market Square Tavern in Williamsburg! As quickly as you can get us there!"

"Market Square Tavern?" she asked in confusion as he took the seat opposite hers.

"Yes. You didn't think we could be married in Bruton's Parish church, did you? We have no license, and wedding banns must be posted there for three Sundays before the minister would wed us. I'll be damned if I'm going to wait that long. I know of an old parson who lives upstairs at the tavern who'll marry an eager couple for the price of a bottle of wine. It's legal—and permanent."

Shivering at the cold finality in his voice, Susanna slumped against the seat in angry resignation as the carriage rounded the corner that took them out onto the main road. She trained her gaze out the window.

Bloody hell! Here she was on her way to be married in a common tavern by a drunken parson to a hateful, lying excuse of a man who would surely make her days a torment for the rest of her life! The fact that she would still be able to honor at least part of Camille's last wish brought her little comfort. What had she done to bring this misery upon herself?

Susanna glanced back at Adam, and was not surprised to find him still glaring at her. "Would you mind telling me how I gave myself away?" she inquired sullenly.

"Purely by accident," he said with little emotion, belying the animosity in his gaze. "Ertha found the painting you hid in the hatbox when she went to put your purchases away on Monday afternoon. That was what she didn't want you to see when she came to the library."

"So it was the portrait," she said almost to herself, cursing the sentiment that had prevented her from tossing it overboard when she had had the chance.

"No, not the portrait itself, although Ertha suggested there might be some deception afoot. Poor woman. I didn't believe her. I told her that an incompetent artist must have painted it to have so misrepresented your features."

Surprised to hear that he had given her the benefit of the doubt, she asked, "What was it, then?"

"Something Ertha wouldn't have noticed because she never learned to read. Your signature."

Susanna stared at him blankly.

"Your signature on the note was not the same as the one I found on the back of the painting. Didn't you know that Camille had written an inscription there to her father?"

"No . . . no, I never looked at the back."

"A foolish oversight. That evidence combined with what Polly Blake told me at the Tates'—"

"Polly Blake?"

"Yes, another waiting-maid who was aboard the *Charming Nancy.*"

"You mean that dark-haired girl you were speaking with near the refreshment table?"

"Then you noticed."

"I chanced to look over once or twice," she allowed with feigned nonchalance, recalling how she had jealously wondered what they were discussing. "But I didn't recognize her from the voyage."

"She didn't recognize you, either, at least not who you really were. All she remembered about you and Camille was that you both had the same honey-blonde hair. I knew then that you were an impostor."

"Yes, I suppose you did." Susanna abruptly fell silent. It seemed she had no one to blame but herself for this wretched turn of events.

"You were right about Celeste. She was the one who told me about your betrothal plans. I believe we both have her to thank for this day's unexpected outcome."

Oh, she knew friggin' well why Adam was grateful, Susanna thought heatedly. Briarwood would soon belong to him. But how could she possibly be obliged to that loose-lipped gossip for the mess her life had suddenly become?

"Cheer up, Susanna. At least you'll be able to live in lavish comfort for the rest of your life. Things could be worse."

Nothing could be worse, she thought resentfully as the fields and woods gradually gave way to the neat white houses of Williamsburg. She refused to waste even a glance on him, watching with dread for the painted sign announcing the Market Square Tavern.

The irony was not lost on her that she would be marrying Adam Thornton after all, the man Camille had dreamed would be a perfect match for her. Except that now the hired man and the waiting-maid were about to play the biggest roles of their lives.

Loving husband and wife.

And nothing could be further from the truth.

# Chapter 18

━━━━━━━━━━━━━━━━━━━⁓◯◯⁓━━━━━━━━━━━━━━━━━━━

"**W**ell, my darling wife, it looks like we have visitors. I hope you have sharpened your story-telling skills. You're going to need them."

Susanna said nothing, avoiding Adam's eyes as his hands encircled her waist and he lifted her easily from the carriage. She glanced with growing apprehension at the dusty black coach also parked in the drive which bore Dominick's family crest, then at the front door, which suddenly opened. Her breath snagging painfully, she was immensely relieved to see it was only Ertha hurrying from the house, followed by Corliss and a half dozen other servants who all appeared equally distressed.

"Oh, Miss Camille, Mr. Thornton! We were wondering when you would get here!" the housekeeper cried, out of breath when she reached them. "Mr. Dominick Spencer arrived over an hour ago, along with Miss Grymes and her brother. They're waiting in the drawing room. They brought us the strangest news . . . they said Briarwood was struck by a fire, but there hasn't been any fire . . . at least not on the main grounds. Has something terrible happened in the outlying fields—"

"Calm yourself, Ertha, nothing terrible has happened," Adam broke in, taking Susanna's arm possessively. She started at his touch, but forced a shaky smile to her lips as he abruptly announced, "We've wonderful news for you. Camille became my bride earlier this afternoon.''

As every mouth in the agitated group fell open, stunned faces turning toward her, Susanna somehow managed to say, "Yes, it's true. Adam and I were married today in Williamsburg. I know this comes as a complete surprise to all of you, but we're very happy and hope you will be, too." Glancing at Adam to find him staring at her, an unfathomable emotion in his gaze, she felt a dizzying warmth flood her body and she quickly turned back to Ertha. "I take it you provided refreshments for our guests?"

"Yes . . . yes, I did, Miss Camille," the house-keeper murmured, appearing more in shock than the others. Corliss, however, was beaming broadly.

"No, Ertha, you mean Mistress Thornton now," the maid corrected, unmistakable relief in her dark eyes, which skipped to Adam. "And Master Thornton."

Susanna almost winced at the sound of her new name. Doing her best to maintain her flagging composure, she requested softly, "Please, Ertha, Corliss, the rest of you, if you must call me 'Mistress,' then use my first name. The other sounds so formal, and I'm sure Adam won't mind . . ."

"Not at all, my love," he said, bending his head to press a light kiss on her flushed cheek. "Anything to please you."

At first startled that he would act with such familiarity in front of the servants, Susanna had to remind herself that as her husband, Adam now had a right to do that and much more. Touch her, embrace her, share her bed . . . oh, she didn't want to think about it!

Perhaps it was enough for him that he was the master of Briarwood now, with the entire Cary fortune at his disposal. She doubted he wanted anything more from her anyway. He despised her. He was just mocking her with his blatant show of affection. Of course he wouldn't want to—

"We should greet our guests, don't you think?" he

asked her, his warm breath tickling her ear. "I'm sure they will be pleased to hear there was no fire."

"Y-yes, we should greet them," she murmured, her legs wooden as they moved to the door, the silent servants parting for them on both sides of the walkway.

Candles had already been lit in the main hall, for the day had grown cloudy and dark with a thunderstorm brewing. Susanna found the cooler air in the house soothing after the heavy, humid air outside, and much easier to breathe. Now if only her heart would stop pounding so furiously . . .

"The drawing room, Ertha?" Adam asked, still tightly holding Susanna's arm, as if he feared she might flee up the stairs. Coward! He *would* leave this mess entirely up to her to straighten out.

"Yes, Master Thornton," the wide-eyed housekeeper replied, then she rounded in agitation on the other servants. "Go on with you! Get back to your chores. You heard there was no fire, so there's nothing to keep you here gawking. Just pass the word along that this is a very happy day for Briarwood. Corliss, take some of the other maids with you and see that Master Thornton's things are moved into Miss . . . Mistress Camille's room, real quick now. Make sure everything looks nice, you hear?"

Susanna wanted to tell Ertha that such a task wasn't necessary, she and Adam wouldn't be sharing a bedroom, but she was distracted as he steered her toward the closed drawing-room door.

"I'll go tell Prue to prepare you a special wedding supper," the housekeeper added, appearing much calmer now that she had resumed command.

"Thank you, Ertha," Adam said, his hand reaching for the knob. "Have it brought up to our room, along with the best wine in the cellar."

"What?" Susanna blurted just as the door was abruptly opened from the inside and she came face-to-face with Celeste.

"I thought I heard your voices!" the young woman exclaimed, her freckled cheeks pink-spotted with exasperation. She stepped backward stiffly as they moved into the room. "Where have you two been? We've been waiting here forever, worried sick about you, and to make matters worse, your servants know absolutely nothing about any fire! Now we'd like an explanation!"

Susanna jumped as the door was shut behind them, her gaze flying to Dominick, who rose to greet her. He was dressed in the finest clothes she had ever seen and an elaborate curled wig, his splendid attire obviously chosen for the occasion of their betrothal; in fact, he would have looked absolutely perfect except for the uncharacteristic sheen of perspiration on his face. Irritation emanated from his every step, clinging to him like the sweet imported cologne he wore.

"Are you all right, my dear?" he asked, his ice-blue eyes growing colder as he noted Adam's hand beneath her elbow. "I'm sure Miss Cary is quite capable of standing on her own without any assistance from you, Mr. Thornton. Kindly release her."

"Now, why would I want to do that?" Susanna heard Adam say calmly, although she felt the tension in his tightening grasp. She sensed what he was about to reveal and wished impossibly that the floor would open up and swallow her whole, leaving this entire tangled muddle behind her.

"I beg your pardon?" Dominick asked, his aristocratic features marked with dark confusion and barely repressed anger at Adam's insolence. "Camille, I demand that you tell this . . . this hired servant of yours—"

"Try husband, Spencer, and you'll be closer to the truth," Adam stated bluntly, his arm winding around Susanna's waist in a clear gesture of possession. She inhaled in surprise as he drew her close to him, but her response was nothing to the horrified gasp that came from Celeste. Momentarily speechless, the pretty redhead's face had become an unattractive shade of pasty white.

"What do you mean, husband?" Dominick said tightly, his narrowed gaze riveting on Susanna.

Say it! Just say it! she screamed to herself, quickly deciding it was best just to blurt out the news. The strained tension in the room was enough to blow out the windows.

"Adam and I were married today," she heard herself say, her voice sounding strangely like someone else's.

"Married?" cried Celeste, while Matthew, his reddened face making a stark contrast to his sister's unwholesome pallor, simply gaped.

"Married?" Dominick rasped, his voice incredulous.

"Yes, in Williamsburg. I—I'm so terribly sorry you had to hear it this way," Susanna sought to explain, more to Dominick than anyone else, "but it came as a total surprise to me as well. I . . . I didn't know Adam held such strong feelings for me, although I had hoped all along that he did—why, ever since I first saw him at the Yorktown docks. And when he heard a rumor from Celeste that Dominick and I were going to announce our betrothal, it finally spurred him to action. He couldn't bear the thought of my marrying another man."

"This can't be true. It can't be," Celeste repeated in disbelief while Susanna, ignoring her, plunged on with her hastily conceived story, despite the silent planter's look of pure fury.

"I'm really very sorry if I've hurt you, Dominick. I never meant to insult or mislead you. That's why I'm so glad you were late today to the races and we didn't announce our engagement. I would never have been able to forgive myself if I had publicly humiliated you. It's just when Adam spirited me from the Tates', saying that there was a fire at Briarwood, and then proposed to me in the Grymes's carriage, I couldn't refuse him. I was so happy to discover that he loved me, the last thing I wanted to do was wait three weeks while the banns were published at Bruton's Parish. We were married in a tavern . . . what was it called, Adam darling?"

"Market Square."

Infuriated by the restrained amusement in his voice while she was quaking in her high-heeled shoes, Susanna nonetheless did her best to continue her impersonation of a giddy bride.

"Yes, that was it! The Market Square Tavern. A delightful old parson who resides there was only too happy to marry us." She held out her trembling left hand to display the thin strip of metal wrapped around her finger. "See? Adam had to improvise and use a bed-curtain ring until we have time to buy a proper wedding band. It was clever of him, don't you think?"

She wasn't surprised when her inane comment was greeted with dead silence.

"Oh, dear, here I am chattering on about my happiness while I can imagine what a shock this must be to you. How terribly insensitive of me." She turned to Celeste and Matthew. "I hope you can both forgive me and that we can remain friends. We've had so much fun these past few weeks that I'd hate to see—"

She didn't get to finish as Celeste burst into tears, flung open the door, and rushed from the room. Mumbling an apology, Matthew ran after her, while Dominick was obviously so angry he could find few words with which to speak.

"I congratulate you, Mrs. Thornton," he said with a stiff bow, pointedly refusing to address Adam directly. "Your husband is a most fortunate man." With that, he brushed past her into the main hall, his footsteps resounding across the floor. Then the front door was closed with cold finality behind him.

"Bravo, my love," Adam said, caressing her waist. "I knew you could do it. Lied like a true expert. I've waited many long years to see that arrogant bastard outdone, and today won't be the last time."

His taunting tone hit Susanna like a cruel slap in the face and she rounded on him. "That man should have been my husband, not you! I'm sure you can well imagine who I think is the bastard here. Go to hell!"

Dashing into the hall before he could stop her, she was so furious that she paid no heed to the startled housemaids coming down the stairway who offered her good wishes on her marriage. Nor did she answer Corliss who asked her if there was anything she needed as they passed each other in the upstairs corridor. Storming into her room, Susanna slammed the new door and drew the bolt, her fingers shaking. Then she flung herself on her bed, dreading the familiar footfalls that she knew would come.

"Open the door, Camille," Adam repeated for the third time, growing more irritated as he was greeted by the same stony silence. He imagined Prue would probably be up soon with their supper, and he didn't want to face embarrassment because his new bride had locked him out of their room.

He had already explained to an understanding Corliss and the other housemaids that their mistress was experiencing the normal fears any young woman might have before her wedding night. But enough was enough, and such rationale grated on him, anyway. He doubted strongly that Susanna was a virgin, despite what she had claimed the other night. He had tumbled enough ladies' maids to know they were a lusty lot, and prone to easily giving their favors if a gentleman caught their eye. Why would Susanna be any different?

Hot desire erupted within him as he recalled the voluptuous beauty of her body and how her skin, glowing like pale alabaster in the moonlight, had been satin-smooth and warm beneath his hands. How many lovers had she known at Fairford? Adam wondered jealously, resisting the urge to pound on the door, knocking firmly instead. How many men had touched her as he had done two nights ago?

She had played the sweet innocent so well, protesting convincingly against his wish to give her pleasure, while all along she had no doubt possessed the experience of a true wanton. The devil take her! Her kisses had told him as much! And how expertly she had spoken earlier that same day of their wedding night being only a few weeks away, when in actuality, she had intended to betray him for Dominick Spencer, a man she thought was good enough to marry while he, Adam Thornton, a mere hired servant, was not.

Well, their wedding night had finally arrived, he thought bitterly, his fury rekindled at the thought of how close he had come to losing her to that murdering scum. But tonight wouldn't be the gentle sexual awakening of her that he had long imagined. He couldn't wait to sheathe himself in her beautiful, treacherous body and ease the torment she had caused him. If by some slim chance she did prove to be a virgin and he hurt her, it would serve her right.

"Damn you, woman, unlock this door or I swear I'll break it down!" he said in a low voice, his patience at an end. "I warn you that you're not entirely safe from prison or the hangman's noose. Ertha may still suspect you despite what I told her last night. If she sees you acting unlike the good and gentle wife her Camille would have been, she'll be convinced all the sooner—"

Adam was suddenly rewarded by the scraping sound of the bolt being drawn. He pushed open the door to find Susanna hastening toward the sitting area on the opposite side of the room from the bed. As she spun to glare at him, her long, honey-blonde curls spilling over her shoulders and down her back, his breath caught deep in his chest.

Standing there so outraged and defiant, her chin lifted high and her creamy skin flushed rose, she looked more gloriously lovely than ever before. He almost regretted that she must play the obedient wife, for he far preferred the rebellious spirit shining from her eyes. He was finally seeing the real essence of this woman, vibrantly passionate and alive, and it made his pulse race like wildfire just to be in the same room with her.

Yet he had only to remember the vehement curses she had hurled at him downstairs, delivered in an unladylike accent reminiscent of Polly Blake's, and he knew he had no choice but to tame her spirit. Their lifelong charade depended upon her proper behavior and so did his revenge, which was of consuming importance to him now.

Since the night of her ball, he had allowed his impossible dreams of love to overshadow his vengeful plans, but no more. In the morning, he would concentrate again on the goal that had driven him for long, bitter years before he had ever seen her face. Surely such a preoccupation would lessen the pain of her betrayal.

"A very wise move . . . opening this door," he said with deadly quiet, shutting it behind him.

When she continued to glare at him, Adam strode purposely across the room. Despite the raised windows, the air was still and warm. He propped open the balcony doors, noting how black and ominous the sky had become, thunder rumbling in the distance. He hoped the coming storm didn't bring a three-day downpour as the last one had. The tobacco would soon be ready to cut, and he didn't want anything to threaten what he had already judged to be a bumper crop.

Turning back into the candlelit interior, he met her truculent gaze. "A word of caution, wife. Don't ever draw that bolt against me again."

"It's my room. I'll do what I please."

"Correction, Camille," he replied, emphasizing the name. "Our room. Yours and mine. From now on, we share it . . . the sitting area, wardrobes, dressing tables, balcony, and, not least of all, that bed."

Her face paled, but her gaze did not waver. Skipping over the charged topic he had just raised, she asked him tartly, "Will you not be calling me Susanna, then, even when we're in the privacy of *our* room?"

"You'll never hear that name from my lips again, nor do I want to hear it from yours. As far as we're concerned, that name was forever laid to rest aboard the *Charming Nancy*. Do you understand?"

Before she could respond, a knock sounded, and Adam strode to open the door, imagining it was Prue. He wanted no more interruptions this evening, and as the cook entered followed by three kitchen maids carrying large silver trays, he quickly checked to see that they had brought plenty of wine. It was going to be a long night.

"Oh, child, I'm so happy for you!" Prue exclaimed, tears glistening in her eyes, the minute she saw Susanna. "Married, this very afternoon! I just knew in my bones there was something going on between you two." She cast a fond glance at Adam. "You've got yourself a real fine man there. 'Course, you already know that, else you wouldn't have married him. Your papa never had anything but good to say about our Master Thornton."

Susanna smiled her thanks, not trusting herself to speak. She didn't know how she was going to suffer through such congratulations from the rest of the servants, however heartfelt, or such absurd assessments of Adam's character. These people had no idea of his true nature!

"That Corliss surely misread your trip to Mr. Spencer's yesterday," the cook continued, shaking her scarf-covered head. "She told me and Ertha this morning that she was afraid you were thinking of marrying that planter. I'm sure glad she was wrong. She saw some mighty awful things at his place that made me shudder—"

"Something smells absolutely wonderful, Prue," Susanna broke in when Adam glanced at her sharply, no doubt realizing that Corliss must have described those same things to her on their way back from Raven's Point. She wasn't surprised that her gabby maid had been unable to keep their secret, but she certainly didn't want to discuss yesterday's events any further. "What did you bring us?"

The cook smiled broadly, lifting one of the domed lids. "One of my specialties, brought out from the smokehouse just for this happy day, Mistress Camille. Bourbon-glazed ham, scalloped potatoes, and buttered green beans fresh-picked from the garden. There's an iced lemon cake for dessert, too, with wild strawberry filling, and the best wine from the cellar, just like you ordered, Master Thornton. I didn't know how much you'd be wanting so we fetched up three bottles.''

Too bad she didn't have any appetite, Susanna thought with regret as Adam ushered the cook to the door, her excited, whispering helpers already waiting for her in the hallway.

"Thank you, Prue. You've prepared us a fine wedding supper," he said. "But I think my bride and I would like to be alone—"

"Oh, my, I'm sorry," the cook interjected, glancing at Susanna with embarrassment. "Here I am, talking on and on. Of course you two want to be alone, it being your wedding night and all. Have a good evening, then."

As Adam closed the door after Prue and drew the bolt, Susanna tried not to panic, reasoning that he must share her room, and her bed, for the sake of appearances. It also made sense that they would retire early, which would give the servants the impression of conjugal bliss.

Actually, she doubted she had anything to worry about. Adam had made no move to touch her or even to come near her all day except when other people were about, which there certainly weren't now. Maybe he would sleep on the divan to avoid coming into contact with her. She felt much calmer now that she had thought through the situation. Yet that didn't stop her heart from leaping in her breast when he met her eyes, his handsome features set inscrutably.

"Very good, Camille. That's exactly how I want you to act from now on around the servants and everyone else, for that matter. No different than you did before I discovered the truth about you. That shouldn't be too difficult, considering your remarkable gift for deception."

Susanna bristled at his mocking tone. "You seem to have deceived everyone at Briarwood as well, Adam, beginning long before I arrived here. Why, even poor Mr. Cary didn't guess what a mercenary bastard you really are—"

"That's another thing you're going to stop," he said sharply, walking toward her. "In light of your upbringing, I'm not surprised you also have a gift for cursing, but you'll do well to sweeten your language from this moment on. A lady doesn't spout oaths like a common guttersnipe. Do you hear me?"

Determined to vent her anger, Susanna ignored what he had just said, despite his uncomfortable closeness. If he insisted she had become an impostor out of greed, then she could bloody well express her interpretation of *his* actions!

"I saw many of Mr. Cary's letters to Camille, Adam. I heard him speak of you the last time he came to England. I think you purposely worked your way into his good graces, leading him to believe you were industrious and trustworthy while the whole time you couldn't wait to possess his daughter and his plantation! You seem to believe that I'm capable of murder. How do I know that you didn't murder Mr. Cary to win what you so coveted?"

He stopped within arm's reach of her, his stunned expression hardening into one of restrained rage.

"It's amazing how close you've come to the mark, my love, but you need to be told the truth. It wasn't me who murdered James Cary for the reasons you describe, but the man you would have married, Dominick Spencer."

"What are you talking about—" She gasped, her eyes widening in fright as Adam suddenly grabbed her shoulders and shook her hard.

"No," he said harshly, his furious gaze burning into hers. "You just listen. Dominick knew James Cary would never allow him to court his daughter so he rid himself of the man, very cleverly staging a hunting accident only one day after he came here to Briarwood to harass James again about the matter. They had a violent argument out in the fields—and if you don't believe me, ask Josiah Skinner. We both saw and heard it. James had no intention of letting Dominick near his daughter, and do you know why?"

Susanna shook her head, in complete shock over what he was telling her.

"Because he believed me when I told him that Dominick was a monster, a cold-blooded killer. I was never going to reveal any of this to you for fear of hurting you, but in light of the circumstances I don't see any reason not to now. After what you did to me, you deserve to know that I'm not the only one who has been manipulated, and why. Then you tell me how it feels."

Wondering wildly at his cryptic words, Susanna struggled to no avail against his cruel grasp as his voice fell almost to a whisper.

"Let me tell you about your precious Dominick, the charming, well-respected gentleman you wanted so badly to wed. I've seen him whip slaves to death without blinking an eye, his face flushed from the pleasure of it. As a punishment to those who disobeyed him, I've seen him use curry combs to scrape away flesh and then add salt to the wounds. And with equal relish, he's cut off the hands and feet of slaves who dared to run away and slashed out the tongues of men, women, and children foolish enough to mumble resistance."

"No," she breathed in horrified disbelief. He rushed on, his eyes tormented in his remembering.

"There's more, my love. Much, much more. I've seen him wrest squalling babies from their mothers' arms and sell them on the auction block. To give you a clearer insight into his despicable nature, he did that to the six children his longtime mistress, Cleo, bore him while I was at Raven's Point. He sold his own flesh and blood into slavery, hating the thought that his superior blood was mixed with a race he so despised. Did you meet Cleo yesterday? She also works as his housekeeper. She's one of the most beautiful women I've ever known. Other than you," he added bitterly.

Attempting to force from her dazed mind the unsettling pity she had seen in Cleo's eyes and shocked to discover the woman was Dominick's mistress, Susanna could make no response.

"I'm surprised Dominick has kept her for as long as

he has," Adam went on. "He must know she hates him. That Satan's spawn must fancy himself in love with her, though it's unbelievable to me that he could care for anything. Cleo told me five years ago, just before I left Raven's Point, that someday she would find a way to break him for selling away her children, but she's obviously failed. Or maybe she simply lost the will to fight . . ."

As Adam fell silent, seemingly lost in memories, Susanna finally found her voice. "How could you have convinced Mr. Cary of these terrible things? He wouldn't have taken your word for such accusations!"

Adam gave a grim laugh, hauntingly hollow, his eyes filled with cold hatred.

"James didn't have just my word. To understand the depths of that man's depravity, he had only to look at what that devil did to me to know I spoke the truth. He had only to hear of how Dominick horsewhipped my father to death right in front of me and my mother, and then how he raped her while two of his overseers held her down. My mother lost the will to live after that and a week later, drowned herself in the York River."

He drew a ragged breath, his voice laden with bitter regret.

"God help me, I was too young to save them, only fifteen. But I swore that one day I would have vengeance, if not by killing that monster, then by finding a way to make him suffer the cruelest torture. I didn't want to marry James Cary's daughter for her land or her fortune, as you so wrongly accused, but for the revenge her wealth could bring me." Adam drew Susanna closer, crushing her against his chest. "Revenge that you will now bring me, Mrs. Adam Thornton."

Though Susanna was horrified by what he had described, she could see in his agonized gaze that he spoke the truth, just as she realized with heartrending clarity that he could never have loved her. What a fool she had been to think that he had pursued her because he cared! In an embittered heart such as his there could be no room for love. He had lied to her to secure his revenge, and that was the most crushing revelation of all.

"There's something else you don't know about your beloved Dominick," Adam added grimly. "Something only his creditors know about him. Even James Cary had no idea that the man was on the verge of bankruptcy."

"Bankruptcy?" she blurted, thinking that this accusation must surely be false. What of Dominick's fine clothes, his luxurious carriage, the costly gifts he had given her which Adam had already told her would be sent back first thing in the morning—

"Why else did you think he wanted to marry you?" he scoffed. "Out of affection? Dominick needed your fortune to pull him out of debt because his addictive gambling has finally gotten the better of him. He's been on the brink of losing Raven's Point for months. His wretched financial state isn't common knowledge only because he's a master at hiding it." Adam laughed dryly. "Think how completely he fooled you, my love. But I've made it my business to know everything about that bastard. A few well-placed bribes have provided me with all the information I needed to plan my revenge. All I required was a very rich wife, and since I now have one, I can finally push him over the edge."

"How . . . how will you do that?" Susanna asked numbly. Her mind spun as she recalled the spartan interior of Dominick's house, the worn furniture, his plain clothes, the meal which had been less than sumptuous . . . and even the many times during their brief courtship when he had disappeared into some planter's game room to play cards . . .

"You will see in time," Adam replied tersely, his hands falling to her waist. "Actually, I believe I should thank you for your cunning deception. It was worth a fortune just to see Dominick's face today when he realized he had lost the one thing that could have saved him from rotting in debtors' prison . . . and to a man he once forced to lick the field dust from his shoes."

"Blackguard! You're as despicable as he!" Susanna

cried, his words shocking her out of her silence. "To think you would so callously use an innocent young woman to suit your own selfish ends! I'm almost glad Camille isn't here to suffer at your hands."

"Leaves a bitter taste in your mouth, doesn't it?" he mocked her. "It's not pleasant to discover that you're valued less as a human being than for what benefit you can bring to someone else. But let's not talk of innocence," he added scornfully, his fingers straying to the ribbon tie at her waist, "as if it's something a former waiting-maid with your passion and beauty might still possess."

# Chapter 19

❦❦

**"W**hat . . . what are you doing?'' Susanna
sputtered in panicked disbelief. She tried
to twist away from him even as he tugged sharply on
the tie and wrenched open the front of her gown, revealing her lace-trimmed stays and hoop-petticoat.

"Surely you can see, my love,'' Adam said, shoving
from his mind the horrible memories he had aroused
and, along with them, any regret over his brutal haste
with her. Fueled by raw anger and overcome with desire, he could not stop himself. "I'm undressing you.''

"No!''

She pushed against him so suddenly that he almost
lost his balance. Grabbing for the chair behind him, he
released his hold on her. As he righted himself, cursing
under his breath, she dashed to the table near the balcony doors where Prue and her maids had left their
supper, and took refuge behind it.

"And since you've seen fit to give me your list of
dos and don'ts, I have one for you,'' she blurted with
furious indignation, clutching her gown together.
"Don't you ever call me 'my love' again! You don't
love me—''

"You're right, I don't,'' Adam lied, certain that he
saw a flicker of pain cross her lovely features as he
slowly advanced upon her, then shrugging off the idea
as impossible. "But I've desired you since the first moment I saw you, and I believe you want me, too.''

"You're wrong!'' she cried. "I detest you—''

254

"You lie," he said, facing her across the table now. He didn't want to dwell on how deeply her words had pierced his heart. He only wanted to feel again the lush wonder of her body pressed against him. "You can't tell me you didn't enjoy the kisses we've shared, the times I've held you in my arms, or the night when you let me caress your beautiful body."

"I didn't! I loathed every moment we spent alone together. I just let you think I liked everything you did to me. You're an easy one to deceive, Adam Thornton."

He shook his head, his senses flooded with the warmed scent of her jasmine perfume. "Such things you cannot fake. I know when a woman's desire is as strong as my own, and no woman I've ever held has a spirit as wanton as yours. Now stop playing the trembling virgin and take my hand. Remember, we're husband and wife now. I have complete rights to your body, just as I have complete charge over your wealth."

Susanna jumped as a sharp crack of thunder rumbled outside, harbinger of an approaching storm that heightened the tension between them.

She couldn't believe this was happening despite how Adam hated her! He had just said so, proving to her at last that he had sought to mislead her as surely as she had misled him.

She didn't want to admit how deeply his words had hurt her, nor would she ever give him the satisfaction of knowing she had actually believed herself in love with him. To think she must spend the rest of her life with this cruel, heartless man! And did he truly think that because she had been a waiting-maid she was no longer a virgin? He must!

"I—I've already given you what you wanted, Adam," she stammered, the lustful way his eyes were raking over her filling her with dread. "Briarwood. The Cary fortune. You can have mistresses if you want, a dozen or more if that's what it takes to satisfy you. I don't care, but just leave me alone. You seem to have forgotten that half of this miserable charade depends upon me. I swear if you touch me I'll go to the county constable and tell him the truth!''

''And settle a noose around your lovely white neck when I counter your truth with mine? I don't think so.'' As he began to stalk her around the table, he threw off his coat, his waistcoat, and then began to work at the buttons on his sweat-dampened shirt until it hung open, his magnificent chest bared to her gaze. ''Come to bed, wife.''

''No,'' Susanna whispered, tripping on the hem of her gown as she tried to maintain a distance between them. She quickly kicked off her shoes so they would not hinder her. ''I'll scream if you so much as touch me—''

''Only in pleasure,'' he countered, his darkening expression suggesting that he was growing more than a little impatient. ''Only in pleasure.''

With a suddenness that made her gasp, he shoved the table against the wall so that she could no longer circle it.

''You have nowhere to run, Camille. The door is bolted. You couldn't manage to open it before I caught you anyway, and I'll throw aside any other chair or table you choose to hide behind. Is an hour or two of sensual delight worth the fuss you are making? It is inevitable that I will have you.''

As Susanna's gaze darted around the room, she realized with a terrible sinking feeling that there truly was no escape.

''No, please, you don't want to do this. I know you don't want me . . .'' She backed up, bumping into the wall with an awful start as he moved toward her, stripping off his shirt and casting it to the floor. Then he stood a mere inch or two from her, so broad and powerful that he blocked out all else behind him, white flashes of lightning reflecting in his eyes.

Her nostrils flared at his musky male scent, arousing in her a heady excitement she could not suppress, and when he took her hand, she felt the strength of his mounting desire course through her fingers.

"You know nothing," he whispered huskily, his intense gaze holding hers. "I want you more than I've ever wanted any woman."

As he braced a powerfully muscled arm against the wall, his chest barely brushing her breasts, she unwittingly lifted her face to his at the same moment that his warm lips captured hers. If she hadn't been pushed to the wall, she would have collapsed, such was the jolt of passion his kiss ignited within her.

He ravaged her mouth, plundering its soft depths with his tongue, and she answered him in kind, unable to help herself. Hearing his groans sent shivers of desire through her. In some distant part of her mind she was aware that he was swiftly undressing her, her gown sliding off her shoulders, her hoop-petticoat, untied from behind, tumbling with a crisp swoosh around her feet. Then she heard the ripping of fabric as he tore her linen drawers from her lower body.

Startled, she opened her eyes at the same moment he grasped her bare bottom and lifted her to him, forcing her stocking-clad legs around his lean hips.

"Adam?" she murmured in surprise against his mouth, but he deepened the kiss, and she forgot everything until she felt his hand slide between their bodies and his warm, insistent fingers circle and tease that sensitive, tingling place at the apex of her thighs.

Gasping with pleasure, she began to tremble as he expertly plied her softness, her hips moving against him in an increasingly urgent rhythm over which she had no control. She wound her arms around his neck and held on to him for dear life, remembering the ecstasy she had felt beneath his touch the other night . . . and wondering with a ravenous hunger if she would feel such sweet rapture again.

"I knew you wanted me," Adam said thickly, kissing her throat as he pressed her to the wall. "You're so hot, woman, so wet . . ."

Unable to wait any longer to possess her, his body ablaze with need, he fumbled at the flap on his breeches and released his hard, engorged shaft into his hand.

Guiding it to the moist, slick center of her, he cupped her firm buttocks with both hands and, capturing her lips again, he plunged himself deeply into her.

Her sharp, muffled cry of pain was not the first thing that told him she was a virgin, for he knew it with swift self-disgust when he unexpectedly felt her maiden barrier give way. Yet he could not stop what he had begun. As her body closed around him like a tight, burning vise, he groaned in pleasure, lifting his mouth from hers to whisper, "Shhh, love, the hurt will pass. I promise."

Adam cursed himself when he saw tears glistening in her wide, stricken eyes, failing utterly to convince himself that he had had every right to believe she had lain with other men before him. Yet now that he knew she had been a virgin, his sudden elation nearly matched that of his burning desire.

She was completely his! She had belonged to no other! With superhuman effort, he slowed his thrusts, determined to give her as much pleasure in this, her first time, as he felt in finally claiming her.

"Does it still hurt?" he asked, kissing her damp cheeks as he slowly embedded himself in her wondrous warmth and then just as slowly withdrew.

To Susanna's amazement, the stinging pain had already receded and was soon blotted from her memory by the incredibly pleasurable sensation of his body moving deep inside hers. She felt full of him, possessed by him, and she could not deny she liked it.

She liked all of it, his strength and the way he held her, his strong fingers gripping her bottom, and the amazing heat radiating from that point where they were joined. She reveled in the muscular hardness of his chest pressed against her breasts, which she wished were freed from her stays and the underlying linen chemise. She wanted to feel the sleekness of his skin rubbing against hers, and she locked her feet behind him to draw him still closer.

"No, it doesn't hurt," she murmured, parting her moistened lips for his kiss. "It doesn't hurt at all."

As his tongue delved into her mouth, their panting breaths merging, he rammed himself into her with new urgency, moving ever faster and faster while she clung to him, moaning raggedly from deep in her throat. She could hear thunder rolling outside, see brilliant lightning flashes piercing her closed eyelids, but it was nothing to the wild tempest inside her. She felt buffeted and storm-tossed, the whirling maelstrom of passion encompassing every charged fiber of her being.

"Tell me . . . how it feels," Adam demanded, his body beginning to shake against hers. "Tell me!"

"Good, Adam . . . so wonderful. Please, hold me closer, hold me . . . oh, Adam!"

She stiffened in his arms, holding her breath as her entire body was rocked by rapturous sensations more intense than she had ever known before. She barely heard him groan aloud for her own cries of ecstasy, but she felt him suddenly shudder from his head to his toes, the powerful throbbing of his body within her only adding to her delirious delight.

"Oh, God . . . Susanna."

Her name was spoken before Adam realized it, and in that bright, blinding moment, he didn't care. Throwing his head back, he exulted in the sheer force of his pulsating release. The sensation of spurting his hot seed into her tightening sheath was a thousand times more heady and tumultuous than what had led up to it.

For long, long moments he just stood there, clutching her fiercely against him, the aftershocks from their pleasure still shaking them both. Only a curtain of cool rain slashing in upon them from the opened balcony doors helped him regain his presence of mind, and he opened his eyes to discover that the downpour had begun in earnest.

"Oh, it's cold!" she squealed in surprise as he withdrew himself from her rain-spattered body and set her feet gently on the floor. While she snatched up her dampened gown and whirled it around her shoulders to cover herself, he adjusted his breeches and then quickly shut the doors, wrestling with them against the fierce, gusting wind. Finally he drew the bolt firmly into place.

Chuckling to himself, his mood lighter than it had been all day, Adam turned to find Susanna staring at him, a horrified look on her face. His laughter died in his throat, his intuition immediately telling him what must have upset her.

"Adam . . . your back. What happened?"

"Something else I had hoped never to have to tell you," he replied evenly, although once again his tone dripped with bitterness. He didn't readily explain, but instead went to the table and poured himself a brimming glass of wine, then promptly drank it down. Helping himself to another, all the while he kept his back to her as if he wanted her to get a really good look.

She swallowed painfully, wondering at his words and unable to tear her eyes away. She was appalled by the severity of his disfigurement, thinking that the vicious lashings she had received at her father's hands might have been inflicted with a feather compared to what must have been used against Adam.

Starting just below his shoulders, his back was crisscrossed with ugly pink scars, raised ridges of healed flesh which gave her the strong impression he had been severely beaten countless times. And now that he was stripped to the waist, she could plainly see that while much of his chest matched the bronzed hue of his face, his sides and back were pale, as if he never completely removed his shirt while working out-of-doors because he didn't want anyone to know what had happened to him.

"Seen enough?" he queried grimly, raising his second glass of wine to his lips as he turned to face her. He took a long draught, then added, "You can touch it if you'd like. You won't hurt me. I can't feel a thing on my back, haven't been able to for years. I think that's what saved me after the hundredth beating."

Shocked, Susanna said softly, "Hundredth?"

"Yes, I quit counting after that. I was only eighteen then, so if you figure I was at Raven's Point for six more years . . ." He shrugged, his voice very low. "I suppose I'm lucky to have any skin left there at all."

"Did Dominick do this to you?" she asked, hoping that he would say no, that it was Dominick's overseers who had flayed him so mercilessly. But she sensed his answer before he uttered it. This must have been what Adam had meant when he said James Cary hadn't had to accept just his word for his horrible accusations. No doubt the planter had taken one look at Adam's back and come to his own grim conclusions about Dominick Spencer.

"What do you think?" was Adam's only reply. Draining his glass, he set it upon the table and reached down to pull off his boots. "You'll see when I take off my breeches that the damage goes much lower, and then there's this . . ."

She started when a triangular chunk of wood with rounded edges tumbled from his right boot.

"I use that to help keep my balance," Adam explained, rolling off his sock. "Fills the shoe."

He paused for a moment to glance at Susanna, his set expression impossible to read.

"I'm not telling you any of this or showing you why I limp to drum up pity. I just think we should discuss this now so you won't have any more unpleasant surprises." His gaze moved meaningfully to the bed, then back to her, falling to the golden thatch of woman's hair that peeked through the edges of her gown. "Then we've got other things to do."

Gathering the gown more tightly around her body, Susanna flushed hotly at his hint of how they would spend the rest of the evening. Yet her flustered thoughts quickly turned to horror when Adam revealed his foot.

She felt a little sick. Only his deeply nicked big toe remained. The rest of his toes, along with a large, slanting portion of the flesh which should have been below them, had been hacked off.

"Oh, Adam . . ."

"It's not a pretty sight, I admit. I probably would

have died if they hadn't stopped the bleeding with a torch—''

''Why?'' she blurted, her hand flying to her mouth. ''Why?''

''I was foolish enough to run away not long after my mother drowned herself. Dominick's dogs found me, then he and his men caught up. They executed my punishment right on the spot. I guess I was lucky, or else Dominick was in a charitable mood. He's been known to chop off the whole foot.''

With sickening clarity, Susanna envisioned the grisly scene. Her stomach pitching, she dashed to the chamber pot in a corner not far from the bed. As she hunched over it, her body wracked by dry heaves, she was grateful she hadn't yet had anything to eat.

''I'm sorry,'' Adam said behind her. ''I shouldn't have shown you outright, but explained it first.''

''No, I'm fine,'' she murmured, straightening to lean shakily against the wall. As he closed the distance between them, carrying two full glasses of wine, she noticed that his limp was far more pronounced now that he didn't have the support of his boot. She accepted the wine with trembling fingers and drank deeply, almost gulping.

''Better?''

She lowered the half-empty glass and wiped her mouth and chin, where some wine had dribbled. ''Yes, I think so. I'm sorry, Adam . . . I didn't mean to—''

''No apologies. I understand.''

They stood there for a long moment, staring silently into each other's eyes, then he took her glass. After setting it on the bedside table next to his own, he drew her with him to the bed, where he gently pushed her loosely draped gown from her shoulders. Susanna didn't protest when he turned her around slowly and, after sweeping her long hair over one shoulder, began to unlace her stays. She stood there numbly as she thought of the man she might have married.

How could she have been so completely fooled by such a diabolical monster? She had always prided herself on her good judgment of character, but in this instance, she had been totally, frighteningly wrong. It was just as Adam had said. Beneath that smooth, devastating charm and those impeccable manners lurked a ruthless, cold-blooded killer.

She shuddered, recalling Dominick's strange statement to her about Corliss on the night of her ball . . . something about slaves knowing their place and that they must be treated with a firm hand. Dear God, if she had married Dominick, she would have subjected all the innocent people under her care to the horrors Adam had described, and herself to endless unhappiness.

No doubt Dominick had had every intention of selling Briarwood to pay his debts. What then of her sworn promise to Camille? In one fell swoop she would have lost everything. No wonder Adam had claimed she would have made the biggest mistake of her life!

She really should thank him, Susanna thought as her stays fell from her body and Adam turned her to face him again. She should thank him for saving her from such a man—

No, he had used her! she reminded herself, looking into his striking brown eyes, which were so filled with desire. He had wanted her only for his revenge, and now, obviously, to satisfy his lust. Damn him, he had lied to her, saying he loved her just to sway her to his purpose!

Yet how could she blame him? a far stronger inner voice asked as he lifted her thin chemise above her head and cast it to the floor. She had hated her father for his cruel abuses, but his beatings had left no permanent scars on her body. His abuse hadn't maimed her for life. She suffered from nightmares, but she could always hope that in time, her bad dreams would fade. Not so the marks that Adam bore. They would be a part of him forever.

She had harshly judged this man for seeking vengeance against another who had not only brutally mistreated him but also been responsible for the horrifying deaths of his parents. Wouldn't she have done exactly the same thing if she had been in his place? She knew she would.

"Woman, you are so beautiful," Adam said softly, gathering her close to kiss her bare shoulders, her throat. "Perfection."

Susanna's eyes dimmed as he knelt in front of her to kiss her breasts, and she tossed back her head so her tears would not spill down upon him.

How much she wanted to tell him that she found him equally beautiful, despite his ravaged flesh. That he was as whole and perfect in her eyes as no other man had ever been to her.

But she kept silent, remembering with blistering pain how he had said he didn't love her. He only desired her and wanted her to play his docile, obedient wife. Nothing more.

Yet that couldn't be all there would ever be between them! Susanna thought desperately as Adam rose and swept her into his arms, then laid her on the bed.

Regardless of the countless lies and deceptions that had brought them together, they were husband and wife now. They would be sharing the rest of their lives. Was she willing to settle for this constant warring and mistrust when there might be a slim chance that they could have much more? She used to think that love wasn't important, that she could be happy without it, but now she wanted Adam to love her!

As he moved away, Susanna watched, awestruck, as he stripped off the last of his clothes, baring his hard, swollen arousal to her gaze. She felt such a rush of excitement that it shook her with its intensity.

Desire was a start, wasn't it? It could lead to love. Maybe after he attained his vengeance against Dominick, Adam might find it within himself to forgive her for misleading him when she had mistakenly believed it was the right thing to do. Maybe then there might be room in his heart for something more than hate, anger, and all-consuming bitterness. She could hope—

"No tears, no pity," Adam whispered huskily, lying

down beside her and blanketing her with his warm, powerful body. He kissed her eyelids, her damp cheeks, then found her mouth, his lips so wondrously demanding that all thoughts fled save one. As she wrapped her arms around him, her hands touching for the first time the roughened, raised scars on his back, she returned his kiss with all the passion she possessed.

Yes, she could hope . . .

# Chapter 20

**"I** believe that concludes our business, Mr. Thornton," said Benjamin Carter matter-of-factly, closing the large ledger in front of him. The stout Yorktown merchant leaned back in his chair and laced his short, stubby fingers over his stomach. "Mr. Spencer's debts are paid in full as far as this shipping firm is concerned."

"And you will relay a letter of our transaction to your London office?" Adam queried, grimly satisfied that the moment of his revenge had drawn that much closer.

"Yes, indeed. One of our ships is sailing this afternoon and that letter will be upon it. My superior will be most delighted with this sudden turn of events. We've been concerned about Mr. Spencer's reluctance to offer any payment against the sums we've advanced him over the years. You've done an overwhelmingly gracious thing in covering his liabilities. Quite commendable." The older man cleared his throat, his double chin jiggling above his frothy white jabot. "Might I ask what has spurred such generosity?"

Adam rose from his chair, telling this merchant what he had already informed a dozen or so others, none of whom were aware that he was making the rounds to every tobacco-shipping firm with which Dominick had ever conducted business.

"It has come to my attention that he is having some monetary difficulty and since my recent marriage has

266

given me substantial means, I decided to make him a small gesture of assistance. It's the least I could do after everything he did for me while I worked at Raven's Point.''

"You're much too modest, young man. Five hundred pounds is no small gesture—''

"And for that reason, Mr. Carter, I would very much prefer that no word of our transaction leave this room. You know that a planter's financial status is his honor here in the Tidewater. Be it five pounds or a thousand, Mr. Spencer may take strong offense if he discovers by some other route than my own admission what has transpired here today. I'm sure he would not want his . . . difficulties to become common knowledge. You understand.''

"Yes, of course,'' the merchant agreed, rising ponderously to shake Adam's hand. "Discreet business arrangements, I'm proud to say, are a hallmark of our firm.'' Clearing his throat again, he rounded the desk and walked Adam to the door. "Please give your lovely wife my congratulations on your wedding. I remember the day she arrived on Captain Keyes's ship. Hard to believe it was only a little over a month ago. I miss that old salt. James Cary, too.''

"So do I,'' Adam said, donning his tricorn. "A good day to you, Mr. Carter.''

"Likewise, young man. Likewise.''

Stepping outside into the bright midday sun, Adam slowly exhaled. His plan of buying up Dominick's debt from the man's creditors was proving as effortless as he had imagined it would be. Not one merchant had asked him any more pointed questions than Benjamin Carter, which confirmed for him that cold hard cash on the table silenced even the most inquisitive of men.

During the week since the wedding he had seen everyone he needed to in Yorktown, Williamsburg, Newport News, and Hampton. Now he had only a few more merchants to visit, which would require an overnight trip to Norfolk starting tomorrow morning.

He didn't like the thought of leaving Susanna alone

at Briarwood for an entire evening, but her presence would only slow his journey. He wanted to travel swiftly on horseback rather than by a cumbersome coach. If all went as planned, by the beginning of next week he would be ready to confront Dominick at Raven's Point. He could hardly wait!

Preparing to mount his chestnut stallion, Adam spied a silversmith's sign down the street and was reminded that he had yet to purchase a real wedding band for Susanna.

She had spent the entire week at home—refusing to accept any of the flood of invitations addressed to Mr. and Mrs. Adam Thornton because, as she had explained to him, she wanted to become better acquainted with the domestic workings of Briarwood—so there hadn't really been any need for her to have a proper ring. But at the Byrds' summer ball on Saturday, an event he had decided would make the perfect occasion to introduce themselves into Tidewater society as husband and wife, it would be an embarrassment for her not to have a ring, and he wished to spare her that. She deserved some reward for complying with the code of behavior he had demanded of her.

In fact, she had complied a bit too well for his liking, Adam thought with irritation as he strode toward the silversmith's shop. She was playing the sweet, obedient wife too expertly. Something was going on in that devious mind of hers, and he didn't know what it might be. All he knew was that her behavior had drastically changed toward him, starting with the morning after their wedding night.

She had actually awoken beside him with a beautiful, sleepy smile upon her face and greeted him not with the sharp, defiant words he had expected, but in a soft, playful tone like the one she had used with him before he had discovered her true identity. And when he had captured her in his arms, overcome with desire for her lush body pressed against his, she had offered no protest, seemingly welcoming his embrace with a fiery passion that fully matched his own.

So she had done all week. They had made love countless times. It had gotten to the point where they elicited knowing smiles from the servants when they retired early to their chamber each night, and the same reaction when they finally came downstairs together at mid-morning. On several afternoons he had even whisked her to their room after arriving hot and sweaty from his journeys to meet with Dominick's creditors, and she hadn't seemed to mind at all.

He couldn't forget what she had said to him yesterday afternoon in the privacy of their chamber after he had returned from Williamsburg, her hands running eagerly over his bare chest.

"I like the way you smell after a long ride, Adam . . . sweat, horses, leather."

Then, with the wanton look in her eyes that never failed to excite him, she had flicked at his nipple with her pink, darting tongue—

"Damn!" Adam muttered to himself, wishing he could forgo the blasted ring and ride straight home. It was a good thing his long waistcoat hid his sudden and uncomfortable arousal. Willing himself to be patient, he entered the shop, determined that this would be the fastest purchase he had ever made.

"Where's your mistress?" Adam asked Corliss as he entered the sunny hall and saw the waiting-maid coming down the stairs carrying some gowns which must be destined for the laundry. "Is she in our room?"

"No, sir, Master Thornton, she's been with Prue in the kitchen since you left this morning."

"Doing what?" he inquired, disappointed to hear that Susanna wasn't even in the house. His ride home had been fueled by the seductive image of what they would do when he found her, whether it be in their chamber, the drawing room, or the library.

"Baking bread, I s'pose," Corliss replied, appearing just as bemused about how her mistress had chosen to spend the day as was Adam. Then, shaking her head, the waiting-maid gave a shrug. "Mistress Camille told

Prue that she'd never done it before and she wanted to learn how.''

Without a reply, Adam threw his hat on the table and left the house, wondering why Susanna was troubling herself with such a chore. Becoming more familiar with the domestic workings of the plantation was one thing, but actually participating in them was another.

Bread-baking was no proper pastime for a planter's wife. He would have to explain to her that her duties were to oversee the household from a discreet distance, and to let the servants do the real work. She probably didn't yet understand the distinction. Yet if she continued on as she was, Ertha would begin to wonder why her gently bred mistress had a stronger interest in such mundane tasks than in the appropriate diversions of a lady of leisure.

As Adam neared the large brick outbuilding that served as a kitchen, the wonderful aroma of fresh-baked bread wafted to him. Although most of the windows were opened to the light breeze, he imagined it must be very hot in there from the summer heat and oven fires.

Preparing himself for the stifling warmth, Adam was almost to the door when it suddenly flew open. His heart lurched as Susanna rushed out to greet him, smiling prettily and carrying a wicker basket covered with a red-checked cloth. No matter how hard he had tried to stifle his powerful feelings toward her this past week, they always hit him with renewed strength whenever he saw her again after being apart for even a few moments.

Damn, if this woman hadn't bewitched him entirely! When she smiled at him like that, as if she was really glad to see him, it was all he could do to remind himself of her callous deception.

''Adam! I saw you ride up to the house,'' she said excitedly, wiping a damp tendril from her flushed face, ''and I was just coming to meet you after Prue quickly prepared us a picnic.'' She turned back the cloth, proudly revealing a crusty loaf of bread. ''Look, I made this myself. Isn't it lovely?''

Adam wanted to say that she was the loveliest thing he had ever seen, but he held his tongue. It wouldn't do to let her know he might be softening toward her. His compliments were profuse enough when she lay naked in his arms, her sea-green eyes liquid with passion. He was surprised that he hadn't yet let slip how much he loved her. He seemed to lose his head at their most intimate moments.

Recalling with an impatient ache in his loins what he had planned for their afternoon, he nodded in answer to her query and asked, "What's this about a picnic?"

"It's such a pretty day, Adam. I thought we could visit that pond you took me to the day after I got here. You know, your favorite place. I've been thinking about it all morning. It was so beautiful there, so cool under the willows, and it was so hot in that kitchen . . ."

She was looking at him so hopefully, he couldn't refuse her, despite his desire to throw her over his shoulder and carry her upstairs to their room like a barbarian with his captive.

And, he reasoned, noting how her simple day gown clung damply to her body, a trip to the pond didn't sound like such a bad idea. Perhaps after their meal, she might be willing to strip off her clothes and join him for a swim . . .

"Done," he agreed, his pulse racing when she threw a bright smile at him that could light any man's heart, even one as suspicious as his own.

"Give me a minute," she said, handing him the basket. "I just have to fetch my straw hat."

As she raced to the house, her skirts fluttering around her slim ankles, Adam wondered anew about her unsettling change of attitude. He could almost swear she was deliberately going out of her way to please him. Maybe she too had imagined them swimming together and what might come afterward . . .

Whatever that cunning wench's plans, Adam thought with sudden unreasoning anger, berating himself for his weakness as he strode to the stable, he didn't trust her. For all he knew, she might be acting so agreeable purely out of pity, for once she had seen his ravaged body on their wedding night, her mood had completely changed toward him.

Yet he didn't want her pity. The only thing he wanted from her was love, and from such a conniving, manipulative woman as Susanna Jane Guthrie, that was impossible. From now on he would watch her with extra care. He didn't trust her as far as he could see.

"Adam, would you like some more apple cider?" Susanna asked, trying to hide her disappointment. It seemed that her plan to build some rapport between them with a lighthearted picnic at one of his favorite places was failing miserably. He had said little to her during their ride here, and now he was acting just as distant, barely touching Prue's savory chicken pie, corn and cucumber relish, or her own freshly baked bread. "I'm sorry I didn't think to bring any wine—"

"Cider is fine," he replied, scrutinizing her as he held out his empty cup. He seemed to be trying to read her thoughts.

She quickly refilled the cup, her hands trembling a little.

Why was he looking at her as if he was angry with her? She hadn't done anything to upset him. Lowering her eyes and sighing to herself, she twisted in the stopper and set the bottle back in the basket.

How strange that the more she tried to please him, the more he seemed to retreat from her. She had done her best this last week to act exactly as he wanted her to, even down to curbing her natural temper which was still pricked that he would have so cruelly lied about being in love with her, but she didn't think she had gained the slightest favor with him at all.

The only time he dropped his guard was during their lovemaking.

Thankfully his desire for her had not flagged; instead, it seemed he couldn't get enough of her, which perfectly matched the way she felt about him. When he held her in his arms, his throbbing body buried deep in her own, it was easy to believe that he could one day grow to love her.

Yet she wanted to feel that same harmony when they were alone like this, sitting close together but not touching. She wanted him to talk to her the way he did when the servants were around, a teasing, affectionate banter she knew was feigned for their benefit but which she desperately wished was real. She wanted to feel as if he might start to trust her, as he had before he had discovered her deception. Oh, she wanted . . . she wanted . . .

You've got to be patient, Susanna Jane, she chided herself, glancing out across the placid pond. Adam hadn't won his vengeance against Dominick yet. She would have to bide her time, then, she hoped, begin to make inroads into his heart. Meanwhile, she would keep on as she had been, trying to rebuild trust between them.

"What are you thinking about?"

His question, almost a demand, startled her, and her wide gaze flew to his face.

"Nothing, really."

"I don't believe you. You were frowning to yourself."

How she hated those words . . . *I don't believe you.* She had heard them so often from him. When would she hear him say, "I believe you" or "my love" again, and mean it?

"I . . . I was wondering how your morning went in Yorktown," she replied, knowing he wouldn't be receptive to what really lay in her heart.

"Well enough."

"You've been traveling so much, Adam. Does it have anything to do with your plans for Dominick?"

Susanna was stunned by the glimmer of suspicion in his eyes. She had only asked him an innocent question!

"That's none of your concern," he answered gruffly. "You might as well know now that I'll be leaving for Norfolk tomorrow morning, and I probably won't be back until Friday night. If it gets late, don't bother holding supper or waiting up for me. You'll need a good night's rest before the Byrds' summer ball on Saturday. We'll be leaving early in the morning to allow us plenty of time to reach Westover before the festivities begin.''

"So you'll be gone tomorrow night?" she asked, not cheered by the prospect of spending a long evening without him. She could already imagine how distressingly empty their bed would feel.

"Yes." Adam was quiet for a brief moment, then asked suspiciously, "Why do you ask?"

"I'll miss you." It was out before she could stop it, but she didn't regret saying the words, despite the shocked expression on Adam's face. His surprise quickly vanished, yet she felt a subdued sense of satisfaction that she could cut through his guard, however fleetingly.

As a tense silence settled between them, Adam shifted away from her and grabbed his riding coat from the grass beside him, as if preparing to leave. An intricately carved object slid halfway out of one deep pocket and Susanna noted with heart-stopping alarm that it was the ivory butt of a pistol.

"You're not going to meet Dominick in a duel, are you, Adam?" she blurted, glancing at him in horror.

"The bastard doesn't deserve such a swift revenge," he replied, shoving the pistol back into his coat. "This is for my own protection."

"Protection?" she queried, her heart pounding faster as stark fear for him gripped her. "From what?"

"I don't plan on meeting the miserable fate that James Cary suffered at Dominick's hands. If he comes looking for me with such an intent, he'll receive a bullet right through his rotting heart."

Susanna was aghast, but then, why should she be surprised? Dominick had murdered Camille's father, or so Adam claimed. If he had killed once, he could kill again. "Oh, Adam, this is terrible. Do you think he will . . . come here looking for you?"

He glanced at her sharply, and his tone was grim as

he replied, "It's possible. I'm preventing him from possessing the one thing he needs to save himself from financial ruin, just as James did months ago. Your wealth would have funded his gambling for years to come. I would say, in fact, that it's likely he'll try to kill me if he can find a way to make it look like another accident."

"How—how did he kill Mr. Cary?"

"Shot him point-blank while he was out hunting alone, then slumped his body over a fieldstone wall and situated his fired musket so that it looked as if James had accidentally shot himself in the gut while trying to climb over."

"How horrible."

"It wasn't a pretty sight." Adam swallowed hard, his voice growing heavy with contempt. "Dominick's no fool. Although I told the constable about his argument with James the day before the death, and although Josiah vouched for me, Dominick escaped any suspicion. A prostitute in West Point swore that he had spent the entire afternoon with her. He knew better than to put Cleo up to such a ruse, even if he could have threatened her into lying for him. No one takes the word of a black slave over the word of a white man, especially one who sits on the governor's council."

"But, Adam, are you absolutely sure that Dominick murdered Mr. Cary?" she asked, knowing her question would upset him but needing to ask it just the same. She had wondered about it since he had first revealed his suspicion, but hadn't dared to ask him until now. "If no one saw it happen . . . and there was no proof—"

"You're right, I have no proof, but you forget how well I know the man," he said, his eyes ablaze. "I know that Dominick killed James as surely as I carry this pistol. You can damned well believe what you want." He snorted in disgust. "Woman, you simply amaze me. After everything I told you last week—"

"I never said I didn't believe you, Adam. I do."

He didn't seem to hear her, and rose in one swift

movement to his feet. Sweeping up his coat, he dug in the opposite pocket and withdrew a small wrapped package. He tossed it into the grass at her feet.

"What's this?" she asked.

"Something you'll need for the Byrds' party. You can't go with that piece of metal wrapped around your finger."

Susanna did her best to ignore his bitterly sarcastic tone as she unwrapped the package, revealing a red velvet box, and then opened the lid. She gasped softly. She had never seen such an exquisite ring, the filigreed gold and square-cut emerald at its center reflecting brilliantly in the sun.

"Oh, Adam, it's beautiful." With trembling fingers, she removed the twisted bed-curtain ring and replaced it with her new wedding band. It fits perfectly. Look!"

But he had moved to the sloping edge of the pond, his back to her. Hurt filled her that he would so pointedly refuse to share in her happiness, and sudden tears stung her eyes. She forced them back, reminding herself miserably that only time could change this impasse between them. Time and her continued patience.

After setting the curtain ring carefully in the box, as she wanted to keep the iron strip for sentimental reasons, she shut the lid and began to gather together the refuse from their picnic. She sensed he was in no mood either to eat or swim . . .

"I don't want you to help Prue in the kitchen ever again."

"What?" she asked, raising her head from her task to find him glaring at her.

"You are now a planter's wife, and planters' wives manage their households from a proper distance, which means they do not participate in their servants' work. Do you understand?"

Her temper flaring, Susanna nonetheless tried to keep it under control. "What do you propose I do with my time, then? I don't know how to do needlepoint, and I'm all thumbs with a needle and thread anyway. I'm not at all musical—"

"You can learn, can't you? You've grasped well enough how to act the part of a lady, wielding a fan and performing the niceties of proper society. The music room is full of fine instruments gathering dust. I'll hire you a music teacher, and I'll order enough stitchery materials from Yorktown to keep you busy for months."

"But I don't like to sew, Adam. I hate it, in fact. To me, it's a waste of time when I could be making myself useful around the house—"

"I don't care what you like or don't like," he broke in with harsh vehemence, approaching to stand only a few feet from her. "Planters' wives work embroidery, play the harpsichord, entertain guests, discreetly direct the house servants' activities, and care for their husbands' and children's needs. Do I make myself clear?"

Susanna stared at him sullenly. Her anger at his insensitivity quickly overcame her excited thoughts of the family they might have together.

"Good God, woman, if you continue baking bread and toiling in the kitchen, Ertha will suspect all the more that you are not her precious Camille!"

"Oh, Adam!" Susanna blurted without thinking, completely exasperated with him. "That doesn't matter anymore! She already knows."

It was too late to clap a hand over her mouth. As Adam's expression of utter incredulity quickly became one of darkening rage, she inwardly cursed her heedless tongue. She had planned to tell Adam what she had done sometime during the next few days, but she had hoped to introduce the topic gently, to prepare him first. So much for that.

"What do you mean, she already knows?"

"I—I told her the truth . . . yesterday morning after you left for Williamsburg. She'd been staring at me so strangely all week, watching my every move, and I just couldn't bear it anymore—"

"You couldn't bear it anymore?" he shouted, grabbing her shoulders and hauling her to her feet. "Heaven help you, woman, do you know what you've done?"

"Of course I do!" Susanna retorted as his fingers bit cruelly into her flesh. Her words tumbled from her mouth in a nervous flood. "I explained everything to her and, though she was understandably shaken to hear about Camille's death she was relieved to know the truth. Poor Ertha had thought she might be going crazy since she saw that portrait. Anyway, she swore not to say a word to anyone. She knows that if Briarwood were ever sold, those servants who aren't free would find themselves on the auction block. They're like her family, Adam, you know that. She promised not to do anything to jeopardize them, and I believe her. Besides, Briarwood is the only home she's ever known. She would have no place to go—"

"I'll tell you where you're going to go," he muttered ominously, sweeping her suddenly into his arms and carrying her to her horse, where he hoisted her unceremoniously into the saddle. "You're going to leave right now and ride straight for home before I do something I might regret!" Flinging the reins into her hands, he ordered harshly, "Get out of here!"

When she only stared at him stupidly, too stunned to speak, Adam slapped her mare's rump. "Go, damn you! Now!"

Susanna held on to the reins for dear life as her startled mount shot out from beneath the willow tree into the full glare of the afternoon sun.

She didn't look back. She kept her tear-blinded eyes fixed straight ahead as she raced for home, her heart thundering as furiously as her mare's flying hooves.

# Chapter 21

❦◇◇◇❧

❝**W**hat are you doing, Corliss?❞ Susanna asked her frowning waiting-maid, who had just entered the bedroom carrying a large leather saddlebag and proceeded to Adam's wardrobe.

❝Packing some clothes for your husband, Mistress Camille. He said for me to tell you that he's leaving for Norfolk today instead of tomorrow morning.❞ The maid clucked her tongue in disapproval. ❝You two must have had some lovers' quarrel. He's in a foul mood, to be sure. He had me fetch Ertha to meet him in the library before he would let me come upstairs, and he told me real angry-like to be quick about filling this bag.❞

Not surprised by this news, Susanna rolled onto her back on the bed and stared blindly at the canopy overhead.

Should she go to him and apologize? she wondered. Now that she had had an hour or so to think about it, she supposed she couldn't blame him for becoming so upset with her at the pond.

He probably thought his plan for revenge had been ruined because of what she had done. But she wouldn't have said a thing to Ertha if she believed there was the slightest chance the housekeeper might have reacted to the truth any differently than she had. Surely he could see that! She didn't want to end up in prison any more than he wanted to lose Briarwood and his chance to get even with Dominick.

❝Ertha sure looked nervous going in to talk to him,

though I can't imagine why," Corliss added, folding several shirts and stuffing them into the saddlebag. "She's been a real puzzle since a few days before you and Master Thornton got married. Sometimes snapping our heads off, other times saying nothing all day. Then all of a sudden yesterday she finally seemed her old self again." The young woman sighed with exasperation. "If she starts grumbling at us again when she gets through talking with Master Thornton . . ."

"I'm sure Ertha will be fine," Susanna reassured her, sitting up. She imagined Adam was just confirming everything she had told him, especially the part about the housekeeper swearing not to tell a soul about what she now knew.

"Did my husband say anything to you about coming upstairs to say good-bye?" she asked.

"Not a word, and maybe you don't want him to," the maid replied, fastening the buckle on the bulging saddlebag. "He looks mighty angry. We don't see Master Thornton like that too often, but when we do, we stay clear out of his way." She hurried to the door. "I better get down there, Mistress Camille, before he starts hollering for me. I've never heard him raise his voice but right now, I wouldn't be surprised if he did."

"Wait a minute, Corliss," Susanna requested, rising from the bed and rushing over to the writing desk. Deciding to heed her maid's warning and unwilling to face Adam's wrath again, she quickly jotted a note of apology, then, after sprinkling it with a few drops of her jasmine perfume, she handed it to the maid. "Please give this to my husband. No, better yet . . ."

Thinking that in his sour mood Adam might not read her note, Susanna undid the buckle and shoved it into the saddlebag.

"Good idea," Corliss said with a small smile, as if guessing her thoughts. "Master Thornton will find it in there tonight when he stops along the way to Norfolk, and after a long hard ride to clear his head, he'll be ready to read whatever you've got to say." Her frown reappeared. "You did say something nice in that letter, didn't you?"

"Yes," Susanna replied, smiling when her maid sighed with relief.

"That's good. I hope you two aren't going to have fights like this very often, Mistress Camille. What with Ertha acting so crazy these past days, and now you and the master mad at each other . . . or from what I see, him being more mad than you, I feel like I'm walking on eggshells around this place."

"Corliss!"

They both jumped at the deep, ringing sound of Adam's voice echoing from downstairs.

"See what I mean?" the maid said as she fled out the door and down the corridor, calling, "I'm coming, Master Thornton!"

Susanna shut the door and leaned upon it, taking heart in the thought that Adam hadn't sounded angry so much as impatient. She waited almost breathlessly, wondering if he might yet come to say good-bye, but when several long moments passed and she still didn't hear his familiar footsteps, she imagined he had already left the house.

Disappointed, she walked out onto the balcony and leaned against the curved wooden railing. Looking out over the beautiful sunlit garden, she thought of the words she had hastily written to him.

*I'm truly sorry I upset you, Adam. If I thought Ertha wouldn't understand, I never would have told her. It's certainly not my intention to thwart your plans. I believe Dominick should pay dearly for what he's done to you. Yours, Camille.*

Sighing softly, she hoped her apology would placate him, at least until she could tell him in person. When he returned from Norfolk, she planned to offer him a special apology he wouldn't forget.

"Thank you, Prue. Everything looks absolutely wonderful," Susanna said sincerely, admiring the exquisite table set with a lacy cloth, gleaming silver service, and fine bone china. A dozen tall white candles graced the candlelabra placed off to one side, surrounded by a fragrant wreath of blood-red roses and delicate baby's breath freshly picked from the garden.

"My pleasure, Mistress Camille. Anything to help you and Master Thornton make up with each other."

"Are you sure our supper will stay warm under those lids?" Susanna asked doubtfully, paying no heed to the cook's reference to her and Adam's quarrel two days ago. She had grown accustomed to the fact that the servants were just as anxious to see things resolved between them as she was. "I'm not exactly sure when Adam will be home, although it should be soon." She glanced at the mantel clock. "It's already eight-thirty. I can't imagine that he'd want to be traveling the roads for long in the dark."

"He'll get here, Mistress Camille, and don't you worry none about the food. It'll keep just fine. My herbed veal pie will taste just as good steaming hot or lukewarm, same as those buttered greens and new potatoes. And the flavors will shine through much better when that peach cobbler has a chance to cool a little. Now if there's anything else you'll be needing—"

"No, Prue, this looks like everything. You go get yourself a good night's rest. You certainly deserve it after preparing this feast."

"No trouble at all, Mistress Camille. Good evening, then."

After the cook left the softly candlelit room, Susanna settled herself in a stuffed chair as comfortably as her taut nerves would allow, and picked up a book of poetry.

She was not surprised when her eyes could not focus on the page. She was both excited and apprehensive, as she had been all day. She had missed Adam desperately, more than she could have ever thought possible, and she couldn't wait until he was home.

Would he still be angry with her? Could she hope he might be glad to see her?

After another futile attempt at reading, Susanna set

down the book. Leaning her head back against the plush brocade, she closed her eyes and listened impatiently as the minutes ticked by.

His heart thumping hard, Adam closed the bedroom door silently behind him, and stepped carefully over to the chair where Susanna was sleeping, her head resting upon the arm cushion and her legs tucked beneath her.

God, how he had missed her! He could not deny it. These past two days without her had been sheer hell.

Despite how angry he had been at her when he left Briarwood late Wednesday afternoon, though his temper had admittedly been soothed by his satisfactory exchange with Ertha, every mile that had taken him further away from her had been an agony, each night he had spent alone the worst torture. The harder he tried to suppress his love for her, the stronger and more insistent it became. This one emotion was a thousand times more powerful than the misgivings, distrust, and cold rationale he had pitted against it. Why, then, wasn't he willing to accept his feelings now that he was finally home with her?

Thrusting away his perplexing dilemma, Adam swept his gaze over her hungrily.

She looked so achingly beautiful in what remained of the sputtering candlelight, her silky hair spilling over the cushion like a cascade of burnished gold, her lovely features half-cast in shadow, her body lushly curved beneath her jade-green dressing gown. He longed to touch her. But he resisted the impulse, reluctantly deciding to wait until he was ready for bed.

Leaving her side, he noticed for the first time the prettily set table and the candles which had burned down to tiny stubs, only a few tiny flames still flickering. How long had she waited supper for him, even when he had told her not to? It was now almost midnight.

He had been delayed in Norfolk by a merchant important to his plan who had gone out of town and returned only late this afternoon. After concluding his business, Adam had caught the last ferry to Old Point Comfort, then had ridden at a devil's pace to Yorktown, where he had stopped briefly for some food and to speak with his attorney, who would be accompanying him to Raven's Point on Monday morning. By then it had already been half past ten, and he had thought Susanna would have long gone to bed. Instead, she had waited up for him . . . why?

Swamped by suspicion whenever he questioned her motives, Adam quietly stripped off his clothes and washed at the basin. It felt good to cleanse the dust and sweat of travel from his body.

The last thing he did was remove the note she had written him from his coat pocket and set it inside the top drawer of his wardrobe. The paper was a bit worse for wear, since he had balled it up after first reading it, but then he had smoothed it out carefully and kept the note upon his person for the remainder of his journey. Why, he didn't know, especially when that niggling suspicion crept into his mind every time he reread it—

Adam grimaced as the drawer grated loudly while closing, and he glanced over his shoulder to find Susanna stirring in the chair.

"What . . . Adam? Is that you?"

He was at her side in a heartbeat. He lifted her gently in his arms as she gazed at him drowsily, and carried her to the bed.

"Shhh, I didn't mean to wake you," he said, throwing back the covers and settling her upon the mattress. "Go back to sleep. We have to get up early tomorrow—"

"I don't want to sleep," she insisted, her eyes like liquid emeralds in the dim candlelight. "I want to hear about your trip . . . I've been waiting for you. What time is it?"

"Midnight."

"Oh, Adam, Prue prepared us a wonderful meal, but she had it brought up at eight. It must be stone-cold by now."

"That's all right. I ate in Yorktown. Did she bring us some wine?"

"Yes"—she began to scoot out of bed—"I'll get it for you."

"No, stay there. I'll get it. Would you like a glass?"

She nodded, then gasped softly, her eyes moving over him. She'd been so dazed from waking abruptly that she hadn't noticed until now that he was naked.

Smiling at her reaction, Adam poured them each a glass of wine and returned to the bed, knowing the wine wasn't all he was bringing to her. He wondered if she would be equally astonished by his hard erection, for his desire had been keenly triggered the moment she had said she didn't want to sleep. Nor did he, now that she was fully awake. Sleep was the last thing on his mind.

"Your wine, my lady," he said teasingly, touching his glass to hers and then enjoying a long draft.

Right now, he didn't want to think of anything but the sweet passion they would soon share. Her dressing gown had fallen slightly open, revealing the full, sensual curve of a creamy breast, and his desire surged even hotter as he realized she wasn't wearing undergarments.

"You'd best take a sip quickly," he bade her huskily when she seemed content to stare at him, a blush warming her cheeks when her wide gaze fell to his fully aroused shaft. "Before I am forced to take the glass from you. I don't want you to spill wine on the bed when I join you beneath the sheets."

She took a deep drink then, her expression becoming wantonly playful as she guessed the intent behind his words.

"I thought you might tell me about your trip first, Adam."

"There's nothing to tell. I went and now I'm home. With you."

Susanna shivered with anticipation, exulting that he actually seemed glad to be with her again. He certainly wasn't angry. Her fingers were trembling so hard that she found it difficult to raise the glass to her lips. She shakily managed one last sip before he set their glasses on the nearby table. She was surprised when he didn't readily join her in bed as he had threatened, but instead held out his hand to her. She looked at him questioningly.

"Stand up, my love. I want to undress you."

She started, hope flaring in her breast, for this was the first time he had spoken the endearment since their wedding night. How far she had come in her feelings toward him since she had defiantly demanded that he never call her "my love" again! Did she dare hope that his own feelings might be softening toward her?

"You will have an easy time of it tonight, Adam," she said softly, her own desire flaring red-hot as she laid her much smaller hand in his callused one and he pulled her up to stand in front of him. "I'm wearing no stays, no chemise, not even any linen drawers. Nothing but my robe."

"I know," he murmured, his free hand disappearing inside her silken dressing gown. Running his palm over her breast, he squeezed it gently. "I had a clue when I saw a hint of bare skin."

"You're very observant," she replied, her breath snagging as his thumb grazed her roused nipple, then circled it slowly.

"Always around you, Camille."

Wishing he would call her by her real name during such intimate moments, Susanna nonetheless knew it was a vain hope. He had sworn never to call her that again, and except for that one time at the height of his pleasure, she sensed that he had every intention of sticking to his word. Then again, she supposed she wouldn't mind so much if he continued to use his familiar endearment, even if he might not really mean it . . . yet.

"Your skin is so smooth. So soft," he said in a low, stirring voice, slipping her dressing gown from her shoulders, only to use it to catch her around the waist and draw her to him. "I love to feel your body touching mine."

"And I, yours." Susanna sighed as her breasts pressed against his broad, sleek chest, finding immeasurable pleasure in his hard muscles. His body was so powerfully built, like sculpted rock, and she always felt so protected in his embrace. He allowed her robe to fall to the floor, the silk drifting like cool water down the back of her legs, and her skin puckered with goose bumps.

"You're chilled. Here, let me warm you . . ." he whispered, his strong hands sliding up her thighs and over her bottom, lingering there to squeeze and caress her, then traveling along her spine, his fingers splaying wide to cover more of her as he added teasingly, "while you warm me." The hardness of his desire pressed urgently into her silken woman's hair. "Hold me there, my love. I want you to touch me . . . I want to feel your hands wrap tight around me."

Delighting in his provocative request, Susanna explored first the sinewed hollows below his hips which she found so fascinating, then she slipped her hands between their bodies and after tugging very lightly at the crisp curls she found there, she boldly curved her fingers around his thick shaft. She smiled as it leapt under her touch. She knew how much her intimate fondling pleased him, and on their wedding night when he had demanded that there be no sexual shyness between them, he had shown her what he liked most.

Cupping in one hand the warm, swollen parts of him that hung below, she began to slowly pump with the other, back and forth, again and again, feeling him grow even more rigid beneath her rhythmic caresses. As a groan came from deep in his chest, she stroked a little faster, a little harder.

"Like this, Adam?" she queried softly, moaning herself as he continued to race his hands over her body. She paused only to wipe the drops of wetness from the tip of his smooth, silken shaft with her palm and then slide her slippery hand anew down the huge length of him. Her other hand lightly squeezed him, her finger-tips rubbing the acutely sensitive space directly behind that which she cupped so gently. "And this?"

"Woman, you've learned far too well," came his ragged response, his body beginning to tremble against hers. "So well that I cannot withstand any more of your magic. Now it is my turn to give you such pleasure."

Susanna gasped as he pushed her gently back against the bed. She guessed what was to come and grew almost light-headed with anticipation. He captured her mouth in a long, deep kiss, his tongue tasting of wine, then whispered against her lips, "Sit down and then lie back, my love. I want you to open your beautiful body to me. I want to see you . . . all of you."

As she did what he asked, in his eagerness he slipped his hand between her lower legs which still dangled off the bed and drew them wide apart, then placed one knee between her thighs so he could bend over her. She stared up into his eyes, which were like burning black coals in the hazy light, thinking he was the most arrestingly handsome of men and how glad she was to be his wife. Then his lips found hers once more, his tongue plunging passionately into her mouth at the same moment his fingertips slid into her wet woman's softness, and her thoughts scattered into fiery slivers of charged sensation.

"Your skin tastes so sweet," he murmured thickly as his mouth trailed a molten path down her throat to her breasts, where he drew hungrily on her erect nipples. "And you smell so damned sweet." As his tongue flicked and tormented her, his teeth nipping her lightly, all the while his fingers kept up their wild assault. Then he left the bed and knelt on the floor. Cupping his hands beneath her bottom, he roughly pulled her toward him. "But I find this hot, fragrant place the sweetest seduction of all."

Susanna almost screamed as he lifted her lower body to his face and buried his tongue inside her, then speared it upwards and circled the tingling heart of her desire.

Tossing her head, her hands gripping his massive shoulders, she began to buck beneath the rapturous torture and begged him to stop. If he heard her, he didn't listen, or else the breathless words flooding from her mouth were an incoherent jumble.

Arching against his lips, the sensation of his panting breaths and relentlessly dueling tongue upon her flesh driving her to distraction, she began to shake, her heels bumping against his back. Suddenly she felt every wondrous sensation funneling to the point of his feverish onslaught and converge deep inside her like a tightly coiled spring.

"Adam . . . I . . . I . . ."

"I know, my love, I know," she heard him answer in her passionate delirium. Through half-closed eyes she saw him rise. He climbed swiftly onto the bed and hauled her on top of him. In the next dazed instant she was facing the headboard and straddling him, her body sinking onto his glorious erection until he filled her completely.

"Kiss me," he demanded hoarsely, pulling her to him and seizing her lips as he thrust powerfully inside her, burying himself to the hilt, only to withdraw and plunge into her again and again. Each time, she felt that coiled spring compress ever tighter . . . tighter . . . until finally her fingers splayed spasmodically upon his sweat-slickened chest and she could only whimper for the incredible rapture exploding within her.

"Kiss me!" Adam whispered against her softly parted lips, feeling his release come upon him so suddenly that he grimaced as if in excruciating pain.

Yet it wasn't pain that gripped him and caused him to stiffen, his shaft throbbing in rhythm with his racing heartbeat within the hot, wondrous tightness of her body, his breath tearing in great gasps from his throat. It was ecstasy, pure, unbounded, and radiantly blinding . . .

How long Susanna had lain collapsed upon his chest he could not say, but when Adam finally found it within himself to speak, he thought she must have fallen asleep.

"Camille?"

She was so quiet, so still, only her breath stirring the glistening hair that covered her face, that he began to believe she had lost consciousness from the sheer intensity of her passion. Wiping her hair from her flushed cheeks, he shook her gently.

"Camille?"

She lifted her head then, slowly, and looked at him with an expression he could not fathom, although her eyes gazed almost pleadingly into his.

"That's not my name, Adam."

His throat tightened, his heart brimming with so many things he wanted to say to her, but he couldn't bring himself to utter a word. If he declared his love for her again and she scorned him for it, he didn't know what he would do.

"It *is* your name. It must be." He almost added that he was truly sorry, but he remained silent, enfolding her in his arms and bringing her with him as he rolled onto his side. As his relaxed body slid from hers, he felt strangely bereft, as if he wished they could remain joined as one forever.

Passion was so damned fleeting. When it was over, love should come into play, sustaining them until the next time desire overwhelmed them. But between himself and this endlessly captivating woman there was only passion, all-encompassing as it was, and he wondered with acute regret if things would ever change and she would also come to accept his love.

Vain hope! On their wedding night she had said that she detested him. Such were the things that he possessed: her desire, which he truly wanted; her pity, which was the last emotion he wanted from her; and her hatred, which he had earned by forcing her into marriage.

Wholly frustrated, Adam willed himself not to dwell upon their seemingly insurmountable impasse. Especially not now, when she lay snuggled so warm and satiated against him, her slim hand resting over his heart and his cheek pressed against her soft, jasmine-scented hair.

Instead he would enjoy this moment, however fleeting. When they were together like this, savoring the sweet harmony after their impassioned lovemaking, it was so easy to imagine that things could be different between them.

"Adam?"

She wasn't looking at him, but at some distant point.

"Yes?"

"Tell me about your life . . . before you came to Virginia, I mean."

Startled by her request, he nonetheless didn't see any harm in answering her. They were married, after all. It seemed that they held few secrets from each other now, other than the one he kept locked so securely in his heart.

"What do you want to know?"

"Everything."

"There isn't much, really," he replied, raising himself on one elbow, while keeping the other arm securely around her. "My father was a miner on the Newcastle coalfield and my mother a seamstress. I worked in the mines, too, starting when I was seven, so I never had much chance to go to school."

"You taught yourself to read and write here at Briarwood, didn't you?" she asked, obviously having surmised that he had been offered no formal education at Raven's Point.

"Mostly," Adam said, recalling his consuming struggle to master those skills within his first year under James Cary's employ, and how when he finally had, he had used most of the wages he had saved to begin his own library. "Cleo managed to teach me a little—"

"Yes, Dominick told me that he'd had her tutored," she broke in softly. "He said so she might help him run his household."

"Whatever his reasons, it was an unusual thing for a white master to do for a slave," Adam replied, finding the topic unpleasant and wishing he hadn't brought it up. "But Dominick always had a soft spot for Cleo, however twisted. When he found out about our lessons together, we both got a beating, but that didn't stop her from writing a letter for me to my uncle in England. She risked a lot to see that it got aboard a ship in Yorktown, doing so practically under Dominick's nose when he took her with him to meet another ship carrying goods he had ordered from London."

"Did you ever receive an answer from your uncle?"

"No. Maybe he never got the letter. More likely he didn't have the money I asked him to loan me so I could buy my way out of my indenture, and was too embarrassed to write and tell me. He was a miner, too, with five children to feed . . ." Adam sighed. "It was a good try, but I didn't bother again."

"I'm sorry, Adam. We won't talk about this anymore. I only asked because I saw your books on grammar and the art of writing when I went to your office. Remember? You started to undress in front of me . . ."

He smiled at his memory of how prettily flustered she had become, but his lighter mood faded when he recalled the lateness of the hour. If they kept talking all night, neither of them would want to get up in the morning for the Byrds' summer ball. "Enough reminiscing. I think we should go to sleep now—"

"No, Adam, I'd like to hear the rest of your story," she insisted. "I won't interrupt again. I promise. Please go on."

He couldn't refuse her when she looked at him so expectantly.

"You said your father was a miner?" she prompted him.

"Yes," Adam began again. "His health began to suffer from breathing in coal dust, he was coughing up blood, and his wages weren't getting any higher, so he decided to try and make us a better life by emigrating to the colonies. He'd heard that America was a land of great plenty, and that a man could become anything he wanted there if he worked hard enough. We didn't have enough money for the sea passage from Liverpool, so we indentured ourselves. The captain of our ship said he would do his best to make sure we all ended up working together at the same plantation when we got to Virginia . . . and he kept his promise.'' Adam sighed, not wanting to go any further. "That's it.''

Silence followed as Susanna pondered what he'd just told her, then she murmured, "Your mother must have been a beautiful woman.''

"She was. With chestnut hair and laughing hazel eyes. But I think I favored my father, except for his sense of humor. I've always been a bit too serious for my own good.'' He drew her closer, entwining a honey tendril around his finger. "I know your mother must have been a beauty to have spawned you.''

"Aye, she was pretty. My father used to curse me up and down because I looked just like her, with the same eyes and hair.''

Wondering if Susanna realized that she had lapsed back into her London accent, Adam decided not to mention it to her. Perhaps her recollections were drawing it from her, he reasoned. Anyway, he liked it.

"What did your father do . . . Daniel, wasn't it?'' he asked her gently, feeling her stiffen against him.

"Yes. He was a foundryman until he lost his job. He never went back to find another. My mother died when I was three. When I turned four my papa sent me out into the streets to beg for him. Sometimes I even picked pockets, but that was only when I hadn't earned enough coins during the day to save myself from a beating.'' She slowly exhaled. "Sometimes he was so drunk that no amount of money made any difference.''

So that was the source of her vivid nightmares, Adam thought, sickened by what she must have suffered at that man's brutal hands. Yet he was also grateful that at least one thing she had told him when she was masquerading as Camille was true.

"So you ran away from him when he wanted to sell you to Keefer Dunn,'' he prodded, hoping not to upset her.

"Aye, when I was twelve. Lady Redmayne and Camille saved me. If they hadn't come along—" She shuddered in his arms, then quickly changed the subject. "I owe everything to Camille . . . Lady Redmayne, too, but especially Camille because she never treated me like her waiting-maid. I was her friend and she was mine, the kind you're lucky to find once in your life." Her low-spoken words throbbed with emotion. "I would have done anything for her. Anything. I owed her so much . . ."

As Susanna's voice faded into a poignant silence, Adam realized with startling clarity how cruelly he had misjudged her. Until now, he had never believed that she and Camille could have truly been close friends, but there was no mistaking the fervent testimony she had just given him. He recalled how Polly Blake had described Camille weeping so bitterly at her waiting-maid's burial. Those had been Susanna's tears for a lost friend . . . a friend whose dying wish she had sworn to honor.

"You know, Adam," she said, meeting his eyes, "I haven't had a single nightmare since we were married. Not even during the past two nights when you were gone." She looked abruptly away then, as if afraid he would read some emotion in her gaze. "You said to me once that you would help chase away my nightmares. I think you already have."

Adam froze against her, unable to believe what he had just heard from her lips.

Why had she said that to him, and so sweetly? he wondered, painfully recalling that evening in the library when he had sworn to protect her with his life and then admitted how much he loved her. A familiar mistrust crept like cold fingers through his mind and body, chilling him to the marrow. Why would she refer to such a moment? Why?

To know that she hadn't masqueraded as Camille out of her own selfish greed was one thing, but she had still purposely deceived him because she had thought he wasn't good enough to marry. He didn't dare hope that there was some affection behind her words, and open himself up for some new treachery.

No, there had to be some other explanation for why she was trying to make him believe her heart was softening toward him. There had to be some dark motive behind her countless attempts to please him, and this sudden, dangerously compelling flattery.

"We've talked enough, Camille," he said, hearing the hard, bitter edge in his voice. "I want you to look your best tomorrow and you won't if you have dark smudges under your eyes. Now go to sleep."

Turning abruptly onto his other side with his back to her, he could feel that she was staring at him in startled surprise, then she sighed in resignation.

"Very well, Adam. Good night."

He didn't answer, closing his eyes and his heart against her once more.

# Chapter 22

"Smile, Mrs. Thornton, or no one will know you're having a good time," Adam whispered in a low aside as they walked from the crowded dance floor to the side of the brightly lit room. He gave her elbow a sharp squeeze to emphasize his words. "I said, smile."

Susanna did her best, but her heart wasn't in it. How could it be, when he had been treating her so callously all day?

She was such a fool, thinking her revelation last night about her nightmares might please him. Instead it had made him so angry that he had scarcely spoken to her until they had arrived at Westover this afternoon. Then it was only to give her these brusque commands on how she was to behave at the home of the most influential planter in the Tidewater, William Byrd, or else to play the doting husband whenever anyone was around to see.

When was she going to realize that Adam didn't trust her? she wondered, cursing her impatience. It would be months before he believed anything she had to say, regardless of when he achieved his revenge against Dominick. Heaven give her the strength to wait that long! When he used such a cutting tone with her, it was all she could do to hold her tongue. Yet if she vented her temper, she imagined it would only drive him that much further away.

Overwhelmed with frustration, Susanna fanned her face with vigor. She was grateful for the lull in the music so she might catch her breath. The eight musicians had kept up an exuberant rhythm for almost an hour now. She felt flushed from her scalp to her slippered toes, not only from the spirited saraband they had just danced, but also from the stuffy warmth of the large reception room that served as the Byrds' ballroom.

Longing to move nearer the wide-opened windows for some fresh air, she glanced at Adam to find he was gazing at her in admiration. Familiar excitement shot through her, the kind she always felt when he looked at her in such a hungry manner.

"That rosy color in your cheeks suits you, my love," he said softly, his gaze straying to the rise and fall of her breasts, swelling provocatively against her daring bodice. "It goes very well with the cream silk of your gown . . . which fits you quite becomingly."

"Thank you, Adam," she replied, mollified that he would say such nice things to her when no one else was near. "I believe that's the first compliment you've paid me all day. I was beginning to believe you hadn't noticed how carefully I had dressed for this evening, it being our first social outing together as husband and wife."

His arresting brown eyes caught and held hers. "As I've told you before, Camille, nothing about you escapes my notice. Nothing."

"Well, you two lovebirds, are you enjoying the party?" came Robert Grymes's blustering voice. As their stout neighbor lumbered up to them, Susanna wished someone would quickly draw his attention elsewhere so that she and Adam might continue the first promising discussion they had shared since last night. But it was not to be.

"Yes, Mr. Grymes, we're having a lovely time," she said, greeting him with a gracious nod. "Aren't we, Adam?"

"Couldn't be better."

Susanna almost winced at the sarcastic tone that had

crept back into his voice. "And you, Mr. Grymes?" she queried, hoping the planter hadn't also noticed.

"Oh, yes, well enough, considering I had to attend alone. My poor Charity and my two youngest sons are abed with summer colds, and Matthew and Celeste are still pining over your sudden marri—" He stopped, clearing his throat in embarrassment. "Forgive me. I meant no insult."

"None taken," Adam answered smoothly. "Our marriage *was* very sudden, and Camille and I feel badly that your son and daughter are suffering undue distress on our account. It was never our intention to mislead them, was it, my love?"

It was Susanna's turn to reply tersely, resenting his pointed barb about her deception even as she remembered all too clearly how jealous Celeste's flirtatious attentions toward him had made her. "Of course it wasn't."

"Please, don't trouble yourselves. I'm sure they'll both get over it soon enough," Robert said in a rush, obviously eager to abandon the topic. "Young hearts mend quickly. Mine was broken a time or two before my beloved Charity consented to become my blushing bride."

"Mine as well," Adam commented dryly.

As Susanna glanced sharply at him, wondering with resentful curiosity who he had known before her who could have possibly broken his hate-filled heart, Robert replied, "There, you see? Happens to the best of us." He chortled, shrugging his rounded shoulders. "Well, I'm off to the game room again. There's a lively round of dice in progress, and so far Dominick Spencer holds the lead in winnings. Amazing thing. He usually has such rotten luck."

Susanna felt Adam's grip tighten painfully on her arm, which seemed to match her own sudden tension.

"Spencer is here?" he asked darkly.

"Yes, arrived about two hours ago, not long after myself. I believe he's been in the game room ever since," Robert replied. "Well, my congratulations on your marriage. I must say you two make a handsome couple. I had that same thought the first time I saw you together at the Yorktown docks, and even wondered then if there might be a chance you'd strike a fancy for each other . . ." He grinned broadly. "Seems my hunch proved right. I wish I had the same luck with the dice."

"So Dominick is winning for once," Adam said almost to himself as the jovial planter ambled away, greeting guests here and there. "Let him enjoy it while he can. Come Monday morning, he'll find his luck has changed."

"Monday?" Susanna asked, sensing from his dark, ominous expression that his moment of revenge was drawing near. Excitement swamped her. She had never imagined it would happen so soon!

Adam didn't readily reply, his eyes narrowing as he studied her face. When he finally spoke, it was not in answer to her astonished query but as if he was purposely avoiding the subject.

"You're still flushed, Camille. Perhaps you would like some refreshment. I could use a brandy or two myself."

"Yes, that would be nice," Susanna murmured, wondering why he was gazing at her so suspiciously. Surely he didn't think that if he revealed his plan to her, she would do something to jeopardize it. She had told him in her note the other day that she had no intention of thwarting his revenge. Why, oh, why couldn't he trust her even in this?

As Adam looped his arm through hers, Susanna gazed longingly at the opened windows across the room, the French lace curtains stirred by a balmy breeze.

"Actually, Adam, would you mind if I waited for you over there rather than accompany you to the dining room? I'm sure it's just as crowded by the refreshment table as it is in here. I feel so warm . . . though I'm sure I'll feel better if I stand by a window for a few moments."

"If you wish," he agreed, concerned. "I won't be

gone long. Would you like some lemon punch or wine?''

"Punch sounds wonderful," she murmured. Her gaze followed his broad back as he wound his way among the chattering guests to the door leading into the hall. She regretted that she hadn't had a chance earlier to tell him how magnificent he looked tonight, too, in his royal-blue coat and matching breeches. Despite his slight limp, he appeared the most virile and physically powerful of any man there.

Susanna felt a sudden rush of desire, thinking ahead to a few hours from now when they would finally be alone in the guest room the Byrds had graciously offered them for the night. She couldn't wait to unfasten the buttons on his silver brocade waistcoat and his white lawn shirt to reach the sensual wonder of his chest, where she would run her hands across those hard, sinewed muscles . . .

Her cheeks burning, she hurried to the window, eager for some fresh air. She actually felt light-headed from the room's stuffiness, and after leaning against the windowsill for a moment and finding no immediate relief despite the light breeze, she decided to step outside into the garden rather than risk the embarrassment of fainting in front of everyone.

Willing herself not to panic, Susanna hurried into the central hall, and although she caught a glimpse of Adam tossing down a brandy as he waited his turn at the punch bowl in the opposite dining room, she feared stopping for even a moment to tell him where she was going. Making her way quickly to the mansion's back entrance, she almost stumbled outside, her hand pressed to her rapidly beating heart as she dragged in gasps of the much cooler night air.

"Are you feeling ill, Camille?"

She froze at the sound of Dominick's voice, his tall, spare form materializing eerily out of the darkness.

"No, I'm fine," she stammered, thinking with alarm that she should return immediately to the house. Yet she still felt so dizzy, she feared she might faint in the hall.

Perhaps a few moments more would make her feel better she decided. She would stay right here by the door. Since there were other guests walking through the darkened gardens, Dominick wouldn't dare to accost her . . . would he?

"You don't look fine to me," he disagreed, stamping out the cheroot he had been smoking. He moved toward her abruptly and took her arm. "Your face is red. I think a walk in the garden might help to clear your head. The house is very warm tonight. Does your husband"—his tone grew harsh—"know you're out here?"

Flustered by his insistent grip on her arm, Susanna blurted without thinking, "No," then, realizing her foolish blunder, she hastily added, "I mean, he's fetching me some lemon punch. I'm sure he'll return shortly."

"Then walk with me, Camille, if only for a few moments. You'll feel much better by the time he joins you."

Before she could refuse, Dominick practically pulled her along with him, directing her away from the lighted safety of the house and toward the now-menacing garden.

"I'm elated that we've found this occasion to talk," he said, holding her uncomfortably close to his side. "When I arrived, I glanced briefly into the reception room and spied you among the guests, but I didn't think . . . things being as they are, of course . . . that we'd find any opportunity to be alone."

"Yes . . . uh, Mr. Grymes mentioned you were in the game room," she said, trying to keep her tone light. The cooler air was gradually reviving her wits, and she quickly determined to deal with this unnerving situation as calmly and rationally as possible. "He said you were having some good fortune with the dice."

"I was," he said tersely, his eyes gleaming in the faint moonlight, "but fortune is fickle, I have found. I decided to soothe my loss with some fresh air, and I'm very glad I did.''

Offering no reply, Susanna swallowed against the nervous tightness in her throat.

Although she was trying to keep a firm grip on her whirling emotions, the farther they walked from the house the more apprehensive she became, her imagination running away with her. Her mouth going as dry as cotton, she remembered all the horrible stories Adam had told her about Dominick's perverted passion for cruelty, and how sick she had felt upon seeing Adam's ravaged back and what remained of his foot. Dear God, was this monster going to do something terrible to her as well?

She couldn't have been more relieved when Dominick suddenly stopped with her almost in the center of the vast garden which stretched all the way to the blackened waters of the James. Could she hope that he wasn't planning to drown her for snubbing him on the day of their betrothal? She sharply inhaled when he faced her, knowing she was trembling and unable to stop.

''Words can't express, my dear, how bitterly disappointed I am that you're not wearing my wedding ring on your finger,'' he said, lightly caressing her upper arms. Susanna felt the raw tension in his touch, which made her think he might want to strangle her instead. ''I've never known a worse moment than when you informed me that Adam Thornton had become your husband. To choose my former servant over me . . . you can imagine my humiliation.''

''I—I told you I was sorry, Dominick,'' she said, chilled by his strange monotone, which was far more unsettling than harsh anger. ''It wasn't my intention to hurt you. When I came to Raven's Point that day, I was convinced that Adam held no affection for me and that I would be wasting my time to wait for him to change his mind. I had fully expected to marry you''—and how much she owed Adam for saving her from this beast! she thought fleetingly—''but when Adam heard the rumor of our betrothal and then declared his love for me, and me loving him all the while—"

"Spare me an account of your misguided feelings for that scum," Dominick snapped, his grip tightening as his facade of gentility shattered. "You should have been my bride, Camille Cary! My wife! Our fortunes should have been joined, not . . . not squandered on some lower-class trash. What could have possessed you to do such a thing? Your poor father must be writhing in his grave at the misfortune you have brought upon what should have been mine!"

"You're hurting me!" Susanna said hotly, her sudden rage that he would say such awful things about Adam, and even dare to mention Camille's father when *he* had been the foul murderer to send the man to his grave, completely overwhelming her fear. "I have apologized to you twice, Dominick. What more can I do? Now release me this instant! My head is much clearer, thank you, and I would like to return to my husband."

"Forgive me, my dear," Dominick said, loosening his grip, although he still held her arms. He took a deep breath, as if trying to regain his composure, and lowered his voice further. "I didn't mean to hurt you. It's just that I've been a broken man since your sudden marriage. I'm in love with you, Camille."

You're not in love with me, you disgusting bastard! Susanna thought furiously, sickened by his touch. All you wanted was the Cary fortune. No doubt you would have cast me into an early grave without a qualm, either!

"You shouldn't be saying such things to me," she objected, trying to twist free of his grasp. "I'm married to another man, Dominick . . . in love with another man!"

"Perhaps," he said silkily, forcing her to face him. "But if anything should ever happen, Camille, know that I would still want you for my wife, despite that you broke my heart. I will always love you. Never forget that."

What did he mean . . . if anything should ever happen? Susanna wondered, although she had a terrible inkling she knew exactly what he was talking about. Fear clogged her throat again, not for herself but for the man she loved more than life.

"You are very kind to think of me, Dominick," she somehow managed to reply, hoping not to give him the impression that she suspected the true purpose lurking in his murderous heart. "But I really should be getting back to the house."

She wanted to run as fast as her legs would carry her! She wanted to find Adam at once and tell him what she had just heard, warn him, protect him. He had been right! Dominick was plotting to kill him!

"Very well," Dominick said with obvious reluctance, finally releasing her. "I'm so glad we had this time to talk . . . to share our deepest feelings. Again, my dearest, don't forget what I said."

"I won't," she murmured, his frightening words burning into her brain.

"Perhaps, then, you will want to enlighten me, my love. I seem to have missed much of your conversation while looking for you."

"Adam!" Her heart pitching in her breast, Susanna whirled to find him standing only a few feet from them. It was so dark she couldn't read his face, but she could easily interpret his wide-legged stance, the set of his broad shoulders, and his furious tone.

"A good evening to you, Mrs. Thornton," Dominick said smoothly, a hint of satisfaction in his voice. "I enjoyed our walk immensely." He didn't deign to say a word to Adam but walked right past him toward the house.

"Adam . . . I can explain," she began, but he cut her off with a curt wave of his hand.

"I already know. You were too warm so you came outside to get some air and who should you find but Dominick, right?"

"Yes! That's exactly what happened. I didn't want to walk with him in the garden, but he took my arm and wouldn't let me go—"

"Save your lies, Camille," he interrupted harshly, grabbing her forearm more cruelly than Dominick had held her. "I don't want to hear any more. Remember? I know what a mistress of deception you are. I should have known that the moment you heard Dominick was at Westover you would conjure up some way to speak with him alone. And how expertly you accomplished it. You fooled even me. Now come on."

"Wh-where are we going?" she asked in confusion, running to keep up with him as he strode with her around the house toward the driveway.

"Home to Briarwood. I'm sure Elias is waiting for us with the carriage by now, our bags loaded."

"But why, Adam? What about the ball . . . and the festivities tomorrow, the picnic brunch and then the horse races? The Byrds prepared a lovely guest room for us—"

"I'm sure by now it's been offered to someone else. I gave Mr. Byrd and his wife our excuses after I discovered Dominick was also missing from the game room. I told them you weren't feeling well and that I thought it best we leave at once. I had already concluded that you were with that bastard, plotting against me. I had only to find you."

Thoroughly shaken by his irrational accusation, Susanna nonetheless attempted to reason with him as he hurried her toward their waiting carriage.

"Adam, you're not making any sense. I would never plot with Dominick against you!" She lowered her voice as they passed some guests strolling along the lantern-lit walkway in front of the house. "Please listen to me. He forced me into the garden. He told me how disappointed he was that I had married you, how I should have been his bride, not yours, and that he loved me."

"How touching."

"No, you don't understand. He told me that if anything ever happened, he would still want me to become his wife. Adam, look at me! He meant that if anything should happen to you . . . you were right about him! I think he's planning to kill you—''

"And no doubt he assured you that it wouldn't be long before you were freed from your forced marriage, didn't he, Camille?'' Adam lifted her into the coach with such anger that she fell hard against the seat. Joining her, he slammed the door with jarring finality as the carriage jolted into motion. "Is that what your precious Dominick meant when he told you so reassuringly not to forget what he had said . . . and you answered that you wouldn't?''

Susanna shook her head numbly, seeing that it was futile to argue with him. His fury had driven him beyond reason. She should have known that if he saw her with Dominick, he would think the worst.

"Did you tell him that I was seeking revenge against him?'' he demanded, not bothering to keep his voice down as the golden light spilling from Westover's many windows and the merry strains of a country dance faded into the distance.

"No.''

"You've never believed a thing I've told you about Dominick, have you? Not a single blessed word. No doubt you think I earned the scars on my body from my own insolence and disrespect for my gracious, aristocratic employer!''

Susanna couldn't answer for the sudden tears choking her. How could she ever have believed Adam might grow to love her? His behavior now proved that he hated her. Why else would he say and think such terrible things about her?

"God help me, woman, you will see on Monday that I have told you the truth! You're going to accompany me to Raven's Point with my attorney and witness the downfall Dominick Spencer has brought upon himself through his wretched excess and incalculable cruelty. Then perhaps you will finally understand that plotting alongside that monster and harboring any hope that he might yet become your husband would have brought you nothing but ruin!''

As tears tumbled down Susanna's flushed cheeks, Adam drew her roughly against him, his hard lips covering hers in a crushing kiss. Desire flared hot within her as acute as the bitter pain in her heart, and when he lifted her skirts and dragged her onto his lap so that she now faced him, her stocking-clad legs spread wide and straddling him, she knew that he meant to take her right there in the carriage.

His tongue ravaging her mouth, his panting breaths as ragged as her own, she heard the impatient tearing of fabric as her lower body was made bare to him. She felt him working at the flap of his breeches, the back of his hand brushing her inner thighs. Then he guided his massive arousal to that slick, hot place that despite his callous haste was crying out for him, and lifted her to receive him, impaling her body.

"Dammit, woman, you are my wife . . . no one else shall have you!" he swore against her lips, thrusting inside her even as she desperately bore down to meet him.

Their thunderous, shared release was instantaneous and overwhelming, their cries of ecstasy and anguish drowned out by the sharp clattering of hooves and the deafening rumble of wheels upon the road leading back to Briarwood.

# Chapter 23

❦

"**L**ook at it, the place hasn't changed at all . . . not even after five long years," Adam said, speaking not so much to a pale, silent Susanna or to William Booth, his equally silent attorney, as he was to himself.

His body tense and his pulse racing, he stared out the window as the lumbering carriage approached the huge, columned house which stood at the center of Raven's Point, each sight and sound sickeningly familiar.

He took in everything. The small slave children hoeing weeds in the tobacco fields alongside adults, their infrequent cries of hunger silenced by sharp cuffs from fearful parents or neighbors. The overseers on their snorting horses, cracking their whips.

The slaves' tattered clothes and half-starved forms, and as he could imagine so well even though the poor wretches were too far away to be seen clearly, their gaunt faces and hauntingly empty eyes. An eerie familiar silence hung like a funeral pall over the main grounds as the coach eased to a stop in front of the mansion. All around them slaves with bowed heads and wearily sagging shoulders were going about their daily tasks, each one as afraid as the other to make a sound for fear of drawing attention to himself.

Only one thing was different, Adam noted, drawing a deep, steadying breath as he mentally prepared himself for the long-awaited moment of his revenge—that hollow rattle of chains as a line of shuffling convicts made its way to the fields. Yet their anxious silence was the same as that of the black slaves whose endless toil they shared.

"Are you ready, Mr. Booth?" he asked grimly, turning his attention to the bespectacled attorney whom James Cary had long trusted with important matters of business and upon whom Adam now relied.

"Quite, Mr. Thornton. Eager to see this matter set upon its course."

"As am I," Adam replied under his breath, his gaze moving to Susanna who sat directly across from him, her eyes downcast. Noting her pallor against the azure blue of her silk brocade gown, he felt resentment flare inside him.

He imagined her wan cheeks were due to her fear of what was about to happen to Dominick, which probably also explained why she had hardly spoken to him since they had left Westover so abruptly late Saturday night. No doubt her hatred of him had multiplied tenfold, far outweighing her pity, because she had made no more efforts to win his favor.

They had scarcely seen each other until this morning, Susanna confining her activities to the house and he spending most of his time in the fields surveying the crops and then sleeping alone in his office, although he had longed for at least the sensual comfort of her body. Even that he had denied himself, deciding resolutely that he would not hold her in his arms again until he sensed she fully realized that everything he had told her about Dominick Spencer was true.

"I can imagine you might prefer to remain in the carriage, Camille, but I'd like you at my side," Adam told her as a young footman hurried down the steps to meet them. "We won't be going into the house. I see no need for any pretense of civility with Mr. Spencer."

When Susanna just nodded, he wondered what the attorney must think of the strained silence between them, then he shrugged it off. He had explained to the man while at Briarwood that she wanted to come along today, believing that what he was doing was right, but that she might appear upset by the unpleasantness of the proceedings. That should suffice. And besides, he had other things to concern himself with right now.

Adam turned to the footman who had swung open the door. "Is your master at home?"

"Yes, but he's still abed."

"No matter. Tell him that Mr. and Mrs. Adam Thornton are waiting for him outside, along with my attorney, Mr. Booth."

"Yes, sir, Mr. Thornton."

As the boy disappeared into the house, Adam helped Susanna down, and Mr. Booth followed. Imagining that Dominick would choose to keep them waiting a good while just to spite him, Adam was surprised when the planter walked outside the front door a short ten minutes later, eyeing them suspiciously where they stood at the base of the broad stone steps.

If Dominick had been abed when informed of their unexpected arrival, his well-groomed appearance gave no evidence of it. His attire was impeccable, every curl in his full powdered wig in place. Adam surmised that the planter had made all haste for his wife's benefit, and with that thought came fresh resentment.

"What a surprise," Dominick said, making no move to come down to greet them. His chilling blue eyes flickered over them one by one, settling appreciatively upon Susanna. "You look particularly lovely this morning, Mrs. Thornton. It is a pleasure to see you again so soon, although I cannot say the same for your husband."

Adam squeezed her arm as a reminder for her to say nothing. He hated the way Dominick's icy gaze was raking slowly, almost possessively, over her. Infuriated, it was all he could do to keep his voice steady.

"This is not a social call, Spencer. Perhaps you have met my attorney, Mr. William Booth?"

Affording the slightest nod to the lawyer, Dominick replied, "I held no illusion that your visit was of a friendly nature, Mr. Thornton. State your business and then get off my land."

"Not your land for much longer," Adam stated bluntly, his blood drumming hot through his veins. At last the goal that had consumed and driven him for so long was come to fruition! "Within the last twelve days I have bought up the entirety of your debt from your many creditors. You now owe me a very substantial sum of money—"

"You've *what?*" Dominick cut him off incredulously, his posture stiffening and his face gone a sickly shade of white. Clenching his fists, he advanced a step toward them. "What insane game are you playing?"

"No game. Mr. Booth?"

The attorney stepped forward, producing several documents from his leather valise.

"Mr. Thornton is hereby suing you for full and complete payment of that amount, Mr. Spencer. The information is all here, if you would care to look at it." When Dominick made no motion to take the papers held out to him, the attorney simply continued. "If Mr. Thornton does not receive the amount owed to him by noon tomorrow, you will be summoned before the county magistrate and your situation made public knowledge. I have every expectation that the court will find judgment in Mr. Thornton's favor and sentence you to debtors' prison, your possessions forfeited to him as payment."

His face now flushed in outrage, Dominick blurted, "You can't do this to me—"

"I can and I have," Adam interrupted bitterly, "and don't think that selling Raven's Point will save you. Even if you auctioned everything—slaves, land, horses, even that emerald necklace—it wouldn't be enough to repay what you owe me. You might have been able to stave off your separate creditors with such a ploy, and perhaps keep yourself afloat until you found some gullible heiress to wed"—he glanced angrily at Susanna—"but nothing will save you now, Spencer. Nothing. Your single debt to me is too large."

"You forget I have friends," Dominick said, descending another few steps. "Very powerful friends who serve with me on the governor's council and in the House of Burgesses. They'll grant me loans."

"You deceive yourself," Adam scoffed. "Once it becomes known how much you owe me and what a notorious spendthrift you are, your so-called friends"—he spat out derisively—"will soon realize they might as well toss their money down a bottomless hole, for it will never be returned to them."

"What of my tobacco?" Dominick added, desperation creeping into his defensive tone. "It's the best crop I've grown in years. It should bring me the market's highest price—"

"Which still won't be enough to save you. Fool, look at the figures cited on those documents! You seem to have conveniently forgotten how much altogether you owed your creditors. I'm surprised they hadn't already sued you for payment, but they probably assumed a gentleman of your high standing could always produce the money. And I'm sure none of them realized how much you had already borrowed from other shipping firms. If they had, you would never have received another penny! Once the magnitude of your indebtedness is made public, I can expect they'll be thanking me profusely for paying them what you owed!"

Dominick's enraged voice rose to a fever pitch. "Damn you, Thornton, you're leaving me no way to redeem myself!"

Adam had never known a more grimly satisfying moment, his hatred for this man so acute he was almost quaking from its intensity.

"Exactly. You'll get no mercy from me. That's what you offered my father when you whipped him to death for stealing food for his family, and my mother when you raped her, destroying her will to survive, and the countless slaves you've murdered out of sheer malice."
His throat became so tight he could barely finish.
"That's what you offered me, you goddamned bastard, each time you brought your studded whip down across

my back. I haven't forgotten your laughter when you cut off part of my foot and threw it to the hounds who'd tracked me.''

Her head pounding, Susanna gasped, sickened. She glanced at Adam in horror, but his burning gaze was on Dominick, and she couldn't help thinking if expressions could kill . . .

"So it's revenge then, is it?'' Dominick demanded.

"Call it what you will,'' Adam answered with deadly quiet. "I prefer to think of it as justice.''

A dangerously charged silence ensued, and then Dominick drew himself up, his eyes leveling on Susanna.

"It appears you've been sorely fooled, my dear. You thought this common scum married you out of love, but you can plainly see what he's been doing with your money. You're nothing but the instrument of his petty vengeance. You would do well to remember that along with everything else I told you the other night.''

Suddenly loathing this man with every ounce of her being, Susanna lifted her chin and met his eyes.

"Is it any worse, Dominick, than what you would have done to me had I married you? Sold my estate to pay your debts and then wantonly gambled away whatever of my fortune remained? That would certainly have been an interesting way to demonstrate your own professed love. No, if I have been used for revenge against a lying monster like you, I consider the money very well spent.''

As the planter's perfect features contorted with incredulity and rage, Susanna felt the warmth of Adam's gaze upon her. Overcome anew by the anguish she had suffered since Saturday night, she desperately hoped her words had finally convinced him that she would never have plotted with Dominick against him.

"Get off my land, all of you!'' the planter commanded, his eyes ablaze. "We'll see whose side the court takes tomorrow afternoon—because you're not going to get a shilling from me, Adam Thornton. You'll discover instead that Virginia law looks more favorably upon a well-respected member of the council than a former indentured servant who believes himself to be a gentleman simply because his fortuitious marriage has given him wealth!''

Glancing at Adam, Susanna was relieved to see that Dominick's insult hadn't affected him. His expression was as hard and resolute as ever.

"If you find comfort in lying to yourself," he replied in a low voice, "then enjoy it while you can. Mr. Booth and I will await you eagerly before the magistrate in Williamsburg." Taking Susanna's arm, he began to steer her back toward the carriage, but he paused to add sarcastically, "If you decide not to appear, honorable councilor, believe me, there will be guards sent to Raven's Point to accompany you to court."

"How dare you threaten me on my property! Leave or by God, I'll take a whip to you and no one would fault me for it!" Dominick ranted at them, shaking his fists.

Glancing at the planter over her shoulder, his mottled face made ugly with rage, Susanna shuddered, silently thanking Adam again for saving her from this brutal man. She spied a movement at an opened upstairs window and was startled to see Cleo, wearing a silk dressing gown, also staring down at them. Though Susanna couldn't read the expression in the beautiful slave's eyes, her tight, close-mouthed smile held sheer triumph.

"Here are the documents, Mr. Spencer," William Booth said tersely, clearly disgusted by Dominick's foul display of temper. He set the papers on the step below the planter and brushed past Susanna and Adam on his way to the carriage.

"You son of a bitch, take your papers with you!" Dominick shouted. "I swear you won't have a legal practice when this is done! I have influence! I—"

"Mr. Spencer!"

The planter's tirade was checked as one of his overseers rode up and reined in his snorting, lathered mount at the foot of the steps.

"Three convicts . . . just tried to escape," the man

rasped, out of breath, sweat dripping down his face.
"We had unlocked their leg chains so they could work
. . . and they bolted across the field. We caught two"—
he jerked his head over his shoulder as another overseer
rode toward them, half-dragging behind him two be-
draggled prisoners bound around their upper chests by
ropes which were tied to the man's saddle—"and I'm
going to set the dogs after the last one. I think . . . he's
hiding somewhere in the field. The tobo's so high we
can't find him."

"Do it, then!" Dominick shouted. "What are you
waiting for?" As the man kicked his mount and rode
away, the planter rushed down the steps to meet the
other overseer, his unwanted guests clearly forgotten.
"Give me your whip!"

"Get into the carriage, Camille. You don't want to
see this," Adam firmly bade Susanna, but she scarcely
heard him, staring in horror as the two unlucky convicts
collapsed in exhaustion on the ground a short distance
away.

One of the men was russet-haired and slight, and he
screamed piteously as Dominick lit into him with a
vengeance, the snapping whip cutting viciously across
his bony shoulders. The other convict, dark-bearded
and of stockier build, gasped for breath on all fours,
then he raised his head, his narrowed amber gaze fixing
upon her. Recognition flitted across his pocked features, but it faded into an agonized grimace when the
whip slashed into his flesh. Yet his eyes never left her
face.

Susanna inhaled sharply, her heart hammering, her
blood roaring in her ears. No, it couldn't be him . . .
It wasn't possible . . .

"I said to get in! Now!" Adam repeated, grabbing
her around the waist and lifting her inside, where Mr.
Booth was already waiting for them. "Drive, Elias!"
he shouted, slamming the door behind him before turning on her. "Good God, Camille, what were you thinking? Dominick is furious enough to flay those poor
bastards alive and you were standing there like a statue,

watching! I can tell you from long experience that it's not a sight you would have enjoyed."

"I—I'm sorry, Adam. It was so awful . . . I didn't mean to stare . . ."

He immediately softened his tone, as if sensing the depth of her shock, and switched his seat to sit beside her. "I know, Camille, I know. Everything happened so fast. It's understandable. Forgive me for being so harsh with you, my love."

Thoroughly shaken, Susanna was scarcely aware of the special emphasis Adam had given his apology, or his endearment, as her mind raced over and over the last few moments. She tried to tell herself that she had only imagined she had just seen Keefer Dunn, but some deep inner instinct screamed that it had been him.

No, no, no, it wasn't him! she countered desperately. Such a coincidence simply wasn't possible. Any number of men might bear such marks from the pox and possess those same amber-colored eyes!

She flinched when Adam's arm encircled her waist and he drew her against him.

"There's no need to tremble, Camille. It's over. Dominick has lost, no matter what he says. By tomorrow afternoon, he'll be on his way to a debtors' prison. Isn't that correct, Mr. Booth?"

"I have every reason to believe that will be the case. The enormity of his debt will sway the magistrate. Mr. Spencer will have many long years to regret the cruelty of his ways."

"As he so justly deserves."

At the harsh satisfaction in Adam's voice, Susanna knew she should be elated. Maybe now there was some hope for them. Maybe now he might set aside his suspicion and begin to trust her. Yet any joy she might have felt was bitterly tempered by what she had seen at Raven's Point.

Laying her head against his shoulder, she closed her eyes and tried to shut out the horrifying image of Keefer Dunn. She should tell Adam about him, but she couldn't bring herself to do it. At least not here, not now, and especially not with the lawyer present. To wrest away Adam's revenge when it was so freshly won? No, she just couldn't do it!

"That's it, my love, just rest. It's been a trying morning for all of us. I'll wake you when we arrive at Briarwood."

But Susanna wasn't resting. She was praying, a terrible, brutally urgent, selfish prayer that the one man who could yet destroy the happiness for which she longed so desperately would not survive Dominick's whip.

*Oh, please, God, please let Keefer Dunn die . . .*

# Chapter 24

Dominick sat alone in his darkened library, the shabby draperies drawn against the bright midday sun. The shadowed room perfectly suited his mood, which was a very dangerous one indeed. He felt trapped, like a wounded animal in a snare, and there didn't seem to be any way he could save himself.

His stomach twisting painfully, bile burning his throat, he again surveyed the legal documents in front of him on the desk. He hadn't wanted to read them at all, but he had forced himself, needing to know the extent of his financial trouble. He had quickly discovered that the situation was far worse than he had imagined.

He could never pay the sum that Adam Thornton demanded. Never. And despite his influence and highly respected position, he doubted the magistrate would rule in his favor. Men had been sentenced to debtors' prison for far less than what he owed. What the devil was he going to do?

Murder wouldn't solve his dilemma anymore, unless he figured out a way to dispatch not only that vengeful scum Adam Thornton but his damned attorney as well, and before noon tomorrow. Then, of course, there was the small matter of Camille calling him a monster, something he had never expected to hear from her lips.

Yet he supposed he should have anticipated it, considering she fancied herself in love with that low-class abomination who thought himself a gentleman. Adam had doubtless filled her head with all kinds of sordid stories and she had swallowed them whole, which was probably why she had slighted him at the Tates'—

Dominick slammed his fist down upon the desk, cursing violently.

If he managed to rid himself of both Adam Thornton and William Booth, he could certainly deal with that little chit and her mewling protests. After a bit of co-ercion and a threat against her life, she would trip down the church aisle with him merrily enough, and then his troubles would be over.

A theft, that's what he could make it look like, he reasoned suddenly. It might be a little risky, but he was a gambler used to taking chances. What other choice did he have anyway? If he was found out, he would rather face hanging than rot for years in some prison cell. But he wouldn't be caught, not if he was careful.

First he would take care of William Booth at his of-fice in Yorktown. Then tonight, he would go to Briar-wood and slit Adam Thornton's throat. After that bastard's death it would be a simple matter to frighten Camille into permanent silence . . . oh, yes, and he couldn't forget the big black buck who had driven them here. If that coachman valued his balls, he would keep his mouth shut, too.

"The devil take you, Spencer, why didn't you think of this sooner?" Dominick muttered under his breath. His plan was so perfect! Here he had been sitting in this library for over an hour since they had left, wasting precious time, although in truth, he hardly remembered their carriage pulling away.

At least in this instance, he was glad those convicts had tried to escape, giving him an outlet for his blind-ing rage. It was amazing how whipping a man to death never failed to soothe his temper. Too bad that third one had been killed by his dogs. The wretch could have joined his compatriot who had survived the lashing for the punishment he planned to inflict first thing tomor-row morning in front of every convict at Raven's Point.

When the rest of them heard the bastard's dying screams, they'd be content enough to hoe weeds.

Dominick rose from his desk, impatient to change out of his blood-spattered clothes and be on his way. He had much to do. A knock came at the door just as he reached it, and he yanked it open to find his head overseer, a broad-shouldered, thickset man, waiting for him in the hall.

"What do you want, Dobson?" he demanded.

"Well, Mr. Spencer, you might think what I have to tell you is a little strange—"

"Spit it out, man! I'm in a hurry."

"It's about the convict I hauled back a while ago to the prisoners' quarters, Keefer Dunn. He's regained consciousness and he's been asking for you, over and over—not just babbling but making some sense. He says he has something important to tell you—"

"And you think I should talk to him?" Dominick cut him off scornfully, remembering how the convict had pleaded the same thing with him until he had been lashed into senseless silence. "You're going soft on me, Dobson, and anyway, the man dies tomorrow morning as an example to the rest of his surly friends. You know that. Now get back to the fields."

"If you'd hear me out, Mr. Spencer. I told him to shut up many a time and even hit him across the face with the butt of my whip, but he kept stubbornly insisting that he see you. He said he knows something about that young woman who was here earlier, and when I told him her name—"

"You did what?" Dominick glared at the man.

"I didn't see any harm in it, and I got the impression it had something to do with why he was asking for you. Well, when he heard that her name was Camille Cary, or used to be before she became Adam Thornton's wife, he yelled out that no, her real name is Susanna Guthrie. He told me that he knew her in London before she went to work as a waiting-maid for a Miss Camille Cary, who was living with her aunt, Baroness Redmayne, at Fairford."

"You're talking gibberish, man!" Dominick shouted, yet he was stunned that a common criminal would know so much about Camille's family background. How had the man stumbled upon such information? The only person he had told any of this to was Cleo, and she wouldn't have dared to say anything to anybody. She knew better.

"Maybe so, Mr. Spencer, but the bloke seemed to know a lot about the lady, and since it's common knowledge even among the slaves that you and Miss Cary had reached a decision to marry right before she suddenly wed Adam Thornton—" Seeing Dominick's scowl deepen, the overseer quickly added, "You made no secret of it, Mr. Spencer. Anyway, I thought you might be curious as to what he's talking about. I know I was. That's why I came here to tell you about it."

A vein in his temple throbbing, Dominick didn't like at all the fact that he was the object of discussion among his laborers, but he had to admit his curiosity was aroused despite that he wanted to leave for Yorktown as soon as possible.

"All right, Dobson, five minutes. That's all I'll give him."

The stench of sweat, urine, and filth in the prisoners' run-down quarters was unbearable, but Dominick, after commanding the disappointed overseer to wait by the door, quickly made his way between the wooden cots to the one where the beaten convict lay on his stomach. When Dominick stopped beside the soiled, foul-smelling mattress, the man slowly turned his head, wincing from the pain that small movement cost him.

"So ye've come, Mr. Spencer. I thought ye might."

Paying no heed to the convict's bare, bloodied back, Dominick grated, "Mr. Dobson said you wanted to see me, Dunn. What is this nonsense about Miss Camille Cary?"

The man licked his cracked lips, his dark-yellow eyes turning shrewd as he answered, "She's not wot she seems t' be, 'tis all."

"And what exactly does that mean . . . not what she seems to be?"

"Simple. I put two and two together when I saw 'er today, recognizing 'er as I did, and I tried t' tell ye when they were drivin' away, but ye wouldn't listen t' me . . ." He shifted on the mattress for emphasis, grimacing, but when he received no words of apology, he grudgingly continued. "She was the girl ye planned t' marry, right? The one who stood ye up fer another man?"

Dominick nodded, angered anew that his private life had become a topic of keen interest to his workers. But like Dobson had said, he'd made no secret of it. From the Tuesday Camille had visited him to Wednesday, when he had arrived at the Tates' to find her gone, he had told several neighbors his good news and a number of the house servants, including Cleo. Word of his upcoming betrothal, and its swift demise, must have flown about the plantation like wildfire.

"Well, ye should be glad ye didn't marry 'er because the chit's an impostor. I don't know 'ow she's done it, passin' 'erself off as 'er mistress Camille Cary, but that Susanna Guthrie was always a clever wench."

"An impostor?" Dominick queried suspiciously. "That's not possible. Camille fits every description I've ever heard of her before she even set foot in Virginia."

"It *is* possible and I'll tell ye 'ow, Mr. Spencer. But first ye must make Keefer Dunn a promise."

Dominick's temper flared. He should have known this wretch would demand payment.

"You're hardly in any position to barter, Dunn. I could just as easily whip the information out of you."

"Aye, ye could, and I could just as easily die on ye, too, like wot happened t' me friend Tommy a short while ago. 'E wasn't strong enough t' take such a beatin' like me, but another so quickly after the first? I don't know that I'd live through it, and then where would ye be? Left hangin', t' be sure."

Realizing this man was a very cunning one, Dominick decided to humor him. "Very well. Name your price."

"Make me an overseer. I'll work 'ard at it, I will, and ye'll find none more loyal. I'll keep these blokes in line as good as any ye've seen. There'll be no more escape attempts because I know 'ow their minds work, and I'll be watchin' 'em like a hawk ev'ry second. Wot do ye say?"

Dominick was silent for a moment, feigning consideration, then he said, "I suppose that could easily be arranged, but what makes you think that whatever you might tell me is of any interest to me now? Miss Cary married someone else. The matter is closed."

"No matter is ever closed when a wench 'umiliates a man," Keefer muttered bitterly, groaning as he lifted himself up on his elbows. "The girl 'umiliated ye, didn't she? She turned ye down fer a man who used t' be yer servant, didn't she? I can't imagine that fine turn of events made ye too 'appy, Mr. Spencer. I've discovered in me year at Raven's Point that yer a man who doesn't like t' be crossed. I would think wot I have t' say is o' great interest t' ye. Per'aps it might help ye t' think of a way t' pay 'er back . . . ye know, fer wot she did t' ye. And in me own way, I'd be gettin' back at 'er, too."

"How so?" Dominick asked, becoming more intrigued in spite of himself.

"Not so fast. Ye 'aven't said yet that ye'll pay me price. Now, will ye or no?"

"An overseer?"

"Aye, with a good 'orse and a whip. I'll work off the five years left t' me sentence, then I'll be on me way and ye'll never see me in these parts again. Are we agreed?"

Hating that he must strike a bargain with a common thief, even if he was only pretending to, Dominick tersely answered, "Agreed."

"I 'ave yer word on it?" Keefer queried, still leery.

"You have my word as a gentleman." As the convict visibly relaxed, Dominick knew he had him. "All right,

Dunn. How do you know that the woman I planned to marry is an impostor?''

"Because by some fluke o' nature, Susanna Guthrie's got the same 'air and eyes as 'er mistress, Camille Cary. I knew Susanna in London, and a fine beauty she was even at twelve years. Ye never forget such a face and figure, and I couldn't believe it when I saw 'er this mornin'. Her father, Daniel, was me good friend, and one night 'e agreed t' sell me 'is daughter fer a night's tumble. The chit ran away when she found out, and as me and 'er father were chasin' her, Daniel was run over by a hackney coach. And who do ye think was inside that fine carriage? Baroness Redmayne and 'er grand-niece, Camille Cary.''

"How did you find out all of this?" Dominick demanded, scarcely able to believe what he was hearing, yet finding it difficult not to.

"A constable was summoned, and I watched ev'rything from a nearby alley, way back in the shadows. The baroness decided t' take Susanna 'ome with 'er rather than send the chit t' an orphans' work'ouse, I s'pose out o' pity. The rest I found out the next day. It's easy enough t' bribe a constable's clerk fer information, Mr. Spencer, and I learned wot I needed t' know.''

When Keefer paused to roll himself on one elbow, grunting in pain, Dominick said impatiently, "Go on, man!''

Throwing him a resentful glance for the misery he was suffering, the convict nonetheless continued. "A few weeks later, I followed Susanna t' Fairford in Gloucestershire t' try and get 'er back. I'd paid good money for that wench! She owed me a tumble! I couldn't get near the manor, but that Sunday mornin' I saw the two girls comin' out o' church lookin' like peas from the same pod. That's wot made me realize today in an instant that me Susanna is now playin' a much cleverer game than pickin' pockets and beggin' as she once did in London. I only wish I knew 'ow she managed it.''

"I think I know," Dominick murmured, everything suddenly making perfect sense to him. "Camille's ship was struck by typhus fever during the crossing."

"There ye 'ave it, Mr. Spencer! The real Camille died, God rest 'er soul, while her waitin'-maid became the lady. Ye 'ave t' 'and it t' her. Susanna's managed quite a swindle."

Until now, Dominick thought grimly, feeling as if a crushing load had miraculously been lifted from his shoulders.

Adam Thornton had married an impostor. Was it possible that he already knew? Could that be why Camille . . . Susanna had so abruptly married that scum? He must have found out the truth about her and, wanting to carry out his revenge, had married her anyway, probably forcing her into it by threat of exposure. Well, now the tables were turned to Dominick's favor for once in his life. Fortune had finally smiled upon him.

"You never said if you got your tumble or not," he prompted Dunn, the woman who called herself Camille now nothing more than a whore in Dominick's eyes. How could she be anything but that, having been both a thief and a beggar, and knowing the likes of this man?

Keefer shook his shaggy head. "One o' me own paid thieves who envied me position in London alerted the parish constable that I was at Fairford, and I was arrested before I got a chance t' talk to 'er, let alone touch 'er. I was carted t' Newgate Prison where I spent five years, then they shipped me 'ere t' Virginia."

"Hard luck."

"Not anymore. I've come a step up in the world, eh, Mr. Spencer?"

"That you have," Dominick said smoothly, moving to the foot of the cot. "Get some rest, Dunn. I'll have one of the house girls bring you some ointment for your back, and a hot meal. She can help you wash . . . and whatever else you might fancy her to do for you."

"That's right decent o' ye. I 'aven't 'ad a woman since I left Newgate, and buggery with the lads 'as never been to me likin'." Keefer glanced at Dobson, who was still waiting in the distant doorway, his pleased expression fading to a scowl. "Do ye think ye could call off yer burly watchdog there? I don't fancy another slam in the face while I'm recuperatin'."

"I'll tell him to leave you alone," Dominick replied, starting to walk away.

"One more thing, Mr. Spencer."

Irritated but trying not to show it, Dominick paused. "What?"

Keefer gestured to the rusty length of chain that bound his left ankle to the cot. "When will this bloody shackle come off me leg?"

"First thing in the morning," Dominick promised, thinking of the deadly punishment with currycombs and salt that he still intended to have enacted. This man couldn't be allowed to live knowing what he did, nor Dobson either, if the overseer chose to give him any trouble. Such astonishing information was for him alone, especially when he was now going to use it to save his own neck and the future of Raven's Point. "There's something I must ask of you, Mr. Dunn."

Appearing startled that Dominick would address him with such courtesy, the convict blurted, "Anythin', Mr. Spencer. Joost name it."

"Don't mention our discussion to your mates when they return from the fields later this afternoon, or to anyone else for that matter, not even Dobson. Until you're out of here tomorrow, you don't want to risk the other convicts finding out that you'll soon be the one wielding the whip over their heads. Oh, yes, and the girl will have to be gone back to the house before they arrive."

Keefer grinned a lusty, gap-toothed smile. "I should be through with the wench by then, and ye' 'ave me word about the other. I'll not suffer a lynchin' just when me luck's about t' change."

Dominick said nothing more and quickly left the building, desperate to escape the foul air. He gestured for his overseer to follow him outside; his eyes were watering when he turned to face the man.

"It was nonsense, Dobson, all of it. Just lies made up to try and save his skin. Say nothing more to that prisoner, do you hear? In fact, don't even go near him. I'm sending over a girl to see to his back and give him a little pleasure before tomorrow morning."

"That's unusual, isn't it, Mr. Spencer?"

"Are you questioning my orders?" he snapped angrily.

"No, sir. Not at all."

"Good. Keep it that way."

Without another word to the startled overseer, Dominick strode back to the house, his thoughts already upon the damning letter he planned to write to Adam Thornton, to be delivered by messenger that very afternoon. If what that fool Dunn had told him was true, and he had every reason to believe it was, then he imagined he would be receiving by nightfall an equally swift reply that met all of his demands.

Murder was no longer necessary, nor must he marry that slut to save himself. Simple blackmail would suffice. Adam and his London whore had fallen right into his hands. They would soon know it was folly to attempt to best Dominick Spencer.

# Chapter 25

"**M**aster Thornton, your wife's up from her nap now," Corliss informed him, popping her head into the game room where Adam had been playing a solitary round of billiards for the past twenty minutes. He had occupied himself with any number of things since arriving home from Raven's Point two hours ago, while Susanna, complaining of a headache, had gone immediately to their room to lie down. Yet his mind hadn't been on his diversions, but upon her.

"Did she say how she's feeling?" he asked with deep concern, hanging up his cue. It had been torture, not allowing himself to check on her, but he had decided to let her rest since she had seemed unable to do so in the carriage.

Besides, he had needed time to sort out his thoughts and emotions. Finally achieving his vengeance had paled against his realization that he had savagely misjudged Susanna about plotting with Dominick. He didn't know how he could ever make it up to her, but he was resolved to try.

Corliss opened the door a little wider, and reproach shone in her dark eyes as she rested her hand on her hip. "Well, she looks better, not half so pale, but she sure doesn't seem very happy to me. I hope you don't mind me saying so, but I wish you two would make up from that fight you had at the Byrds' party. I can't imagine that it could have been anything so serious to keep you fussing at each other two days later!"

"I'm not angry anymore," Adam said honestly, thinking the maid's outburst was wholly justified. Things had been strained and uncomfortable at Briarwood since Saturday night, not only for himself and Susanna, but obviously for the servants as well, and it was time harmony was restored.

"I'm very glad to hear that, Master Thornton, but maybe you might want to go upstairs and tell Mistress Camille, too. She's the one who needs to hear those words."

"You've read my mind exactly, Corliss. Would you run out to the kitchen and tell Prue that my wife and I will be taking dinner in our chamber this afternoon? Supper as well, for that matter."

"I'd be happy to!" the maid said, beaming. She whirled and fairly flew through the music room to the hall beyond, then he heard the front door close behind her.

Leaving the game room, Adam's own smile was fleeting as he turned his thoughts again to Susanna and the fervent apology he had been mentally rehearsing.

He had been such a bastard to her! If she threw his apology right back in his face he wouldn't blame her at all, but he planned to tell her again and again, a thousand times if necessary, until she believed he was truly sorry for the callous way he had been treating her.

Her biting words to Dominick had sent a shock through him, convincing him at last that his suspicions had been of his own making. She had told him she would never plot against him and she hadn't. He had won his revenge and now it was time to think of the future. Their future.

Susanna might hate him, but he loved her desperately, and it was time she knew exactly how he felt about her. He couldn't go on deceiving himself. He needed her as he needed air to breathe, and if he was very, very patient, maybe her desire, pity, and even her hatred for him might evolve first into affection, and someday, if he was lucky, into love. But for now their reconciliation needed to start somewhere, and it would have to start with him—

"Master Thornton!" came Corliss's breathless voice behind him just as he reached the stairs.

He turned to find the maid standing inside the doorway, her expression strained and anxious. She must have burst right in, for the young footman had barely caught the door before it crashed into the wall.

"Corliss, what's wrong?"

"I was on my way to the kitchen, but there was a man outside who just rode up the drive, calling out and asking where he could find you. When I heard he'd come all the way from Raven's Point, I came right back in to tell you." She glanced over her shoulder. "Here he comes now!"

"Move out of my way, girl," the sweat-soaked rider said coarsely, pushing her aside. "I asked you to find your master and you skittered off on me—"

"Don't touch her!" Adam commanded, his deep voice ringing in the hall. Recognizing the man as one of Dominick's overseers he'd seen that morning, he strode angrily to the door, although he softened his tone as he addressed the wide-eyed maid who had retreated to stand next to the equally startled footman. "Go on to the kitchen, Corliss."

"Yes, sir, Master Thornton," she murmured, giving their rude visitor a wide berth as she fled from the house.

"If you ever have cause to visit Briarwood again," Adam warned, his eyes dangerously narrowed, "remember that I don't take kindly to abuse of my servants. Do you understand?" When the overseer nodded silently, Adam demanded, "What's your business here?"

The man reached into his coat pocket and thrust a wax-sealed letter at Adam. "This is from Mr. Spencer. He told me to wait for your reply."

Feeling a twinge of apprehension, Adam took it, saying tersely, "Then do so by the stable. You can get water from the trough . . . and don't forget what I said about my servants."

Without replying, the overseer stomped from the house while Adam broke the blood-red seal and ripped open the letter.

Scanning the brief contents, he was suddenly oblivious to everything around him except the words screaming in triumph from the page, the first floridly written line in particular . . . *Does the name Keefer Dunn mean anything to you, Mr. Thornton?*

"No. This can't be happening," Adam told himself.

He read the short letter again, this time more carefully, his hands shaking from the fury swelling within him and the chilling sense of betrayal clutching like icy fingers at his heart.

Susanna had done this to him. She must have told that bastard on Saturday who she really was. How else would Dominick have known that name? No other explanation was given in the remaining lines:

> Since I strongly suspect that you're familiar with the name, these are my terms. If you wish to continue your charade as the husband of "Camille Cary," plan on paying well for my silence. I shall expect a reply this evening with your full agreement not only to absorb my debts, but also to award me a substantial annual sum, to be arranged later, which will support me in the grand style deserving of a man of my social standing. Be assured, Mr. Thornton, that if I don't receive a satisfactory reply before I retire for the night, I will expose your charade with great pleasure before the magistrate tomorrow. Then who shall find himself in prison?

> D. S.

"Damn you, Susanna Guthrie," Adam whispered, the gloating tone of the letter fanning his rage. "Damn you!"

How could he have been such a fool? he berated

himself, crushing the paper in his fist. He had thought she hadn't plotted against him . . . that finally, together, they could begin anew. He should have known that a clever, quick-witted actress such as she would find a way to thwart him, despising him as she did.

He had fully anticipated that Dominick might attempt some treachery before they met in court tomorrow, and he had been prepared to face it, his loaded pistol accompanying him wherever he went. But he would never have suspected after what Susanna had said today at Raven's Point that his revenge would turn to ashes because of her!

Enraged, Adam took the stairs three at a time.

Susanna and Dominick must have staged that outrageous and convincing performance this morning because of William Booth's presence. Why else would they have gone to such trouble? Dominick knew he couldn't have said anything about Keefer Dunn in front of the attorney. He would have foiled his only chance to save himself, the chance that had been granted to him by Susanna.

Yet how did she figure into the scheme? Adam seethed furiously, storming down the hall. Dominick hadn't mentioned her once in that letter. Was this only a temporary trap until those two could figure out a way to get rid of him permanently and still make it look like an accident? God in heaven, that she would do this to him, that she could betray him so mercilessly . . . the woman he loved!

Adam shoved open the door so violently that it slammed against the wall, sending several small framed landscapes crashing to the floor. His gaze flew to where Susanna, seated at her dressing table, spun on the cushioned stool to face him, her eyes wide and alarmed, their startling hue a perfect match for her jade-green dressing gown. Her brush slipped from her slender fingers and thudded to the carpet.

"Adam . . . ?"

Fear clutching at her for the murderous expression twisting his handsome features as he slowly approached her, Susanna felt as if her heart was beating in her throat.

"Adam?" she repeated when he didn't answer, his angry eyes daring her to look away. "What's happened? What's wrong?"

"This is what's wrong!" he spat, tossing the crumpled letter onto her dressing table. "Read it!"

Forcing her numbed body to respond, Susanna picked up the balled paper with shaking fingers, and began to smooth it out.

"Who . . . who is it from?"

"Just read it!"

Spreading the crinkled letter in front of her, she could scarcely focus her eyes upon it. The first thing she noticed was the initials at the bottom, and her heart sank, cold dread seizing her. Then she saw the name Keefer Dunn in the first line. She turned her head away, unable to read further.

Dear God, the worst had come to pass. Her selfish prayer had gone unheeded.

"Adam, I was going to tell you," she began, looking up at him imploringly. "I—I just didn't know how to do it. I knew how much your revenge meant to you, and I couldn't bear the thought that you might not obtain it because of me. I still can't believe it was him—"

"What the hell are you talking about?" Adam cut her off so angrily that she jumped, gasping in fright. "Did you read the letter or not?"

"I . . . I can't," she said, shaking her head. "I saw the name Keefer Dunn . . . and I couldn't go on."

"Then I'll read it for you," Adam said, snatching up the paper, "and listen well, my love, for you are the cause of this!"

As he rushed through the letter, his hate-filled tone cut into Susanna's heart like a razor-sharp knife.

The situation was as bad as she had imagined. No, worse. Keefer Dunn must have identified her to Dominick and then told everything about her, probably in an attempt to save his own miserable life. Now Adam would never complete his revenge, and he was blaming her, but it wasn't her fault. Fate had worked against them, thrusting in their path a man she had hoped never to see again.

"Adam, I'm truly sorry this has happened," she said, rising from the stool to face him, "but you can't say it's my fault. If you hadn't made me go with you this morning, you'd still have your revenge. How could I have known that Keefer Dunn was a convict at Raven's Point?"

His eyes widening, Adam suddenly threw back his head and laughed, a harsh, humorless sound. Startled by his unexpected reaction, she went on nervously.

"It was a horrible trick of fate that Keefer tried to escape today . . . that he was one of the men dragged to the house to be whipped. He recognized me the moment he saw me, and I recognized him"—she shuddered, remembering—"those dark-yellow eyes, like a snake's, and his ugly pocked face behind that scraggly beard. I tried to tell myself it wasn't possible, but it was him, Adam, and I should have told you sooner—"

"Good God, woman, do you expect me to believe this tale?" Adam shouted, grabbing her by the arms and shaking her hard. "A trick of fate? I knew you would come up with some fantastic story, but this . . . this is incredible!"

Susanna gasped at him in astonishment, tears smarting her eyes.

"And don't dare start crying either, because it won't work," he railed at her, his hands tightening their painful grip. "What a consummate actress you are to summon tears so effortlessly. I have to grant it to you, Susanna Guthrie, you're as clever and devious as they come."

Stunned even more that he would call her by her real name, she pleaded, "Adam, you're hurting me . . . I don't understand—"

"There is no Keefer Dunn at Raven's Point, and you damn well know it!" he thundered, releasing her so abruptly that she fell against the dressing table, upsetting perfume bottles and other toiletries. "You told Dominick that name at the Byrds' party, and everything else about yourself, didn't you?"

"No, that's not true!" Susanna cried, anguished that he would make such a preposterous accusation. Why, why did he never believe her?

"You told him I was going to seek vengeance against him, probably soon, and then you came up with the perfect way to save him, didn't you? A way to keep me mum until you and your precious Dominick could silence me permanently."

"Adam, this is madness!" she insisted, backing up as he advanced upon her, his expression so black that she feared he might strike her.

"Those words you said to him this morning were all part of your act, weren't they? You two make an ingenious pair, maybe you deserve each other. But I don't plan on giving either of you the satisfaction."

She bumped into the wall, hitting her head hard. Still he stalked her, until suddenly he stopped within arm's reach of her. His voice was bitterly quiet.

"And to think that just before I received the letter I was on my way up here to apologize for accusing you of plotting against me. To tell you that I wanted us to start over . . . to tell you that I—" He didn't finish, choking on his words, and for a fleeting instant Susanna thought she saw a wetness glistening in his eyes until he blinked several times and said hoarsely, "Damn you, woman. This is twice you've made me the fool."

"Adam . . . Adam, please listen to me," she said, her throat tightened painfully against the tears threatening to overwhelm her. "I didn't plot against you, I swear it! We can still start fresh. We don't have to let Dominick do this to us!"

"To us?" he scoffed. "He made no mention of you in that letter."

"I—I don't know why he didn't," Susanna admitted, confused, her words coming in a desperate flood, "but he meant both of us! Adam, we can go to Williamsburg right now and confess everything to the magistrate. The court might punish us, but when they hear the truth, maybe they won't. I know we'll lose Briarwood but after what happened today, I don't think we were ever meant to have it. Yet you can still have your revenge! The Cary money you paid to Dominick's creditors will have to be returned, and then they'll go directly after him for payment. He'll still end up in a debtors' prison, Adam, don't you see?''

''Why would I agree to give up everything I've worked so long and hard to gain and start over with nothing, and with the likes of you?'' he lashed out at her. ''No, my love, you're going to remain as Camille Cary and the mistress of Briarwood until the day you die, whether you like it or not. And if I ever discover again that you've plotted with that monster against me . . .''

Susanna gasped in terror as he brought her hard against his chest, plunging his fingers through her hair to pull her head back cruelly.

''We're going to play out this deadly game with Dominick Spencer and give him exactly what he wants until I can find a way to best him. What a merry race it will be! Him, hoping to find a way to kill me so he can have you and your fortune, and me, thwarting his every move. One day I will have my vengeance, my beautiful, treacherous wife. This *I* swear.''

As Adam's mouth came down savagely upon her own, his powerful arms enveloping her in a crushing, heart-rending embrace, Susanna felt all hope die within her. She would never have his love, only suspicion, mistrust, and hate . . . and she knew she couldn't bear it. Not for a lifetime. Not for another moment.

''No . . . !'' she cried against his mouth, biting his lower lip hard. As, cursing, he abruptly loosened his hold upon her, she wrenched away from him so violently that she would have fallen if she hadn't grabbed the opened balcony door.

Regaining her balance and spinning around to face him, she edged along the door until she felt nothing but air, the afternoon sun warm upon her back and the strong breeze stirring her hair. With the balcony behind her, her desperate gaze flew to the door across the room, her only means of escape, then back to his face.

"So this is how it's going to be from now on," Adam said, a dangerous gleam in his eyes as he wiped the back of his hand over his mouth. "Biting, kicking, scratching. I can't say that the challenge doesn't intrigue me—"

"It's not going to be any way!" Susanna broke in defiantly, trying to choke back the scalding tears that were almost blinding her. Trembling with hurt and fury, her embittered words tumbled from her lips in a wild, agonized torrent.

"You don't deserve to touch me, Adam Thornton, and you never will again! I refuse to spend the rest of my life with a man such as you, a man who can't love, a man who won't relinquish his insane lust for revenge. I should have known that no matter what I did and no matter what I said, you would always think the worst of me. Well, you can have your precious Briarwood and the Cary fortune and Dominick's blackmail of you, and you're welcome to them! I don't want any part of this charade, and I don't want any part of you!"

"You're confusing matters here," Adam said, moving slowly toward her, his gaze stormy as he stepped from the shade of the room into the bright sunshine streaming through the open doors. "Love has never been a concern between us, only desire, yet you hurl it at me like an accusation."

"You're right, it never was a concern!" Susanna cried, retreating onto the balcony as he kept advancing on her until she could go no further, halting abruptly against the wooden railing. Her heart breaking, she could not stop herself from flinging at him, "That's why I can't believe I ever fell in love with a man like you! How could I have ever been such a bloody fool as to hope that someday you might come to love me, too? You're too full of hate to care about anything but your revenge!"

Adam stopped cold, feeling as if he had been struck

hard in the face. He stared at her in total astonishment, at those beautiful green eyes which were filled with such torment and defiance, at the tears streaming down her flushed cheeks, at the palpable tension in her stance, as if she was about to flee past him for the door.

"What did you say?" he demanded softly, wanting to hear her startling words again so that he would know he hadn't imagined them.

"It doesn't matter!" she threw back at him, swiping a damp tendril from her face. "You have nothing to fear from me anymore, Adam Thornton. No more foul plots to uncover, no more worries that I might go to the constable and tell him the truth about Camille. I'm leaving for England on the next ship sailing out of Yorktown, and then you'll not have Susanna Jane Guthrie to worry about any longer. You can tell your fine Tidewater friends that I've gone back to my aunt's at Fairford, or tell them I died suddenly, I don't care! Just get out of my bloody way!"

"You're not going anywhere," Adam said, his heart thundering. God help him, she had said she loved him! He had heard it! Yet was it the truth, or just another of her many lies? Dammit, he had to know! "You're going to stay right here and answer me—"

"No, you can't stop me!"

She dashed past him with such agile quickness that he almost didn't catch her; grabbing a handful of jade silk he hauled her back and enfolded her thrashing body in his arms. He wasn't prepared for the wild ferocity of her struggles, and when she kicked him hard in the shin, he lost his balance, pitching into her.

He saw a blur of green silk and white flailing arms as Susanna lurched backwards . . . heard wood cracking and splitting, and her terrified gasp of surprise. Then she was gone and he was left alone on the balcony surrounded by an eerie, ominous silence.

Feeling as if his heart had stopped beating, Adam rushed to the shattered railing. She lay on her stomach twelve feet below him, her body inert and limbs askew, her face deadly white against the green grass.

"Susanna!"

He didn't think, only reacted. Wrenching aside the splintered wood, he jumped, feeling excruciating pain shoot through his right ankle as he landed. But he paid it no heed, falling to his knees and gathering her unconscious form into his arms. Her breathing was frighteningly shallow. Tears stung his eyes when he saw the scarlet blood matting her glistening hair where her head had grazed the edge of the bricked path.

"Oh, God. Susanna . . ."

In shock, he rose with her and, hugging her to his chest, he limped on his badly turned ankle to the double French doors. He couldn't believe they were bolted, then he remembered he had ordered all doors and downstairs windows to be locked, just in case Dominick decided to pay them an unwelcome call . . .

Wasting no time, Adam smashed his fist through the glass and, ignoring the stinging cuts in his knuckles, he unfastened the bolt and flung open the door. Swallowing against the fear and terrible anguish that gripped him, he staggered inside and began to yell . . . for Ertha, for Corliss, and for the footman to run like hell to the stable and saddle his horse so he could ride into Yorktown for the physician.

# Chapter 26

**“I**’ll sit with her, Master Thornton, if you want to go and talk to that man from Raven's Point. After I saw the physician on his way home, the man said to tell you that he can't wait much longer before he has to leave. It's almost sunset, and he hasn't gotten any answer from you yet to take back to Mr. Spencer.”

Jolted from his exhausted haze by Ertha's voice, Adam realized he had forgotten all about the overseer in the horror and then sweeping relief of the last few hours. He glanced from Susanna's ashen face to the housekeeper's. Strain showed around her dark-brown eyes, which held concern but, thank God, no judgment.

“You'll stay here until I get back?” he asked, reluctant to leave Susanna's side for even a moment. “I won't be gone long.”

Ertha nodded as she smoothed the satin spread tucked up under Susanna's arms. “You don't have to rush. There's nothing you can do here anyway. Maybe after you speak to the man, you might want to get some rest. Corliss will help me keep watch when she returns from fetching you something for supper.”

“I'm not hungry, and the last thing I want to do is sleep,” Adam replied.

“Now, Master Thornton, you know the physician said it could be hours before your wife wakes up. It's a miracle she wasn't hurt no worse than some bruises and that nasty cut on her head . . . no broken bones and, thank the Lord, no broken neck. It was the thick grass that saved her.''

''Yes. A miracle,'' Adam agreed, wondering how a sorry son of a bitch like himself had been found deserving of such a precious thing. He rose, wincing at the pain in his tightly bandaged ankle, and relinquished his chair beside the bed to the housekeeper, who sat down with a heavy sigh.

''I just wish she wasn't so pale,'' Ertha murmured, laying her wrinkled hand on Susanna's forehead, then, adding as she glanced up at Adam, ''and I wish things weren't turning out as they are, that there was something I could do about all this, some way I could help. I don't know what troubles between you and Mistress Susanna''—sighing again, she continued—''I mean Camille, caused this terrible thing to happen, but I have a strong feeling it has something to do with why that man is waiting for you outside.''

''It does,'' Adam replied with grim honesty, but he said no more as he limped to the foot of the bed and gazed upon Susanna, stark emotion welling in him. How beautiful she was . . . and how horribly close he had come to losing her forever.

Her impassioned words still rang in his head, fueling the unanswered questions that tormented him. Unanswered questions that would give him no peace. It sickened him that even now, he could not bring himself simply to believe that she might love him. So much hurt and deception had gone between them. They had both suffered so much. Yet there was a way he could find out if she had spoken the truth . . .

''I'll be back soon, Ertha,'' he said, turning from the bed.

''Whatever you say, Master Thornton, but I still think you should get some rest. You were injured yourself, you know.''

Adam didn't answer as he left the room, the weight of the pistol he kept hidden in his coat pocket bumping against his thigh.

\* \* \*

"Good thing you came out of the house when you did, Mr. Thornton. I was just getting ready to leave," the overseer said testily, reining in his restless mount by the front walk. "I heard about the accident. I guess that's as good an excuse as any for keeping me waiting here all afternoon. Is your wife going to recover?"

Ignoring the man's callously stated and all-too-personal question, Adam said, "If you want to talk to me, get down off your horse."

"Look here, I don't see any reason for that," the man objected, scowling. "Just give me your reply to Mr. Spencer's letter and I'll be on my way. He told me a simple yes or no would do nicely, so which one is it?"

"I said to get down," Adam repeated calmly despite his thundering pulse, withdrawing the pistol from his coat pocket and pointing it at the overseer's startled face. "Now!"

"All right, Mr. Thornton! All right!" The man jumped down, his swarthy coloring marked by a distinct greenish pallor. "I—I don't see why you're getting so upset—"

"Shut up and listen!" Adam ordered, leveling his weapon at the man's stomach. "Now I want an answer to my question and I want it fast. Do you have a convict by the name of Keefer Dunn at Raven's Point?"

"I—I don't know. There are so many of them—"

"Think very, very hard."

"Like I told you," the overseer echoed nervously, beads of sweat breaking out on his forehead. "I don't know, and Mr. Spencer said not to say anything more to you, just to hand you the letter and get your reply."

"But Mr. Spencer won't be the one with the ball in his gut, will he?" Adam queried, cocking the pistol with an ominous click. "I can assure you, a stomach wound is a gruesome way to die—"

"All right! Don't shoot me!" the man blurted, backing into his horse, which whinnied sharply, tossing its head. "Keefer Dunn's been at Raven's Point for a year now, but if you were thinking of trying to see him, God knows why, you're out of luck.''

His hand trembling, Adam had to tighten his grip on the pistol. Susanna hadn't lied to him! Oh, God, what had he done to her . . . ? Filled with self-loathing and bitter remorse, he forced himself to focus on the matter at hand, although he wanted nothing more than to rush back to her side.

"Why is that?" he demanded, his blood roaring in his ears.

"The bastard tried to escape this morning and since he survived the lashing Mr. Spencer gave him, he's going to be executed first thing tomorrow as an example to the rest of the prisoners." The overseer gulped for air like a fish, his Adam's apple bobbing. "You must have seen him, Mr. Thornton! He was one of the two men dragged back to the house while you were talking with Mr. Spencer."

"Describe him. I don't remember."

"Stout build, bearded, pocked face like he suffered bad with the pox, and the strangest eyes I've ever seen on a man. A real freakish dark-yellow color."

The man's hasty description, matching the one Susanna had given him, made Adam all the more desperate to return to her. His heart aching, he muttered, "Get back on your horse."

The overseer scrambled into the saddle, his hands shaking as he took the reins. "Wh—what do you want me to tell Mr. Spencer? About the letter, I mean?"

"Tell him to meet me here tomorrow morning at ten o'clock and we'll go over the arrangements he requires," Adam replied tightly, a determined plan taking shape in his mind. "If that isn't acceptable, he'll just have to wait. My wife's recent injury will prevent me from leaving Briarwood anytime soon. Do you have that?"

"I heard you, Mr. Thornton," the man agreed, anxiously eyeing the pistol still pointed at his gut. "Tomorrow morning, ten o'clock, the arrangements he requires. I take it that means you're in agreement with what he told you in the letter?''

"Yes. Now get the hell off my land.''

The overseer didn't need to be told twice. Jabbing his horse with his spurred boots, he took off around the drive and never once looked back.

Impatiently waiting until the man disappeared from sight, Adam released the cock on the pistol and returned the weapon to his pocket.

Oh, he was in full agreement, all right, he thought grimly, limping back into the house and up the stairs. But only with the part about seeing the magistrate.

Judging from the depth of Dominick's greed, Adam guessed that the accursed bastard would throw aside all caution and be here well before ten o'clock tomorrow, his fingers itching to touch the first installment of his ill-gotten wealth. Adam couldn't wait to see his expression when Dominick discovered he would soon be caressing cold prison bars instead, and that Adam would be personally escorting him to Williamsburg. As Susanna desperately had tried to tell him after he had so unjustly accused her, that would be vengeance enough.

Entering their room, Adam knew when he saw Ertha keeping faithful watch by the bed that she deserved to know what was going to happen tomorrow. Everyone at Briarwood would be affected by his decision. But he had no other choice than to admit everything to the magistrate.

Their charade couldn't continue, not if he hoped to convince Susanna that he wanted her only for herself. The precious gift of her love was worth more to him than Briarwood, worth more than any revenge the plantation could give him. Once, he had told himself that he would be content just to have her at his side for the rest of his life, but now there was an all-important difference.

He didn't want the heiress to the Cary fortune; he wanted Susanna Jane Guthrie, waiting-maid. He would never call her Camille again.

"Has she stirred?'' Adam asked, noting with acute

relief that some faint color had returned to Susanna's pale cheeks.

"Just once," Ertha answered, "though she didn't open her eyes. She whispered something several times, whimpering like, then she fell quiet again."

Deeply regretting that he hadn't been there to hear it, Adam sat on the edge of the bed and took Susanna's limp hand in his bandaged one, squeezing it gently. "What did she say?"

"Only your name, Master Thornton. Adam."

Susanna's eyelids fluttered open, but she quickly shut them against the excruciating throbbing in her head. Having no clear sense of why she was in such pain, she lay very quietly for several long moments, then she tried again to open her eyes.

"Where . . . ?" she whispered to herself as her fuzzy vision gradually focused. She saw the cream-colored canopy overhead and, feeling smooth satin beneath her fingertips and soft pillows behind her aching head, she suddenly had the strangest sensation that she had experienced all this before. Girlish words spoken long ago surfaced and echoed in her befuddled mind . . . *Yer angels, ain't ye? I've died and gone straight t' 'eaven!*

Yet there were differences, Susanna began to note, her hauntingly vivid memories colliding with reality. Only a single candle sputtered in this much larger room, and there was no cheery fire in the distant hearth. The windows were open, a cool breeze billowing the white curtains.

She carefully turned her aching head to the right, afraid to move too quickly lest she suffer more pain.

The walls were papered, but not with that pretty rose pattern. She frowned. No, this couldn't be the same room. And she didn't hear any female voices, neither Lady Redmayne's proper tones nor the lilting brogue of Mary the waiting-maid. Susanna cautiously shifted her head to the left. There weren't any voices at all and no wonder. No one else seemed to be in the room but

Adam, who was sound asleep on the divan pulled next to the bed—

"Adam," she breathed, tensing. Instantly old memories faded, and she knew exactly where she was, just as she was assaulted by a shocking realization of why her body hurt all over.

They had been having a dreadful argument . . . he had accused her of the most horrible things. She had shouted at him, saying she was a fool to have fallen in love with him, saying she was leaving at once for England. She ran past him, but he dragged her back and then . . . then he violently shoved her into the balcony railing! She distinctly remembered saying to him right before he pushed her that he could tell his friends she had suddenly died . . . and he must have taken her suggestion to heart! Dear God, he had tried to kill her!

Stricken with fear, Susanna's sudden consuming thought was to get out of that room and far away from Adam as quickly as possible. She gave no heed to the fact that she wore only a thin nightrail or that she possessed no money. She had her costly wedding ring, which she was certain would buy her some clothes and passage back to England. That was all she needed.

Holding her breath, she eased back the covers and slid from the bed, wincing at the terrible pain in her head and the aching soreness in her limbs. Fleetingly grateful that she had suffered no broken bones in that terrifying fall, she focused intently upon the door and, swaying slightly from her skewed sense of balance, she passed as silently as a wraith across the carpet.

Once, Adam shifted on the divan and she froze, certain that he would wake and spy her trying to escape.

Her half-dazed mind raced wildly—what would he do to her? She had obviously frustrated his scheme by surviving her plunge from the balcony. Would he try to smother her with a pillow, or was it enough that she now knew he was capable of murdering her and he could use it as a threat to force her to his will?

Susanna didn't resume her desperate flight until he sighed heavily in his sleep, his shadowed face turned away from her. Shivering in the cool night air wafting in from the windows, she slowly turned the latch and drew open the door just enough to squeeze through. Then she closed it with a soft click, overwhelming relief flooding her bruised body as she fled down the hallway to the stairs.

She paused on the landing, remembering that there was always a footman at the front door. Taking the first few steps with great caution, her bare feet making no sound, she heard the man snoring deeply and sensed she would not wake him if she went out the back way.

Her head pounding anew from her exertions, she raced down the rest of the stairs and along the darkened hall to the French doors. She was surprised to find one side boarded up, a large pane of glass missing. The bolt was also drawn, and fumbling at it, she managed to open the other door and escape into the black night.

With only the faintest sliver of moon to guide her, Susanna knew it must be very late, for a heavy stillness hung over the main grounds. Even the distant servants' quarters were silent, everyone having gone to bed.

As she hurried around the house and made her way through the enveloping darkness to the stable, she wished she had taken a moment to whisk a dressing gown around her bare shoulders. Her flimsy silken garment was no match for the coolness of this early September evening, although the fresh, sweet-smelling air was helping to restore her wits and sense of balance. Then, hearing the sudden snap of a branch close behind her, she forgot her teeth-chattering discomfort and ran all the faster, knowing that wild creatures roamed the grounds freely at night.

She exhaled with relief when she reached the stable and pulled back one of the doors, assailed by the pungent aromas of horses, straw, and oiled leather. Expecting to find herself alone, she was startled to see Zachary Roe, the building's manager, step from a stall where pregnant mares nearing their time to foal were usually kept. He raised his lantern high, and seemed equally startled to see her.

"Mistress Camille, what are you doing out here?" he queried, studying her flushed face with concern. "I heard what happened to you this afternoon. You should be abed."

"I—I need a horse, Zachary. Would you kindly saddle my mare?"

"Pardon me for asking, ma'am, but for what? It's so dark tonight, nobody in his right mind would want to be out riding. Let me walk you back to the house—"

"No!" she said, hurrying past him to the stall where her snow-white mare was contentedly munching oats. "If you won't do as I ask, I'll saddle her myself."

"But Mistress Camille—"

"That's all right, Zachary. I'll assist my wife."

Gasping, Susanna spun to find Adam standing just inside the stable door, his powerful, broad-shouldered form casting a huge shadow against the planked wall and upwards toward the ceiling.

"You! Don't you dare come near me!" she demanded, panicked, her eyes darting for anything she might use as a weapon against him. She spied a pitchfork that had been left propped against a nearby stall, and grabbing the tool with aching arms, lowered it threateningly.

"Zachary, would you leave us?" Adam suggested calmly, although he felt anything but calm.

He had never experienced such a scare as when he had abruptly awoken at the sound of the door clicking shut to find Susanna gone from their bed. Realizing she had fled, he had followed the sweet scent of her jasmine perfume downstairs, then had spied her white nightrail through the trees the moment he stepped outside the back door. He would have caught up with her sooner if not for his blasted ankle.

The spry stable manager glanced from Susanna back to Adam, his relieved expression showing he was only too eager to oblige. "Yes, sir, Master Thornton, I think I will." Setting the lantern on a bench, he muttered on his way out, "Lucky thing that mare won't be foaling until tomorrow. Good evening to you."

Too intent upon Susanna to make a reply, Adam saw the stark fear in her wide, beautiful eyes, and he knew with intense regret that he had put it there.

He couldn't blame her if she now thought the worse of him. He certainly hadn't given her any benefit of the doubt since their marriage. He began to move cautiously toward her, not so much because of the pitchfork she wielded, but because he didn't want to upset her further. She had already endured so much at his doing.

"Susanna, I'm not going to try and touch you. I just want to talk," he said soothingly, noting that she was swaying a little, obviously still suffering the aftereffects of her fall.

"We have nothing to discuss!" she countered, backing away a few steps. "I told you before you shoved me from the balcony that I was leaving for England, and I mean to do it! You can't make me stay here!"

"Is that what you think . . . that I pushed you?" Adam asked, cut to the quick and knowing he deserved all his present misery.

"Yes, and I don't doubt that you'd do it again, knowing how much you hate me—"

"I don't hate you, Susanna," he said, emotion swelling in his chest. "I love you."

Stunned, Susanna felt the pitchfork slip in her hands, and she almost dropped it before quickly recovering herself, although she couldn't stop hot, bitter tears from springing to her eyes.

"You lie!" she accused him hoarsely, amazed that he would carry his cruelties so far. It was beyond belief.

"I'm not lying, Susanna. I've known I was in love with you since the night of your welcome ball—"

"Not me!" she blurted, tears now tumbling unchecked down her cheeks as she pointed her pronged weapon at him. "Camille Cary!"

"No, it was you, the warm, enthralling woman beneath the charade. I fell in love with you, Susanna Jane Guthrie. You!"

Shaking her head, Susanna was trembling so badly she feared her knees might buckle beneath her. She wanted so desperately to believe him, to trust the raw emotion blazing in his eyes, but she couldn't bear to suffer more miserable heartache.

"Why can't you just let me go?" she demanded in a plaintive whisper. "I'll never trouble you again, and you'll have everything you ever wanted, even the chance to win your revenge against Dominick."

"I don't want anything but you, Susanna," he insisted. "Aren't you listening to me? I said I love you! That's why I can't allow you to leave. I need you!"

"But the balcony—"

"A terrible accident! When you kicked me, I lost my balance and fell into you. Oh, God, when I thought that you might be dead . . ." Adam couldn't seem to finish. He stepped even closer to her and for the first time, she noticed how badly he was limping. "You said you loved me, Susanna—"

"I lied," she said, his gaze holding her captive even while her mind was screaming to run back out into the night while she still had the chance.

"That was no lie . . . and neither was what you told me about Keefer Dunn. *I've* been the bloody fool all along, Susanna, not you! I couldn't give up my suspicions because you betrayed me once, and it made me accuse you of plotting against me. I was going to tell you that I loved you earlier today, then I received that letter and ruthlessly accused you again . . ." His piercing brown eyes full of torment, he finally added in an impassioned voice, "Can you find it within your heart to forgive me?"

Susanna lowered the pitchfork to the ground as if she had forgotten she held it. She had never felt so torn.

She wanted to fling herself into his arms and admit again the love that was threatening to overwhelm her. Yet she also knew with certainty that she would never be everything to him as he claimed, not when he still sought revenge against Dominick. With such hatred in his heart, he would never fully trust her. There would always be the chance that his suspicions might once more raise their ugly heads, and she couldn't bear to see him turn against her so furiously again.

"I—I can't, Adam," she began. But the words were no sooner spoken than he lunged toward her and, knocking the pitchfork from her hand, swept her into his arms.

"No! I don't believe you!" he cried, his gaze burning into hers as he crushed her against him. "What would you say if you knew that tomorrow I planned to admit everything to the magistrate in Williamsburg, just as you pleaded for me to do this afternoon? That tomorrow you and I would start fresh with nothing but our love between us. When you're well enough to travel, we'll begin anew by retaking our vows as husband and wife, not as Adam Thornton and Camille Cary but with the beauteous Susanna Jane Guthrie as my bride. Would that change your mind about me, my dearest love?"

Dumbstruck, Susanna could manage only a whisper. "You . . . you would do that for me?"

"I would do anything for you, Susanna, except allow you to leave me. For then, I would surely die." He tenderly caressed away her fresh tears, cradling her face in his hands. "Tell me, love. Do you forgive me now?"

She nodded, her throat so constricted she could not speak. She had never known that such infinite happiness was possible on this earth, and she felt drunkenly giddy with it, her limbs suddenly so weak she was grateful for his powerful embrace.

"That's not good enough," he murmured, bending his head to poignantly kiss her damp cheeks, her eyelids, the tip of her nose. Then he tilted up her chin and lowered his mouth until his parted lips were barely brushing her own, his breath warm upon her. "I must hear you say it, Susanna," he demanded huskily. "Tell me . . . please."

Somehow she found her voice, answering him with all the passion her soul possessed. "Yes. I forgive you, Adam."

"That," he whispered hoarsely, tears shining in his

# Chapter 27

**❝I**t's almost nine o'clock, my love. Though I would like nothing more than to remain here in bed with you all morning, I have to leave for Williamsburg.''

Stubbornly pretending she hadn't heard him, Susanna snuggled closer against Adam's broad chest. She inhaled his warm, musky scent, still basking in the sensual afterglow of their gentle lovemaking.

His tender kisses and caresses this morning and last night, after they had returned together from the stable, had been like a soothing tonic to her bruised body. Wondrously enough, her head hardly ached at all anymore. Love held such incredible power to heal. She shivered deliciously when he pressed his lips to her temple.

''Did you hear me, Susanna?'' He chuckled softly when she shook her tousled head, but his voice held an edge of seriousness as he lightly stroked the small of her back. ''You know that what I have to do cannot wait for another day.''

''Oh, Adam, I know,'' she said, ''but I don't want to be apart from you, not even for a minute. Why won't you let me go with you?''

''I've already told you a dozen times, love,'' he murmured, kissing her brow. ''The physician stated quite emphatically that you must remain in bed for a few days, at the very least until he visits again tomorrow.''

''But I'm fine, other than a little pain right here . . .

oooh!'' She sucked in her breath as she gingerly touched the swollen cut on the side of her head. If she had wanted to prove to him that she was feeling better, that wasn't the way to do it. ''I ran to the stable last night without any ill effects,'' she added hastily. ''And saw to your needs quite adequately when we returned . . . as I did again this morning.''

''More than adequately,'' Adam agreed with a roguish smile, ''but a long and bumpy carriage ride would be far more tiring than the gentle ride we just shared.'' When she opened her mouth to protest, he put his finger to her lips. ''Shhh, now. No more arguments.'' He sobered, his eyes staring into hers. ''You'll have your chance to speak to the magistrate soon enough, maybe even tonight if he's willing to accompany me back to Briarwood.''

*If* you come back to Briarwood, Susanna thought unhappily as he fell silent, purposely avoiding the darker issue that they had already discussed, the slim chance that they both might spend the night in prison. Instead he kissed her soundly on the mouth and then, tossing back the covers, left their bed, grimacing as he put weight on his wrapped ankle.

''You shouldn't have jumped, Adam,'' she chided him softly, having heard the explanation for his pronounced limp and his bandaged hand last night on their way back from the stable.

''It seemed the thing to do at the time,'' he tossed back in a lighter tone, although his ruggedly handsome features had become somber, his thoughts already upon the day's coming events. Almost to himself, he added, ''I don't need this anymore,'' and undid the bandage around his knuckles. Then, flexing his stiff fingers, he walked to the washbasin where he began his morning ablutions.

Chilled by the cool breeze wafting in a nearby window, the cloudy morning portending rain, Susanna drew the covers over her breasts and watched him raptly, marveling at his physical beauty. The scars he bore only heightened his masculinity in her eyes, and despite his disfigured flesh she could see the amazing play of sinewed muscle across his powerful back and shoulders as he washed and shaved.

Even more amazing was the wonderful harmony between them and the utter contentment she felt in knowing that he loved her and she loved him. It was a dream come true, no matter the pall still hanging over their happiness. She had to believe that everything would work out. Otherwise she couldn't bear his leaving her to make the journey to Williamsburg alone.

"Remember not to say anything to the servants about what's taking place today," Adam reminded her as he tied his thick mahogany hair into a queue and hastily dressed. "Ertha is the only one who knows I'm seeing the magistrate and why, and I've asked her to keep the news to herself until we receive the court's ruling. If all goes well, there's always the chance that we might be allowed to stay on at Briarwood to run things until Lady Redmayne decides what she wants to do with the property, which could be months from now. At least that way life here will bear some semblance of normalcy until the inevitable sale of land and slaves begins."

Sickened by the thought, Susanna murmured, "Oh, Adam, I wish there was something we could do for them."

"I know. So do I," he replied grimly, coming back by the bed to pull on the coat he had left draped over the divan. "If we're granted leave to remain here, I plan to do everything in my power to see that they're sold to honorable men and that those who are free are able to find new positions. Other than that, there isn't much else we can do." Reaching into a pocket, he pulled out his pistol and proceeded to check it carefully.

"Why do you still need that?" she queried in alarm.

"Until that bastard Spencer is in prison, I'm not going to take any chances," Adam answered, returning the ornate weapon to his coat.

"Now I *am* frightened," she admitted, flinging her arms around his neck as he sat beside her on the bed.

"Don't be, my love," he said, brushing a kiss on her cheek. "Everything will work out. You must trust that I know what I'm doing."

"I do trust you, Adam—" She stopped abruptly, remembering something. Searching his eyes, she asked, "Did you ever send a reply to Dominick's letter? You've never said anything about it."

"Don't trouble yourself with these details, Susanna," he replied almost evasively. "Now I want you to lie back"—he pushed her gently onto the pillows—"and rest as the physician ordered. Will you promise me to do this?"

Sighing reluctantly, she nodded.

"Good. I might not be back until late, so don't feel you must wait up for me—"

"Don't be ridiculous, Adam Thornton!" she said with feigned annoyance, tears smarting her eyes. "Of course I'll be waiting up for you." As he bent to kiss her, his lips so warm and passionate upon her own, her arms flew around him again and she hugged him fiercely, not wanting to ever let him go. "I love you," she whispered against his mouth, her heart full to bursting when he fervently echoed her words. Then he was pulling away from her, caressing the side of her face as he rose from the bed.

"Rest now. I'll have Corliss bring you something to eat."

Her throat too tight to speak, she could only watch him stride from the room . . . leaving her alone, to wait.

"Lord, it's so good to see you awake, Mistress Camille," said Corliss, her expression strangely subdued, although her dark eyes showed relief as she set the breakfast tray upon the bedside table. "You sure struck a fear in me when I saw you yesterday so still and pale in Master Thornton's arms and your head bleeding like

it was. I thought we'd lost you. I almost fainted myself.''

''No, I'm still here,'' Susanna replied quietly, feeling deep regret as she was reminded by the way Corliss
had addressed her that the maid had no idea of what
was going to happen today.

Wishing she could say something to prepare the
young woman for what might lie ahead, Susanna nonetheless squelched the impulse, knowing Adam had
asked her not to. Corliss seemed upset about something
already anyway, and she didn't want to add to her
waiting-maid's worries. She rose to a sitting position
and settled into the pillows Corliss fluffed and then
propped for her against the headboard.

''I saw you frowning just now, Mistress Camille. Are
you having a lot of pain?''

''No, only a little,'' Susanna said, although in truth
her head seemed to be hurting her more now that Adam
had left. She reasoned that her apprehension was probably making it so, combined with missing him terribly.
He had been gone only half an hour, but it felt like
forever, the ticking clock and the relentless sound of
rain pelting against the windows making it impossible
to sleep.

''Well, Prue's herb tea should make you feel better,''
Corliss murmured, pouring the steaming liquid into a
delicate porcelain cup and handing it rather shakily to
Susanna, spilling some over the rim into the saucer.

''Corliss, what's wrong?'' she asked, taking the cup
before any hot tea sloshed on her.

''Nothing . . . nothing at all,'' the maid blurted a bit
too hastily, wiping her hands on her starched apron as
she surveyed the tray. ''Let's see now . . . there's two
poached eggs here for you, a slice of honey ham, a
basket of wild blueberry muffins, and some of Prue's
cinnamon butter.''

Wondering if perhaps Corliss had heard something
from Ertha, which might account for her odd behavior,
Susanna set the cup on the table and touched the maid's

arm. "Corliss, I know you. You're not acting like yourself this morning."

"I didn't sleep well last night, Mistress Camille, worrying about you and all. But I know I'll get over it soon, just seeing how much better you are." The maid uncovered the plate and, adding a few plump muffins from the basket, handed it to Susanna. "You should eat now, before it gets cold. Meanwhile, I'll go fetch you some nice hot water so's you can bathe."

"You don't have to rush." Susanna glanced out the window. "The rain's coming down harder now. Why don't you wait until it lets up a little?"

"Oh, don't you worry none about that. I've got a kitchen boy waiting for me downstairs with a big umbrella."

Heaving a soft sigh as Corliss hurried around the bed to fetch the pitcher from the washbasin, Susanna bit thoughtfully into a muffin. Something was troubling her maid. But what?

Quickly deciding that Ertha wouldn't have willfully gone against Adam's orders and unable to come up with any other reason why Corliss might be upset, she concluded it must be due to what the maid had told her.

"Corliss, I'm really much better," she reassured her as the young woman reached the door. "You don't have to be so anxious about me."

"I know, Mistress Camille, and I'm glad to see it. Is there anything else I can bring you when I come back? Something more from the kitchen? Some playing cards from the game room? You might want some diversion to occupy yourself while you're not sleeping."

"A few books would be nice if you wouldn't mind fetching them from the library. The ones I've been reading are on that small table by the window—"

"Oh, dear, I'm sorry, Mistress Camille, but I can't go in there right now. Master Thornton's got a visitor—" Gasping, she clapped her hand over her mouth, her eyes wide.

"Corliss, what are you talking about?" Susanna

asked, confused. "Hasn't Adam left yet for Williamsburg?"

The maid lowered her hand slowly. "Uh, no, but the carriage is already out front. I 'spect he'll be leaving soon, though I can't rightly say for sure . . ." She opened the door. "I'll go fetch that hot water now."

"Wait a minute, Corliss, you said he had a visitor. My husband didn't tell me he was seeing anyone this morning. Surely this must be unexpected. Who is it?"

"Master Thornton asked me not to say anything to you, Mistress Camille. He said it would only worry you, and what with you needing your rest—"

"Corliss, I demand that you tell me," Susanna said sharply, struck by a chilling intuition. Why would Adam have said that unless . . . unless . . . "Who's down there with him?"

Sighing as if realizing there was no way to get out of it, the maid blurted in a rush, "That planter you were thinking of marrying. Mr. Spencer."

Stunned, Susanna's mind sped wildly.

Why had Dominick come here and why had Adam allowed him into the house? He had told her that until Dominick was in prison, he wasn't going to take any chances. But they were downstairs in the library, alone. That was taking a chance, wasn't it? She couldn't think of a worse one.

Suddenly a darker concern pressed in upon her, strangling her breath and making her heart pound.

Unless Adam had wanted Dominick to meet him here . . . unless he planned to do something rash . . . take justice into his own hands. He had sworn to her that one day he would have his vengeance, hadn't he? Was challenging Dominick to a duel what he had meant? Had Adam perhaps lured that monster here by sending a reply that he would meet all of his demands? Dear God, no, this couldn't be happening! He could be seriously injured, or . . .

"How long has Mr. Spencer been here?" Susanna demanded, tossing her plate onto the tray with a crash and vaulting so abruptly from the bed that she staggered dizzily, a sharp pain shooting through her head. Not allowing herself to even consider the grimmer prospect that Adam might be killed, she ran to the wardrobe. "How long, Corliss?"

"Only since I was about to bring your tray upstairs . . . no more than a few minutes ago. What are you doing, Mistress Camille? You should be in bed!"

Susanna flung open the doors and grabbed the first gown she touched, dreading that at any moment she might hear the sound of pistols firing from the back lawn. "Quick, help me dress! I have to get downstairs!"

"But Mistress Camille—"

"No questions, Corliss! Please! Just help me!"


"You bastard! So this meeting was nothing but a trick," Dominick said through clenched teeth, his eyes bloodshot with fury.

"One you brought upon yourself." Swept by grim elation that his nemesis had played so easily into his hands, Adam kept his pistol trained squarely on Dominick's heaving chest. "Fool! You let your selfish greed overpower your reason. You thought you knew me so well, thought I would do anything to keep Briarwood for myself, even if that meant paying you blackmail for the rest of my life. But you were wrong, and now you're going to pay for your reckless miscalculation. Start moving to the door! My carriage is waiting to take us to Williamsburg."

"You're the fool, Adam Thornton!" Dominick spat, remaining right where he was. "Surely you realize the magistrate will throw both you and your London slut Susanna Guthrie in prison for your charade—"

"Call her that again, Spencer, and my finger just might slip on this trigger." Adam was sickened that Spencer would even say her name. "True, the court might do that, but I doubt it. I imagine the magistrate will simply be glad to have this matter cleared up and Briarwood returned to the proper heir's hands. There can be some reward in honesty."

"Honesty?" Dominick scoffed, his face livid. "Petty revenge is driving you. Don't you see, man? We could all profit from our arrangement, there's certainly enough Cary wealth to go around, but you're going to throw everything away just so you can see me suffer!"

"Exactly, so save your deal-making for the court," Adam countered bitterly. "Though I seriously doubt they'll listen to any scheme you propose. No, I fully expect that they're going to lock you inside a cell and toss away the key while your estate is sold bit by bit to satisfy your anxious creditors. I only wish you were going to find a noose lowered around your neck, not only for Keefer Dunn's murder earlier this morning, scum that he was, and one to which you so callously admitted, but James Cary's as well. Why don't you admit you killed him, too, and clean the slate?"

"That's one satisfaction you'll never have," Dominick said, his hand moving suddenly to the sword hilt protruding from the vent in his coat.

"Draw it even an inch, and you die," Adam warned, pointing the pistol at Dominick's forehead. "And don't think I wouldn't shoot you with the greatest relish. Ease your hand away . . . that's it, and walk very slowly to the door. Once we're outside, my coachman Elias will have the pleasure of binding your wrists so you won't be causing me any more such trouble. But for now, just keep walk—"

Adam was startled into shocked silence when the door suddenly burst open, and he watched in disbelief as Susanna rushed into the room.

"Adam, please stop! You can't do this!"

"Dammit, Susanna, get out of here!" He lunged to thrust her from the room, but his twisted ankle prevented him from moving quickly enough. Dominick reached her first and with a great heave, pushed her into Adam. They both toppled to the floor, Adam landing hard on his back and Susanna sprawling on top of him, the pistol knocked from his hand. It slid across the carpet and came to rest under a chair, well out of his reach.

"I'll teach you to threaten me!" Dominick raged, drawing his sword and advancing upon them. "I see this as a clear case of self-defense, and so will the court. Now, I have only to kill you and then I'll marry the bitch myself!"

"Roll out of the way, Susanna! Move!" Adam cried, hurling her with all his might off his body one way and then wrenching a side table down on top of himself to use as a shield just as Dominick struck the first blow.

Sent tumbling across the floor, the room spinning crazily around her until she pitched into the desk, Susanna lay dazed while the sounds of servants yelling in the hall, vehement curses, and splintering wood rang around her. Gasping for breath, her entire body aching, she managed to roll onto her side. Her eyes widened in stark horror at the sight of Dominick hacking wildly at what little remained of the tabletop which Adam, pinned to the floor by the crazed fury of his attacker's onslaught, held in front of him.

"No! Stop it!" she screamed, hauling herself to her feet and running at Dominick, who paused only long enough to fling her away from him.

She fell on all fours, tears stinging her eyes, but she wiped them away when she spied the pistol only a few feet from her. As she clawed for it, her only thought was to get the weapon back to Adam before it was too late. Then she heard him yell out in pain at the same moment that her hand closed around the engraved butt, and she twisted to find Dominick's bloodied sword coming down for a final blow.

"Damn you, Dominick! No!" A deafening report echoed around her, her hand vibrated and acrid powder smoke burned her eyes just as Elias rushed into the room and lunged at Dominick, who, clutching his shoulder, crumpled to his knees and collapsed unconscious onto Adam.

"Get him off! Get him off!" she cried, dropping the pistol to scramble on hands and bruised knees to Adam's side. As the huge black man lifted Dominick bodily and threw him against the wall, she saw that

Adam had been slashed diagonally across the chest. Bright red blood seeped from the wound visible through the torn edges of his clothing.

"No, God, no," she moaned, ripping away his waistcoat and shirt to expose the eight-inch gash. Quickly she tore off a wide piece of her linen skirt to staunch the flow of blood.

"It's all right, love," she heard him say hoarsely, and was astonished that he was speaking at all. He tried to smile at her, grimacing instead. "I don't think . . . he cut me very deep."

"Oh, Adam," she whispered, her heart aching. "You told me you were going to Williamsburg—"

"I was, Susanna, but with Dominick. I wanted to see the bastard's face when he realized that he'd lost . . . I wanted to take him with me to court so we would face the magistrate together . . ."

As he groaned raggedly and then fell silent, his head lolling back on the floor, Susanna realized with heightened fear that he had lost consciousness. Seized by sheer panic that he might die, she pressed harder upon the wound, which wouldn't stop bleeding.

"Let me help, Mistress Camille. I want to help," came Corliss's teary voice beside her while Elias's deep baritone made her jump.

"Mr. Spencer's out cold, Mistress Camille. He won't be getting up and going nowhere, but I'll call for some men to come in and watch him just the same. Then I'm going to ride like the devil to Yorktown and fetch the physician."

"Yes, go! Go as quickly as you can, Elias!" she pleaded, caressing Adam's pale cheek with trembling, bloodstained fingers while Corliss applied her wadded apron to Adam's chest. "I'm so sorry, my love . . ." She choked, overwhelmed with inexpressible regret as she glanced back to where he had been wounded. "So sorry for causing this terrible thing to happen. I shouldn't have run into the room like I did, but I was so frightened for you—"

"Susanna," broke in Ertha's shaky yet urgent voice

next to her ear. "There's a lady just arrived, and she's asking for Camille. I'll stay here with Master Thornton . . . his wound looks bad, but he's as strong as they come. He'll pull through this well enough." Ertha tugged upon her arm. "Did you hear me, Susanna? I think you'd best go out and greet her before she comes in here. I have a feeling it's important—"

"Who's Susanna?" Corliss exclaimed in confusion. "Lordy, Ertha, don't give out on us, too! You're talking to Mistress Camille!"

"No, I want to stay here," Susanna insisted, ignoring her maid's outburst and wondering how the housekeeper could dare ask her to leave Adam's side at a time like this. "I have to stay with him—"

"Will someone kindly tell me what is going on . . . Good heavens, Susanna Guthrie, is that you? I should have known you'd be in the center of this melee!"

Her heart seeming to stop, Susanna incredulously lifted her eyes to Lady Redmayne's indignant gaze.

"Well, young woman, what do you have to say to explain this horrible mess? And where's Camille? Where's her husband, Adam Thornton? I've never been so relieved as when I heard of their marriage from the constable in Yorktown—then I come here to find their household in a total uproar! Why, it looks as if I've stumbled onto a battlefield! Now I want an explanation, and I want it this very instant!"

Her whole world crumbling around her, Susanna could only murmur numbly, "Oh bloody, bloody hell . . ."

# Chapter 28

 

**66 I** still can't believe Lady Redmayne is here at Briarwood," Susanna murmured to Adam, who half-reclined beside her on the bed, pillows propped behind him and the covers drawn to his waist, a thick white bandage encircling his bare chest. She nestled closer against his comforting warmth, her cheek resting against his broad shoulder. "That she came all this way on the strength of a letter she received only a few weeks after Camille and I left England, and from a woman she didn't even know . . . Cleo, no less!"

"I believe it, knowing how much Cleo hated Dominick," Adam replied, drawing her closer, his arm securely around her waist. "She finally found a way to pay him back for selling off her children. I can imagine the baroness's reaction when she read Cleo's charge that he had murdered James Cary to clear the way so he could marry Camille and save himself from bankruptcy. I'm not surprised Lady Redmayne threw aside her prejudices and booked passage on the next ship bound for Virginia so she might prevent such a marriage. You told me she dearly loved her grandniece."

"She did," Susanna answered softly, recalling how the baroness's stern facade had crumbled so piteously when she had learned that Camille had died from fever.

It had been long hours now since Susanna had composed herself enough to tell Lady Redmayne the full story of everything that had happened since she and Camille had sailed from Bristol. Twilight had fallen outside upon a day that had begun cloudy and wet and had ended with a glorious sunset. As far as Susanna knew, the baroness was still sitting in the drawing room, alone with her grief as she had tearfully requested. Even Mary Sayers, Lady Redmayne's longtime waiting-maid who had accompanied her on the voyage to Virginia, had been asked to leave.

"It's a good thing Cleo mentioned Dominick's private diary in her letter and where it was hidden in his library," Adam continued, his voice deep and husky. "The court would never have taken a slave's word for the murder if the constable hadn't found that journal and its gloating entry about James's death."

"Yes, and I'm glad that when he and his men came here to arrest Dominick, the constable made a point to show Lady Redmayne that her accusation was well-founded." Susanna heaved a small sigh, glancing up at him. "She started crying again when she saw the diary. I think she loved Mr. Cary, too, despite the resentment she'd held against him for so long. She's totally alone now—the last of the Cary family."

A pensive silence rose between them, broken only when Adam spoke again.

"If Dominick hadn't been here at Briarwood this morning while the constable went directly to search his house upon the baroness's insistence, he might have destroyed the evidence before they ever found it. Now he's going to hang, and he can only blame himself for ever allowing Cleo to learn to read and write. His twisted love for her proved his undoing."

Susanna shivered, wondering what was going to be her and Adam's fate. They still planned on admitting everything to the magistrate and taking whatever punishment the court, and Lady Redmayne, now deemed warranted. But what that might be, they still had no clue.

Other than her explanation for why she had come to Virginia, the baroness had said little to Susanna while she recounted her tale, instead staring out the window with tears streaming down her lined face. Yet Susanna had taken some comfort after she had finished when she had sensed no anger or resentment from the older woman, receiving instead a few pointed questions that had caught her completely off guard.

"What are your feelings for Adam Thornton?" Lady Redmayne had queried, her tear-dimmed hazel eyes intent on Susanna's face.

"I love him," she had said honestly, her own eyes growing wet as she thought of him receiving care upstairs from the physician who had pronounced his wound serious but not life-threatening. "If he had died today . . ." Unable to go on, she had stared down at her folded hands.

"And what will the two of you do now?"

"Marry again, this time using my own name," she had answered. She had purposely skipped over any talk of possible punishment, fearing even to raise the subject. "Then we'll start a new life somewhere, maybe on Virginia's frontier. There's land to be had in the west, good land waiting to be settled. All that really matters to me is that Adam and I are together."

To her surprise, the baroness had brusquely dismissed her then, giving her no idea what she planned to do with them.

Suddenly growing apprehensive, Susanna threw her arm tightly around Adam's lean waist, wondering with dread if tomorrow they might find themselves separated by prison walls.

"Adam," she murmured, her voice catching as she hugged him fiercely, "I'm so sorry about what happened this morning. So terribly sorry. I should have trusted you. I thought . . . I thought you were going to challenge Dominick—"

"It doesn't matter, my love," he broke in gently, kissing her forehead. "All that matters is that you brought Dominick down and saved my life. But now we're starting over, remember? From this moment on, all of that is behind us. Let's think only of the future. Our future."

"Oh, I want that so much," she said. "You know,

Lady Redmayne said the strangest thing when she first walked into the library this morning, something about being so relieved when she heard from the constable about your marriage to Camille—''

''I think she probably meant she was simply glad to discover there had been no wedding between her grand-niece and Dominick,'' Adam interrupted her, giving her a reassuring squeeze.

''I don't know,'' Susanna persisted, a wild hope flaring in her heart that it might mean something more. ''Lady Redmayne knew from Mr. Cary's letters to Camille that you were his plantation manager, Adam. By rights, she should have been enraged by such a match, considering the rules she had droned into Camille's head about marrying into wealth and position. Yet she didn't seem in the least dismayed when she said your name.''

''Susanna, I don't think it's wise that we read anything into Lady Redmayne's words. From what I've heard about her bluntness, I'm sure she'll clearly state her position toward us when she's ready. Other than that, we can only wait—''

He stopped at the sudden knock on the door, a firm, no-nonsense rap. Susanna immediately rose from the bed and, casting a nervous glance at Adam, hurried across the candlelit room, taking only an instant to smooth her hair and secure her dressing gown more tightly around her before she opened the door.

''Your ladyship,'' she murmured, trembling with apprehension at the inscrutable expression on the baroness's face. Almost forgetting herself, she dropped a quick curtsy. ''Please . . . come in.''

''Thank you, I will,'' said the petite older woman. Her black gown rustled as she swept into the room, her posture as gracefully erect as ever despite her advancing age. ''I hope I'm not disturbing you.''

''Not at all, my lady. Adam and I were just talking . . .'' Susanna's voice trailed off as the baroness seemed not to have expected any objection to her presence but moved directly to the bed.

''I need a chair, Susanna.''

She hastened to obey, her seven years as a lady's maid coming to the fore. As she returned with the chair, she noticed Adam's frown and imagined he didn't like the sight of her waiting upon another person.

As the elegant woman sat down and folded her hands primly in her lap, she added, "I believe some introductions are in order, Susanna."

"I'm Adam Thornton," Adam spoke up before Susanna could reply. "It's a pleasure to meet you, Lady Redmayne. I've heard a great deal about you."

Susanna winced, wishing she had instructed Adam on the proper way to address a baroness. But it was too late, and she doubted he would have listened anyway. He was a stubborn, proud man who demanded to be met on his own terms.

"And I know a great deal about you as well," Lady Redmayne countered cryptically, although her patrician features held no irritation. "I'm glad to see that you're feeling much better than when I saw you last, being carried upstairs by that hulking black man."

"Elias."

"Yes, Elias. He seemed protective of you, quite loyal. It surprised me. I'd heard that these slaves usually despise their masters."

"Some do," Adam answered frankly. "But I've found that treating others with respect usually begets the same, as James Cary also believed."

"Indeed."

Thinking that things weren't exactly getting off to the best start and wishing Adam would soften his tone, Susanna moved to the bedside and took his hand, squeezing it gently in reproach. When he squeezed hers back, she felt some reassurance.

"I'm truly sorry, Lady Redmayne, that you had to learn about your grandniece's death in such an unexpected manner," Adam said, obviously having taken Susanna's cue to heart, for his voice was filled with sincere regret. "We had planned to write you a letter after meeting with the magistrate—"

"Yes, it has been a day fraught with the most unsettling confessions," the baroness broke in quietly, her eyes suddenly glistening. Lowering her head for a moment, she cleared her throat delicately against the hoarseness that had crept into her voice, then she looked up, squaring her shoulders. "I have a confession to make myself."

Gripping Adam's hand tightly, Susanna felt her nervousness mounting as Lady Redmayne withdrew a worn, folded piece of paper from a side pocket buried in the black satin material of her gown.

"This letter was written to Camille by her father shortly before his death and arrived only days before she was due to leave Fairford. I deliberately kept it from her because it held sentiments I did not wish her to see." The baroness leveled her gaze upon Adam. "It's about you, Mr. Thornton, every single word." Her ringed fingers were shaking as she handed him the letter. "You may read it later at your leisure, I'm giving it to you to keep, but for now I would prefer that you simply listen to what I have to say."

"As you wish," Adam answered, glancing at Susanna as he released her hand and took the paper.

"My nephew held a great fondness for you, Mr. Thornton, and it's echoed in each line of that letter. He looked upon you as a son, and he wanted you and Camille to marry, believing you would do well by both her and Briarwood. And although I know now of the vengeful motive that had driven you to prove to James that you were worthy to wed his daughter, I am sure he wouldn't have faulted you for it; he loved you that much. You'll find that he states he had intended to share his feelings and hopes with Camille when she arrived in Virginia, but something compelled him to write to her instead. I can only imagine that he must have had some premonition . . ."

As Lady Redmayne paused again to collect herself, Susanna's thoughts skipped back to that balmy July afternoon when Adam had asked if he might court her. She hadn't believed James Cary would have given a common hired man his blessing, but the planter had, and here finally was Adam's proof.

"That is why I couldn't allow Camille to read the letter," the baroness continued. "Despite my nephew's wishes, I didn't think you would make a suitable husband for her, Camille being an heiress—which I mean as no insult to you personally, Mr. Thornton—"

"None taken," he murmured.

"Yes, well, to be blunt, I had my sights for her set much higher. I trusted that I had taught her well enough about the importance of choosing a proper husband, that once you made your marital intentions known to her, she would reject you outright." Her eyes began to mist, her voice suddenly catching.

"But I can't tell you, Mr. Thornton, what James's letter came to mean to me when I learned of his foul murder and that horrible man Dominick Spencer's intentions toward my beloved Camille. It was the only thing during that endless ocean crossing that gave me any hope. I can't even count how many times I reread that letter, especially the words about how stubborn you were, how hardworking and persevering, and I prayed day and night that you were using that same dogged persistence against any objections Camille might give you about your courtship of her. You can't imagine my trepidation when I disembarked from that ship early this morning and went straight to the town constable's house and rousted him from bed, only to hear that you had married my grandniece almost two weeks ago . . ."

Susanna felt a terrible lump rising in her throat as Lady Redmayne's teary gaze fell upon her. "I'm sorry it was me, your ladyship, truly I am. If I could have taken the fever from Camille and put it upon myself, I would have done it gladly. I didn't want her to die . . ."

"Heavens, dear child, I know that," the baroness murmured, pulling a black handkerchief from her sleeve to dab at her eyes. "And I know how much Camille loved you, like a sister. You were the only one who could make her truly laugh, and every time I heard it, I thanked God you had stumbled across our path in

London. I fear I was too hard on her, wishing she could shed her shyness and be more like you. I hope she knew that I only wanted the best for her—''

"She did, my lady, she did," Susanna interrupted fervently, grateful for the warmth and strength of Adam's hand once again grasping her own.

Lady Redmayne rose from the chair, her handkerchief now limp and sodden. "Forgive me. I didn't come here to make such an emotional display, only to explain myself and tell you both that I have no intention of hauling you before any magistrate. As far as I'm concerned, this is a family matter, and I consider both of you my family now. You're all that I have left connecting me to the ones I loved."

Her limbs suddenly gone weak with relief, Susanna sank down next to Adam, scarcely noticing that his arm had slipped around her waist.

"I have only one question to ask you, Mr. Thornton," the baroness added, drawing back her delicate shoulders as her expression regained a good measure of its sternness. "Do you love this young woman?"

"I do," Adam answered, his voice throbbing with intensity. "She's everything to me. I need nothing else as long as she is by my side."

"Good. It is just as I expected. Tomorrow I shall journey into Williamsburg and visit the magistrate myself, where I will explain everything and then have documents drawn up to deed Briarwood over to you. James had hoped that someday you might have this plantation, knowing you would make it prosper, and so you shall. Then I plan to visit the parish church and see that the proper wedding banns are posted and the wedding license obtained. If Camille wanted you, Susanna, to carry on in her stead as the mistress of Briarwood, I can do no less than to honor her dying wish. She was right. No one deserves it more than you."

Completely stunned, Susanna looked at Adam, who appeared as astounded as she was.

"Now, if you'll both excuse me, I must retire," Lady Redmayne said, appearing suddenly very weary, although a faint smile curved her lips. "I imagine it's going to be a very hectic few weeks, planning the wedding and all the parties that must go with it, and seeing a bit of this colony of which James was so proud. I must admit, I never expected to find Virginia so agreeable, despite the unwelcome downpour that greeted Mary and me as soon as we came off the ship. Quite civilized, too. Well, good night."

As the baroness began to walk to the door, Susanna quickly left Adam's side to catch up with her, saying, "I'll show you to your room, my lady." She was surprised when Lady Redmayne waved her back to the bed.

"There's no need to accompany me, Susanna, I can find my own way down the hall," she insisted. "Go care for your handsome betrothed and look to yourself, for that matter. From what I've heard from Ertha, whom I took the liberty of reassuring I might add, and that charming young Corliss, you two have had quite an interesting past few days. Lovers' quarrels, spills from balconies, sword fights . . ." She shook her gray head. "You should both be abed, resting!"

"All—all right, your ladyship," Susanna murmured, offering another curtsy.

"That's another thing, my dear," Lady Redmayne added kindly as she opened the door. "From now on, please call me Aunt Melicent, and the same goes for you, Adam. Remember, I said we're family now. That means no more curtsying, too. Sleep well."

Then the baroness was gone, leaving them alone, yet Susanna stood rooted to the floor. She could hardly believe everything that had just happened . . . their good fortune was simply unheard of. Yet it had happened! She didn't have to pinch herself to know that it was true. She and Adam could stay at Briarwood! It was going to be their home!

"Come here, my love," she heard Adam say behind her, his beloved voice only heightening her incredible joy. She spun to find him staring at her hungrily, his eyes warm and glittering in the candlelight. "There's something I want to ask you."

She rushed toward him but stopped just out of his arm's reach, for his expression had suddenly become most serious, taking her by surprise. "What is it, Adam? Is something wrong?"

"Only if I don't hear the right answer from your lips. Come closer so I can touch you."

She did, his hand sliding around her waist, then he gently pulled her down to sit facing him on the bed. "Answer to what, Adam?"

Reaching up to tenderly cradle her face with one hand, he stared deeply into her eyes. "Will you marry me, Susanna Jane Guthrie?"

As her heart swelled with infinite love for this man, her first impulse was to shout out "Yes!" and hear it ring all around them. But instead she could not resist murmuring playfully, wanting to draw out this rapturous moment, "Only on two conditions."

He smiled roguishly and adopted her teasing tone. "Name them."

"I cannot simply be a lady of leisure, Adam. Needlework and playing the pianoforte aren't enough for me. I want to work for my keep. Make myself useful."

"Done."

"As easily as that?" His very nearness was sending tremors of excitement racing through her.

"How can I refuse you anything, my love?" He caressed her silken cheek with his thumb, rejoicing in his heart that this beautiful, enchanting woman had come into his life. "And your second condition?"

She smiled wantonly, leaning forward to brush the lightest yet most seductive kiss upon his lips. "I want a proper courting before we wed, Adam . . . the kind any woman would dream about."

"I'll show you the stuff of which a woman's dreams are made," he said huskily, pulling her on top of him so that she straddled him. Ignoring the twinge of pain his movement had cost him and thinking that to have her astride him so appealingly was well worth any discomfort, he traced her full, inviting lips with his fingertips. Then slowly, he drew her face toward him until their mouths were almost touching. "But first, Susanna Jane, you must give me your answer."

"Yes, Adam Thornton, I will marry you," she whispered, pressing her soft lips to his. In that brilliant, shining moment, he had never felt more loved, or more whole.

# Avon Romances—
## *the best in exceptional authors and unforgettable novels!*

**HIGHLAND MOON**  Judith E. French
76104-1/$4.50 US/$5.50 Can

**SCOUNDREL'S CAPTIVE**  JoAnn DeLazzari
76420-2/$4.50 US/$5.50 Can

**FIRE LILY**  Deborah Camp
76394-X/$4.50 US/$5.50 Can

**SURRENDER IN SCARLET**  Patricia Camden
76262-5/$4.50 US/$5.50 Can

**TIGER DANCE**  Jillian Hunter
76095-9/$4.50 US/$5.50 Can

**LOVE ME WITH FURY**  Cara Miles
76450-4/$4.50 US/$5.50 Can

**DIAMONDS AND DREAMS**  Rebecca Paisley
76564-0/$4.50 US/$5.50 Can

**WILD CARD BRIDE**  Joy Tucker
76445-8/$4.50 US/$5.50 Can

**ROGUE'S MISTRESS**  Eugenia Riley
76474-1/$4.50 US/$5.50 Can

**CONQUEROR'S KISS**  Hannah Howell
76503-9/$4.50 US/$5.50 Can